BROTHERBAND

BOOK 6

THE GHOSTFACES

Also by John Flanagan

BROTHERBAND CHRONICLES

Book 1: The Outcasts

Book 2: The Invaders

Book 3: The Hunters

Book 4: Slaves of Socorro

Book 5: Scorpion Mountain

THE RANGER'S APPRENTICE EPIC

Book 1: The Ruins of Gorlan

Book 2: The Burning Bridge

Book 3: The Icebound Land

Book 4: The Battle for Skandia

Book 5: The Sorcerer of the North

Book 6: The Siege of Macindaw

Book 7: Erak's Ransom

Book 8: The Kings of Clonmel

Book 9: Halt's Peril

Book 10: The Emperor of Nihon-Ja

Book 11: The Lost Stories

Book 12: The Royal Ranger

RANGER'S APPRENTICE: THE EARLY YEARS

The Tournament at Gorlan

SKANDIA AND ITS NEIGHBOURS
Frozen Sea
Northern Wastes
WESTERN OCEAN
Greystone Forest
SKANDIA
Hallasholm
ENDLESS OCEAN
SONDERLAND
Eastern Steppe
Stormwhite Sea
Skorghijl
TEUTLANDT
PICTA
Castle Araluen
Narrow Sea
HIBERNIA
ARALUEN
MAGYARA
ALPINA
GALLICA
CELTICA
IBERION
ASLAVA
TOSCANA
ENDLESS OCEAN
Narrows of Ikbar
The Constant Sea
Sea of Rostov
N
Socorro
ARRIDA

PHILOMEL BOOKS
an imprint of Penguin Random House LLC
375 Hudson Street, New York, NY 10014

First published in Australia by Random House Australia in 2016.

Library of Congress Cataloging-in-Publication Data
Names: Flanagan, John (John Anthony), author. | Title: The ghostfaces / John Flanagan.
Description: U.S. edition. | New York : Philomel Books, [2016] | Series: Brotherband chronicles ; book 6 | "Companion to the bestselling Ranger's Apprentice." | "First published in Australia by Random House Australia in 2016." | Summary: When a massive storm at sea blows the Brotherband crew off course to a land so far west Hal cannot recognize it from his maps, they face an unknown enemy. | Identifiers: LCCN 2015050312 | ISBN 9780399163579 | Subjects: | CYAC: Seafaring life—Fiction. | Adventure and adventurers—Fiction. | Pirates—Fiction. | Friendship—Fiction. | Courage—Fiction. | Fantasy. | Classification: LCC PZ7.F598284 Gho 2016 | DDC [Fic]—dc23
LC record available at https://lccn.loc.gov/2015050312

Printed in the United States of America.
ISBN 9780399163579
3 5 7 9 10 8 6 4 2
U.S. edition edited by Michael Green.
U.S. edition designed by Amy Wu. Text set in 13/18-point Centaur MT Std.

A Few Sailing Terms Explained

Because this book involves sailing ships, I thought it might be useful to explain a few of the nautical terms found in the story.

Be reassured that I haven't gone overboard (to keep up the nautical allusion) with technical details in the book, and even if you're not familiar with sailing, I'm sure you'll understand what's going on. But a certain amount of sailing terminology is necessary for the story to feel realistic.

So, here we go, in no particular order:

Bow: The front of the ship, also called the prow.

Stern: The rear of the ship.

Port and starboard: The left and the right side of the ship, as you're facing the bow. In fact, I'm probably incorrect in using the term *port.* The early term for port was *larboard,* but I thought we'd all get confused if I used that.

Starboard is a corruption of "steering board" (or steering side). The steering oar was always placed on the right-hand side of the ship at the stern.

Consequently, when a ship came into port, it would moor with the left side against the jetty, to avoid damage to the steering oar. One theory says the word derived from the ship's being in port—left side to the jetty. I suspect, however, that it might have come from the fact that the entry port, by which crew and passengers boarded, was also always on the left side.

How do you remember which side is which? Easy. *Port* and *left* both have four letters.

Forward: Toward the bow.

Aft: Toward the stern.

Fore-and-aft rig: A sail plan in which the sail is in line with the hull of the ship.

Hull: The body of the ship.

Keel: The spine of the ship.

Stem: The upright timber piece at the bow, joining the two sides together.

Forefoot: The lowest point of the bow, where the keel and the stem of the ship meet.

Steering oar: The blade used to control the ship's direction, mounted on the starboard side of the ship, at the stern.

Tiller: The handle for the steering oar.

Sea anchor: A method of slowing a ship's downwind drift, often by use of a canvas **drogue**—a long, conical tube of canvas closed at one end and held open at the other—or two spars lashed together in a cross. The sea anchor is streamed from the bow and the resultant drag slows the ship's movement through the water.

Yardarm, or yard: A spar (wooden pole) that is hoisted up the mast, carrying the sail.

Masthead: The top of the mast.

Bulwark: The part of the ship's side above the deck.

Scuppers: Drain holes in the bulwarks set at deck level to allow water that comes on board to drain away.

Belaying pins: Wooden pins used to fasten rope.

Oarlock, or rowlock: Pegs set on either side of an oar to keep it in place while rowing.

Thwart: A seat.

Telltale: A pennant that indicates the wind's direction.

Tacking: To tack is to change direction from one side to the other, passing through the eye of the wind.

If the wind is from the north and you want to sail northeast, you would perform one tack so that you are heading northeast, and you would continue to sail on that tack for as long as you need.

However, if the wind is from the north and you want to sail due north, you would have to do so in a series of short tacks, going back and forth on a zigzag course, crossing through the wind each time, and slowly making ground to the north. This is a process known as **beating** into the wind.

Wearing: When a ship tacks, it turns *into* the wind to change direction. When it wears, it turns *away* from the wind, traveling in a much larger arc, with the wind in the sail, driving the ship around throughout the maneuver. Wearing was a safer way of changing direction for wolfships than beating into the wind.

Reach, or reaching: When the wind is from the side of the ship, the ship is sailing on a reach, or reaching.

Running: When the wind is from the stern, the ship is running. (So would you if the wind was strong enough at your back.)

Reef: To gather in part of the sail and bundle it against the yardarm to reduce the sail area. This is done in high winds to protect the sail and the mast.

Trim: To adjust the sail to the most efficient angle.

Halyard: A rope used to haul the yard up the mast. (Haul-yard, get it?)

Stay: A heavy rope that supports the mast. The **backstay** and the **forestay** are heavy ropes running from the top of the mast to the stern and the bow (it's pretty obvious which is which).

Sheets and shrouds: Many people think these are sails, which is a logical assumption. But in fact, they're ropes. Shrouds are thick ropes that run from the top of the mast to the side of the ship, supporting the mast. Sheets are the ropes used to control, or trim, the sail—to haul it in and out according to the wind strength and direction. In an emergency, the order might be given to "let fly the sheets!" The sheets would be released, letting the sail loose and bringing the ship to a halt. (If *you* were to let fly the sheets, you'd probably fall out of bed.)

Hawser: Heavy rope used to moor a ship.

Way: The motion of the ship. If a ship is under way, it is moving according to its course. If it is making leeway, the ship is moving downwind so it loses ground or goes off course.

Lee: The downwind side of a ship, opposite to the direction of the wind.

Lee shore: A shoreline downwind of the ship, with the wind blowing the ship toward the shore—a dangerous situation for a sailing ship.

Back water: To row a reverse stroke.

So, now that you know all you need to know about sailing terms, welcome aboard the world of the Brotherband Chronicles!

John Flanagan

COMPANION TO THE BESTSELLING

RANGER'S APPRENTICE

BROTHERBAND

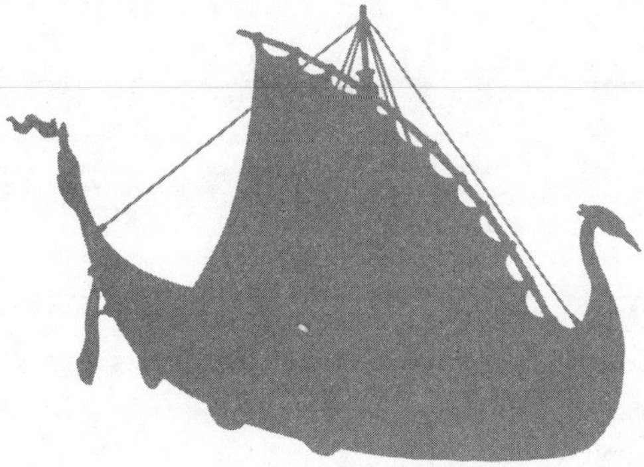

BOOK 6

THE GHOSTFACES

JOHN FLANAGAN

PHILOMEL BOOKS

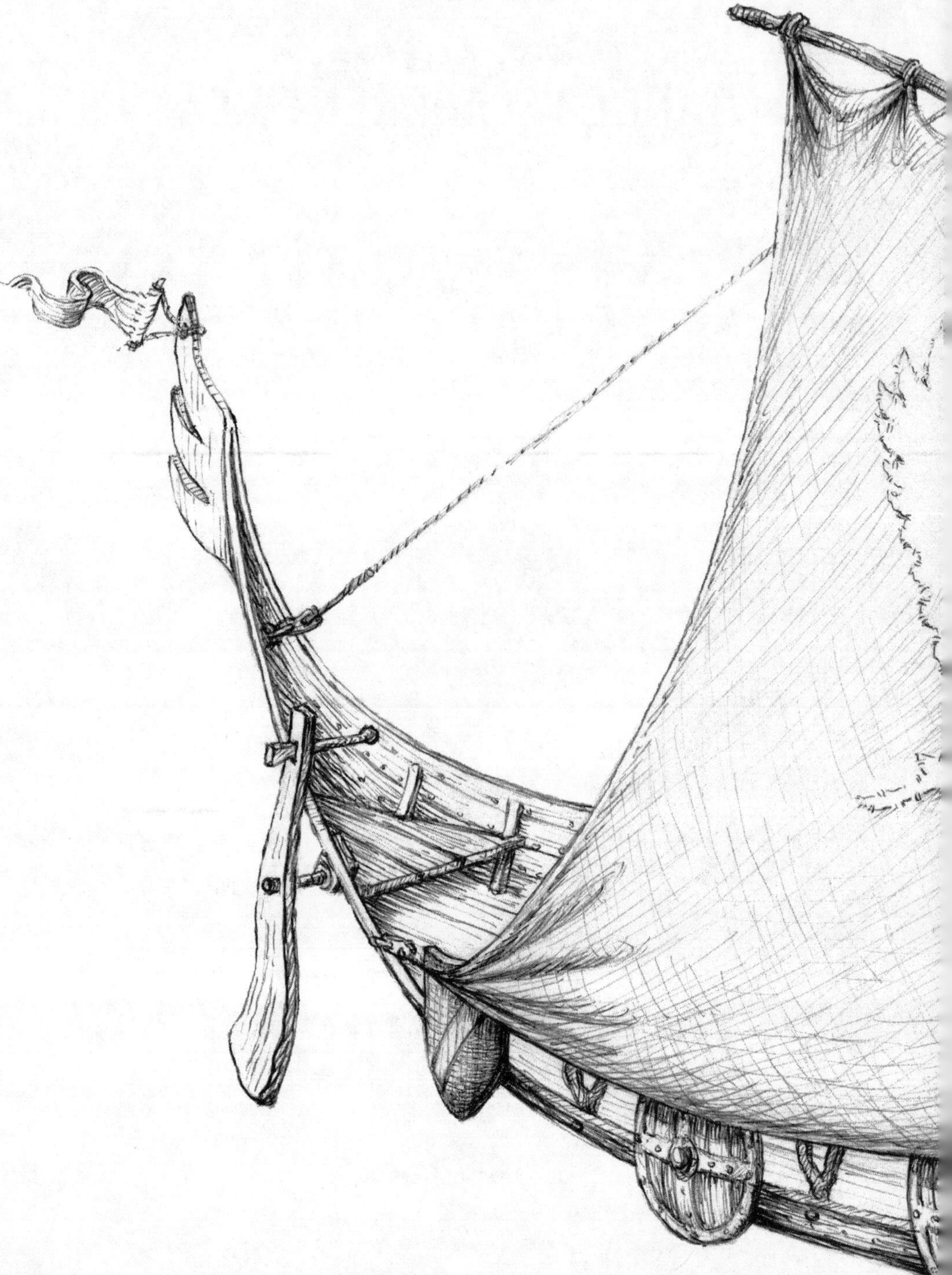

PART ONE

THE STORM

chapter one

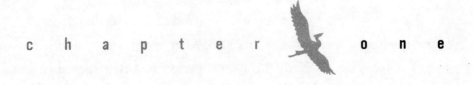

I don't like the look of that," Thorn said, wrinkling his nose as he sniffed the damp salt air.

He and Hal were standing on the breakwater of the small harbor that served Castle Dun Kilty in Clonmel. The castle itself was several kilometers inland, but the harbor was home to a small fishing fleet that provided food for the castle and its surrounding village. In addition, it was a haven for courier ships bringing messages to King Sean, ruler of Clonmel.

Heron was one such ship. She had delivered a signed and sealed set of official papers to the king, a renewal of the treaty between Skandia and Clonmel. She had also delivered similar documents to three other kingdoms farther down the Hibernian coast. Erak liked to use the *Heron* for such tasks. She was fast and handy, and Hal was a reliable navigator.

Now, however, their task was completed and it was time to head for home. But the weather wasn't altogether promising.

The two friends studied the gray, racing seas that surged past outside the harbor walls, driven by the stiff north wind.

Thorn sniffed again. "It'll be a wet, rough passage north to round the tip of Picta," he said.

Hal shrugged. "We've been wet before," he replied, and then grinned. "It's part of a sailor's lot, they say."

"No sense in getting soaked for the sake of it," Thorn said. "If we wait a day or two, this might blow itself out."

"Or it might get worse, and then we'll find ourselves trapped here, with a hard beat north into the wind and sea. We could be caught here for a week or more."

"We'd be dry," Thorn said.

Hal shook his head. "We'd be bored to tears as well," he said. "There's precious little to do in the town here." He paused, studying the racing waves once more, looking to the north, then came to a decision. "We'll go," he said. "Let's get the crew on board."

They strode briskly back around the breakwater to the small town. There was an inn there where the Herons had been accommodated while they carried out their diplomatic mission. The others were finishing their breakfasts in the taproom when Hal and Thorn entered, allowing a gust of cold wind to swirl around the room and set the fire flaring in the grate. Eight pairs of eyes looked up at them expectantly.

"We're going," Hal told them.

"About time too," Stig said. He shared Hal's opinion of the

lack of entertainment in the little port. Stefan, Ulf and Wulf gulped down the rest of the nourishing porridge the innkeeper had served them. The rest of the crew had finished eating, but they took final sips of the inn's excellent coffee, knowing it would be their last for some time.

Hal glanced at Edvin. "Are we stocked up?"

Edvin nodded. "Provisioned and watered, ready to go," he said, then added, "Although I'd like to pick up a few loaves of bread."

Once they were at sea, they'd be subsisting on hardtack biscuits. It was always good to have a supply of soft fresh bread at the start of the voyage. Hal nodded assent and Edvin hurried out, heading for the bakery a few doors away. The rest of the crew gathered up their rucksacks and other personal belongings and straggled out the door.

"Take a reef in the sails before you hoist them," Hal called after Ulf and Wulf. "That wind is getting up."

The two sail trimmers nodded. It made sense to do this before they hoisted the sails, rather than have to lower them again to lash a fold in them and reduce the sail area.

Hal waited behind to check the reckoning the innkeeper had ready for him. He ran his finger down the list of charges—so many rooms for so many nights, and a tally of the meals his crew had eaten. He signed off on the bill and handed it back. They were on a diplomatic mission and the bill would be sent to Castle Dun Kilty.

"Thanks for the hospitality," he said to the innkeeper.

"Always a pleasure to see you," the innkeeper replied. The Herons had provided him with good business at a slack time of the year. Then he couldn't help grinning. "Although there was a time I'd never have said that to Skandians."

Hal smiled in return. Not too many years ago, the presence of a wolfship in the harbor would have been accompanied by a lot of unpleasantness, and the skirl wouldn't have been signing for the food and drink consumed by the crew. He would have simply seized it at sword point—along with the inn's taking for the week.

"Different times," he said. He picked up his own kit bag from where he had left it earlier in the morning and tossed it over his shoulder as he exited. The cold wind whistled round the harbor, and he quickened his pace as he headed for the jetty where *Heron* was moored.

Edvin was a few meters in front of him, carrying a net of fresh loaves. He jumped lightly down from the jetty onto *Heron* and stowed the bread in the central watertight section of the hull. Even inside the bay, the unruly sea was causing the little ship to jerk at her moorings and setting the wicker fenders squealing as she snubbed against the ropes holding her to the jetty.

Hal made his way aft, stowed his kit bag in his personal space and stepped to the steering platform. He glanced at Stig.

"All ready?" he asked, although he knew the answer. Stig was an efficient first mate.

"Whenever you are," Stig replied.

Hal unlashed the restraining rope on the tiller and looked around the harbor. There were no other ships moving. The boats of the little fishing fleet were cozily tucked up in their moorings farther down harbor.

Very wise of them, he thought bleakly, pulling his sheepskin collar up higher round his neck in anticipation of the wet journey ahead. He reached inside his jerkin and produced his woolen watch cap, emblazoned with the heron symbol. He pulled it tight down round his ears and glanced up at the wind telltale on the mast. The wind was on their beam, from the port side.

"Starboard sail," he ordered, and Stefan and Jesper bent to the halyards, sending the slender, curving yardarm up the mast and letting it clunk into place. Ulf and Wulf were watching him expectantly.

"Cast off for'ard!" Hal called to Thorn in the bow. Thorn released the for'ard mooring rope and the bow began to swing out, away from the jetty.

"Cast off aft," he said to Stig, then, "Sheet home!"

The ship gathered way almost immediately as the twins hauled the sail tight. She curved away from the jetty, buffeting her way through the short, steep waves. Hal let her slide away to starboard, heading diagonally across the little bay. The tiller vibrated under his hand, and, as ever, he marveled at the sense that he was in control of a living being.

When he judged the angle was right, he brought the bow round to port and the twins reacted immediately, hauling the sail in tighter. Now *Heron* was angled to the left of the harbor mouth. But she'd make leeway, falling off to the right under the force of the wind, so that when they reached the harbor mouth, she'd be heading straight for the center of the gap. Hal couldn't have articulated how he knew where to head the bow so they would arrive at that exit point. It was a combination of instinct and experience, and his intimate knowledge of his ship's performance and handling.

The ship passed between the two granite breakwaters, heading into the open sea. Instantly, the wind force increased as they emerged from the shelter of the harbor, and the ship began to heel to starboard. Ulf and Wulf, without needing to be told, eased the sheets to reduce the pressure in the sail, and the *Heron* came upright once more. She rose to the first of the rollers, then slid down into the trough behind it, smashing into the following wave and drenching the deck and its occupants with a shower of white water.

"What price a warm, dry inn now?" Thorn called.

Hal grinned at him. "I can set you ashore again if you like," he said. "We'll come back for you next summer."

Heron swooped up the face of another roller, then slid down the back, sending more spray across the decks. Those not on duty huddled under tarpaulins, hastily snatched around them.

Hal grinned to himself. It was cold. It was wet. And he loved it. This was what his life was meant to be, he thought, the freedom of movement that a good, seaworthy ship gave him. The exhilaration of meeting and taming the wind and the sea.

Then a shower of spray hit him in the face, and he spluttered and coughed. A hand nudged him and he dashed the spray out of his eyes to see Lydia beside him, holding out a tarpaulin cloak.

"Cover up, idiot," she said, "before you drown."

She took the tiller while he hauled the cloak around him. He smiled at her gratefully.

"Thanks, Mummy," he said.

She raised an eyebrow. "Mummy yourself," she muttered, then

sought shelter in the leeward rowing benches. A wave broke over the bows and water surged the length of the deck. Kloof, fastened by a length of rope to the mast, snapped at it and tried to bite it as it swirled around her. She seemed to be enjoying herself, Hal thought.

They spent the rest of the morning tacking back and forth as they made their way north along the coastline. By midday, they had left Hibernia behind and could see the dim gray coast of Araluen and Picta to starboard. It was wet and cold and uncomfortable but that was a minor concern to the crew. They were young and hardy and they were used to conditions like this. They had sailed in wet, icy weather virtually since they could walk. Skandians didn't stay in port because of a bit of cold weather.

And besides, they were heading home and that was sufficient reason to put up with a bit of discomfort.

In the early afternoon, they rounded the northernmost point of the coast of Picta, and Hal, after giving himself plenty of sea room, set a course to the east. The wind was on their port side now and they were on a reach, possibly their best point of sailing. The *Heron* swooped and skimmed over the rollers like her namesake, and they all felt the elation that came with sailing fast and heading for home.

Mid-afternoon, Thorn left his customary position at the foot of the mast, where he huddled with Kloof, sharing her warmth, and paced back to the steering platform. The rest of the crew were following Lydia's example, crouching in the leeward rowing well, wrapped in cloaks and tarpaulins, heads down and chins tucked in to conserve warmth.

Thorn gestured with a thumb to the north. "I really don't like the look of that," he said.

Hal followed the direction of his thumb. A black line of thick, heavy storm clouds, shot through with flashes of lightning, blotted out the ocean.

It was still a long way away. But it was coming straight at them.

chapter two

Hal glanced quickly to starboard. The gray, rugged line of the Picta coast stretched across the horizon. He wouldn't clear it by the time the storm reached them, and then they'd find themselves on a lee shore, with the wild wind and sea driving them down onto the rocks of the coastline. He came to a rapid decision.

"Going about!" he yelled. When he was sure he had the crew's full attention, he signaled to port. "Go!"

He hauled on the tiller, and the *Heron* swung smoothly into the eye of the wind, then across it. Simultaneously, Stig and Stefan brought the starboard yardarm and sail down, then hoisted the port sail as the bow came round. Ingvar, Lydia and Jesper all manhandled the loose, flapping mass of the starboard sail, gathering it in and lashing it into a tight bundle. The wind filled the port sail and the twins hauled in on the sheets, hardening it into a tight, smooth curve and driving the ship forward with renewed urgency. A wave smashed against the starboard bow, showering them all with spray. They ignored it, save for Kloof, who barked delightedly and snapped at the flying salt water.

Heron was now racing at full speed toward the west. Hal glanced from the coastline to the approaching mass of the storm. They'd clear the coast of Picta with time to spare, but beyond that, farther to the south, lay Hibernia. He needed sea room. The moment the storm hit them, they'd begin to lose distance downwind and he wanted to be well clear of the Hibernian coast when that happened.

Thorn made his way aft and stood beside him, his eyes fixed on the storm front. More lightning flashed among the black clouds, and this time, Hal could hear the distant rumble of thunder.

"You'll need to get that yard down before the storm hits," Thorn told him, and Hal nodded. The slender, curving yardarm and its big sail would never stand up to the force of that raging wind.

"For the moment, I need the speed it gives us," he said. "We need to get clear of the Hibernian coast. The faster we go, the sooner that will be."

Thorn chewed his lip. Hal was right, he thought. And he trusted the young man's judgment. Hal would pick the right time to lower the sail.

Hal gestured to Stig, who was watching them. The tall youth came aft to join them, walking easily along the plunging deck without need for handholds.

"Something in mind?" he asked.

"I'm going to wait till the last minute to drop the sail," Hal told him. "Get the sea anchor ready and get the storm sail ready to hoist."

The storm sail was a small triangular sail that was hoisted on the forestay of the stubby main mast. It would give them steerage-way in the high winds, without overstressing the mast or rigging. Stig nodded and returned to the bow, where he called Stefan to help him rig the sea anchor. This was a long, conical-shaped canvas drogue, with its wide end held open by a circle of light, pliable cane. When heaved over the bow, it would hold the ship heading into the wind and slow their downwind drift until Hal could get her under way again with the storm sail.

Once it was ready, lying in the bow beside its coiled rope, Stig and Stefan began clipping the retaining rings of the storm sail onto the heavy forestay, then attached the halyard that was permanently rigged so they could haul it up. When all was ready, Stig rose, turned toward Hal and waved.

"Now we wait," Hal said. He wondered whether he should try to edge the ship to the north to give himself a little extra sea room. Then he realized that this would slow his westerly movement. Better to use the speed he had to clear the Hibernian coast, he thought. Any northing he gained would be quickly negated by the storm. He glanced nervously at the coastline. They were crossing it quickly. Another fifteen minutes and they'd be clear. If the storm gave them fifteen minutes.

"Wind's veering," Thorn told him. "It's shifted to the northeast."

That was definitely good news. If the wind was coming from

the northeast, their downwind path would be southwest, which would take them away from Hibernia and into clear ocean.

And that might make all the difference, he thought.

Suddenly, the *Heron* was engulfed in a howling, battering, almost-living force as the wind slammed into the little ship, driving spray and solid water with it so that they were blinded by the sheer mass of it.

The storm had covered the remaining distance with incredible speed, hitting them with full force.

Heron heeled wildly to port, her leeward gunwales driven momentarily under, shipping huge amounts of water. Hal opened his mouth to bellow orders, but the crew were way ahead of him. Ulf and Wulf released the halyards, spilling the air out of the sail and letting it flap wildly, cracking and smacking like a giant whip. At the same time, Stig heaved the sea anchor over the bow while Stefan and Ingvar lowered the port yardarm and gathered in the sail. Stefan suffered a vicious cut to his forehead from one of the wildly whipping ends of the sail, but in a few moments, they had it under control, with the other available crew members throwing their body weight on it to contain it.

Heron jerked upright once the sail was released, rocking wildly and sending seawater sloshing from side to side in the rowing wells, but the central watertight section did its job and gave the ship a reserve of buoyancy. The sea anchor was taking effect too, hauling the ship's bow around to face the wind and sea.

Clearing the spray and salt water from his eyes, Hal could see Stig heaving the storm sail up into position. Then he felt the tiller come alive as the storm sail took effect and the *Heron* began to claw her way diagonally across the storm. Hal knew that they'd still be losing distance downwind, but they were angling out to the west, and there was a good chance that they'd be clear of the Hibernian coast by the time they reached it.

He hoped.

He flinched as there was a massive flash of lightning, followed almost immediately by a deafening detonation of thunder. Kloof, lashed to the mast, howled in fear.

Thorn leaned closer to Hal. "She didn't like that," he shouted.

Hal grinned nervously in reply. "I wasn't too fond of it myself," he said. He was glad Kloof's reaction had distracted the others. Nobody seemed to have noticed that he had actually jumped in fright at the sudden flash and boom.

He felt his skin tingling and the hair on the nape of his neck rising. Thorn obviously felt it too.

"Another one coming," he warned. Almost instantly, there was a blinding flash and a deafening crack as a lightning bolt struck the sea close by. The water steamed briefly, but the vapor was snatched away by the roaring wind.

Again Kloof howled her displeasure. Hal shook his head and blinked. His retina was imprinted with the aftereffect of the flash, seeing a jagged purple shape for some seconds after the actual event. He was vaguely aware that lightning usually centered on the highest point available and wondered why it hadn't hit their mast. He leaned closer to Thorn and said as much, but the old sea wolf shook his head and pointed to the massive waves marching past them.

"Waves are higher than the mast is," he said and Hal realized he was right.

They shot down the back of one of the waves, then climbed laboriously up the next face. As they smashed through the crest, they were suddenly exposed to the full force of the wind again. *Heron* was laid over on her beam ends once more, then she righted and slid down the back of the wave, moving into its wind shadow and slicing her bow into the water in the trough. Twin explosions of spray fanned out either side of the bow as she buried her nose into the sea, then slowly came up. Seawater surged along the deck and out through the scuppers as she began to climb the next wave.

It was a monster—one of those freak waves that rise up in a storm that are half again as big as their fellows. Hal realized that the wave was higher than the length of the ship and, as *Heron* climbed and her speed began to drop off, he had a heart-stopping moment when he thought she would lose forward momentum and slide backward into the trough. Then she surged through the face of the wave some three meters from the top, smashing the water aside, shaking herself like a soaking-wet dog and then plunging down the far side.

Again, the bow bit into the sea in the trough. Again, spray and solid water exploded out to either side. Stig, making his way aft, seized hold of the standing rigging, wrapping his arms and legs around it as water surged thigh deep down the length of the ship.

As the wave passed, he released his grip and staggered the last few meters to the steering platform.

"She's holding up well," he said.

Hal had to admit he was right. *Heron* was riding the massive waves and thundering wind like the seabird she was named for. But superstition warned him not to appear too positive. The gods of the sea had a way of punishing such hubris, he thought.

"So long as the storm sail holds and we don't spring a plank or two," he said.

Stig dashed water out of his eyes and frowned at him. "You're a cheery soul," he grumbled.

Hal shrugged. There was always the chance—with the violent impacts the ship was suffering as she smashed down into the troughs of the waves—a plank could be started and the ship could spring a leak. He didn't think it would. After all, he'd built the boat himself and knew every join and every rivet in the hull. But it *was* possible.

He glanced astern and felt his heart rise into his throat. The coastline was much closer now, closer than he would have thought possible. Even as *Heron* continued to claw her way up and through the waves, the storm was driving her backward toward the lee shore.

There was nothing he could do about it. He was holding her on the best possible course, covering as much distance to the west as they could. His arms ached with the effort of holding the tiller but he wasn't prepared to turn it over to one of the others. It was his ship, after all, and his responsibility. And when he discounted any false modesty, he knew he was the best man for the task at hand. He was a more skillful helmsman than any of his friends.

Thorn's left hand gripped his shoulder and he nodded his head astern. Hal swung to look again in the direction indicated. He felt a jolt of fear as he saw a line of black rocks jutting like fangs from the sea, at one moment hidden from sight by the spray bursting around them, the next rearing their razor-sharp heads above the surface, as if searching for the ship bearing down on them.

The three friends were silent. Hal measured the bearing to the rocks by closing one eye and keeping the sternpost aligned with them. After a minute, he realized the angle was changing, slowly, but sufficiently to let them slide past.

"We're going to miss them," he said.

Thorn and Stig looked doubtful as *Heron* reared up another wave face and smashed through and down. For a few moments, the snarling, threatening rocks were hidden from sight. Then, as they soared up the next wave, they could see that the reef was now to starboard. They would slide by safely. Not by much, but by enough.

Hal flinched as one of the rocks emerged from the seething ocean only a few meters from their stern, then seemed to race away down the starboard side of the ship. It had been a close thing, he realized.

There was another vivid flash of lightning and a crashing roll of thunder a few seconds later. But this one was farther away than the previous lightning strike and he considered it dispassionately. Stig gained his attention and pointed to the Hibernian coastline, now well to the east.

"We're past it," Stig said.

Hal nodded emphatically. He heaved on the tiller and swung the ship's head to the west, the wind filling the storm sail and heeling *Heron* over under the pressure.

"Let's get some sea room," he said, and headed his ship out into the unknown wastes of the Endless Ocean.

chapter three

Days passed and the storm continued unabated.

"How long can a storm like this last?" Stefan asked Thorn. The crew were huddled together in the meager shelter of the port rowing well, draped in tarpaulins, in a vain attempt to keep dry. Hal and Stig were by the steering platform, Hal's hands still clenched around the tiller, Stig with his feet braced wide for balance and his arm around his friend to keep him steady on his feet. It had been days since Hal had managed any meaningful rest. He had snatched the odd catnap from time to time when Stig or Thorn could persuade him to relinquish the tiller. But the slightest change in the ship's motion, the occasional jolt from a wave slightly out of the normal rhythm, would have him back on his feet in an instant, seizing the tiller and taking control once more.

Thorn looked up at the gray sky, full of scudding clouds, and immediately wished he hadn't as cold water trickled down his neck through a gap his movement had opened.

"Days," he said.

"It's been days already," Jesper pointed out. Thorn looked at him, this time moving carefully to avoid another shot of water down his neck.

"Weeks then," he said. "Knew a storm like this once that lasted more than two weeks."

"As bad as this?" Stefan asked.

Thorn considered his answer, then shook his head. And cursed as the unthinking movement released more water inside his clothes.

"No. This is the worst I can remember."

"That's comforting," Lydia mumbled, sitting with her head lowered and a tarpaulin cloak pulled up tight around her face and neck.

Interesting, Thorn thought. She had less sailing experience than any of the others. They had all been raised on boats and on the sea. Yet she seemed to have a stolid confidence that they would make it through the storm. A lot of girls in her position would have been reduced to gibbering terror, he knew, then realized a lot of men would be the same.

"You're not worried?" he asked her.

She raised her eyes to meet his. "Yes. But there's precious little I can do about it, so there's no point letting it get on top of me," she said. "Besides, you're all constantly telling me that Hal is the best helmsman you've ever seen. I'm sure he'll bring us through it."

That was certainly true. But Thorn wondered how long Hal

could continue like this. He'd been at the helm virtually since the storm had hit them. His eyes were red-rimmed from salt water and fatigue, and he was hunched over the tiller like an old man. Sooner or later, one of them would have to relieve him. Hal needed sleep—hours of it—whether he liked it or not.

Thorn glanced sideways at the young skirl. As he did, he saw Hal lurch and stumble with an unexpected movement of the ship. Stig moved quickly to steady him and Hal muttered a silent "thanks" to his friend. He shook himself and stood erect, blinking those sore, red-rimmed eyes and stamping his feet to stimulate the blood flow in them. His legs and feet must be aching, Thorn thought. Within a few seconds, Hal's upright stance sagged once more with weariness and he was again left supported by Stig's muscular arm.

"That's it," Thorn said to himself. He cast aside the tarpaulin cloak and clambered onto the deck of the ship, lurching toward the two figures at the steering platform as the ship jerked and jolted under him.

Stig looked at him, a question in his eyes. Hal remained staring doggedly forward, his hands locked on the tiller.

"He's out on his feet," Thorn said.

Stig nodded agreement. "I know. But he won't rest. I've already offered to spell him but he just shakes his head and says he's fine."

"Which he is obviously not," Thorn replied. He took hold of Hal's right hand and tried to lever it from the tiller. The young skirl's grip tightened, locking his hand on to the smooth wood. Thorn released his own grip and leaned closer to his young friend.

"You've got to take a break," he said.

Hal's lips moved soundlessly.

Thorn gestured at the waves surging past, lifting and lowering the ship in a regular rhythm. *Heron* was riding the storm comfortably. They had taken in the sea anchor some hours ago, letting the storm sail propel her. If they lost ground downwind now, it didn't really matter. There was no dangerous shore to leeward—nothing but the endless sea itself. She was still heaving herself up each wave, then sliding down the far side, showering the decks with spray as she cut through the crest and then plunged deep into the trough. But the motion, violent as it was, was regular and predictable.

"She's under control now," Thorn continued, his lips close to Hal's ear. "Stig can take her. You should rest in case the weather gets worse."

The red-rimmed eyes looked at him. The boy was exhausted, Thorn thought. In fact, he was way past exhausted. Again, Thorn tried to pry one of Hal's hands free from the tiller, and, this time, Hal reluctantly let him do so. Thorn's words must have penetrated to his brain and he had realized the sense behind them. Thorn began to work on the other hand and glanced at Stig.

"Take the helm," he said and the first mate took over the tiller as Thorn pried Hal's other hand free. With his arm around Hal, Thorn gently led him away from the steering platform and down to the leeward rowing benches.

The others reached up to help him into the meager shelter.

"Get a dry blanket," Thorn told Edvin.

The medic opened a hatch in the watertight center section of the ship and produced a more or less dry blanket. Then, he and Thorn stripped off Hal's sheepskin vest and woolen shirt and began to rub him hard with the blanket, working away until his skin glowed red from the friction and the blood began to return to his flesh. His lips had been tinged with blue, but now the violent rubbing with the blanket had got his circulation going once more and the skin returned to its normal color. Wulf had delved into another locker to produce a dry shirt.

When Hal was dressed again, Thorn draped the blanket around him and pulled him in close, wrapping his arms around the skirl. Edvin draped Thorn's tarpaulin cloak over both of them. Hal shivered violently and then collapsed against Thorn's comforting bulk.

"Get some sleep," the one-armed sea wolf told his young friend. His voice was surprisingly gentle and comforting, and Edvin glanced at him curiously. He was used to Thorn being noisy or sardonic. This was a caring side of him that he rarely let show. Thorn glanced up, realized Edvin was watching him, and guessed what the boy was thinking.

"He'd keep going till he dropped if we let him," he said, nodding his head toward the now-resting Hal.

"We'd better keep an eye on Stig as well," Edvin told him.

Thorn nodded. "That's true. He's been up there in the wind and cold almost as long as Hal has been." He swiveled on the bench to check Stig. The big youth seemed all right, he thought. Stig caught him looking and grinned reassuringly, then ducked his head as another cascade of spray broke over the bow and drenched him.

Thorn let Stig stay on the tiller for another hour, then moved to spell him, carefully handing off the sleeping Hal to Ingvar. "Should be plenty of body heat there to keep him warm," he said.

Ingvar, big and amiable, smiled agreement.

The storm continued to howl around them, setting the standing rigging humming with the force of the wind. They continued their endless sequence of climbing a wave face, then plunging down its back, only to begin another staggering climb, until the repetitive motion seemed to encompass their entire world. Their minds were numbed by it, as their bodies and hands were numbed by the bitter cold.

Thorn stayed on the tiller for two hours, as the already-dim daylight faded into darkness. Occasionally, lightning would still crack through the black clouds, lighting up the lines of the ship for a brief second. Then the boom of thunder would deafen them, and Kloof would bark angrily in reply. But the lightning flashes were becoming less and less frequent.

Thorn handed over the tiller to Stig again once night had fallen. They looked at Hal's sleeping form.

"We'll let him sleep as long as he can," Thorn said. "He needs the rest."

It was during Stig's watch that they noticed the flickering blue light that shimmered at the top of the stumpy mast and spread along the rigging. The first mate called out a warning as he saw it, thinking that the mast had somehow caught fire in the storm. Thorn stood, swaying with the motion of the ship, and studied it. The rest of the crew muttered in alarm at the sight.

"It's Loki's Fire," Thorn called. "Liar's Fire, they sometimes call it."

Loki was the god of lies, and well-known as a trickster. The blue flames were not fire at all, but merely a phenomenon that sometimes occurred in a thunderstorm at sea. Thorn had seen it several times before on voyages and he knew the blue, flickering flamelike light was harmless.

Stefan eyed it uncertainly. "Looks like real fire to me."

Several others in the crew agreed, their voices nervous.

Thorn smiled at them. "If it were fire, the mast would have been burnt up by now," he pointed out.

The crew subsided, their fears calmed but not entirely dismissed. The blue light had been flickering on the mast and tarred ropes for several minutes now, with no sign of any deterioration in the material.

"I've seen that in the forest a few times," Lydia said, "although I never knew what it was called. Thorn's right. It can't hurt us."

That seemed to settle the rest of the crew. If Lydia wasn't worried by the strange light, they weren't going to let it rattle them. But, mollified as they were, they still continued to cast doubtful looks at the strange light until it abruptly disappeared, as quickly as it had come.

"I kind of miss it now," Jesper said after the deep blackness of night settled around them again. "It was pretty."

Then a rogue wave, sliding unseen at an angle to the normal swell, smashed into their starboard bow, laying *Heron* over and dumping spray and solid water on her decks. The ship shuddered, then righted herself. Hal was instantly awake, alerted by the changed motion of the ship. He cast aside the tarpaulin cloak that covered him and looked round in the darkness.

Stig had the ship back on course, and she was climbing yet another mountain of water as it bore down on them. But there were tons of water in the rowing wells now, more than the scuppers could cope with. The ship felt sluggish and heavy as she labored up the wave. Hal sprang lightly up onto the deck and moved to take the tiller from Stig. The first mate gratefully relinquished it to him. He had taken the full force of the wave. It had winded him and drenched him at the same time.

"Didn't see that coming," he complained.

"Get yourself dried off," Hal told him. "I'll take her for a while."

He was obviously reinvigorated after his long rest. Stig headed for the rowing wells, in search of a dry blanket.

Thorn sighed and gestured to the rest of the crew.

"Grab a bucket each," he said. "We're going to have to bail her out."

chapter four

They sailed on through the dark hours of the night, alternately climbing and sliding down the massive swells, with the wind howling at them like a wild, living creature.

Their lives took on an inevitable sequence—climb up, smash through, swoop down, bury the bow in the sea, then begin the next laborious climb.

It was uncomfortable and unpleasant, but the early venom of the storm had abated a little and now they were confident that, barring the unexpected, the ship would handle the conditions safely.

The wind was still too strong for Hal to risk hoisting the slender, curved yardarms or setting more sail. The tiny storm sail stretched drum-taut against the wind and gave them steerageway in the plunging seas. But, even though the little ship was pointing northwest, they all knew that their real course was southwest, as the wind and waves drove the ship before them.

It was an unnerving feeling for the crew. They were being driven farther and farther into the vast expanse of the Endless Ocean, a place where none of them had ever sailed before. But, as Lydia had stated, there was little they could do about it, so worrying over the matter would achieve nothing. In fact, it was her calm acceptance of the situation that allowed a lot of them to retain their equanimity. In such situations, panic and fear can become contagious. But this time, it was calmness and stoicism that spread among them.

They were in a routine now. The steering position, exposed to the wind and spray on the upper part of the rear deck, was potentially the most exhausting—with the exception of those times, thankfully infrequent, when they had to bail. Hal, realizing that he couldn't possibly take on the task of steering on his own, organized a roster between himself, Stig, Thorn and Edvin.

Edvin, of course, had trained early on in the *Heron*'s first cruise as a relief helmsman. He didn't have the physical strength of Hal, and certainly not Stig or Thorn. But he had a deft touch on the tiller and sense of the ship's rhythm that helped him keep her on course with a minimum of movement of the rudder. He anticipated the ship's movements as the sea swirled around her. And, by anticipating, he needed to expend less effort to correct her.

Lydia watched him, admiration in her eyes. She had moved up close to the steering platform to keep him company, realizing that steering could be a lonely task.

"You're good at this, aren't you?" she said.

Edvin flushed, and smiled at her, pleased that she recognized his skill in handling the ship. "It's easier to keep her going where you want if you don't let her go where *she* wants."

Lydia thought about that and nodded seriously. "That's a good way of looking at it." On previous cruises, she'd taken her turn at the helm. Hal believed every crew member should be able to steer a course, no matter what their individual skills might be. He and Stig had been at pains to get her to develop the anticipation that Edvin grasped so easily. The tiller required constant small adjustments as the water flowed around it, she had learned. If you let the wind or the waves push the ship off course, it took twice the effort to get it back on course again.

Of course, knowing it and being able to do it were two completely different matters.

"Would you like a drink?" she asked.

Edvin nodded eagerly. Steering was thirsty work, in spite of the cold and damp conditions. "What's on offer?" he asked. He grinned and the dried salt on his cracked lips stung.

"There's water. Or water," Lydia told him.

He made as if he were considering the choice. "Better make it water," he said finally.

Of course, there was nothing hot to drink, much as they would all have loved to have something. With the deck rearing and plunging the way it was, it would be madness to light a fire on board, even the small gimballed oil burner that Edvin had in his cooking kit.

Lydia dropped into the rowing well and poured him a beaker of cold water from a water skin, leaning over to shield the beaker from the salt spray that cascaded along the deck with monotonous regularity. She climbed back to the main deck and handed the drink to Edvin. He sipped deeply. It was cold, of course, and very refreshing because of it. But with the second sip, he frowned slightly. There was a distinct salt taste to the water now, courtesy of the spray that had fallen into it. Lydia saw his expression of slight distaste.

"Sorry," she said, guessing the reason. "Hard to keep that salt water out of everything."

"Can't be helped," he replied, draining the beaker quickly to prevent any further contamination.

He studied the sky, taking in the unbroken dark gray of the clouds and the way the wind kept the telltale at the masthead whipping out in a virtually straight line.

"Can't say the weather's improving," he muttered.

But it was, albeit in increments so gradual that it was hard for them to notice the change.

By the fourth day, the wind had dropped from the howling, unpredictable force of the first two days to a steadier pattern, without the sudden, terrifying and potentially lethal gusts and lunges that had threatened to overwhelm the ship if the crew let their attention wander.

There was still plenty of danger in that wind, and plenty of brute force. But it no longer seemed to be trying to catch them unawares. It was simply there, as a backdrop to their day.

And so they sailed on. Four days. Then five. Then six. And with every hour and every day that passed, they were driven deeper and deeper into the unexplored vastness of the Endless Ocean.

On the sixth day, the sun actually appeared. Hal watched it travel through an arc above them. He had never seen the sun as high as that before. He took several measurements, using his hinged sighting stick. Even without an accurate determination of the time of day, he knew that they had come farther south than he had ever been before.

Maybe farther south than *anyone* had ever been.

He was sitting in the rowing well, slapping his arms back and forth against his body to restore a little warmth to them, when Stig approached him, a worried look on his face.

"What's the problem?" Hal asked.

Stig glanced round, making sure that none of the other crew members was in earshot. "We're running low on water," he said in a subdued tone.

Hal frowned, not understanding. "How can that be? We're still on the first cask. We've a full second cask to go after that."

The *Heron* carried their drinking water in two large casks below deck in the watertight center section. Each day, Stig would fill a large water skin and keep it handy on deck for crew members to drink from. As a matter of course, they had refilled both casks before they left Hibernia. One would have been enough to see them home, but Hal preferred to err on the side of caution. You never knew what might happen, after all—as their current situation showed only too well.

"The second cask has sprung a leak. The water's been seeping away." Stig shook his head angrily. "Don't know how it happened. Maybe all the lurching and banging loosened a stave."

As first mate, it was Stig's task to attend to such matters as supplies and equipment. Hal could tell that he blamed himself for the leaking cask.

"How much have we lost?" he asked. That was the vital matter.

Stig considered the question. "We've maybe a third of a cask left," he said. "And a little less than that in the first cask."

"First thing to do is stop the leak," Hal said.

Stig made a dismissive gesture. "I've taken care of that. It was hard to see where the leak was actually coming from, so I transferred the remaining water to the first cask."

"There's no problem with that, is there?" Hal asked anxiously. If one cask was damaged, it was all too possible that the other might be as well. It wasn't likely, but it was possible. And Hal had been at sea long enough to know that if something was possible, it might well happen—and all too often, it did. But Stig reassured him.

"No. It's sound. I've checked it three times. Point is, two-thirds of a cask would be enough to get us back home in normal conditions."

He paused meaningfully. Hal got the point. He eyed the gray, racing waves overside.

"But these aren't normal conditions," he said.

"No indeed," Stig agreed heavily. "We have no idea where we are, and no idea how long it'll take us to get home."

"Which makes it hard to figure out how much water we'll need," Hal finished for him. They sat in silence for a few minutes, then Hal came to a decision. "We'll cut the normal daily ration by half," he said.

Stig looked doubtful, although he was glad the decision wasn't his. "Will that be enough?"

Hal shrugged. "I honestly don't know. We've been blown a long way west and south. And we're continuing to be so. We'll have to see how long these conditions keep up and how long it'll be before we can begin to head northeast again." He scratched his chin thoughtfully. "We'll go to half rations for a while and see what develops. Let the others know," he added. He didn't want them finding out when it came time for their daily water ration to be doled out. Better to let them get their grumbling and complaining over in advance.

Stig pursed his lips. Hal could see he was still chafing over the fact that he had allowed this to happen. He patted his friend's arm.

"Don't beat yourself up over this," he said. "It wasn't your fault."

Stig shook his head disgustedly. "I'm your first mate. I should have checked sooner."

Hal shrugged philosophically. He wasn't going to argue the point too much. Technically, it *was* Stig's job to keep track of details like this, and the fact that he blamed himself was, in a way, a good thing. He would never let a similar situation arise in the future.

If we have a future, a niggling little voice said in Hal's mind. He shook his head to clear it.

"Tell the others," he repeated, and Stig made his way for'ard to where the rest of the crew were sitting, huddled together for warmth.

Predictably, it was Jesper who was first to complain about the news.

"How did that happen?" he demanded in an injured tone when Stig told them of the leaking cask. The big first mate fixed him with a steely glare.

"How it happened doesn't matter," he said. "What does matter is that it *has* happened. And we're on half rations until further notice."

"Maybe it'll rain," Ingvar suggested. "We should be ready to catch any rainwater if it does."

Stig gave him an appreciative nod. "Good thinking, Ingvar. Jesper, Stefan, rig one of the spare sails to catch water if we get some rain."

"Why me?" Jesper wanted to know. Listening, Hal raised his eyes to the storm-wracked heavens.

"Because I said so," Stig replied.

Jesper sniffed disparagingly. "That's not an answer," he muttered.

Stig moved a little closer to him. "Well, how about this? Because I'm the first mate and if you don't do as I say, I'll give you a thick ear."

There was a long silence between them. Finally, Jesper looked away and moved toward the locker where spare sails were stowed.

"Yeah, well, that's kind of an answer," he admitted sulkily.

chapter five

On the eighth day, the storm finally decided to have mercy on them. The howling wind and driving spray abated. And the *Heron* no longer shipped green water over her bows every time she plunged into the troughs at the back of each wave.

But while the force of the storm dissipated and gave the crew a welcome respite from alternately huddling in the rowing wells and bailing out the water that came on board, there was no change in the relentless southwestward drive of the wind and sea. *Heron* continued to drift downwind. The wind direction was completely foul for the course they would need to take them back toward Hibernia, and eventually Skandia.

Thorn and Hal crouched by the steering platform as Stig kept the ship headed at an angle to the prevailing sea and wind. They appeared to be traveling northwest but all three of them knew that, while that was their heading, they were still drifting downwind and down sea to the southwest. The wind, while no longer the shrieking, malevolent force that had battered them for eight exhausting days and nights, was still blowing half a gale and seemed determined to prevent them making any progress toward their homeland.

"Do you think there's any chance that it might change?" Hal asked Thorn. The old sea wolf was the most experienced sailor among them. He had seen wind and weather patterns all over their known world.

But the problem was, they were no longer in their known world. The Endless Ocean was an unknown quantity, an enigma to them all. Wolfships had skirted its easternmost edge in times past. But none had ventured as far into the vast, heaving gray mass as they had.

Or at least, if any ship had, it hadn't returned to tell the tale.

Thorn hesitated before answering. He wrinkled his nose and sniffed the air, peering into the northeast where the wind and waves originated.

"Frankly," he said at length, "I have no idea. I don't know these waters and I don't know the weather systems here. All I can say is, why should it change? It's been blowing from the northeast for eight days now. I can't see any sign that it might suddenly shift. And we'd need it to veer ninety degrees to do us any good."

"So for all we know, it could continue like this for another eight days," Hal said.

Thorn shrugged. "Why stop at eight? It could keep on like this for weeks. It's obviously a massive weather front that's driving it. Sorry I can't be more encouraging."

Hal chewed on a frayed fingernail, then glanced at Stig. "How are the crew?" he asked. In a situation like this, as skirl, he had to remain a little aloof from the crew. He couldn't discuss things with them or share his thoughts. If he had to make hard and unpopular decisions, it was best if he maintained his distance. That way, his orders and his decisions wouldn't become a topic for debate and discussion. But Stig was able to stay closer to the crew and act as Hal's eyes and ears among them.

"Well, you know I cut the water ration again yesterday. We're down to two beakers a day." Hal frowned. He'd known that Stig was going to cut the ration again, but he hadn't known what the result would be. "That's getting pretty meager. How did they take it?"

"They didn't like it," Stig said. "Who would? But they can see why it's necessary. They're not children, after all. And if they complain to me, it helps get it all off their chests."

"Cursed if I know why it hasn't rained," Thorn put in, glaring at the low clouds still whipping overhead, driven by the wind. "Orlog knows there's enough cloud up there for a deluge."

"Maybe it will," Hal said. His tone indicated how little chance he gave it of happening. Things never happen when you need them, he thought. But he didn't express the sentiment aloud. Quarter rations of water was a serious step. It was barely enough to sustain the crew. They had plenty of food, of course, but without water, nobody felt like eating too much. And lack of water would affect them far sooner than lack of food.

"Even if the wind did shift," he said, after a few minutes'

silence, "it'd take us at least another eight days to get back to where we started."

"More," Stig pointed out. "We'd be beating into the wind, zigzagging back and forth and having to cover twice the distance we've come."

"So maybe ten, twelve days," Hal said.

Stig nodded agreement. "At least. And we'll be out of water in three."

Thorn was watching his young friend carefully. "You've got something in mind?"

Hal took a deep breath, then committed himself. "I'm thinking we should hoist the mainsail and head west."

"West?" Thorn said, disbelief all too evident in his voice. "Farther into the Endless Ocean?"

"That's just a name," Hal said. "And it exists because nobody has ever sailed out into it. But think about it. There must be something out there."

He gestured vaguely to the western horizon, and the others followed the direction of his pointing arm. Thorn looked skeptical. Stig looked concerned.

"But what if it really is endless?" Stig asked.

Hal shook his head scornfully. "Why should it be? No other ocean goes on forever. There's always land somewhere."

"But this is the Endless Ocean," Thorn put in mildly.

Hal shook his head impatiently. "It's just *called* that. Certainly it's big. But mapmakers tend to be poetic. They'd never call it the Big Ocean. The Endless Ocean has a much more dramatic ring to it."

"It has a decidedly scary ring to it, if you ask me," Stig said.

Thorn switched his gaze back and forth between the two friends as they spoke. Finally, he said deliberately, "I think Hal is right. We're doing nothing here but bobbing up and down like a cork, constantly being swept farther south and west. We'll soon run out of water and then where will we be?"

"What if the wind changes?" Stig said stubbornly.

Thorn shrugged. "We can always put about and head back toward Hibernia if it does." He paused. "But we've established that even if the wind does change, we'd run out of water long before we got there."

"And if we head west, we'll make good speed," Hal added. "We'll be on our best point of sailing, and the wind is certainly strong enough. We could find land in a day or so, who knows?"

"Nobody. And that's the point," Stig said.

"Well, we can keep sitting here, going up and down and backward and getting nowhere. Or we can try to do something about it. I'd rather do something than sit and wait to die of thirst."

He looked around at the gray, sullen sea. It was ironic, he thought, to be talking about dying of thirst when they were surrounded by millions of square kilometers of water.

"I suppose you're right," Stig said, slowly coming round to Hal's point of view. "But I think that this is one occasion when we should consult the others. It's their lives we're dealing with, after all. They deserve to have a say."

"I don't like doing that," Hal said. "It could set a bad precedent."

"Normally, you'd be right," Thorn said. "But normally, you'd make a decision like this based on facts and knowledge. This time, you're acting on instinct. I agree with Stig. For once, the crew should be included in the decision."

Hal realized that his friends were right. If he headed west, he was taking an enormous risk. He had nothing to back up his belief that there must be land out there, somewhere.

"All right," he said. "Let's get them together."

The crew assembled in the stern. Stig kept control of the tiller while Hal put the position to them, and laid out his idea of turning west and hoisting full sail.

He was greeted by shocked looks, as he'd expected. The concept of heading out into the unknown was a radical one. Jesper, naturally, was the first to argue against it.

"You want to sail farther away from home?" he said incredulously. "Farther out into the Endless Ocean?" He shook his head, looking at Hal as if he were mad.

"As I see it," the skirl explained calmly, "it's our best chance of finding land. We're certainly not going to do it sitting here."

Now that he'd had time to absorb the idea, Ingvar spoke up. "I admit I was a bit shocked when you just suggested it," he said. "But, thinking about it, it seems the only logical thing to do."

"Logical?" Jesper erupted indignantly. "What's logical about sailing farther away from home—into the Endless Ocean? The *Endless* Ocean," he repeated for emphasis. "That means it goes on and on *forever*."

"Nobody knows that," Edvin said quietly. He knew their situation was dire. But, as far as he was concerned, Hal was offering the best possible alternative.

"Nobody knows it doesn't either," said Jesper. In truth, he

wasn't so skeptical about the idea. But Hal's suggestion had just driven home to him how bad their position really was. It had made him face the very strong possibility that they would all die out here, thousands of kilometers from home.

"Let me see if I've got this right," Lydia said. They all turned to regard her. In her time with the crew, she had become a trusted and respected member. She had an analytical mind. Her life as a hunter had trained her to weigh possibilities and decisions. Even Jesper wanted to hear what she had to say. Deep down, he trusted Hal to make important decisions. But this was one of the most important they had ever faced, and usually the young skirl could support his ideas with facts and solid reason. This time, he had no facts to back up his idea.

"We've got water for three days?" Lydia said, looking at Stig. He nodded confirmation. "If the wind changed, where would we be in three days? I mean, is there any land to the east that we could reach in three days?"

Since she was addressing him, Stig shook his head. Hal felt it was better to stay out of this conversation. His position was already clear.

"None," Stig said. "You've seen what's to the east. Hibernia is the closest land and that's maybe ten days away, at least."

"By which time we'll be out of water," she said.

Stefan interrupted. "By which time we'll be *dead* from lack of water. It's not as if we've had a lot in the past few days."

She nodded at him. "Good point." Then she returned her gaze to Stig. "And if we go west? Is there land there?"

The tall first mate hesitated, then shrugged. "We just don't know."

"But we do know there's nothing to the east," she stated and again he agreed.

"That's right."

She thought about what he had said, then looked at Thorn. "Thorn, what do you think? Does this ocean just go on forever? Or is it possible there's land to the west?"

"Of course it's possible," he said. "In fact, it's a pretty logical assumption."

"How's that?" Lydia asked.

"Well, we all know the theory that the world is a huge saucer, supported on the back of a giant tortoise," he said. It was a popular myth, although he wasn't sure that he believed it. Several of the others obviously did, however. He saw them nodding quiet agreement.

"Then think about this. We know that to the east, there's Hibernia, Araluen and then the huge landmass of the continent leading to Aslava and the Steppes. It makes sense to believe that there must be a similar landmass to the west to counterbalance it. Otherwise, the world would overbalance and tip off the tortoise's back."

Jesper opened his mouth to say something, then stopped and closed it again, considering what Thorn had just said.

"Well, at last somebody's making sense," he said finally. He looked at Hal. "Why didn't you say that in the first place?"

chapter six

With the wind on her starboard beam, *Heron* positively flew across the ocean, reeling off kilometer after kilometer as she went. The perpetual, and slightly nauseating, pitching as she rode up and down each successive wave was gone, and the relentless pounding into the waves, taking them head-on, was a thing of the past. Now she swooped at a diagonal angle to the waves, shouldering her way through the crests and sliding down into the troughs. She rolled and pitched, certainly, but the rhythm of her movement was exhilarating. She was alive. The rigging creaked and groaned in a constant song. At last, the crew felt they were actually going somewhere.

The problem was, they still had no idea where that might be.

Irrationally, Hal had hoped that they might see some sign of land in the first day. They had certainly covered plenty of distance. But as the night fell and the following morning broke over them, there was nothing in sight but the endless sea around them, stretching to the horizon in all directions.

Stig doled out the miserly pittance of water to the crew. Hal tried to refuse his, but the entire crew protested when he did.

"We're in this together," said Wulf. "And we need you as healthy as possible."

The others mumbled agreement and Hal submitted to their will. He slowly let the small portion of water slide down his throat, trying to make it last as long as possible.

"Not sure how healthy that'll keep me," he mused, his voice thick, as he handed the empty beaker back to Stig. It was getting difficult to talk, he noted. All of their voices had thickened and coarsened as their throats and mouths were left swollen and dry. The momentary effect of the small portion of water they were given twice a day did little to relieve the feeling.

The lack of water was making him lethargic too. He had to force himself to take his position at the helm when his turn came, asking himself why he bothered, when they could all be dead within a week.

Stefan had at one stage suggested they might try to drink small quantities of seawater. "At least it's water," he said. But Thorn quickly scotched that idea.

"Get rid of that thought!" he said, his voice muffled by the dryness in his mouth and throat. "I've seen crews go mad doing that."

Stefan looked down, embarrassed by his own suggestion. For a second or two, it had seemed to make sense. But he saw now how right Thorn was. Seawater would only make their raging thirst feel worse.

"Maybe it'll rain," Wulf said hopefully.

"Maybe it won't," Ulf replied.

Another night passed. The wind remained constant and *Heron* continued to speed westward. The rising sun the following morning seared their eyes with its red glow. Slowly, it rose up the eastern sky. Once again, Hal was concerned to see how high it sat in the sky before beginning its descent once more.

"Bear left!" Jesper was in the bow, keeping a lookout.

His sudden shout roused Hal, and he realized, guiltily, that he had actually dozed off at the tiller. Now, with Jesper's warning, he shoved the tiller bar over and the ship swung instantly to the left. A black mass passed down the starboard side—long and shining wet, almost submerged, with a crooked branch sticking up into the air. A dead tree trunk, he realized, watching it dully. Had they hit it at the speed they were traveling, they could have shattered *Heron*'s bow.

Might have been a good thing, he thought. At least that way, they'd get it over quickly, without the lingering agony of thirst and the unbelievable weariness they were all feeling.

He sank back into his lethargy. He realized now that he had been wrong. There was no land to the west. This ocean really was endless and they would sail on into it until they were dried-out husks hunched over in the ship. A ghost ship with a crew of dead men—and one woman, he amended.

Lydia had felt the sudden alteration in the *Heron*'s course. So had the others, but none of them were alert enough to be bothered commenting on it.

"What was that?" she asked. Although with the dryness of her mouth and thickening of her tongue, the words came out sounding more like "Wha' wa' tha'?"

Hal shrugged. "Just a tree trunk," he said, his tone showing his total disinterest in the matter. "Nearly hit it."

Lydia frowned. She sensed there was something significant here, but she couldn't figure what it was. She pushed her brain to think, but it responded slowly and ponderously. Thinking was hard work. It was easier not to think. Probably better not to think, as well. When she expended energy thinking, all she thought of was water. Finally, a small light of intelligence burned in the back of her mind.

"Where did it come from?" she asked.

Hal glanced at her dully, a little annoyed to be roused from the torpor that was creeping over him. Now he had to think, to work out what she was asking. Where did what come from? And what did it matter, in any event?

"What?" he asked eventually, realizing that she was going to insist on an answer.

Lydia waved a weary hand at the sea over the side.

"The tree trunk. We nearly hit it," she reminded him. She was irritable in her turn, thinking that Hal was being intentionally annoying.

"I know that," he replied.

She gestured angrily at him once more. "So where did it come from?"

"Up for'ard," he replied tartly. "Nearly hit our starboard bow. Would have sunk us in all likelihood."

She glared at him, wondering how he could be so dense. He was usually quite intelligent, she thought.

"I mean, where did it come from? It was a tree. A tree has to grow somewhere before it falls into the sea."

"Well, how the blazes would I know where it grew? I'm not an expert on—" He suddenly stopped, as the import of what she was saying struck him like a battering ram. His mouth hung open for a few seconds. "It was a tree," he said eventually.

"I think we've established that," Lydia replied.

He waved his hands defensively. "But you're right. It had to grow somewhere. Trees don't just appear in the middle of the ocean. It had to come from land. An island. Or something bigger."

He lashed the tiller in place and clambered awkwardly onto the bulwark, holding on to the backstay for balance. Even as he did so, he realized how badly he had been affected by dehydration. Normally, he would have sprung lightly onto the railing. Today, he struggled to make it. But he shielded his eyes and peered ahead into the gathering gloom, hoping against hope that he might see land.

"Well?" said Lydia expectantly.

He shook his head, downcast. "Nothing but the sea," he told her.

She frowned. "But it must have come from somewhere," she insisted. He climbed stiffly down from the railing and took the tiller again.

Thorn, who had noticed the little scene being played out, walked aft to join them. "What is it?" he asked.

"There was a tree," Hal told him. "It came out of nowhere and drifted past us."

Thorn looked at the two of them. The meaning of Hal's words wasn't lost on him.

"If there was a tree, that means there's land," he said.

"We know," Lydia replied. "The question is, how far is it? And which direction?"

"I guess we'll have to wait for morning to find out," Thorn said. "It's getting too dark to see anything now."

Hal came to a decision. He called to Stig, who wearily made his way aft to join them. He raised his eyebrows in an unspoken question.

"How much water is left?" Hal asked him. Stig pursed his lips, then licked them, dry and cracked as they were. The very mention of water reminded him of how thirsty he was.

"Two or three liters," he said. "Enough for two beakers each . . . maybe."

"Dole it out," Hal said.

Stig looked at him in surprise. "All of it?"

Hal nodded. "All of it. I'm sick and tired of having my mouth thick and parched. Let's all have one decent drink. Tomorrow morning, we're going to sight land."

Stig's surprised look turned to doubt. He wondered whether Hal had lost his senses. "We are?"

Hal nodded definitely. "We are."

But they didn't.

Dawn found them swooping steadily across the heaving ocean, with no sign of land in any direction. Buoyed up by Hal's unreasoning optimism, the crew had lined the bulwarks since first light, scanning the horizon ahead. Jesper clambered painfully up to the lookout position on the bow post. But even his keen eyes couldn't see a trace of land.

The memory of the night before, of the luxury of having one long, satisfying drink, was behind them now. They knew there was no more water, and with that knowledge, their mouths grew dry and tongues grew swollen once more. Speech was difficult, so for the most part they remained silent.

They sat in the windward rowing well, downcast and dejected, heads lowered, shoulders hunched. The true enormity of their situation now faced them. But none of them begrudged Hal's impetuous decision to drink the last of the water. Better to enjoy one last meaningful drink than to eke out the remaining few drops, they all thought.

Such was the measure of their despair that none of them noticed the gull when it first landed on the tip of the yardarm, spreading its wings for balance before folding them neatly away and beginning to preen itself. It had been there for over ten minutes when it finally emitted a loud squawk and launched itself into the air, plunging almost immediately into the side of a wave to capture the fish that its keen eyes had seen just below the surface.

It bobbed on the heaving ocean as it tossed the fish it had caught, turning it so it would be easier to swallow, then gulping it down.

"It's a gull," said Edvin.

Lydia regarded him incuriously. "So?"

He pointed at the bird as it shook itself. "A gull. Not an albatross or a frigate bird. They can fly hundreds of kilometers from the land—way out into the oceans. But a gull stays close to land."

As he spoke, the white-and-gray bird raised itself from the surface and flapped its wings vigorously, taking flight almost immediately. It gathered height and flew in a large circle to approach the ship again. Now twenty eyes were fixed on it. For a moment, it seemed about to land on the yardarm once more.

Ulf rose up, waving his arms violently, and yelled in a cracked, croaking tone, "Shoo! Get out of it! Go home!"

Startled by the sudden movement, the gull wheeled away and steadied on a course to the west. The Herons looked at one another, and hope sprang up in all their hearts.

"He's going home," said Ulf.

Wulf, as ever, chose to bicker with his twin, even at a time like this. "How do you know it's not a she?"

Ulf let his shoulders slump wearily. "All right. *She's* going home," he amended. "Home to dry land." His uncharacteristic lack of protest was a sign of how weary he truly was.

"And all we have to do is follow her," Hal said.

Stig grinned through cracked, dry lips. "How do you know it's a she?"

Hal didn't answer. He had already brought the bow round to follow the exact course set by the rapidly disappearing gull.

chapter seven

Half a day had passed since they had sighted the seagull. The bird had long ago flown out of sight, and the ship continued to slide through the sea in its wake. Their initial excitement had died away, followed by disappointment and dejection as no sight of land eventuated.

Stefan sat downcast on the deck, idly kicking his legs back and forth as they dangled down into the starboard rowing well.

"I wonder if this is what happened to *Wolfbird*," he said, more to himself than anyone else. *Wolfbird* had disappeared several years previously, after sailing out past Cape Shelter into the Frozen Sea.

Thorn looked keenly around the circle of glum faces. They needed something to shake them up, he thought, to snap them out of this renewed bout of apathy.

"I believe *Wolfbird* was taken by a giant sea monster," he said artlessly.

Not one of them thought to ask him how he knew that. There had been no word of *Wolfbird* since she had passed beyond Cape Shelter. But the mention of the giant sea monster drove all other thoughts from their mind.

"Sea monster?" Jesper said. "What kind of sea monster?"

"A big one," Thorn told him. "Enormous, in fact. *Big* hardly does it credit."

"But what did it look like?" Stefan asked.

Amazing, Thorn thought. They've gone for this story hook, line and sinker. He searched his mind for some of the wilder stories he had heard from sailors in the past.

"Kind of spade-shaped," he said, "with a huge staring eye on either side of its head. And it had fourteen long, bendy legs—like an octopus's tentacles," he added, warming to his theme. "And a beak like a parrot's—big enough to tear a man in two."

"Could it talk like a parrot?" Edvin asked.

Thorn turned his gaze on the brotherband's medic. Edvin's expression was skeptical, and Thorn grinned to himself. Edvin wasn't one to fall for tall tales. He'd probably seen the basic flaw in Thorn's story.

"No," Thorn said, pretending offended dignity. "It could not talk like a parrot. But it could grab a ship and tear it in two."

Edvin raised an eyebrow. *I'm on to you,* the expression said. Thorn winked at him.

The others were still digesting his assertion that the monster could seize a wolfship and rip it apart.

"What would a monster like that be called?" Ulf said in an awed tone, visualizing the giant creature Thorn had described.

"Anything it wanted to be," Thorn told them. He was about to let them off the hook and say there was no such thing as a sea monster when there was a massive disturbance in the water twenty meters off their starboard side. A giant black creature slowly emerged from the depths. The water swirled around its glistening body and massive head, and one eye seemed to be rolled toward them, watching them. It was at least half again as long as *Heron* and it kept pace with them easily, sliding along on a parallel course.

Then, with a whistling roar, a huge spurt of water vapor erupted from the top of its head and the wind blew a cloud of reeking, fishy spray down upon them.

Thorn felt the hairs on the back of his neck rise in fear. It was as if the monster had appeared in answer to his joke. He wasn't normally a superstitious man, but now he thought he might have tempted fate too far by mentioning sea monsters in this mysterious, unexplored ocean.

For a moment, there was silence on board. Then, with cries of alarm, the crew scrambled across to the port side, away from the apparition—as if a further four meters would protect them in the event that the giant creature decided to attack. Hal leaned his weight on the tiller, swinging the ship away from the huge fish and snapping orders to Ulf and Wulf to re-trim the sail. The beast mirrored their course change effortlessly, maintaining the twenty-meter separation between it and them.

"Thorn?" Hal called nervously. "What is it?"

But the old sea wolf, for once, had no answer. His eyes were fixed on the huge fish. Its left eye—he assumed there was another on the right side of its head—seemed focused back on him.

They heard a massive, whistling intake of breath, and the monster slowly arched its back and slid beneath the waves again, driving itself under with a huge fluked tail and leaving a swirling patch of disturbed water behind.

As it departed, the Herons dashed back to the windward side of the ship, craning over the railing, trying to see into the gray water, looking for some sign of the great beast. They broke into an excited, fearful chatter, all speaking at once, all voicing their wonder at the sight they had just seen. While Thorn's talk of sea monsters had enthralled them, none of them had *completely* believed it. Sea monsters were, after all, the stuff of myth and legend. They might or might not exist. Or so they had all believed until now. Now they had proof that huge animals did dwell in the depths of the ocean, and the knowledge unsettled them all—even Hal and Edvin, who had been inclined to be skeptical about Thorn's story.

Thorn himself was shaken. Up until now, the largest sea animal he had ever seen had been a bull walrus—but that faded into insignificance compared with the monster they had just sighted.

It was a sobering, and disturbing, moment for all of them. None of them doubted the fact that, had it wanted to, the great fish could have smashed their ship to splinters.

So intent were they on searching the ocean around them for any sign of the monster's return that Lydia's announcement came as a shock to them all.

She had climbed onto the bulwark at the very edge of the bow to search for another sight of the fish. Seeing nothing, she raised her gaze to look farther afield.

"I think I see land," she said, a note of wonder in her voice.

The excited chatter about the whereabouts of the sea monster was instantly stilled. The crew turned toward the bow, moving forward along the deck to join Lydia. A long, dark gray line stretched across the horizon ahead of them, reaching as far as they could see to either side.

"It's a cloud," Jesper said.

But Lydia shook her head. "Don't think so," she countered. "I've made that mistake twice before. This looks more substantial, more solid than any of the clouds I've seen."

Thorn had sprung lightly onto the upwind bulwark, holding on to the rigging to maintain his balance.

"I think she's right," he said, after a few seconds. "That definitely looks like land to me."

The sea monster was immediately forgotten as a topic of discussion. Now the crew clamored out their agreement with Thorn and Lydia—with a few reserving judgment. Hal was one of the latter group. He felt that if he did believe it was land, and it turned out that he was mistaken, the disappointment would be too much for him to bear. But as the ship plunged farther to the west, the dim gray line began to take on harder focus and, finally, he joined in the chorus of relief.

"It's land," he said. "It's definitely land. We've finally made it."

Thorn looked at his young friend, unable to keep the smile of relief from his face.

"Wherever *it* may be," he said.

chapter eight

Exciting as it was, sighting land did nothing to relieve their most pressing problem—their lack of drinking water.

As they came closer to the coastline, they could see no place where they might be able to go ashore. The land stretched north and south in an unbroken line of rocky cliffs, with trees growing thickly on top. The waves beat against their bases, sending towers of white spray high into the air in a constant rhythm.

"Plenty of trees and vegetation," Edvin said hopefully. "That means there must be water somewhere."

"All we have to do is get to it," Stefan said, and they all strained their eyes to see some kind of landing place. But there was none.

They were barely four hundred meters from the cliffs, traveling at right angles to the land. Soon they would have to turn to port or starboard to make their way along the coast. The choice could be vital. They needed an inlet or a bay, somewhere they could find freshwater. Such a spot could be a few kilometers in either direction. Or it could be twenty or thirty kilometers away. There was nothing to guide their choice.

Thorn and Hal exchanged a glance. "Which way?" Thorn asked.

Hal considered the matter for a few seconds and, as he almost always did, automatically looked up to check the wind direction on the telltale. It was still out of the north, as it had been for days. He knew that, of course. But checking to make sure was an instinctive action with him.

"South," he said. "If we go north, we'll be tacking back and forth into the wind. This way, we can run before it on one tack."

He shouted his sail orders to Ulf and Wulf as he let the bow fall off to port. They released the sheets, letting the big port-side sail swing out almost at right angles to the hull. The wind filled it as they tightened the sheets a little, and *Heron* drove to the south.

"Eyes peeled, everyone," Hal ordered. "We don't want to miss an entrance if there is one."

The crew lined the starboard rail, peering intently at the shore that passed by them. For some time, there was no break in the cliffs, no sign of any inlet or bay that would let them approach the land.

When it came, they very nearly missed it. There were two close-set headlands, with a third sited well inside, opposite the opening, and giving it the appearance of an unbroken coastline. It was Stefan who recognized the lack of breaking waves across the fifty-meter gap and, peering more closely, saw that there was a narrow inlet just visible.

"There!" he shouted, pointing.

Hal heaved on the tiller so that the *Heron* swung to starboard, Ulf and Wulf compensating for the new angle across the wind by sheeting home and flattening the sail. Stefan moved aft to the steering platform and pointed to the gap in the rocks.

"See?" he said. "There's a way in there. Must be a small river."

Hal nodded, his eyes riveted on the almost invisible gap.

"Get the oars ready," he told Stig. "I don't think I want to go careering in there under sail."

Stig nodded and shouted a series of commands to the crew. The ship was filled with the rattle and clunk of the oars being unstowed and then placed into the oarlocks. The crew members took their places on either side, ready to begin rowing.

Hal waited until they were a bare hundred meters from the river mouth and nodded to Stig. The first mate called for Ulf and Wulf to bring the sail down and stow it, then to take their places in the rowing wells. With the sail down, the ship gradually lost way. She was almost at a stop when Stig took his own oar and called for the first stroke.

Seven oars dipped into the water as one, then heaved the little ship forward. Hal felt the renewed life in the tiller as she started to move, swooping up the long ocean rollers at an angle, cutting through the crests and sliding down diagonally into the troughs once more.

They made ground swiftly to the inlet. Lydia, with no rowing duties, was in the bow, keeping a keen eye out for hidden rocks or shoals. But the way in was clear.

The tall cliffs towered above them on either side, blocking the sunlight and casting deep shadows over the water. Then they were through the entrance and Hal cried out in surprise at the sight that greeted him.

He had assumed that the narrow gap in the cliffs was the mouth of a river. Instead, it turned out to be the entrance into a massive, wide bay, at least four kilometers across. Straight ahead was the long, narrow promontory that had seemed to fill the gap between the heads, but on either side, the bay swelled out into a huge natural harbor, fringed by heavily treed shores.

The crew, hearing his exclamation of surprise, looked over their shoulders and paused in their stroke. Angrily, Stig urged them on again and they went back to work. But they continued to look over their shoulders at the huge enclosed space of water that now surrounded them.

"Looks like a river to the north," Thorn called and they all swung their gazes that way.

There was a gap in the trees that might well have been a river mouth. Hal nodded, but continued to look for another water source. The river, if it was one, and not just a shallow inlet, would be tidal. They'd have to travel several kilometers inland to find freshwater.

"To the south," he said, pointing.

On the southern curve of the vast bay's coastline, he could see the pale sand of a long beach. And, issuing from the cliffs above it, a shower of sparkling water fell down the rock face. Unconsciously, he licked his dry lips at the sight of it, as did several of the others.

He swung the *Heron* to the south and the rowers drove her on with renewed energy. They had all seen the silver sparkle of water cascading down the cliff to the beach below. That meant freshwater ready to hand.

The seawater gurgled and thumped under the hull as the *Heron* gathered speed. They cruised smoothly across the bay, watching that sparkling, gushing source of drinking water, licking dry, cracked lips at the thought of drinking unlimited amounts of it. Only Thorn kept his wits about him.

"Keep a good lookout," he said, his voice rasping. "There could be people here."

That thought hadn't occurred to them, and they began to sweep the shoreline with their eyes, looking for some sign that there were people here—people who might not be altogether welcoming.

But the shoreline seemed deserted and the peacefulness of the bay, after the rush of wind and waves on the open sea outside, seemed to wrap itself around them, giving them a sense of security.

"Can't see anyone," Hal called.

"Doesn't mean there's no one here," Thorn replied. "When we reach the shore, don't go dashing off to get water. Keep your weapons handy while we make sure this place is as deserted as it looks."

Lydia looked at him and nodded agreement. She unclipped her atlatl from her belt and took a dart from the quiver slung over her shoulder, casually fitting its base into the hooked receptacle on the end of the handle.

Stig glanced inboard, making sure his ax was ready to hand. His shield was slung on the bulwark beside him. The others mirrored his action. Edvin reached out to where his sword was hanging by the side of the rowing well. He loosened it in its scabbard, raising it a few centimeters, then resumed his two-handed grip on his oar. Seeing these actions, Hal made sure his crossbow was close by. He was already wearing his sword, with the scabbard slung over his shoulder.

"Do you always expect the worst?" he asked Thorn with a grin.

The old sea wolf raised an eyebrow. "Always. That way, you're never disappointed."

They were twenty meters off the beach now. Hal could see it was coarse sand and small pebbles, colored a dirty white. The bottom shelved as they came closer.

"Beaching positions!" he called.

Jesper ran in his oar and stowed it, then sprang to the main deck and ran lightly for'ard, to where the beach anchor sat on its coil of rope. Ulf and Wulf joined him, staying slightly behind him and arming themselves with their axes. Their shields, which had been hanging from the bulwarks beside their rowing positions, were now slung across their backs, leaving their hands free.

Once they were all in position, Lydia moved for'ard as well, her atlatl held casually, a dart nocked and ready to cast at the first sign of danger.

Hal made a hand gesture to Stig.

"In oars!" the first mate yelled.

Stefan, Edvin and Ingvar obeyed, raising the dripping oars out of the water, then lowering them to stow them along the line of the hull. A few seconds later, the bow grated onto the coarse sand and ran up it for a few meters, before tilting to one side on the keel. Instantly, Jesper was over the side, running with the beach anchor until he reached dry sand above the tide line, and driving the flukes of the anchor into the sand. Ulf and Wulf went over the side a few seconds behind him, flanking him. They had their weapons ready and kept their eyes scanning the silent trees at the edge of the beach. Lydia moved to a vantage point on the bow and Thorn tied off the anchor line to a wooden cleat on the starboard bulwark.

Now, without the creak and rattle of the oars, and the sound of the seawater sliding around the hull, they became aware of another sound—the liquid splashing of water on rocks as the waterfall cascaded down, barely fifty meters from where the ship lay beached.

Hal and Stig exchanged a glance. Hal felt an immense weight lift from his shoulders. They had come through. They had found land and, even more important, a source of freshwater. They would survive—at least for the time being.

Stig, guessing his thoughts, inclined his head and grinned. He realized, with a little surprise, that he had never really doubted the fact that Hal would bring them through the days of peril and hardship they had faced.

The young skirl tied off the tiller and slung his crossbow and quiver of bolts over his left shoulder. The others made way for him as he paced down the length of the ship to the bow, then they fell in behind him.

Thorn moved aside as Hal slung his legs over the bulwark and let himself drop to the hard, wet sand. He moved a few paces up the beach, hearing the dull thuds of the others following him. He stopped level with Jesper and the twins. The three crew members were still scanning the trees fifty meters away. There was no sign of anyone watching them. The harsh cry of a bird broke the stillness, and the wind eased softly through the tops of the trees, setting the tall narrow trunks swaying in unison.

Thorn, Stig and the others stopped a few meters behind him. Like him, they were intent on the shadows beneath the trees, looking for the first sign that they might not be alone on this unknown land.

Jesper broke the silence, his voice sounding unnaturally loud and somehow intrusive. “What do we do now?”

Hal glanced at him and gave him a tired grin.

“I don’t know about you,” he said in a dry, rasping voice that was barely audible, “but I’m going to get a drink.”

chapter nine

There was an immediate surge of motion as the group started toward the waterfall. But Thorn's voice stopped them in their tracks.

"Stand fast!" he roared. They responded immediately to the note of command in his voice. He glared at them, then continued. "We'll go in formation. Arrowhead, forming on Stig. Keep your eyes open and your weapons ready."

He knew all too well that a wild rush to get water would leave them vulnerable to ambush, if there were any potential enemies nearby. Distracted by the prospect of easing their maddening thirst, they would be easy targets. It was a tribute to the years of drilling under his command that their discipline held now and they formed into an inverted-V shape, with Stig at the point. Hal and Ingvar stood to his left and right and the others fanned out behind them. Thorn nodded, satisfied.

"Move out, Stig," he ordered and the big first mate led the way, jogging through the soft sand, his steps causing the coarse grains to squeak together as they were compacted, then released.

The crew moved up the beach, with Thorn bringing up the rear. Their eyes scanned the surrounding trees.

As they drew closer to the spot where the waterfall splashed onto the rocks, among a series of sparkling pools, Jesper couldn't stand it any longer. He broke ranks and raced up the beach, throwing himself facedown in the first of the pools and lapping at the water like a dog.

"Blast you, Jesper," Thorn muttered. The others heard the angry tone in his voice and maintained their formation. As they reached the water, Thorn gestured to Lydia.

"Lydia. Keep watch with me."

He reasoned that the girl's long experience of stalking and hunting would make her sense of personal self-discipline stronger than the others'. She nodded and stepped back as the others waited.

"All right," he said gruffly. "Get to it."

They broke ranks immediately and dashed toward the nearest pool, where Jesper was still lying belly down, sucking in great quantities of water. Edvin, ever the planner, had brought their drinking mugs with him, and the water skin. He handed out the mugs to them now and they filled them, standing or kneeling in the shin-deep, beautifully cold water, and drank. Then they refilled them and drank again. Edvin filled his own mug and took a deep draft. Then he filled two more and took them to where Thorn and Lydia stood guard.

The old sea wolf acknowledged his thoughtfulness with a nod. Lydia allowed him a beaming smile. "Thanks, Edvin," she said.

Then she couldn't wait any longer and let the first draft of cold, refreshing water slide down her parched throat.

Thorn followed suit, taking a deep draft. Then he lowered the mug. "Not too fast too soon," he warned them. "You'll just throw it all up if you do."

And of course Jesper, who had been facedown in the water, sucking in huge gutfuls, chose that moment to do just that. Fortunately, he managed to clamber to his feet and move away from the pond before he threw up on the rocks nearby, his stomach and throat heaving.

Thorn watched him, one eyebrow raised. "There's always one," he muttered.

"And it's usually Jes," Lydia replied, smiling.

They exchanged a conspiratorial glance and shrugged, before beginning to scan the land around them again. Then Hal and Stig approached them, having slaked their thirst with several mugs of water. Hal jerked a thumb at the pool.

"Your turn," he said. "We'll keep watch."

Thorn nodded gratefully. "Let's g—" he began, but Lydia was already dashing to the water, kneeling to fill her mug, throwing her head back to drink it, letting it slide slowly down her throat. Grinning, Thorn allowed his own iron self-discipline to relax and hurried to follow suit.

There were cries and moans of pleasure from the crew as they had their first real drink of water in days. And it was fresh, cold water, not stale and moldy after weeks in a cask. With their immediate yearning assuaged, they filled their mugs and moved to sit on the rocks fringing the series of small pools, drinking slowly, appreciating the taste and sensation of wetness in their mouths and throats, feeling their dry, swollen tongues slowly returning to normal.

Jesper sat to one side, head down, retching and belching. Edvin filled a mug and started toward him. Thorn held out a hand to stop him.

"Leave him," he said. "He'll be all right and it'll teach him a lesson."

But Edvin's role as medical orderly gave him a feeling of responsibility for the crew's physical welfare. He hesitated, then moved around Thorn.

"I'll just take him this mug," he said.

Thorn shrugged. "Suit yourself. I'd tend to throw it at him."

Edvin grinned and continued to where his crewmate sat, hunched over and groaning. He prodded Jesper's shoulder with the mug to get his attention.

"Here, Jes," he said. "Just sip this slowly."

Jesper looked up at him, took the mug and drank deeply. Edvin put a hand out to pull the mug away from his lips.

"Slowly, I said!"

Jesper shook his head. "I'm fine," he said, then let out a resounding belch.

Lydia raised an eyebrow. "Well, if there's anybody within ten kilometers, that should let them know we've arrived."

Once they had drunk their fill of the fresh, cold water, they made their way back to where the ship was beached.

Hal trudged wearily along the sand, measuring distances with his eye, looking for a suitable campsite. The obvious choice was near the water source. Not only would that give them an uninterrupted supply of water, but the high, rocky cliff where the water ran down would protect their rear in the event of an attack.

He paced backward a few meters, then held both hands out at arm's length, looking from side to side to see where a protective fence could be sited. His arms suddenly felt tired and he let them droop. His shoulders followed. He shook his head to clear it, and made a mark in the sand with his heel. This would be the forward extent of their fence, he thought. Then he stopped. What would they use to build the fence? There weren't sufficient rocks nearby to construct a solid wall. He shook his head again. He was bone tired, and the problems of building a secure camp suddenly seemed too much for him.

"What are you doing?"

It was Thorn, standing close by him, a concerned expression on his face.

Hal took a deep breath. "We'd better get started on a camp—and build a protective fence around it."

Thorn shook his head. "No. *We'd* better get started on that," he said. "Stig and Lydia and I can handle that. It's time you got some decent rest."

"But I'm the skirl," Hal began to protest.

Thorn nodded agreement. "That's right. And when we're at sea, you're in total command. But on land, you can hand over the responsibility to me and the others."

"I don't . . . ," Hal started again, but Thorn took his arm and led him to one of the nearest rock outcrops.

"Sit down," Thorn ordered, and Hal, after a moment's hesitation, obeyed. Suddenly his legs felt very tired.

"Hal, you're worn-out and you need to rest. You've been carrying us all on your shoulders for weeks now. You've made all the hard decisions."

"But that's my job . . ."

Thorn nodded patiently. "When we're at sea, yes. And you've handled it brilliantly. You've brought us through safely. But now we're ready to take over. To take some of the load off you." He studied the young man keenly, seeing the strain on Hal's face and the utter weariness in his eyes. Thorn understood, more than any of the other Herons, how heavy a burden command could be. There was a physical side to it, of course. But more than that, there was a mental load that a skirl carried—the need to make life-or-death decisions for his crew, to be always ready to take control in times of danger. It could wear a person down, he knew. And he could see that Hal, after weeks of danger and uncertainty, was nearly at the end of his tether.

Ingvar, who had been dispatched by Thorn to the ship, appeared at his side, carrying a roll of blankets.

"Here's Hal's bedroll, Thorn," he said quietly.

Hal looked at the big lad, not comprehending. "My bedroll?"

But Thorn forestalled him. "Thanks, Ingvar. Spread it out here." And, as Ingvar complied, Thorn turned back to Hal. "Lie down and get some good, solid rest, Hal. I'll wake you when we need you."

The bedroll, spartan as it might be, looked incredibly inviting. Hal crawled under the blankets and pulled them up to his chin.

Ingvar knelt, felt under the blankets and found Hal's feet, then removed his boots.

"That's good," Hal said dozily. "Maybe you're right, Thorn. I'll just have twenty minutes, then I'll . . ."

He didn't finish. His eyes closed and he let out a little sigh of pleasure—a sigh that turned into a soft snore.

"Yeah. Twenty minutes," Thorn said, smiling. Then he turned to Ingvar. "Let's start building a camp."

Thorn marked out a semicircle in the sand with a pointed stick. The two ends of the line abutted the cliff face and the line itself enclosed a space ten meters by thirty.

"I want a two-rail fence built on this line," he said. "I want it a meter eighty high, with uprights every five meters. We'll fill it in with brush and bracken to give us a reasonable barrier. If we can find some thornbush, that'd be ideal." He looked critically around the bay, then at the ship, beached on the sand at the water's edge. "I'm not happy with *Heron* being so exposed to view," he said. "I think we might move her into that inlet."

He indicated a narrow inlet that was close to the southern end of the proposed fortification. It was barely ten meters wide and overhung by trees growing on either bank.

He turned to the crew. "Stig, Stefan, Edvin. Come with me and we'll get the ship refloated. Ingvar, start cutting logs for the fence. Lydia, you can go with Ingvar and keep watch. Someone might get curious if they hear trees being cut down."

They set to their various tasks with a will. Once the ship was refloated, Thorn took the hawser and waded waist deep into the water, holding the rope over his shoulder and hauling on it to drag the ship stern-first along the few meters of beach to the entrance to the inlet.

"If we have to leave in a hurry, we won't want to waste time turning her around," he explained.

The *Heron* bobbed along obediently behind Thorn. Once she was afloat, there was very little weight for him to move, but Stig waded in to join him.

The inlet was a narrow indentation in the beach, extending back barely fifteen meters. But that was ample space to conceal the *Heron* from unfriendly eyes. They took a mooring line to each bank and hauled her in under the trees. Once she was in place, her bow facing out to the large bay, they moored her securely to the two banks and left Edvin to conceal her with hacked-down branches.

Then they returned to the campsite. Ingvar had cut the first half-dozen uprights for the fence. They carried these to the line Thorn had drawn and began digging deep, narrow post holes in the sand. Thorn walked up the beach to the tree line, where Ingvar was at work, stripped to the waist, his arm and body muscles rippling. He grunted lightly with each stroke of the ax, and Thorn was mildly impressed to see how deeply each ax stroke bit into the wood.

Lydia was a few meters away, patroling among the trees, watching inland. Kloof kept pace with her, nose raised, sniffing the air, her nostrils quivering.

"Anything to see?" Thorn asked her quietly.

She shook her head. "So far, not a thing. Although if there's anyone within half a kilometer, they'd be hearing Ingvar's ax strokes."

She was right, Thorn thought. The big boy was driving the ax blade deep into the larger saplings that he was felling, and each blow rang loudly, the sound echoing and reechoing around the forest. He grunted.

"Keep your eyes open," he said. "I'll send the others up to collect the posts and rails."

He strode back through the thick sand, noting that the first three uprights were already in position, Stig having driven them deep into the sand with a large wooden mallet from the ship. Thorn caught Jesper's eye and beckoned to him.

Jesper glanced away guiltily, unwilling to meet Thorn's gaze.

"Jesper," Thorn called softly, "I'd like a word with you."

The soft tone and easy words were deceptive. Jesper sauntered across the sand to where Thorn waited, the thumb of his left hand thrust through his broad leather belt.

"Yes, Thorn?" the former thief said, trying too hard to be casual. He knew what was coming.

Thorn smiled at him, then moved closer, so that their noses were ten centimeters apart. The smile faded and the old warrior spoke in a voice that wouldn't carry to the crew members working on the fence.

"If you ever—*ever*—break discipline again like you did today, I will kick your backside so hard your eyes will pop out of your head."

Jesper hung his head, unable to meet Thorn's burning gaze. "Yes, Thorn," he muttered.

But Thorn wasn't letting him off so lightly. "Are you clear on that?" he demanded.

Jesper nodded his head. "Yes, Thorn," he repeated, still unwilling to look the older man in the eyes.

"We're a long way from home, Jesper," Thorn continued. "We don't know where we are and we don't know what or who we might encounter. We *have* to be able to rely on each other. We *have* to maintain our discipline as a group. If we don't, people could die. If one person lets the others down, it could mean the end for all of us. Is that clear?"

"Yes, Thorn."

"Blast you, Jesper, look at me when you talk to me!"

Reluctantly, Jesper raised his head to meet Thorn's gaze. The anger he saw there was nothing short of terrifying.

"I'll warn you once. If your laziness or lack of discipline is the cause of any of the others being injured or killed, you will answer to me. Is that clear?"

Jesper nodded. He had no doubt that Thorn meant what he was saying. But a nod wasn't enough for Thorn.

"Say it. I want to hear you say it. Do you understand?"

Jesper licked his lips. Suddenly, they were dry again, as they had been for the preceding week. But the reason now wasn't lack of drinking water. It was fear.

"I understand, Thorn," he managed at last.

Thorn held his gaze in silence for ten long seconds, then nodded fiercely.

"Make sure you do."

PART TWO

THE BEAR

chapter ten

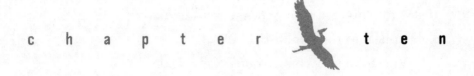

By nightfall, the perimeter fence of their enclosure was completed. They had yet to fill in the spaces between the two rails with brushwood and saplings, but that would be done in the morning.

Thorn called a halt to their work as the shadows lengthened across the small camp, and the crew set about building small individual shelters for the night, using cut branches to form frameworks and covering them with canvas from the ship. Edvin and Ingvar built a fireplace for a cook fire. Edvin hung a small cauldron from an iron triangle, placing it so that the iron cook pot hung low over the fire.

Stefan walked thigh deep into the waters of the bay and began casting a fishing line into the choppy waves. He'd cut a whippy rod from a grove of willows in the inlet and had a selection of lures hooked into his vest, trying them one after another to find one that might appeal to the local fish.

"Where did they come from?" Stig asked idly.

Hal, now awake and refreshed after the first deep, uninterrupted sleep he'd enjoyed in weeks, nursed a cup of coffee—luckily they had a good supply after their stop in Hibernia. He smiled at Stig's question.

"Stefan always has his fishing gear with him," he said. "He's addicted to the pastime."

Stig nodded. "I've noticed how that happens to people."

They were interrupted by a shout of triumph from the angler. They looked up to see his rod bending and quivering as a captive fish tried to break free of his hook. Stefan played the fish for a few minutes, allowing it to exhaust its strength against the springy resistance of the rod. Then he brought the rod in and began hauling his line in hand over hand. There was a flurry on the surface of the water a few meters from the shore as he managed to bring the fish closer. Once it was on the surface, he backed away up the beach, dragging it out onto the sand, where it lay flapping and jumping. He grinned at the two watching him.

"It's a bream," he announced. "And a good one."

"We can use it," Hal said as Stefan knelt beside the fish and quickly dispatched it with a blow from a rock. He tossed it in a rock pool to keep it cool, then rebaited his hook and walked into the water, casting out once more.

Over the next fifteen minutes, Stefan felt a regular succession of jerks and tugs on his line as fish attacked his bait. His fishing rod was rudimentary, but he managed to land another three of the bream, all of them fat and well fed.

Then the brief flurry of activity died away, and he made cast after cast with no reaction, his bait floating untouched on the surface of the bay.

"You've scared them off," Stig called.

Stefan shook his head, frowning. "Sometimes it just happens this way," he said. "They move on to another feeding ground."

"Where there isn't a giant two-legged monster jamming a hook in their mouth and dragging them ashore," Stig suggested.

Stefan shook his head once again. "No. I think it just happens this way."

He began hauling his line in, winding it round the fishing pole as it came. Hal gestured at the four fish in the shallow pool beside Stefan.

"Let's clean those and take them up to Edvin," he said. "Might as well have them while they're fresh."

"You can't beat fresh fish," Stig said in agreement.

They gave Stefan a hand gutting and cleaning the fish at the water's edge. As they threw the entrails and offcuts into the water, tiny fish darted around them, seizing fragments and flashing away at high speed. Stefan tied the four cleaned bream onto a loop of twine, strung through their mouths and gills, and they trudged up through the heavy sand to the half-completed palisade. They stooped under the top rail and stepped over the lower one, making their way to the rear of the enclosed area, where Edvin had built his cook fire. He had brought stores from the ship and arrayed the various casks and pottery jars in a neat stack to one side. He was chopping onions, his sharp knife sliding smoothly through them and separating them into neat discs. He looked up as they approached, smiling as he saw the four substantial fish Stefan was carrying.

"Nice work," he said. "I'll do them tonight."

Hal sat on a nearby rock, eyeing Edvin's handiwork. His mother was a cook and he could appreciate Edvin's knife skills, slicing the onions quickly and precisely, and not allowing them to separate into ragged pieces—as they always seemed to do when Hal tried to chop them.

"How are we placed for supplies?" he asked, eyeing the neat stack of casks and jars behind the cook.

Edvin had been expecting the question. One of his first acts, once he was released from the task of building the palisade, had been to take inventory of their food supplies.

"Actually, we have plenty," he said. "After all, I restocked before we left Hibernia and I laid in enough food for the journey home."

He paused. The word *home* had a bittersweet ring to it. Then he shook his head distractedly and continued.

"Most of the fresh food is gone, of course," he said. "I had nets of vegetables and bread, but they were either spoiled by the salt water, or washed overboard. We've plenty of dried or smoked food, though: pork and beef, hard biscuit and a couple of sacks of dried peas. We needn't go hungry."

There was a note of dissatisfaction in his voice as he listed their supplies.

Hal raised an eyebrow. "But?" he queried.

Edvin shrugged. "But it's going to be pretty boring eating," he said. Edvin prided himself on providing good, interesting meals to the crew, and hearing their exclamations of appreciation. In their current situation, cast up on an unknown shore and hundreds of leagues from home, good, nourishing and varied meals would go a long way to maintaining the crew's morale.

Hal appreciated the fact as well. He nodded and turned to where Lydia was sitting, five meters away, outside the small canvas tent that Ulf and Wulf had constructed for her—though in truth she was more than capable of building her own shelter. She had her back against a rock, her eyes closed.

"Are you asleep, Lydia?" Hal called.

"Fast asleep," she replied, her eyes remaining closed.

Hal grinned. "I wonder, could you sleepwalk over here for a few minutes?"

With a small sigh, she reluctantly opened her eyes, rose to her feet in one smooth, graceful movement and joined them. She had already guessed what Hal might want to discuss and his words confirmed it for her.

"D'you think there's likely to be game around here?" he asked.

She cast her gaze around the surrounding terrain. "I'd be surprised if there weren't," she said. "There's freshwater and plenty of greenery and ground cover. I imagine there'd be deer and rabbits around. And probably some form of wildfowl. Plus I heard a strange bird in the trees earlier this afternoon. Made a kind of *oggle-oggle-oggle* sound. I went to see if I could spot it but it dashed away. From the noise it made going through the undergrowth, I'd say it was pretty big."

Hal glanced at Edvin. "Deer, rabbits and a big bird going *oggle-oggle-oggle,*" he said. "How does that sound to you, Ed?"

Edvin grinned. "Sounds good. Although I'll reserve judgment on any bird that goes *oggle-oggle-oggle.*"

"It could be delicious," Hal told him.

Edvin shrugged. "Or it could be like the mythical bongo bird with its iron-hard flesh. It takes hours to cook and it's a tricky process."

"What do you do with it?" Lydia asked.

Edvin replied with a completely straight face. "You find a rock that's the same size as the bird and put them both in a pot. Then you boil them together for four hours."

"Four hours?" Lydia was skeptical but Edvin nodded emphatically.

"Four hours. Then you throw the bird away and eat the rock."

Stig and Hal, who had heard the old joke before, both burst out laughing.

"It's the way you tell it, Edvin," said Stig.

Lydia, realizing her leg had been severely pulled, raised an eyebrow at the cook. "Well, I'll try to get an *oggle-oggle-oggle* bird for the rest of us tomorrow. You don't have to eat it."

"What will I eat?" Edvin asked and she eyed him for several seconds before replying.

"I'll catch a rock for you. You can eat that."

The following morning, Lydia left camp shortly after breakfast, while the rest of the crew returned to work on the palisade, cutting large bunches of brushwood and dragging it in to camp, then weaving it in and out between the two fence rails to fill in the gap between them.

As she was checking her atlatl and her quiver, making sure she had several of the darts she used to hunt birds, Hal wandered across from his shelter to join her.

"Maybe you should take Ingvar along," he suggested. "These woods seem quiet enough, but you never really know."

She smiled as she loaded the darts into her quiver, sliding them in between layers of sheepskin that would keep them from rattling.

"He's a dear," she said, "but he'd be a big drawback hunting. Even with those vision goggles you made him, he tends to blunder along, stepping on twigs and fallen branches and bumping into trees. He'll scare off any game within half a kilometer."

Hal conceded the point, but he was still reluctant to let her go on her own. "Maybe Stig could—"

Lydia laid her hand on his arm to stop him. "I'm perfectly capable of looking after myself," she said. "And if I do run into trouble, I don't want someone else slowing me down while I get away. Remember, I've been doing this all my life."

He grinned, realizing she was right. "Okay then. But take care. And keep your eyes open."

"That's what hunters do," she said.

chapter eleven

Lydia made her way into the cool green of the forest. The early sunlight filtered down through the thick canopy of trees and, as she drew farther away from the camp, the clatter and thump of axes and hammers, and the sound of crew members calling to one another, were gradually muffled by the intervening forest, until they died away altogether.

She paused a moment, enjoying the silence that enveloped her, appreciating the sense of being alone. While she loved the brotherband members dearly, and regarded them as her brothers, sometimes she longed for the days when she was on her own, stalking silently through the woods of her homeland and looking for signs of game. Her eyes misted for a moment as she thought of her home, and of her grandfather, who had been her companion since her parents died many years ago. He too was dead now, killed in the raid mounted by the pirate Zavac.

She shook her head to drive the moment of nostalgia away. Her life now was a good one, she thought. She had friends and a place in the crew. She was a valued member, admired for her skill in tracking and her accuracy with the atlatl.

"Some people wouldn't mope about that," she told herself quietly, then moved off again, her eyes scanning the ground in front of her and the brambles and bracken to either side. She was following what must have been a game trail, formed by animals as they pushed through the undergrowth to the water holes by the beach. It was barely half a meter wide in some places, and she had to turn sideways to slip between the narrow tree trunks.

She paused as she caught sight of a scrap of brown on one shoot growing off a trunk. She leaned closer, touched it and studied it closely. It looked as if an animal had brushed against the trunk and left a piece of fur behind. The scrap was over a meter from the ground, so it must have been a long-legged animal.

"A deer," she muttered, pleased to see evidence that her supposition was correct. She dropped to one knee and scanned the forest floor. It was thick with leaf mold that concealed any tracks. But in one clear spot, she saw an imprint left by a cloven hoof.

Her heart beat a little faster, as it always did when she found herself on the trail of a game animal.

She rose to continue, then caught sight of a small mound of black pebblelike objects. Rabbit droppings, she realized, and she smiled.

"Deer, rabbits and fish in the bay," she said softly. "We won't go hungry."

She frowned. You have to catch them first, she cautioned herself mentally. She paused and deftly set two snares on the path, scattering a handful of dried peas from Edvin's supplies around each, then continued on her way. A few meters on, she noticed several thin branches broken on the trunk of another tree, at around the same height that she had seen the scrap of fur. She studied the broken twigs. The sap inside them was oozing slightly. The deer, if it was a deer, had passed by the point only recently.

Maybe ten, fifteen minutes ago, she thought. The sun wasn't strong enough yet to dry the sap. Later in the day, as it moved directly overhead, its heat would seal off the broken ends.

She quietly withdrew a dart from her quiver. In a habit born of long practice, she checked the razor-sharp broadhead. No sense throwing a dart if the point wasn't sharp, she thought. Satisfied, she clipped the notched end of the dart into the spur of the atlatl and kept it close by her body, ready to throw, but held vertically so it wouldn't snag on the undergrowth.

She continued in the direction the deer had followed. The narrow path twisted and turned, but always seemed to return to one basic direction. There was a rustling sound from the undergrowth ahead and she stopped in mid-stride, her right foot having just made contact with the ground, the bulk of her weight still on the left.

Carefully, moving infinitely slowly, she tested the ground under her right foot. The thin sole of her knee-high boot allowed her to feel the ground underneath and she checked for any sense of a twig or fallen branch that might snap when she put her full weight on it. Feeling nothing, she advanced another pace, repeating the action with her left foot. Then another, always checking, always pausing.

The rustle came from the undergrowth ahead once more, louder this time as she drew closer to the source. She concentrated on making her movements even more stealthy, gliding through the thick-growing trees and tangled undergrowth with barely a sound. The noise ahead of her had changed now to a rattling that, from past experience, she knew came from a deer clashing his antlers against the branches of a tree. At some stages of the year, they did that to remove the annoying coating, known as velvet, that could build up on their antlers.

Or sometimes, it might be caused by a young stag testing his fighting moves against the branches of a tree before taking on a more dangerous, live opponent.

It proved to be the latter. As she advanced, she became aware that the light ahead of her was becoming brighter, indicating that she was coming to a clearing in the trees, where the sun had more direct access to the forest floor.

The clearing, when she reached it, was a roughly circular shape, possibly formed by animals as they sought to create a place to shelter from the winter storms. Or maybe just formed by chance. In either case, there was a young buck dancing lightly on his hooves on the far side, lowering his head to slash and strike with his half-grown antlers at the trees. As she watched, he trapped a young branch between his antlers and twisted his head and neck quickly, snapping the branch off and letting it fall. Then he leapt backward, ears pricked, eyes alert, as if looking for a riposte from the tree.

Slowly, Lydia drew back her arm, bringing the dart up to the horizontal, preparing to cast. At this range, she couldn't possibly miss.

She must have made some slight noise as she moved. Perhaps the leather of her sleeveless overjacket made an infinitesimal creak, or her sleeve brushed against a branch without her noticing.

The young stag reacted instantly, springing back from the tree and pivoting to look in her direction, his muscles tensed and quivering, ready to flee.

Lydia froze, the dart half drawn back, and for a few seconds she and the deer faced each other. She knew that the animal wasn't sure of her presence. She was still in shadow and he was in the brighter sunlight that filled the clearing. The wind, what little there was, was blowing across the clearing, from left to right, so she knew he couldn't make out any alien scent coming from her. As long as she didn't move, she wouldn't alarm him.

It was a familiar situation for her. Just wait. Don't move. Wait for the deer to relax and go back to concentrating on his tree enemy. Her right arm, half raised, was in a most uncomfortable position, neither relaxed nor fully extended. But she had spent years teaching herself to ignore discomfort when hunting. She smiled inwardly. People thought of hunting as a high-energy, high-action pastime. All too often, it was a stand-still-and-don't-move-a-muscle pastime.

The impasse continued. The deer's large ears were cupped to pick up the slightest sound, and they twisted from side to side, seeking any possible threat. His legs and body were still tensed, the muscles twitching from time to time.

Lydia remained as relaxed as she could, without moving any part of her body. She ignored the growing ache in her right arm and concentrated on breathing as quietly as possible. She wondered whether the deer, in its heightened state of awareness, could sense the beating of her heart. Her pulse seemed deafening in her own ears and surely, she thought, the animal must hear it.

She dismissed the notion as fanciful. Her arm, extended

halfway up and back, was beginning to really ache now. But she knew if she moved a muscle, the deer would be gone in a flash, before she could complete her swing and cast the dart.

Come on, she willed it silently. Relax. Put your head down. Crop some of that delicious sweet grass at your feet. But the deer seemed to have an almost infinite capacity to remain alert. To make matters worse, its gaze was fixed on the spot where Lydia stood. Any movement at all would be instantly visible. Her only chance of remaining unseen was to be totally, absolutely stock-still.

Then, gratefully, she became aware that the tension was ebbing from the deer. His ears relaxed initially, ceasing their constant twitching back and forth. Then the trembling in his muscles ceased.

Any minute now, she thought, mentally rehearsing the movements of her cast. Her eyes focused on a spot just behind the animal's left foreleg, where she knew the heart was situated. One quick cast and the deer would be instantly dead. She felt the usual twinge of regret at the thought of killing such a beautiful creature. She didn't hunt for sport or for the thrill of it. She hunted for food, out of necessity. And she always had a moment of regret when she brought down a target.

But that was fifty kilograms of meat standing opposite her—two or three days' good eating for the crew. And she couldn't pass that up out of any mistaken sense of regret.

Come on, relax, she thought. And, as if in answer, the deer began to lower its head, a centimeter at a time. She felt a surge of triumph. Just one more minute, she told herself, and I'll be able to—

Oggle-oggle-oggle!

The raucous cry rang across the clearing, and, in a movement faster than her eye could follow, the deer pirouetted and leapt away through the trees. She heard it crashing through the undergrowth as it made its escape, the sound gradually fading away.

She released her pent-up breath in a sigh of frustration as a ridiculous-looking bird waddled into the clearing from the trees to the right.

It had a large, heavy body and she guessed it would weigh somewhere around twelve kilograms. It was covered in black and white feathers, with a spectacular round, fan-shaped tail. The long neck was bare and serpentine and the head that surmounted it was remarkably ugly, with a red wattle hanging down over one side of its beak.

Oggle-oggle-oggle! it warbled once more and stalked out into the center of the clearing, clearly full of its own importance. It stopped and turned to look at her. She hesitated for a second or two.

There's a lot of meat on you, she thought. So long as you're not like Edvin's bongo bird, we'll get a couple of meals out of you.

And with that thought, she finished her drawback and sent the dart flashing across the clearing. She didn't have time to substitute it for one of her blunts and, in any event, this was a large creature. The dart transfixed the bird through the breast, and, with one last choked cry, it was hurled backward, collapsing on the leaf mold beneath its feet. It twitched its legs once or twice, then lay still.

She knew that some of the meat surrounding the wound would be spoiled, but it was only a small amount compared with the total. She stepped across the clearing to claim her prize. The deer would have to wait till another day. But at least now she knew that there *were* deer in the forest.

She withdrew the dart from the bird's body. It had gone clean through, she saw. That meant spoiled meat at the entrance and exit wounds. She wiped the blood from the dart and replaced it in her quiver, then hoisted the big bird by the legs and turned for home.

"Edvin can clean you," she told it.

The bird said nothing.

As she retraced her steps, she was delighted to see a large rabbit in one of the snares she had set earlier. It jerked and twisted as she approached, and she seized it and quickly broke its neck with a sharp blow from the heel of her hand. She untangled it from the snare, reset the thin rope loop and scattered a few more peas around. The other snare was untouched so she left it as it was.

Straightening, she noticed a mark on one of the trees that she had missed earlier. It had been on the reverse side of the tree as she moved through the forest, but now it was facing her and she made her way closer to study it.

It was actually a series of marks—four parallel gouges in the bark. She had seen this sort of mark before, but usually it was on both sides of a tree trunk. It was above her head, over two meters from the ground.

She reached out a finger to touch it. The sap was dry. It was an old mark, possibly made several days prior. It was made by a bear dragging his claws through the bark, either to sharpen the claws or to mark his territory. A big bear, she thought, seeing the height of the scars from the ground. He'd be nearly three meters tall, she thought in awe. She had never seen a bear as large as that in Skandia, although the old sailors talked of great white bears that lived in the permanent snow and ice to the north that were as big as this.

Suddenly, the hairs on the back of her neck prickled. She had the distinct impression that she was being watched. She reached for a dart and drew it from the quiver. She had felt this instinct before and had learned not to discount it. It wasn't always accurate, but it had been correct enough times in the past.

Slowly she turned, half expecting to see a massive bear a few meters away. But there was nothing.

Still, she could sense eyes upon her. Something, or someone, was watching her. Keeping her head still, she scanned the surrounding trees with her eyes, searching for a sight of the hidden observer—human or otherwise.

Nothing.

Realizing she was making the common mistake of searching at her own eye level, she raised her angle of sight and swung her vision from side to side once more. Again, nothing. But still she felt the presence.

Then she dropped her gaze to ground level and scanned. And saw something. In a damp patch of earth that was clear of the ubiquitous leaf mold, there was a long indentation in the ground beside a tree. She moved closer and went down on one knee to study it more closely. It was about twenty-five centimeters long by ten wide. Rounded at both ends and flat along its lengths.

It was the imprint left by a human foot in a soft, heelless shoe.

chapter twelve

Lydia emerged from the tree line and stopped to observe the progress that had been made on the construction of the palisade. More than two-thirds of its length was now filled in by a thick tangle of brushwood and small branches. The crew were working diligently to complete the rest of the barrier. Ingvar and Stig were hacking down bushes and small saplings, Stefan and Jesper were dragging them to the unfinished end of the fence and Hal, Thorn and the twins were threading them through the two horizontal rails, intertwining them to form an almost solid obstacle.

Edvin was the only crew member not engaged in fence building. He was crouched among his cook pots by the fire. A small iron cauldron hung over the glowing pile of coals, suspended from his iron tripod. Steam escaped from a gap he had left between the pot and the lid.

Lydia stooped under an unfinished section of the fence and approached him, tossing the heavy carcass of the bird toward him.

He raised his eyebrows, impressed. "That's a respectable-size bird," he said.

She nodded. "I just hope it's edible. I had to use a warhead dart on it, I'm afraid. Some of the meat will be spoiled."

Edvin was examining the bird, running his hands over it and feeling it. He discounted her apology. "No harm done. There's plenty of meat there."

"Just so long as it's not tough as goats' knees," she said. He felt the flesh of the bird again and pursed his lips.

"It feels pretty fat and meaty," he said. "I wouldn't be surprised if it's good eating. I take it this is the now-famous *oggle-oggle-oggle* bird?" he added, with a smile.

"That's it," she replied. Then, remembering, she took the rabbit that she'd tied to her belt and tossed that by the fire as well. "There seem to be rabbits in the area too."

"Excellent." Edvin looked pleased. He could picture himself preparing a few varied and interesting meals for the brotherband. "I'll slip away this afternoon and see what I can find in the way of wild greens," he said.

She held up a cautioning hand. "Don't go too far. And don't go alone. I saw the tracks of a bear out there—a very big one."

Edvin raised his eyebrows. "I suppose it couldn't all be good news. If we have rabbits and oggle birds, I guess we have to have bears as well."

"I'll warn the others," she said. She nodded farewell to Edvin, who was already beginning to pluck the feathers from the large bird, preparatory to gutting and cleaning it, and walked back to where the crew were building the barricade. Thorn and Hal were nearest her, bending and twisting lengths of sapling between the two rails. The old sea wolf was remarkably dexterous with his hook, she noted. He looked up as she approached.

"Any luck?" he asked.

She shrugged. "Remains to be seen. I got one of those big birds and snared a rabbit. Plus I just missed a deer. So there appears to be plenty of game around. Unfortunately, not all of it is friendly."

Hal, who had been bending a sapling length behind the top rail of the fence, stopped and looked at her as he heard those words.

She continued. "There's a bear somewhere around—a big one. Bigger than any I've seen. I'd say he'd be three meters tall, or maybe more."

Thorn whistled softly. "That is big. Did you catch sight of him?"

She shook her head. "No. I saw his marks on a tree, where he'd been clawing the bark. Thing is, he'd only been doing it with his right paw, which indicates that his left paw is wounded or crippled."

"Which would make him even more dangerous," Hal said as she paused to let that information sink in.

She glanced at him and nodded. "Yes. A wounded bear is not something to trifle with," she said.

Thorn sensed she had more to add. "Is that the extent of the bad news?" he prompted.

She shook her head. She stepped a little closer to the two of them and lowered her voice so that Ulf and Wulf, working several meters away and bickering good-naturedly, couldn't hear her.

"I saw human tracks as well," she said.

Thorn stood upright and leaned against the fence. He frowned thoughtfully. "How many?"

She shrugged. "I only saw one footprint. But it was definitely human. Whoever it was, he was wearing a soft shoe, without a heel—some kind of animal-hide slipper, I'd say."

Hal and Thorn exchanged a quick glance. It had been too good to be true, Hal thought. A place like this, with freshwater, plenty of game and firewood, would almost certainly be inhabited.

"I also had the sense that someone was watching me," Lydia added. Both her companions took the comment seriously. Lydia wasn't the type to let her imagination, or her nerves, get the better of her. They trusted her instincts.

"You didn't actually see anyone?" Hal asked.

"No. But I could *feel* eyes on me. You know how you can, sometimes?" She looked earnestly at Thorn. "I wasn't imagining things," she said a little defensively, and he shook his head, dismissing the idea.

"I didn't think you were," he said. "You've been a hunter long enough to develop that sixth sense that tells you when you're not alone. Besides, there was the footprint."

There was a silence among them as they considered the import of what she had told them. Thorn abruptly broke it, coming to a decision and straightening up from where he leaned against the fence.

"All right," he said briskly, "we'd better let the others know. From now on, nobody goes into the forest alone." He saw Lydia start to raise her hand in protest and altered the command. "Aside from you, Lydia. You know how to stay concealed, and you're smart enough to avoid that bear if he shows up. In the meanwhile, we'd better fashion a few bear spears."

"We've got half a dozen spears in the ship," Hal pointed out, but Thorn shook his head.

"They're fine for fighting against men. And we may as well have them handy in the camp," he added as an afterthought. "But a bear as big as Lydia said this one is will need something longer and stronger. We can make them from saplings, sharpen the points and harden them in a fire, then hammer crosspieces through them behind the points."

Lydia was nodding agreement but Hal had a question. "Crosspieces?" he asked. "What sort of crosspieces?"

"Iron spikes driven through the spear," Thorn told him. "If the bear charges and you can catch him on the point, the crosspiece will stop him sliding down the shaft and getting you."

"Will a bear do that?" Hal asked and both his friends nodded.

"Oh yes," Thorn told him. "I saw it happen once on a hunting trip in the mountains behind Hallasholm. The bear was so intent on getting to the man who had put the spear into it that it just kept going forward. The spear went right through and out the other side."

"Which must have killed it," Hal protested.

Thorn nodded. "It did. But not before the bear had taken the hunter's head off with one swipe of its paw. That bear seemed to die with a smile on its face."

Hal frowned, picturing the scene as Thorn had described it.

He knew the old sea wolf was prone to exaggeration when it came to tales about hunting and fighting. But he sensed that this time he was serious.

"I'll dig out some spikes from the ship's supplies," he said. He kept a supply of nails, rivets, iron ingots and other odds and ends on board the ship.

"In the meanwhile, we'd better let the others know what's going on," Thorn said. He put his fingers in his mouth and emitted a piercing whistle. Along the beach, the Herons all stopped what they were doing and turned to face him. He beckoned them in with his good arm, and as they straggled toward him, he called to Edvin.

"Edvin! How's lunch coming?"

The cook looked up at him and cupped his hands around his mouth to reply. He didn't have Thorn's wind- and wave-quelling bellow.

"Ready when you are, Thorn."

"Ten minutes," Thorn replied, then, as the crew assembled, he waved them closer. There was a water skin hanging on the fence and several of them helped themselves to it. The freedom to drink as long and as often as they wanted to was a pleasant novelty after their weeks of reduced water rations. Once they'd drunk, they dropped to the sand, sitting cross-legged in a half circle around Thorn, Hal and Lydia, waiting to hear what their battle leader had to tell them. When he had their attention, Thorn began.

"First of all," he said, "we're not alone here. Lydia saw human footprints in the forest."

"One footprint," Lydia corrected him, but he waved the comment aside.

"I think we can assume that we're not dealing with a one-legged hermit," he said. "If there was one footprint, we'll take it that there'll be others. And we can also assume that whoever left it was trying to conceal his presence—otherwise you would have seen more."

Lydia cocked her head thoughtfully. "I suppose that could be so," she admitted.

Thorn pressed on. "Let's take it that it is. As you know, it's always better—"

"To assume the worst," chorused Ulf, Wulf, Jesper and Stefan. It was one of Thorn's favorite mantras.

He allowed himself a small grin. "I'm glad that's sunk in. You people may finally be learning something. Now another thing, there's a bear wandering around in the woods as well."

That news caused a flurry of comment from those listening. What kind? How big? Where did you see him? They all wanted to know more details and Thorn held up his wooden hook to quiet them. He glanced at the slim girl standing beside him.

"Lydia?" he said, making a gesture for her to take over.

"I don't know what kind," she said. "I didn't see him. I saw his claw marks in the bark of a tree." She paused and several of the crew nodded. They were familiar with those sort of marks. "But . . ." She paused, making sure they were all listening. "From the height of the marks, I'd say he's at least three meters tall."

Jesper whistled incredulously. "Three meters?" he said. "I've never seen a bear as big as that."

"Neither have I," Lydia told him. "And I'm not in any hurry to see him now. He was clawing the bark with his right paw only, which indicates to me that his left paw is injured. And an injured bear—"

"Is a dangerous bear," finished the former chorus.

Like Thorn, she allowed herself a smile. "Exactly. If you see him, don't do anything to provoke him."

"Like what?" Wulf asked, and before she could answer, Ulf did.

"Like letting him see your ugly face," he said. "That'd be enough to send a bear into an attacking frenzy."

"My ugly face?" Wulf said indignantly. "What about your ugly face? You're twice as ugly as I am!"

"So, you admit you're ugly?" Ulf shot back. The entire exchange was pointless. Neither boy was ugly, and more importantly, they were identical.

Wulf drew in breath to reply, but Thorn took a half pace forward.

"I think we'll leave it at that," he said. There was a dangerous gleam in his eye, and Wulf decided that it might be wise to agree. He made an uncertain gesture in the air and sank back onto his haunches. Ulf grinned, delighted to have the last word. Thorn looked away from the twins and addressed the group as a whole.

"We'll need to make some bear spears," he said. "Good, strong poles about three meters long. Make one each, sharpen the points and harden them in the fire. Hal will drive spikes through them."

They all nodded. They could see the wisdom of the idea.

"And we'll need to build some beacon fires along the beach, about ten meters out from the palisade. Use light brushwood and lots of tinder. We want them to burn easily and brightly if we need them."

"What are they for, Thorn?" Jesper asked. He was a little hesitant, as he seemed to have a habit of rubbing Thorn the wrong way with his comments. But Thorn thought it was a fair question and he never begrudged explaining his tactics to any of the crew.

"Just in case someone comes calling," he said. "If we're sitting inside the fence, looking into our own fire, we'll be night-blind. This way, if someone's on the beach, we can light the beacon fires and illuminate them." He glanced at Hal and Lydia. "You might make up some fire arrows and darts for your crossbow and atlatl," he said. They both nodded. "The fires will also be handy to make the bear keep its distance if it comes prowling around," he added, making eye contact with Jesper.

The former thief nodded, his question answered.

"Now, let's have lunch, then get back to it," Thorn said. "We've got spears to make, and a barricade to finish. And I suggest we do everything we can to make it bear-proof."

chapter thirteen

By sundown, the palisade fence was finished. Hal, Thorn, Stig and Lydia inspected it, satisfying themselves that it was an effective barrier.

"Even a bear would have trouble getting through that," Hal said, eyeing the tangle of brushwood and sapling, with the sharp pointed ends of branches pointing in multiple directions. He seized hold of a section of brush and heaved at it. It didn't move. It was solidly built and interwoven to provide strength.

"A bear's stronger than you," Thorn told him.

Hal grinned. "Maybe, but I'm smarter."

Thorn's eyebrow shot up. "That remains to be seen," he said. But on the whole, he was satisfied that the fence was as strong as they could make it. He glanced out to the beach, where four large mounds of firewood—light kindling and dried brushwood—had been placed at intervals along the line of the fence.

"Is that bear likely to come nosing around?" Stig asked.

Thorn shrugged and looked at Lydia. "No reason why he should, is there?" he asked. He was prepared to defer to her greater knowledge.

Lydia considered the question thoughtfully. "No way to know, really," she said. "Bears do as they please. He might be scared off by the activity and noise of the campsite. Or it might make him curious to find out what's going on. One thing," she added. "We should make sure Edvin knows not to leave any food leftovers inside the palisade. That'd bring the bear faster than anything. If he's got leftovers, I'll tell him to stow them up a tree outside the campsite."

Stig studied the fence critically. "So, could a bear get through that?"

"I think a bear could get through anything we could build—if he wanted to," Lydia told him.

Stig raised his eyebrows. "You're such a comfort."

Hal glanced around the deserted beach. The daylight was fading rapidly. He shifted his gaze to the forest, where the shadows were deep and dark under the trees. Somewhere in there was a bear, he thought.

"I think we'll double the watch tonight," he said.

From the campsite came the soft sound of voices raised in song. The crew were sitting around Edvin's cook fire, singing and sniffing the savory odors coming from the large bird Lydia had shot. Edvin had jointed it. It was too large to cook in one piece over his small cook fire. The wings, legs and thighs he was roasting over coals, while he split the big body in two, then coated it in bark and mud and placed it in a fire pit, heaping coals over the top. The fat sizzled and spat from the meat over the coals, causing flames to flare up from time to time. Edvin eyed it proprietorially.

"Plenty of fat there," he said. "That should mean it's tender and good eating."

Indeed, if the smell was anything to go by, the bird would be delicious; the crew watched the cooking pieces eagerly as Edvin turned the spit over the fire. They'd been working hard all day and their appetites were well and truly honed.

Stefan began a new song and they joined in. He had a fine tenor voice and his shipmates were content to let him lead the song, joining him on the chorus. It was a song about being far away from home.

Ulf, thinking of his mother and her comfortable little cottage in Hallasholm, was momentarily overwhelmed with nostalgia and surreptitiously raised a hand to wipe away a tear.

Wulf, who was similarly affected by the words and the haunting melody, snorted disdainfully. "Hah! Has the song made you sad, crybaby?" he asked, glad of the chance to disguise his own feelings with an assumed attitude of scorn.

"Just got something in my eye," Ulf said defensively, making a more obvious movement to rub his eyes and disguise the tears.

"I'll bet," his twin replied scornfully.

Ulf looked steadily at him. "You'll have my fist in *your* eye if you don't shut up."

Wulf opened his mouth to retort but he was silenced by an angry growl from Ingvar, sitting close by.

"Shut up, the pair of you," he said.

They looked at Ingvar in surprise, which deepened as they

realized that tears were rolling freely down his cheeks. He too had been affected by the song and was totally unabashed by the fact. Ulf and Wulf exchanged an uncomfortable look. Ingvar was as brave as a lion, they both knew—big, strong and terrifying in battle. If he wasn't ashamed to show a little emotion, why should they be? Wulf raised a hand and wiped a knuckle over his eyes. Ulf, on the brink of making a sarcastic comment, decided not to.

Lydia's huge bird was an unqualified success. The meat was tender and delicious, particularly the pieces that had been baked in the coating of mud and leaves. The meat, dark in some places and light in others, peeled away easily from the bones, and both light and dark meat were equally tasty.

They ate it with fried onions and some of the dwindling supply of potatoes they had laid in before they left Hibernia. Unfortunately, several of the sacks of potatoes had gone moldy, spoiled by the salt water that had washed aboard during the storm.

Ingvar sat back and licked the grease from his fingers. "Well, if you can get more of those oggle birds, Lydia, you'll make me a happy camper."

She smiled, remembering how the bird had waddled into the clearing, full of its own sense of self-importance.

"I should be able to manage that," she said. "They don't seem to be too bright." She paused and added thoughtfully, "But I'd really like to get that deer I missed. That would keep us stocked with meat for three or four days. I might go looking for it tomorrow."

Thorn looked up at her. "I'll join you."

She frowned. "I thought you said—"

He held up his hook to stop her. "I know what I said. But I'd like to get a look at this bear if possible. It could become a problem."

Leaning back against a log, the warmth of the fire on his face, Hal nodded to himself. He was well fed. His crew were safe. And for the moment, the task of organizing their camp lay with Thorn. The young skirl was happy to leave that responsibility to his older friend. It was a welcome relief after having been in charge for days and nights through the fury of the storm. For a moment, Hal considered suggesting that he might go along with Thorn and Lydia the following morning. Then he shrugged and discarded the idea. The time would come when he'd have to take charge again, he knew. Until then, he could leave the responsibility and the worry to the others.

He looked across the bay to where the rising moon lit a silver path across the water. It's really quite beautiful, he thought.

He glanced up at the sky. There were constellations there he had never seen before. Those that he recognized were far to the north. Suddenly, he felt a long way from home.

It rained during the night and the crew pulled their blankets tightly around them as they huddled comfortably in their low tents. Hal listened to the soft patter of rain on the canvas a few centimeters from his face. Before too long, they'd have to build a more substantial shelter, he thought—something along the lines of the large canvas-covered cabin they'd constructed during their brotherband training days.

Stefan and Edvin, who had the first watch, prowled along the fence line, wrapped in tarpaulin cloaks to keep out the rain.

"Hope that bear doesn't show up," Stefan said. "Those beacon fires will be useless in this rain."

Edvin looked up, letting a light scatter of drops fall on his face. "I don't know," he said. "Hal coated the wood with a lot of pitch. That should burn easily enough. Besides, bears are too smart to go out in the rain. They leave that sort of thing to idiots like us."

Stefan said nothing, but winced as a runnel of cold water found its way inside his cloak and ran down the back of his neck.

The rain had stopped by morning, and as the sun rose over the bay, the tents steamed as the moisture dried out of them. Edvin was already at the cook fire and the welcome scent of coffee drifted over the small settlement. Gradually, figures rolled out of their blankets, crawled out of their low tents and ambled up to the cook fire, where the coffeepot was sitting in the coals to one side of the main fire.

Their eyes were bleary and their hair was tangled and awry. In spite of the early, low-angle sun, the morning was chilly. But gradually the hot beverage sent its warmth seeping through their bones, bringing them fully awake. The smell of frying salt pork and hot griddle cakes raised their spirits even further.

The crew had erected a canvas screen for Lydia around one of the small pools and she sheltered behind it as she washed and bathed. By unspoken agreement, the rest of the crew waited until she had finished, then followed suit in the larger pools. Lydia, her face glowing and her hair damp, sat by the cook fire and wolfed down slices of hot salt pork wrapped in a griddle cake.

"You keep supplying food like this, Edvin," she said, "and I might have to marry you someday."

The cook-cum-medic grinned easily at her. "Kind of you to say so," he replied. "But I've had better offers."

"I'll marry you, Lydia," said Stefan cheerfully. He was the first of the boys back from the pools and was pouring himself another cup of coffee, blowing on its steaming surface to cool it.

Lydia eyed him speculatively. "You can't cook," she said at length.

He shrugged, unabashed. "I have other, hidden talents."

She smiled. "Very well hidden, I'd say."

As the rest of the crew straggled back down to the cook fire, hair wet and faces red with the cold of the water and the friction of rubbing with rough towels, Thorn emerged from his tent and rose to his feet, scratching himself.

He's like a bear himself, Lydia thought, as he strolled over to the fireplace, sniffing and stretching.

"You ready to go hunting?" he asked her, accepting a mug of coffee from Edvin.

She nodded, but glanced toward the water pools under the cliffs.

"I'm ready," she said. "Are you going to wash first?"

He wrinkled his nose, rubbed his hand over his face and shook his head.

"Naah. Washing is for them that's dirty," he said.

chapter fourteen

Once breakfast was finished, the crew broke up into smaller groups. Hal led Stig, Stefan and Jesper off to the inlet. He wanted to inspect *Heron*'s bilges. He had a suspicion that she had been taking in water. After the pounding she had taken during the storm, she might have sprung a plank or two. They would need re-seating and caulking with pitch and oakum—a substance derived from unraveling old lengths of rope.

To do that, they'd need to locate the sprung planks, then tilt the ship to expose them. They could do this by hauling in on hawsers running from the mast to trees on either bank of the inlet.

Thorn and Lydia headed off into the forest, in search of another deer. Thorn trusted Lydia's instincts when she said she thought someone had been watching her. But he wanted to see for himself and to get a better idea of the country inland of their campsite.

Ingvar stayed with Edvin, helping clean the breakfast dishes. They packed the rest of the food away, securing it tightly under canvas covers and in small wooden casks. Even without Lydia's warning, they were well aware of bears' propensity to seek out food left uncovered. Then Ingvar took the food scraps and climbed over the barricade by way of the rough stile they had erected the day before—two ladders tied together at the top and placed one each side of the fence. He disposed of the scraps by the simple expedient of hurling them into the sea. As the bread and fragments of pork hit the water, myriads of small fish swarmed around them.

Ulf and Wulf had been prepared to spend a day relaxing on the sand, enjoying the sun. But before he left the camp, Thorn had glanced at Edvin's supply of firewood.

The stock was running low, Thorn thought, and even though he knew Edvin would replenish it himself without complaint, he felt that Edvin already did more than his share of the campsite tasks, cooking for them all, cleaning up and tending any minor wounds or illnesses they might suffer. He had jerked a thumb at the twins as they stretched out on the sand in the rapidly warming sun.

"You two. Get more firewood for Edvin," he ordered.

Ulf opened his mouth to protest, took one look at Thorn's face and nodded. "Yes, Thorn," he said meekly.

"Take one of the bear spears and keep your wits about you," the old sea wolf ordered, and turned away to stride after Lydia.

"Why didn't you tell him where to put his firewood?" said

Wulf pugnaciously. Ulf noticed that he waited until Thorn was out of earshot before he said it. And even then, he kept his voice low.

"Why didn't *you* tell him?" Ulf replied.

Wulf shrugged. "Obviously, he was talking to you."

"And how is that so obvious?" his brother wanted to know.

"If he'd been talking to me, he would have said 'please.' He respects me."

Wulf selected one of the long, sharpened poles the crew had prepared the previous day, inspecting the cross-spike that Hal had hammered through it. He sighted down it, checking that it was relatively straight, and was apparently satisfied.

"You'd better get the firewood carrier," he said to his twin. This was a large square of canvas with rope handles on either side. The user laid it on the ground, piled firewood into it, then picked it up by the handles, wrapping the canvas round the firewood to secure it for carrying.

"And what will you be doing while I'm cutting and collecting firewood?" Ulf wanted to know.

Wulf gave a small shrug. "I'll be keeping a watch out for that bear. You heard Thorn tell me to take a spear."

"I didn't hear him say please," Ulf said sharply. "So he must have been talking to me."

Wulf shook his head. "He was definitely talking to me. The please was implicit."

"The please was nonexistent," Ulf told him. But he gathered the firewood carrier anyway, rolling it up and cramming it under one arm. They negotiated the stile over the boundary fence and headed for the forest, waving good-bye to Ingvar and Edvin.

They continued their bickering as they made their way into the shadows under the trees. It was second nature to them, and if they had been asked what they were arguing about, neither of them could have said.

But as they entered the trees, the bickering died away and both boys became instantly more wary. The forest was an unfamiliar and strangely disturbing place. The trees were tall and grew thickly together, creating blind spots and deeply shadowed areas where anything could be lurking. When they were building the barricade, the crew had collected most of the deadfalls and kindling that lay close to the campsite, so now the twins had to go farther afield in search of suitable firewood. The trees seemed to close in behind them, masking the cheerful, familiar sound of waves breaking on the beach. Without realizing it, they began to talk in lowered tones, afraid of disturbing the stillness of the forest.

Ulf spied a good pile of deadfall underneath one of the older trees. They were branches that had dried and fallen off in the wind—or under the influence of their own weight. He stepped quickly forward and laid the firewood carrier out on the forest floor.

"Keep an eye out for bears," he said. He reached toward the pile of dead branches and grabbed a large bunch in both hands. As he went to pull them free, he heard a violent buzzing, rattling sound from the wood and he sprang back.

"What was that?" Wulf demanded. He'd turned in time to see his brother leap back from the pile of wood.

"The wood rattled at me," Ulf told him, his voice unsteady.

"Don't be an idiot. How can wood rattle at you?"

Ulf pointed at the tangled pile of dead branches and gestured an invitation. "See for yourself," he said. "Try to pick it up."

But Wulf had heard the rattling buzz and it had a decidedly threatening sound to it. He wasn't putting his hand anywhere near it. Stopping a few meters away, he thrust the bear spear forward, pushing it in between the branches and twisting it so that the transverse spike caught in a Y-shaped fork.

The rattle sounded again—louder and more insistent this time. Wulf drew back the pole, dragging the forked limb with it and disturbing several of the other branches at the same time.

The rattle increased in pitch and volume, and he distinctly felt two sharp impacts against the end of the spear. Twisting it free of the branches, he withdrew it rapidly and they both stepped back.

The rattling stopped.

Wulf brought the sharp end of the spear closer and held it up for inspection. There was a small stain of viscous liquid on the end, just before the burnt, hardened point.

Ulf crouched, shading his eyes from the sunlight filtering through the trees, and peered under the pile of branches. There was something there, he saw. Something mottled and brown, that blended into the colors of the bark and leaf mold. As he peered more intently, it took shape.

It was a snake, lying coiled up, with its head and tail both rising out of the ends of its thick body. As he watched, the tail vibrated, and a low, warning buzz sounded. The tail seemed to be constructed of a series of hard rings, and as the snake moved its tail rapidly from side to side, these rattled together. He edged toward it a pace. The vibration increased in speed and the rattle went up in volume and pitch. He stepped back and the sound subsided.

"It's a snake," he said. "It has some kind of rattling thing on its tail."

"I thought so," Wulf said loftily. He never liked to look as if he was hearing anything he didn't know.

Ulf looked at him and shook his head.

"I suppose it's venomous," Wulf continued.

His brother jerked a thumb at the liquid staining the end of the spear tip. "Unless that's wild honey, I'd say it is," he said sarcastically.

Wulf dropped the lofty, knowing tone and studied the spear tip once more, taking care not to touch the thick liquid. "What should we do?" he asked.

Ulf had a ready answer. "Leave it alone. It only rattles when we come near it. It's warning us off. If we leave it alone, it'll stay where it is."

"What makes you so sure?" Wulf asked.

Ulf gave him a long-suffering look. "Well, it's stayed put so far, while we've been disturbing it. Stands to reason that if we simply walk away, it's not going to come after us."

"Maybe we should kill it," Wulf said uncertainly.

His brother gave him another pitying look. "What with?"

Wulf looked down at the bear spear, but before he could speak, Ulf forestalled him.

"You'll never get at it with that sharpened stick," he pointed out. "There are too many branches in the way. If you go poking around in there with that, it's possible it'll come darting out and attack us."

"We could kill it with our saxes," Wulf suggested, dropping his hand to the hilt of his saxe knife. "We could lop its head off." The idea appealed to him. He'd teach that snake to go rattling at him, he thought. But again his brother offered a scornful suggestion.

"You can try it if you like. But I wouldn't go pushing my hand through that tangle of deadfall, saxe or no saxe. That's getting altogether too close to it."

"So what do you suggest we do?" asked Wulf, with the tone of someone who has presented a series of good ideas only to have them disregarded by someone with none.

"I told you. We should simply walk away and leave it alone. Listen," Ulf said, pointing to the tangle of dried wood. "Since we've been talking, and not poking around where the creature lives, it's stopped its rattling."

"All the same, it tried to bite me," Wulf protested.

"It tried to bite your stick," Ulf told him. "And if you went poking around me with it, I'd likely do the same thing."

Wulf regarded him with interest. "You'd bite a stick if I poked you with it?" he asked. He seemed to be contemplating the idea.

Ulf met his gaze for several seconds without speaking. "No. If you tried to poke me with a stick," he said, "I'd bite *you*."

There was something in his voice that told Wulf he was serious. He discarded the idea of poking him with the bear spear. "So what should we do about it?" he repeated.

Ulf sighed. Sometimes it was like talking to an infant, he thought. "We walk away. We ignore it and it will ignore us. We haven't heard a peep out of it since we've left it alone."

"It doesn't peep. It rattles. Or buzzes," Wulf said, remembering how high-pitched and urgent the rattle had become as he shoved the stick farther into the bushes. Then he added thoughtfully, "Of course, it may be trying to lull us into a false sense of security. I've heard snakes do that. It may be waiting for us to walk away, and when we do, it might come chasing out after us. And I've heard snakes can move very quickly when they want to."

"So?" Ulf challenged.

"So what do we do if it chases us?"

"I don't know what you'll do. But I'm going to run away."

"Can you run faster than a snake? I've heard they're very fast," Wulf repeated.

"I don't need to run faster than the snake," Ulf said, in tones of sweet reason. "I just need to run faster than you."

There was silence for a moment. Then Wulf asked: "And what will you tell our mam? Will you tell her you ran off and left me to be bitten by a rattling snake?"

"No. I'd tell her that I ran away and you bravely threw yourself on the snake to save me. I'd tell her you died a hero, and we'd both shed a tear for you."

Of course, they both knew that neither of them would ever desert the other in the face of danger. And they knew that either of them would willingly give his life for the other. But neither mentioned the fact.

chapter fifteen

In another part of the forest, Lydia had found the trail of a small group of deer.

Their tracks wound through the close-growing trees, and from time to time, one or another of the animals left a small tuft of fur on the sharp edges of twigs. They also broke small branches as they pushed through, leaving them bent back and oozing sap.

That fact alone was enough to tell Lydia that the tracks were fresh.

"Three of them," she said in an undertone. "Two females and a fawn."

"How can you tell?" Thorn answered, also speaking in a lowered voice. It wasn't that either of them was overawed by the dimness and brooding silence of the forest, as the twins had been.

Lydia had spent half her life tracking animals through the dimness beneath trees and felt thoroughly at home here. As for Thorn, he wasn't the impressionable type. He didn't react to atmosphere. He looked for facts and hard evidence—which was why he asked the question of Lydia.

She knelt and pointed to two hoofprints in the leaf mold. They were so close, they almost overlapped.

"These were made by two different animals," she said. He inclined his head, about to ask a question, when she elaborated. "See, they're only two centimeters apart. They couldn't have been made by one deer. It had to be two, with one following the other closely."

He nodded, understanding. It was simple when someone explained it, he thought. Then he realized that most things in life were.

"You can see that one print is slightly bigger and deeper," she continued.

Thorn bent closer and peered intently at the two prints. In fact, he couldn't see that at all. But he grunted as if he could.

Lydia glanced at him. "Can't you see that?" she asked incredulously. To her, the two prints were so obviously different that she couldn't understand how anyone could miss the fact.

"Well, maybe a bit," Thorn prevaricated.

She shook her head. "So, which is the bigger?"

He put out a hand to the two prints, let it hover over them and then touched the front print. "That one," he said, trying to keep a questioning note out of his voice.

Lydia sighed and said nothing.

"Is that right?" he asked, knowing from her reaction that it wasn't.

"You have to ask?"

He shrugged. Then he froze, his hand outstretched to the two small impressions in the leaf mold. Out of his peripheral vision, he had seen a faint, almost imperceptible movement in the trees to their left as a shadow flitted from one patch of cover to the next. With a superhuman effort, he refrained from turning his head to look at the spot where he'd seen it.

"So how do you know about the fawn? Don't look. But I just saw someone following us," he added, in the same conversational tone.

Lydia stiffened slightly. For a moment, she said nothing, gathering her wits, then replied, "Deer tend to snag their chests and shoulders on twigs and branches as they pass through—those are the widest parts of them, after all. And some of the tufts of hair on the trees here are a good bit lower than the others—barely at thigh height. So one is considerably smaller than the others. Which direction?"

There was no real need to continue their conversation about the deer. The chances were that if anyone was watching them, he or she wouldn't be able to understand them. But it helped maintain the matter-of-fact tone of their voices.

"Off to the left, about fifteen meters and a little behind us," Thorn said, reaching down to trace one of the footprints with his forefinger as he spoke. Lydia did the same, as if showing him a salient feature of the print.

"Just saw it move again," she said quietly. "Whatever it is."

Their pantomime of studying the tracks seemed to have lulled their watcher into a false sense of security, she thought.

Thorn straightened his back and rose to his feet, groaning slightly as he did and rubbing both hands into the small of his back. "You don't think it's a person?" he asked.

She rose lithely from her crouching position. She didn't groan or rub her back, Thorn noted ruefully. She pointed through the trees, in the direction in which the three deer were traveling.

"Don't know. I didn't get a clear enough look," she replied.

Thorn twisted his mouth, gnawing at the end of his mustache. He hadn't got a clear look either. But his instincts told him it was a human movement, not an animal. An animal *wouldn't* have moved, after all. Animals were smart.

"I think it's a person," he said.

Lydia started off through the trees once more, following the deer. "What should we do?"

He considered the question for a second or two. "Nothing," he said. "We keep doing what we're doing. So far they haven't bothered us."

"He said, just before a spear came whistling out of the shadows," she said sarcastically and he shrugged his shoulders.

"If they wanted to attack us, they've had plenty of opportunity," he pointed out. Lydia accepted the fact, but it didn't stop her nerves from tingling and she ached to turn around for a good look at the trees behind them and to their left.

The opportunity to do so came a few minutes later. She sighted sunlight through the trees, indicating that a clearing was up ahead. And a clearing could mean that the deer would stop to graze. She tested the wind. It was in a perfect position for them, dead ahead, blowing their scent away from the deer. She turned back to Thorn.

"There's a clearing up ahead," she said. "Go slowly."

As she turned and spoke, she was just in time to see a shadowy form slip back into the shelter of a clump of man-high undergrowth. That was definitely a person, she thought. An animal wouldn't have the instinct to move into cover. It would either freeze in place or turn and flee.

"All right," she said. "I saw him that time. He's about twenty meters away and hiding in the bushes. What do we do?"

Thorn considered the question for a moment, then decided. "We keep doing what we're doing," he said. "First item of business is to get one of those deer."

"If you say so. Odds are they'll have stopped in that clearing, so tread quietly."

Lydia, with years of practice, made virtually no sound as she slipped between the trees. Thorn made a few slight sounds, but for a big, bulky man, he was surprisingly light on his feet. She had noticed this on previous occasions with him, but it never failed to impress her how quietly he could move.

She drew a dart from her quiver and fitted it to the atlatl handle. Remembering the previous day's hunt, she raised it and drew it back, ready to throw. That way, if the deer were in the clearing, she wouldn't have to make any preliminary movement that might unsettle them.

With her left hand, she gestured for Thorn to stop. She continued to the edge of the clear space among the trees.

The deer were there, grazing on the far side of the clearing, about fifteen meters from where she stood in the shadows. Two does, she saw, the younger and smaller one with the fawn beside her, butting its head up into her body to nurse. The other was older and heavier, and she was busily cropping the long grass. Something alerted her and her head came up, ears twitching, nostrils sniffing the air, testing it for an alien presence.

In a second, they'd be off, Lydia knew. There was no time to waste. Targeting the older of the two adults, she drew back the final few centimeters and cast. The dart flashed across the clearing as the now-alert deer tensed to turn and run. It sliced into her left side, behind the shoulder, and took her cleanly in the heart. The tensed legs and muscles collapsed and the doe fell without a sound onto the grass.

The other doe and the fawn didn't hesitate. They bounded into the trees and Lydia heard them crashing through the undergrowth as they made their escape.

"Got one," she called softly.

Thorn came level with her, taking in the fallen brown body across the clearing. He drew his saxe, stepping into the clearing.

"I've got an idea," he said as he moved toward the dead deer and dropped to his knees beside it. "We'll field dress it and leave a joint hanging in the tree as a gift to our silent watcher. That way, he'll know we're friendly."

"That's good thinking," Lydia said. But she put a hand out to prevent him starting to work on the carcass. "That saxe is too big for the job," she said, drawing her razor-sharp skinning knife. "I'll skin it and gut it and you can hack off one of the rear legs with your saxe."

She went to work and he watched her deft movements as she separated the deer from its skin, then opened the body cavity and carefully removed the stomach and entrails, making sure not to puncture the thin walls of the intestines or gall bladder with her knife.

She made a neat pile of the guts, laying them on the recently removed skin of the deer. Then she gestured to the naked, glistening carcass as she wiped the blood off her hands on the thick grass. Already flies were buzzing around the entrails she had piled to one side.

"Take off a leg," she said.

Thorn drew his saxe—he had re-sheathed it when she went to work with her skinning knife. He took hold of the deer's left hind leg with his right-hand gripping hook and lifted it up, exposing the hip joint.

In just two powerful, accurate strokes, he severed the leg. He held it up, looking admiringly at it.

"Plenty of meat there," he said. "I hope our hidden friend appreciates it."

He brandished the joint toward the direction where they had last seen their secret observer.

"This is for you," he called in a raised voice. He smiled at the wall of green shadows. Then he turned to wedge the leg into the fork of a tree some two meters from the ground.

Which was when they heard the low, rumbling growl.

It came ninety degrees away from the direction Thorn was facing. He froze, still holding the leg aloft, and they both turned to see a massive brown shape force its way through the trees into the clearing, snapping several saplings like twigs as it came.

"Orlog's teeth!" he said softly. "It's huge."

Even on all fours, the bear was immense. It stood at least a meter and a half high at the shoulder.

Then it reared onto its hind legs and towered above them, although still twenty meters away. The left forepaw hung uselessly beside it, but the right one was pawing angrily at the air, the curved claws slashing like black scimitars. The fur was thick and brown and matted, with half a dozen old scars and bare patches, evidence of combats fought long ago. The teeth, when it bared them to snarl once more, were huge and yellow. It must have been three and a half meters tall, Thorn thought, and for several seconds he stood frozen, his blood like ice water in his veins.

"Put down the leg," Lydia said softly. "Lay it down in front of you and back away."

He did as she said and looked to see if the bear was advancing. So far, it remained where it was, but it roared now, a shattering, nerve-chilling sound that seemed to fill the forest. It clawed at the air again with its right paw. The left, obviously trying to join in, made a tiny movement.

"Don't make eye contact with it," Lydia warned. She was already backing toward the trees behind them, her eyes lowered. Thorn hastily complied.

"Back away," she repeated and Thorn, eyes down, slowly took a pace backward. Then another.

"Don't let it know you're afraid," Lydia told him.

"I think it's already guessed," he said through gritted teeth. The bear dropped to all fours again and began to shuffle forward, eyes fixed on the carcass of the dead deer.

"Do bears eat deer?" Thorn asked. The bear looked up and snarled, curling its lips back from those massive yellow teeth.

"I think this bear will eat anything it can catch," she told him as they continued to back away from the monster. Thorn looked ruefully at the ground beside the deer's carcass, where he had laid his bear spear down. Not that a piece of sharpened stick would stop this brute, he thought.

"There's a tree root behind you," Lydia warned him. If he fell, the bear might rush to take him. He felt carefully with his foot as he continued to step back, finding the root and stepping over it.

"Thanks," he said breathlessly.

The bear reached the deer carcass and pushed tentatively at it with its right front paw. It lowered its head and licked at the drying blood that smeared the spot where Thorn had severed the deer's leg. Then it raked the separated limb toward itself. Holding the leg awkwardly between its crippled left paw and the uninjured right one, the bear took a huge chunk of meat from the leg with its massive teeth. It sat beside the deer, holding the joint across its body, and took another huge bite. It snarled appreciatively, its attention now focused on the thirty kilograms of fresh meat in front of it, the intruding two-legged creatures forgotten.

Lydia and Thorn continued to back away, listening to the crunching and growling as the bear demolished the leg, then started on the rest of the deer.

"Curse it," said Lydia. "I can't keep losing deer this way."

Thorn looked at her bleakly. "We've got a bigger problem than that," he said. "After today, it's going to associate us with fresh meat."

chapter sixteen

Stig and Ingvar had the second watch that night, from midnight to three in the morning. They patrolled along the inside of the barricade, peering out at the beach before them. The moon had set hours ago and now the bay was lit only by stars. But they were brilliant and there was plenty of light.

They'd considered patrolling separately but decided to stick together. Thorn and Lydia had told the group about the bear and the mysterious observer, so they knew it was important to keep a sharp eye on their surroundings. Ingvar was armed with his long voulge—the spear-axe-pike combination that had become his standard weapon. Stig had his ax thrust through a metal ring on his belt and carried one of the long bear spears. He looked at it doubtfully.

"From the way Lydia described the bear, it'll take more than a pointy stick to see it off," he remarked.

Ingvar smiled. "That's a pointy stick with a crosspiece," he said. "That makes all the difference. You'll be glad of it if the bear tries to climb over the barricade."

Stig was about to caution his big friend not to say such things. Putting ideas like that into words often seemed to make them come true, he thought. But at that moment, they heard a violent crashing and snarling from the southern end of the fence.

"Come on!" said Stig and the two of them broke into a run, heading for the source of the noise.

There was a massive form against the fence, gripping it with one forepaw and trying to clamber up onto it. But as it did so, it came into painful contact with the dozens of sharpened ends of branches and saplings that protruded outward. And the tangle of light saplings and brush gave it no useful purchase, collapsing under its weight as it tried to climb over. The fence shook and vibrated along twenty meters of its length as the bear struggled with it.

"Loki's beard, that's big!" said Ingvar. He had a sudden flash of understanding how normal-size people felt when they saw him.

Stig dashed forward, the wooden spear in both hands raised to shoulder height. He lunged at the bear, putting all the weight of his body behind the stroke. The point caught the bear in the shoulder. It didn't penetrate the bear's thick fur, but it jabbed painfully and the bear roared in pain and anger. It swatted at the spear with its right paw and spun it out of Stig's grip. The force of the blow numbed his hands. He paled. This was a serious opponent, he thought. He retrieved the spear and began a rapid series of darting jabs at the bear's head and neck, aiming for the eyes and the soft flesh around the mouth.

"Get a torch from the fire!" he shouted at Ingvar. Ingvar had cut at the bear with an overhand blow of the voulge. The razor-sharp blade drew blood along the bear's upper arm, but unfortunately it was on the already-damaged left side. As the blade bit into its flesh, the bear swung around and batted the shaft of the voulge, knocking it out of Ingvar's hands. He stepped back, then nodded to Stig and took off at a run for the fireplace, grateful for the viewing spectacles Hal had made for him months ago.

Even so, in the uneven starlight, he stumbled several times and once fell full length on the cold sand. It had been warm earlier in the day, under the sun, he recalled. Strange how it had lost its heat so quickly.

There was movement in the camp as people rolled out of their tents, calling to one another, asking what was happening. Kloof galloped back and forth, barking. There was a rising note of alarm in her bark.

"It's the bear!" Ingvar shouted. "It's trying to climb the palisade!"

He grabbed two large burning brands from the fire and turned to retrace his steps. He had a quick glimpse of Hal turning back to his tent and reappearing with his crossbow and quiver. Then he was running back the way he had come, picking his way with a little more care this time, the burning torches in his hands spewing out showers of red-hot sparks behind him as he ran.

The bear was still roaring its frustration at Stig as the first mate jabbed and stabbed his spear at it, never leaving it in place long enough for the creature to smash it with that mighty forepaw. Ingvar saw it manage to clamber up almost to the top of the barricade, where it towered high above Stig in the night, seeming to blot out the starlight. In another second, he thought, it would come tumbling over inside the barricade.

And then all hell would break loose.

Acting instinctively, Ingvar drew back his right arm and hurled one of the flaming torches at the monster's head. The torch struck it on the shoulders, and the flames, subdued momentarily as the torch spun end over end through the air, sprang to violent life once more.

The bear recoiled, crashing over backward from its precarious perch on the barricade and hitting the sand with a mighty, earth-shaking thud.

Its fur had caught fire in several places and it beat at the flames, its howls of anguish rising higher as it shambled away from the barricade, down the beach and toward the southernmost of the piles of firewood. The torch Ingvar had thrown fell to the ground within the tangle of saplings and brushwood. Ingvar reached into the barricade with his voulge, hooking the burning brand out onto the sand before it could set the fence ablaze.

"That'd be all we need," he muttered.

He was conscious of someone arriving beside him at a run. He looked around and saw Hal, lowering his crossbow to cock the string and setting a bolt into the loading groove.

"That won't stop the bear," he said, but Hal gestured to the lump of pitch-soaked rags on the head of the bolt.

"Light it up," Hal ordered.

Ingvar, understanding his intention, used the remaining torch to light the oil-soaked rags. The flame flickered for a moment, then flared into bright life as the oil caught.

Hal raised the crossbow, sighted quickly and released. The flaming bolt became a tiny red coal as it streaked across the intervening space toward the beacon fire where the bear had run. Then, when it hit, the flame came alive again. For a moment, they could see the yellow tongue of light among the pitch-soaked firewood.

Then the pitch and the tinder caught in a *WHOOMPH* of flame, throwing the dark form of the bear into stark relief.

Frightened by the sudden explosion of fire close beside it, the monster threw back its head and snarled in terror. Then it dropped to all fours and lumbered away, back toward the forest from which it had come, never pausing, never looking back.

Hal let go a huge sigh of pent-up breath as he watched it go.

"We can't go on like this," he said. "We're going to have to do something about that cursed bear."

chapter seventeen

For the next few days, it seemed that the problem with the bear had been solved, for they saw no further sign of it.

Perhaps, Hal thought, the shock of having the beacon explode into flames a few meters away had convinced it that the two-legged creatures were best avoided. Thorn maintained his directive that nobody, other than Lydia, should venture into the forest alone. Various groups went out from time to time, bringing in firewood and, under Edvin's direction, searching for edible plants and wild vegetables. After hearing of the twins' encounter with the rattling snake, they took great care not to reach under any fallen trees, rocks or piles of deadfalls.

Lydia resumed her solo hunting expeditions and finally returned to the camp with a medium-size deer.

"I actually saw plenty," she told Hal. "But there's no sense in killing more than we can eat, and the meat would only spoil if we left it."

Hal rubbed his chin thoughtfully. "We could always salt it or smoke it," he said, but Lydia dismissed the idea.

"Why smoke meat when we can find plenty of it fresh?" she asked. "As I said, the forest is full of game."

"We're going to have to start doing it sometime," Hal told her. "We'll need to lay in a supply of dried or smoked meat for when we head home."

It was the first time he had made any mention of a return journey, and although Lydia had known deep down that one day they would have to leave, having the concept mentioned brought it into sharp focus. She hadn't thought much about it in the preceding few days.

"When will we be doing that?" she asked. She didn't ask the other question that sprang to mind—*how will we do that?* They'd been driven hundreds, probably thousands of kilometers off course by the huge storm that had engulfed them. She wouldn't have a clue how to head for home.

"Not for a while," Hal told her. "It's still winter and I don't want to try crossing the Endless Ocean while there's a chance of hitting winter storms."

"But when you do—or rather when *we* do—how will you know which way to go?"

Lydia was a total adept when it came to finding her way through a forest—or any other form of landscape if it came to it. But her inherent sense of direction failed her on the ocean. To her, it was a trackless, watery waste. And it tended to hurl bucketfuls of cold water on you if you didn't stay constantly alert.

Hal smiled. He was weaving fine beech saplings together to make a new tiller attachment for the ship. The old one was fraying badly, he'd noticed.

"The stars," he told her. He gestured toward the sky above them. "I don't recognize a lot of the ones we see now, but I can still spot some of my old friends in the northern sky. They'll lead us home."

He sounded confident and that reassured her. She knew he was a master navigator. Even Thorn, with all his years of experience, deferred to Hal's knowledge of the sky and wind and sea, and his instinct for sensing currents that could take the ship off course. She'd noticed that Hal had been quiet since they had reached this strange land and she had feared that the storm had driven the confidence out of him.

"It's another reason to wait until winter is over," he added. "In summer, the stars move south, so I'll be able to see my familiar signposts a lot easier."

"Move south?" she asked. "How do stars move south?"

He shrugged. "I suppose they decide they want a warmer climate," he said. Then he added seriously, "We don't know why they do it. We just know that they do. In the meantime, keep bringing in fresh meat."

She nodded. She had heard and seen several of the big oggle birds over the past few days. But she had become a little obsessive over bringing down a deer and had ignored them. It might be time to take a few of them for Edvin's cook fire, she thought. The last one had proven to be delicious.

She nodded toward the dressed deer carcass lying at her feet.

"I'll take this up to Edvin," she said. "We can have venison tonight."

Hal grinned. "That'll make a difference from salt pork," he said, and turned back to his tiller attachment.

She made her way through the campsite, replying to the greetings from the other members of the crew, who were engaged in building a more permanent form of accommodation for their extended stay. They had cut saplings to form a hut-shaped framework and were now covering it with canvas at the sides, and interwoven pine branches on the roof. It looked snug and waterproof. Stig, as first mate, was the de facto foreman of the crew and in charge of the building of their shelter, although the overall design had been laid out by Hal. Lydia had been amazed by the speed at which the hut was taking shape, until Hal had revealed that the hut was almost identical to the one they had all built on the first day of their brotherband course, and they were drawing on that experience.

One corner of the hut had been screened off—to form a small private room for her, she knew. She smiled to herself. She enjoyed the way her brothers took extra trouble to make her comfortable and preserve her privacy. It made her feel special and well regarded. Thorn saw her crossing the sand and laid down the hammer he was using to nail several cross-ties into place. Even working left-handed, she thought, he was still capable of driving nails neatly into place, with a minimum of hammer strokes and without the sort of off-angle blows that would bend the nails out of shape.

"No sign of our giant hairy friend?" Thorn asked as he came over to walk beside her.

Lydia smiled. "Not until you came up and started talking to me."

"You're getting altogether too smart with your words," he told her, then continued in a serious tone. "But no sign of the bear?"

She shook her head. "We may have finally scared him off."

He looked at her sidelong. "Do you really think that?"

She paused, considering her reply. "No. I think he'll be back eventually. We're going to have to figure out what to do about him."

Thorn nodded. "Don't know what that'll be. None of our weapons really seem to bother him."

"I suppose I could put four or five darts into him," she said thoughtfully. "That'd kill him eventually. But it'd be a slow, unpleasant death and I really don't want to do that."

Thorn had noticed this trait in her. She was a hunter, and a highly efficient one. Yet she took no joy in killing and tried to make her kills quick and clean. The idea of leaving a bear with half a dozen wounds cutting him up inside, and bleeding him slowly to death, was against all her instincts. He admired her for it.

"Still," he said, "it may come to that." She nodded briefly, knowing he was right. He changed the subject.

"How about our other friend?" he asked. "Any sign of him?"

"Nothing," she said. "I checked several times but there was no sign that anyone was out there with me."

He scratched his beard. "Maybe they've watched you long enough to know you're simply hunting for game," he said. "And that you're no threat to them."

"That could be it," she agreed.

They were close to the cook fire now, and Edvin looked up, smiling as he saw her burden. "Venison!" he said happily. "I take it you didn't have to give this one to a bear?"

He stepped forward and took the deer from her. She passed him a parcel of the liver and tongue, wrapped in a section of the animal's skin.

"And some delicious offal!" he added. He knew that some people declined to eat these parts of an animal, but to him they were a true delicacy.

"Do you need a hand jointing that deer?" Thorn asked.

Edvin nodded. "I'd appreciate that."

Thorn drew his saxe and got to work, removing the haunches first, then the fore shoulders. While he set them aside, Lydia cut the rumps off. Then Thorn went to work with his saxe again, cutting the rib cage into racks of chops. In a short time, the deer was reduced from one carcass to a selection of cookable pieces.

As they worked, Lydia told Thorn of her conversation with Hal.

"Hal's talking about heading back to Skandia," she said.

Thorn nodded, a satisfied look on his face. "Good. I hoped he'd start thinking that way. I was a little worried that he was feeling lost—figuratively as well as literally. That storm could have sapped his confidence badly."

"I get the feeling that he was glad to turn over responsibility for the camp to you and Stig," she said, and Thorn agreed with her.

"That's the way we do things. We each use our skills and experience where it's best suited. Hal has a lot of responsibility riding on his shoulders when we're at sea, and he had to make a pretty tough decision when he chose to head west. That sort of thing can make a man start to doubt his own judgment. We need him fit and confident. None of us can do what he does when we're at sea." She noticed a slight note of pride in Thorn's voice. He loved the young skirl like a son, she knew, and he was inordinately proud of Hal's skill at the tiller and at reading the stars and sea currents.

"How good is he?" she asked. She had always simply assumed that Hal was a superlative helmsman and navigator, but she had no real basis for comparison.

Before Thorn could answer, Edvin, who had been an interested witness to their conversation, interrupted.

"I'd say he's a genius," he said. "We all have some knowledge of navigation and ship handling. But Hal takes it way beyond what the rest of us can do. He's an absolute natural. He has the most amazing sense of what's about to happen, and he's incredible when it comes to judging angles and drift. He can put a ship exactly where he wants it to be, within a meter of space. Wouldn't you agree, Thorn?" he said, finally deferring to the old sea wolf's greater experience.

Thorn nodded. "If we're going to make it back to Hallasholm—and I believe we are—it'll be because of his skill and instincts." He grinned cheerfully. "If it were my job to get us home, I wouldn't even know where to begin."

Lydia opened her mouth to reply but, before she could, they were interrupted by an all-too-familiar sound—the roaring of an angry bear.

"Oh, Orlog's hairy armpits!" she said, an oath she had picked up from the crew. "He's back."

chapter eighteen

There was an explosion of activity in the camp as the crew raced to collect weapons and then scrambled over the barricade, heading for the sounds made by the obviously enraged bear.

Kloof raced up and down inside the fence, barking furiously and looking for someone to help her over the ladder. Finally, when there was a clear path, she solved the problem for herself by scrambling up the inner ladder and launching herself off the top, landing light-footed in the soft sand and racing toward the forest north of the campsite.

Stig had been the first to react, and as he ran through the heavy sand, he became aware of another sound that had previously been masked by the bear's angry roaring. It was a high-pitched sound, a frightened sound.

It was the sound of children crying out in fear.

As he recognized it for what it was, he redoubled his efforts. He heard feet pounding in the sand behind him and glanced over his shoulder to see Thorn and Hal. Thorn had a large shield clamped on his right arm and was carrying an ax in his left hand. Hal was balancing one of the long spears they had fashioned, although prior experience had shown them to be relatively ineffective. Stig had his battleax.

Jesper went past them as if they were standing still. He had always been the fastest runner in the crew—due in no small part to his previous occupation as a thief. He had a bear spear as well, balancing it at the midpoint and carrying it in a horizontal position.

"There are kids there!" Stig shouted to the others, and they nodded. They'd heard the high-pitched screams as well.

The roaring and screaming were both louder now and they turned toward the fringe of the trees. Through the shadows, they could see violent movement. Then the scene became clearer. Just inside the line of trees, the bear was standing by one of the mottled-bark trees, throwing its massive weight against the slender trunk with a series of resounding crashes. Four meters up the tree, just out of the bear's reach, were huddled two small children—a boy and a girl. Stig had a quick impression of black hair, worn long, and brown-skinned faces. And two pairs of terrified eyes.

As the Herons watched, the two children tried to haul themselves higher, to get farther away from the bear's clutches. But as they moved, the huge beast crashed its weight against the trunk once more, shaking the entire tree and causing the lower child, the girl, to momentarily lose her grip and begin to fall. She screamed in terror, and her companion grabbed her by the back of her shirt, hauling her to safety. The bear roared in anger and renewed its efforts to shake them loose. For a dreadful moment, it seemed that the two children, off balance and without a secure grip on the tree, were about to tumble down to the ground next to the raging bear.

Then Jesper intervened. He dashed forward, switching his grip on the bear spear, twirling it to hold it above his head like a javelin. He paused when he was only five meters from the bear, sighted, drew back his arm and yelled as loud as he could, hoping to distract the bear from its immediate quarry.

"Hey, bear! See how you like this!"

He hurled the heavy spear at the bear with all his strength, putting his whole body behind the cast.

The spear hit the bear in the ribs, beneath its reaching right forepaw. It didn't penetrate—the point wasn't sufficiently sharp for that. But it slammed into the animal's side, causing it to stagger a couple of paces and relinquish its grip on the tree.

It threw its head back and emitted a shattering roar, curling its lips back from its huge yellow teeth. Then it dropped to all fours and lunged at Jesper, who was now unarmed.

The fleet-footed ex-thief had noted the bear's injured left forepaw. Instinctively, he knew it would be less agile in a turn to the right, pushing off from the left. He leapt to the bear's right. As it tried to follow him, it inadvertently put weight on the useless left paw and stumbled, snarling in fury as the darting figure in front of it eluded it once more.

Stig dashed toward it and swung a horizontal blow with his ax. He had seen Jesper's ploy and he attacked from the bear's left. The bear, seeing him coming, rose to its full height, teeth bared. Stig swung another blow at the bear, catching it on the left forepaw. Blood spurted from the wound but it did little to impede the bear's fighting abilities, as that paw was already damaged and useless. The creature swung at Stig with its right paw and he raised the ax to parry with its long shaft.

That was a mistake. The ax spun out of Stig's hand under the force of the blow and he hastily backed away.

The bear had no chance to follow him. Thorn was charging in from the right, swinging his own ax in his left hand. He caught the bear in the rib cage and heard a howl of pain and fury. Then the bear swiped at him with its right paw, in a lightning-fast blow. He managed to raise the big wooden shield that he had clamped on to his hook and block the blow. But the force of it drove the shield into his own ribs and hurled him from his feet, sending him flying several meters. As the bear went to follow up its advantage, it found Hal blocking its way.

The skirl held his long bear spear in a two-handed underhand grip. He raised the point now, darting it at the bear's face and eyes in a series of rapid jabs. The bear, big and clumsy as it might appear, was remarkably fast. It leapt backward, swaying to one side to avoid the fire-hardened point, and swiped at the spear with its forepaw.

But Hal was expecting the move and he had darted the spear back out of reach. Before the bear could recover, he jabbed again, once, twice, three times in rapid succession. Confused and frustrated by the blinding speed of his thrusts and withdrawals, the bear gave ground.

Dimly, Hal was aware of his crew rallying around him. Stefan and Edvin were half carrying, half dragging the semiconscious Thorn back toward the palisade. Ulf and Wulf, both armed with spears, were waiting for their chance to engage. Kloof raced in big circles around the bear, baying furiously. When the opportunity arose, the big dog would dart in behind the bear, jaws snapping and tearing. Blood now flowed from half a dozen wounds on the thick, matted fur. But none of them were mortal and they tended to serve only to enrage the beast further.

Hal jabbed again at the bear's face. But the mighty beast, cunning after years of combats, was aware of his tactics now, and as the spear came in, it swayed to one side, then snapped its powerful jaw shut on the spear shaft as the point slipped past its face. Hal felt himself jerked forward by an irresistible force. He staggered, then the bear inadvertently saved him. It chopped its right paw down on the spear shaft, snapping it in two pieces with a resounding *CRACK!*

Suddenly released, Hal sprawled back on the ground, backpedaling as fast as he could to take himself out of the bear's reach. Kloof sensed her master's danger and launched a frontal attack on the bear to distract it. One mighty forepaw caught her in mid-leap and sent her flying, howling in shock and pain. Her thick coat saved her from serious injury but she was badly bruised. She hit the sand heavily, rolled several times, then rose painfully to her feet, ready to protect her master once more. Hal could see that, in her wounded, bruised state, she wouldn't have the speed to evade the bear's blows.

"Get out of it, Kloof!" he yelled. His voice cracked with tension as he desperately waved her away. She saw that he was safe for the moment and limped away as Ulf and Wulf charged in with two more spears.

Wulf, like Hal, chose to jab and stab with his spear. Ulf hurled his with all his force. The bear calmly batted it away, then trapped his brother's spear and snapped it like a twig.

"These things are useless!" Wulf said, throwing the shattered haft aside.

Stig, whose ax was lost somewhere in the undergrowth, stood uncertainly beside the twins, his saxe drawn. The big knife would be virtually useless against the bear, he knew, but it was the only weapon he had to hand.

Hal scrambled back to join them. Jesper stood to one side, ready to dart in if needed.

For a moment or two, there was an impasse, as the bear swung its head from one tormentor to another, trying to decide which one to attack first. The Herons were content to let it wait. None of them were keen to commit to close combat with it. They'd all tried and seen their attacks fail.

Then Lydia and Ingvar, who had been standing back planning an assault, saw their opportunity. Two darts whipped past Hal's head, barely a meter away, and struck the bear in the chest, plunging deep into the flesh and muscle there, then sagging painfully. As the bear roared in agony, Ingvar charged.

He had forsaken his voulge for one of the heavy saplings intended for the frame of the cabin they were building. He swung the massive beam overhand as if it weighed no more than a twig, and brought it crashing down on the bear's head.

Momentarily stunned, the bear was driven to a seated position. Then, as it rose, Ingvar made the mistake of trying to repeat the blow. The bear deflected it so that it slammed into its shoulder. Painfully, but not mortally. And as the beam hit the bear, it flicked it with its lightning-fast forepaw.

Ingvar, off balance from following through on his stroke, felt the beam twitch in his hands. Then, disastrously, the butt end flicked upward and raked across his face, opening a deep cut and hitting the frame of his spectacles, spinning them off his face and leaving him blinded.

Hal saw the danger immediately. He dashed forward and grabbed the huge boy's hand, dragging him clear. As the bear reeled, trying to refocus its own vision, Ulf and Wulf dashed in.

Ulf had retrieved the spear he had thrown earlier and he jabbed at the bear with it. Still dazed, and bleeding from several wounds, the bear gave ground. But it was far from defeated, Hal saw, and was gathering its strength for another onslaught.

He had a sudden flash of inspiration.

"Scatter, everyone! Get back behind the palisade!" he yelled. "Jesper, try to lead it to the ship!"

On board the *Heron,* he realized, was the only weapon that could stop the ravening animal. He grabbed Ingvar's hand once more. The big boy was searching in vain for his lost spectacles.

"Leave them!" Hal barked. "Come with me! Run!"

As the others scattered, heading for the dubious safety of the palisade, he dragged Ingvar into a lumbering run through the sand, heading along the front of the fence toward the inlet where *Heron* was moored. Ingvar stumbled several times, but Hal, with the strength of desperation, kept him on his feet and running.

Jesper, sensing what Hal had in mind, danced in front of the bear as it hesitated, dimly trying to decide which of the fleeing figures it should pursue. Jesper helped the decision along. He'd picked up several large, jagged rocks and now he hurled two of them at the bear, hitting it on the nose and forehead.

"Hey, bear! Yaah! Yaah! Come on, you ugly brute!" he shouted, and danced light-footed past it, just out of reach.

The bear snarled at him, its other tormentors forgotten. Then it dropped to all fours and lumbered after him.

It moved clumsily, but it was deceptively fast and Jesper only just managed to avoid its murderous lunge. He ran a few paces at top speed to give himself a bit of clear space, then glanced to where the others were scrambling to safety, Stig leaning back over the fence at the top of the ladder to drag Kloof inside.

They were all safe now except Hal and Ingvar, who were pounding their way through the sand.

Jesper darted in toward the bear once more, hurling another rock and yelling. It rose to its hind legs, towering over him, and he dived to one side, rolling in the sand to avoid the blow it aimed at him. As he regained his feet, the bear lurched after him.

He danced around it, forcing it to turn through a circle to follow him, then rapidly reversing his direction so it had to turn back. The bear roared in fury.

"Oh, shut up!" he said, and threw another rock. A quick glance told him that Hal and Ingvar had reached the end of the palisade and were plunging into the trees, taking the narrow path that led to the inlet.

"Time to move," he said and ran lightly after them. He checked over his shoulder to make sure the bear was following. Intent now on his light-footed figure and infuriated by the ease with which Jesper had avoided its attacks, the bear would now follow him into a fiery pit. On all fours once more, it pounded after him, forcing him to check and dodge several times to avoid it, as he led it constantly toward the narrow path in the trees.

Hal and Ingvar reached the channel of water where the ship was moored a few meters from the bank. They stumbled through the shallow water and hauled themselves up and over the bulwarks. Taking Ingvar's sleeve once more, Hal led the way for'ard to the bow, where the Mangler crouched, covered in its canvas wrapping.

There was no time to untie the leather thongs holding the canvas cover in place. He drew his saxe and slashed quickly at them, then pulled the cover clear.

"Cock it!" he shouted.

Ingvar reached forward, took the two levers and drew the heavy cord back until it clicked into the cocking spurs. As he was doing this, Hal fumbled open the ammunition locker and selected one of the massive, iron-tipped bolts, dropping it into the loading groove and engaging the notched rear end with the cord.

He dropped into the seat behind the weapon and swung it to the left, where he knew Jesper and the bear would appear.

A few seconds later, they heard pounding feet and angry snarling. Jesper shot into view and headed for the side of the ship. The bear was only five meters behind him, shambling quickly on its three good legs.

There was no time for a shot. The two figures were past his line of sight too quickly, with Jesper heading for the waist of the ship. They felt the *Heron* rock as he heaved himself aboard. Then felt it lurch violently as the bear, waist deep in the water, slammed into the hull just behind him.

They were too far astern for Hal to bring the Mangler to bear. He had a sudden fear that they'd be trapped on the ship by the huge, vengeful beast.

Then Jesper saw the problem and acted instinctively. He leapt from the bulwarks, launching himself high in the air over the bear's head, hitting the bank and somersaulting to regain his feet, then darting toward the bow.

The bear, impeded by the meter-deep water, moved slowly to follow him, then regained firm ground and gathered speed.

Jesper, in an amazing show of courage, took a sharp turn from the bank and plunged into the water again, huddling close under the raised bow. The bear paused on the bank and reared up to full height again, giving Hal a perfect shot.

The Mangler gave its ugly *SLAM!* as Hal triggered it. The heavy bolt shot forward and took the bear in the center of the chest, punching through flesh and shattering bones, sending the huge animal reeling back to crash over in the thick undergrowth. It made one unsuccessful attempt to rise, then its eyes glazed over and it fell back, stone dead.

Hal collapsed against the smooth wood of the Mangler, the tension leaking out of him like air out of a punctured bladder. Ingvar dropped a congratulatory hand on his shoulder. Neither of them said anything.

A hand appeared over the bulwark, followed by Jesper's grinning face as he hauled himself on board.

"Well, that was easy," he said.

chapter nineteen

When they returned to the spot where they had first seen the bear, there was no sign of the two children it had been chasing. Hal, Jesper and Stig looked around, searching for some sign of them. There were a few child-size footprints in the sand at the base of the tree, but they were quickly lost in the confusion of the leaf mold that covered the forest floor.

"Maybe Lydia can track them when she's finished," Stig suggested.

Lydia was at the inlet, where Hal had shot the bear with the Mangler. She had volunteered to skin the animal. The massive bearskin would be useful if the weather turned cold.

"We could probably get two cloaks or a couple of big blankets out of it," she had said, surveying the huge body. "They'd be handy on board ship in bad weather."

Ingvar had offered to help her with the task and she had accepted gratefully. It would take a lot of hard work and muscle to lift and turn the huge body for skinning, and for pulling the skin away from the body.

"Can you eat a bear?" he'd asked, eyeing the huge mound of potential meat.

Lydia had pursed her lips doubtfully. "People do. But it's an awfully strong taste. And with all that muscle I'd guess this one would be pretty tough to chew."

Hal looked around the spot where they had last seen the children. "I'm guessing there's a settlement or a village of some sort relatively close by," he said. "Maybe through the forest."

Up until now, the risk of running into the bear had precluded any extensive exploring, although they knew the area was inhabited after Thorn and Lydia had spotted their mysterious follower. The question was, who were the inhabitants and how many were there?

Stig peered into the dimness beneath the trees, shading his eyes to block the bright overhead sun so he could see more clearly.

"Should we go looking for them?" he asked.

Hal considered the idea, but shook his head after a few seconds. "I think we'll wait for them to come to us. So far they've shown no sign of hostility and they might resent it if we go barging around." He paused uncertainly. "Let's see what Thorn says when Edvin is finished with him."

Thorn had been hit hard by the bear, whose sweeping blow caught his shield and drove the ironshod rim into his ribs. He was badly bruised at best and possibly had a cracked rib. When he came round, Edvin sat him down by the cook fire, stripped off his shirt and began binding the ribs tightly with a long, linen bandage. As Thorn obediently held his hands in the air for the process, Edvin sniffed distastefully.

"Whew!" he exclaimed. "Maybe you should wash more often."

Thorn glared at him. "Washing is for them as is dirty," he growled.

Edvin raised his eyebrows. "I think you qualify for that group now," he told the old sea wolf. "Maybe you could give yourself a bit of a sponge-down when I'm finished."

Thorn grunted. But he couldn't really disagree. When he'd raised his arms, he'd become conscious of the fact that he was less than dainty. Not that he'd admit to that, of course.

Edvin continued to wind the linen bandage around his ribs. He'd started without too much pressure, but as layer after layer wound on, the bandage became more and more restrictive.

"Take it easy," Thorn managed to gasp. "I can hardly breathe."

"That's the general idea," Edvin told him. "When you breathe, your ribs move as they expand and contract. If they're cracked, which I think they are, the ends will rub against each other and they'll never knit. This way, you have to keep taking shallow breaths to stop them moving and give them time to heal."

He nodded a greeting to Hal and Stig as they strolled up to the cook-fire site. The two sat down on one of the large logs that had been placed by the fire, forming a convenient seat.

Edvin stopped winding the bandage and Thorn lowered his arms, grateful for a rest.

"How am I expected to fight in this condition?" Thorn grumbled.

Edvin looked at him, unsmiling. "You're not. People with

cracked ribs are supposed to convalesce. Not fight—particularly when fighting involves swinging a whacking great club or an ax. Neither pastime is recommended for healing ribs."

Thorn scowled. He knew he would never get the better of Edvin in this discussion. The medic was dealing from a position of strength. He knew what he was talking about. Thorn was merely grumbling.

"Scowl all you like," Edvin said calmly. "The sooner you take it easy, the sooner those ribs will heal."

Reluctantly admitting defeat, Thorn raised his arms again. "Keep winding," he said. "Let's get it done with."

Edvin eyed Stig and Hal and shook his head. "He's such a gracious patient," he said. "*Thank you, Edvin. How kind of you to help heal my ribs, Edvin. Tell me what to do, Edvin, and I'll do it.*"

He spoke with a fair approximation of Thorn's gruff tones and both the younger men grinned.

Seeing Thorn was done arguing with the medic, Hal leaned forward and addressed the old sea wolf.

"What should we do about the local people?" he asked. "They must have a settlement somewhere nearby."

Thorn pursed his lips. "Leave them be," he said decisively. "They'll come to us when the time is right."

"What makes you think so?" Hal asked.

Thorn shrugged and immediately winced in pain. Edvin muttered an inaudible imprecation. Then Thorn recovered and, speaking more carefully, he said, "Well, we did save the lives of two of their children," he said. "They were about to become that bear's next meal."

"Probably would have, too, if it hadn't been for Jesper," Stig said.

Thorn looked thoughtful. "Yes. He did rather well, didn't he—dashing in to throw his spear at the bear, then leading it away."

"He did even better at the ship," Hal said.

Thorn, of course, hadn't witnessed the way Jesper had decoyed the bear so that Hal could get a shot at it with the Mangler. He looked questioningly at Hal.

"The bear had got behind us," Hal explained. "We were in the bow and it was trying to climb aboard in the waist. Jesper actually somersaulted over it to get it away from the ship, then ran to the bow and brought the bear to where I could get a clean shot. He'd backed himself up against the hull of the ship to do it. If I'd missed, he'd have been Jesper on toast for that bear."

Thorn shook his head at the words. "It never ceases to amaze me," he said, "how someone can drive you mad—questioning constantly, disobeying orders, complaining and whining all the time—then the moment comes and he turns out to be a full-blown hero."

"I guess there's more to him than we all realize," Edvin said without looking up from his bandaging.

Hal nodded. "I guess so. Just when you have him pegged as an annoying whiner, he puts us all to shame."

"That's how people are," Stig said wisely, and they all looked at him.

"Oh, is that so?" Hal asked him. "Who else have you noticed behaving in such a manner?"

"You," Stig said without hesitation. "One moment, you're banging on about raising and lowering the sails, sheeting home, letting them fly and so on, and driving everyone crazy. Next minute, you find a safe anchorage like this for us." He swept his arm around the big bay and grinned at his skirl. "Just when we were all ready to throw you overboard."

"Oh, do forgive me," Hal said in a voice heavy with sarcasm. "Did I disturb your rest during the nasty storm? Was it all too inconvenient for you?"

"A little." Stig grinned. "In future, try to modify your behavior when you're frightened by a little breeze, will you?"

"I wasn't frightened," Hal said. And, when they all regarded him with disbelief, he continued. "I was terrified. There's a big difference."

Hal returned to his original question. "Anyway, Thorn, why do you think we should wait for the locals to come to us?"

Thorn took an experimental breath. He had to admit that he felt a lot less pain with his ribs tightly bound and held in place. The restriction was somewhat uncomfortable, it was true. But it was a lot better than the sharp, stabbing pain he'd been feeling before. He nodded his gratitude to Edvin.

"Thanks, Edvin. That feels a lot better."

Edvin shrugged, more than a little surprised at the change in Thorn's manner.

Then the older man replied to Hal's question. "If we did go off exploring," he said, "I'd want to go fully armed. And with a fair number of us along. We never know what we're going to run into, after all."

He paused and Hal nodded. "That sounds reasonable to me."

"To you, yes. But think how it would look to the local

inhabitants. We'd look like a war party and they might resent that. And the odds are, they outnumber us."

"You and Lydia could go alone," Stig suggested. "She can be very stealthy and she could probably keep you out of sight—clumsy as you are."

Thorn turned a stony gaze on the tall first mate. Stig grinned unrepentantly.

"Amazing how disrespectful people become when you're injured and unable to swing a club," Thorn said. "As you say, Lydia can be stealthy when she wants to be. But the watcher still managed to find us and follow us yesterday, and he was stalking her the previous day as well."

"So we sit and wait?" Hal said. He tended to agree with Thorn but it was good to have his opinion validated.

Thorn nodded. "We'll give it another day or two and see what turns up. After that, we'll look at matters again."

"One good thing," Hal said. "With the bear taken care of, we can go back to single watch-keepers at night. So we'll all get a little extra sleep."

"And that's something I'm in favor of," Stig said heartily.

chapter twenty

Hal was dozing comfortably on his bedroll, his blankets wrapped around him. He had enjoyed a full night's sleep. Now that there was no need for a double watch, he had exempted himself from sentry duty the night before. There were plenty of people to take care of that.

Now he was luxuriating in that best of all sleeping moments. He had woken early, as the first light was appearing over the bay, realized that he had no immediate responsibilities to attend to, turned over with a contented sigh and gone back to sleep.

"Nothing like it," he murmured contentedly. It seemed his eyes had barely closed when he felt a hand shaking his shoulder. He frowned under the blankets.

"Go away," he growled, hoping that if he sounded forbidding

enough, whoever it was would leave him alone. But Stefan, for it was he who had roused him, was insistent.

"Hal, you'd better come and see this."

Reluctantly, Hal tossed back his blankets and sat up, rubbing his eyes. The crew had completed the large sleeping hut, and he had a privileged position by the doorway. He glanced at the sun now. It couldn't have been more than ten minutes since he'd decided the world owed him more rest. A quick look around the interior of the hut showed him that most of the crew were still in bed asleep. So much for stealing a little extra warmth and relaxation, he thought. He stood up and pulled on his trousers and sheepskin jacket. He paused to buckle on the heavy leather belt that held his saxe in its scabbard and, yawning, followed Stefan toward the barricade.

Thorn, who elected to sleep separately from the rest of the crew, was crawling out of his low, one-man tent. Even though Stefan had kept his voice to a whisper when he roused Hal, Thorn had been aware of it.

"He sleeps with one eye open," Hal commented. Then he amended the thought. "One ear open, at any rate."

"What's happening?" Thorn asked.

Hal shrugged. "Ask Stefan."

"We have visitors," Stefan said, pointing to the barricade.

Those words banished the last vestiges of sleep from Hal and Thorn. Hal increased his pace, heading for the stile that led over the fence. The thought occurred to him that, if Stefan had left the barricade to rouse him, he mustn't feel that the newcomers posed any threat to the camp. Nevertheless, he hurried, and Thorn, some meters behind him, broke into a trot to catch up.

"There," said Stefan, as they reached the rough ladder leaning against the interior of the fence. The outer ladder had been raised for the night and brought inside the stockade.

Hal mounted the first few rungs to see more clearly, looking in the direction that Stefan had indicated.

"Well, by the great tortoise that holds up the world," he said, "will you look at that."

Standing some fifteen meters from the barricade, close by one of the beacon fires, were three men. Two of them were young and muscular-looking—warriors, Hal guessed. They were flanking a smaller, older man who stood between them.

They were all dressed similarly. They wore long, fringed overshirts of what appeared to be deerskin leather, belted at the waist. The shirts reached to just above the knee and beneath them they wore leggings of the same material. Their feet were shod in soft, fleece-lined, flat-soled shoes.

They were brown skinned and strong featured, with dark hair worn long and plaited into braids on either side of their heads. The older man's hair showed streaks of gray and he wore a large eagle feather at the back of his head, held in place by a plain leather headband.

The two younger men carried round, hide-covered shields and wooden spears, with what appeared to be stone heads. All three wore knives in their belts.

As they saw Hal's head appear over the palisade, the older man spoke a brief command. His two companions stooped to lay their spears and shields on the sand. Then all three stood erect, with their hands raised over their heads, palms outward toward the stockade in an obvious demonstration of the fact that they were now unarmed and came in peace.

"Let's go talk to them," Hal said, and started up another rung in the ladder.

Thorn placed a hand on his arm to stop him. "Not so fast," he said. "Stefan, run and get Lydia. And tell her to bring her atlatl and darts. Then wake the others. Bring them here and tell them to bring their weapons."

"You're not expecting trouble, are you?" Hal asked. "There are only three of them, after all."

"There are only three that we can see," Thorn pointed out, as Stefan pounded back to the sleeping tent to rouse the crew. Lydia had a small cabin to one side of the communal sleeping area. Stefan stopped there first and they heard him talking urgently to her. A minute later, she emerged, pulling on her leather overjacket and carrying her quiver in her left hand. She ran lightly down the sand to join them.

"What's happening?" she asked.

Hal nodded toward the three figures standing on the beach, arms still raised.

"The locals have arrived," he said. "I'm going out to talk to them."

"I'm going with him," Thorn said. "You stay here, and at the first hint of trouble put a dart through that gray-haired one in the middle."

Lydia nodded, drawing one of the long, heavy projectiles from her quiver.

"I can do the other two as well, if you like," she said.

Thorn grinned at her. "I'll leave that to your judgment," he said. "We don't want to start a bloodbath."

By this time, Stig, Ulf and Wulf had arrived, with Stefan close behind. The rest of the crew were struggling blearily out of their blankets. Hal quickly told Stig what was going on and what he intended. As he did, the big first mate took a step toward the ladder.

"I'm coming with you," he announced, but Hal shook his head.

"You stay here and take command if there's any trouble," he said.

Stig looked rebellious for a moment, then yielded the point. It didn't make sense for the three senior members of the crew to all put themselves at risk.

"All right," he said. "But don't take any chances."

Hal couldn't help a grin touching his mouth. "Like going out to talk to three armed strangers?" he said. "No, we won't do that."

"There's a point," Stig said. "How do you plan to talk with them? Do we know what language they speak?"

Hal paused as he heaved the outer ladder over the fence and placed it in position. "We'll manage," he said. "We'll use sign language if we have to."

Thorn followed him up the ladder as Hal started down the other side. "I'm good at sign language," he said. "I can sign things like *No trouble or I'll bash you.*"

For the first time, Stig noticed that Thorn was wearing his fighting club-hand, instead of the utility hook that Hal had fashioned for him. Useful, the first mate thought. This way, Thorn could appear to be unarmed, while he was wearing a truly devastating weapon on the end of his right arm.

Hal had climbed down the outer ladder and stood waiting for Thorn to join him. As the old sea wolf stepped down, Hal removed his saxe from its scabbard, held it up, then placed it point first in the sand. Thorn, after a moment's hesitation, did the same.

"Feel naked without it," he muttered out of the side of his mouth as the two stepped out together toward the three newcomers.

"You're not exactly unarmed," Hal replied, "with that great head-bashing knob on the end of your hand."

Their footsteps squeaked in the fine dry sand as they approached the three unmoving figures. The strangers still stood with their hands raised high above their heads, but as Hal and Thorn stopped, facing them and a few meters away, the older man uttered a brief command and they all lowered their arms to their sides.

"Hal?" Lydia's voice called from the barricade.

Without looking, Hal knew that Lydia would have fitted the dart to the end of her thrower and was standing at the top of the ladder, poised and ready to throw.

"It's all right, Lydia," he said, without taking his eyes off the center man.

The older man's eyes had flicked away from Hal as Lydia had called out. A wary light had come into them, but now Hal could see him relax. Obviously, Lydia had lowered the threatening dart.

For a few moments, Hal studied the three men. They had dark eyes and prominent cheekbones. Their noses were strong and aquiline. All three were clean-shaven, but their black hair was long and parted in the middle of their heads, shaped into braids that hung down either side. The clothes they wore were skillfully made and neatly stitched. The material looked soft, supple and expertly cured. The leader's long overshirt was richly decorated with colored beads and long quill-shaped needles set in intricate patterns. Their soft shoes were bound in rawhide thongs and came up past the ankle to mid-calf.

He realized that, while he had been taking stock of the three strangers, they had been doing the same with him. He hesitated, not sure how to open communications. There was a trading sign language that was used through the Stormwhite Sea and beyond, for those remote areas where people didn't speak the common tongue. But he doubted it would be understood here. He decided on the simplest opening gambit he could think of.

He pointed to himself, and spoke. "Hal," he said. "I am Hal."

He saw a light of comprehension in the three sets of dark eyes studying him. Encouraged, he half turned and rested his hand on Thorn's shoulder.

"Thorn," he said. "This is Thorn."

The older man nodded once and repeated the names.

"Hal . . . and Thorn," he said, gesturing to each of them as he spoke.

Hal was delighted that he had been understood. He nodded, smiling. "Yes," he said. "Hal . . . Thorn." Again, he pointed to himself and to his companion.

But Thorn had noticed the additional word the older man had used.

"He said *and,*" he said softly to Hal. The skirl turned to him, not quite understanding the significance. Thorn repeated the statement.

"He said *and*," he said. "You didn't say *and*. How did he know *and*?"

Hal was taken aback, realizing that Thorn was right. The stranger had used an extra word—and used it correctly. Maybe, he thought wildly, *and* was a universal word. Then his surprise doubled as the gray-haired man continued, speaking slowly and precisely in the common tongue.

"I am Mohegas," he said, "of the Mawagansett people. These are my nephews."

chapter twenty-one

Hal was so shocked at hearing the man speak the common tongue that he actually recoiled a pace. He looked to Thorn, who appeared equally surprised. Then he turned back to the gray-haired man—Mohegas, he corrected himself.

"You speak the common tongue?" he said. It was a question, not a statement. Mohegas allowed a faint smile to touch his grave features, then composed them again.

"Not very good," he said apologetically. "But some. I speak some."

"How did you—"

Mohegas interrupted him. "We have one of your people with us. A White Hair like you." He touched his own hair with his left hand as he spoke. While his hair was almost black, although streaked with gray, Hal and Thorn were both fair-haired, as were most of the crew. Even Edvin, whose hair was a slightly darker shade than the norm, had hair that was a light shade of brown. Compared with the dark tresses of the three men facing him, Hal thought that "White Hair" was a fitting description.

Of greater significance was the fact that a White Hair, presumably a Skandian, was living with the Mawagansett people. Hal frowned as he tried to think who that might be. He couldn't think of anyone who had gone missing recently—or at least anyone who wasn't accounted for. Mohegas saw his expression and guessed at his thoughts.

"He joined us twelve sun cycles ago," he said, then corrected himself. "Twelve years, you would say. He has taught many of our tribe the common tongue, even the children."

Which explained why Hal couldn't think of anyone who might be the mysterious White Hair. If he'd been here twelve years, Hal still would have been a boy when he first went missing.

Thorn, however, was a different matter. "What is his name?" he asked.

Mohegas switched his gaze to the old sea wolf, sizing him up, taking in the hard muscles, the graying blond hair and the massive club-hand on the end of his right forearm.

"We call him Polennis," he said. "In your tongue, that would mean 'Man Who Swims.' He calls himself . . ." He paused, trying to recall the man's Skandian name, which hadn't been used for many years, then succeeding. "Or-wik? No, Or-vik."

It was a common enough name and Thorn shrugged. For the moment, he couldn't recall any Orvik who had gone missing twelve years prior. But then, he couldn't recall a lot of events from that period of his life. He had seen most events over the rim of a brandy tankard. He looked at Hal.

"Doesn't ring a bell with me," he said.

Hal nodded. "He may not even have come from Hallasholm," he said. "He could have come from anywhere in Skandia."

"At first, we thought you were Ghostfaces," Mohegas continued. "But then we watched you and saw that your skin was naturally pale." He paused, then explained, with an expression of distaste. "Ghostfaces have skin like ours, but they paint it white."

"Ghostfaces," Hal mused. "They sound like good people to avoid."

Mohegas continued. "We have been watching you. We watched you hunting," he said, looking at Thorn, who nodded.

"We saw you watching us," he said, and Mohegas smiled again.

"Then we saw the bear chase you—you and the girl." He looked at the stockade, where Lydia was still poised at the top of the access ladder. Hal glanced back with him. She was resting the atlatl dart across one bent knee, apparently relaxed, but ready to throw in a second.

"It wasn't my most dignified moment, I have to say," Thorn replied.

"Then, yesterday, you risked your lives to save two of our children," Mohegas continued. "The bear nearly got you then." He addressed this remark to Thorn, who instinctively touched his still-aching ribs.

"It did indeed," he replied.

"But then you all joined together to fight the bear. You two, and the tall one. The two who look the same. And the one who is always complaining."

"They *have* been watching us," Hal said in an aside to Thorn.

"And then you killed the bear," Mohegas said. There was a note of wonder in his voice. "How did you do that?"

Of course, Hal thought, the final battle with the bear, on board the *Heron* moored in the inlet, wouldn't have been visible to anyone observing from the forest near the campsite.

"We have a very powerful weapon," he said. "We call it the Mangler and we used it to shoot the bear."

Mohegas nodded gravely. "It must be powerful. That bear has been terrorizing our people for over a year. None of our weapons were much use against it and it has killed three of our warriors."

"Well, we're glad we could help out," Thorn said. "It was causing us our share of trouble too."

"And you saved our children. We had told them not to come and spy on you. We told them the bear was prowling in the area. But they are children, after all, and inclined not to listen."

"Children are like that," said Hal loftily.

Thorn regarded him with amusement. It wasn't too many years since Hal had been a child himself, and one who was constantly getting into trouble.

"For this, you have our thanks. And for ridding us of the bear, of course. But mostly, for saving our children. That is the most important."

Hal inclined his head in a shallow bow of acknowledgment. "As we said, we're glad to be of service." He felt a small surge of pride as he recalled how his crew had rallied together to protect the two Mawagansett children clinging desperately to the tree as the bear raged below them. There had been no need for him to issue any orders; everybody simply joined forces to save the children, regardless of their own safety.

"We want to name you as friends of the Mawagansett. And we are here to invite you to our village for a feast of gratitude. The two children you saved, Minneka and Lahontas, will express their thanks. They will apologize for putting you all in danger and they will serve you during the feast."

"There's no need for that," Hal said, but Mohegas nodded gravely.

"Yes. There is. They disobeyed their parents. It will do them good to make amends."

Thorn grinned. "That's a good point," he replied. "It's good for naughty children to make amends for their sins."

"They are not bad, you understand," Mohegas told him, thinking that perhaps he had given them an incorrect impression. "They are just headstrong and curious."

"Knew a boy like that myself once," Thorn told him.

Hal decided that it was time to get the old sea wolf off the subject of headstrong boys he had known in the past. "We'll be delighted to come and join your feast," he said, giving Thorn a warning glance. "When do you want us to come?"

"This evening. After sunset," Mohegas told him. "I will come to show you the way to our village just before dark."

Hal nodded. "We'll be ready then."

Mohegas hesitated, looking from Hal to Thorn, then back again. "Forgive me for asking," he said, "but which of you is the leader of your people?"

"He is," Thorn said promptly, laying his left hand on Hal's

shoulder. "He's the commander of our ship and the leader of our brotherband."

"Yet you are the older?" Mohegas said. In his world, authority tended to equate with seniority in years.

Thorn smiled. "But not the wiser," he replied easily. He had no qualms about admitting to Hal's authority over him.

"Thorn is our battle leader," Hal explained and Mohegas nodded. Among the Mawagansett, the war leader and the chief of the tribe were often separate positions.

"You have the look of a warrior," he said, allowing his glance to drop to the massive club that Thorn wore on his right arm. He paused, allowing this information about these mysterious visitors to sink in. Then he made a sign to his two companions. They stooped and retrieved their shields and spears.

"It's all right, Lydia," Hal called, without turning. He knew that the moment their hands had touched their weapons, Lydia would have readied her atlatl. Mohegas's faint smile told him he was correct.

"She is a warrior too," the Mawagansett elder said.

Hal nodded. "One of our best."

Mohegas raised a hand in farewell.

"I'll return for you before sunset," he said. Then he uttered a command to his two companions and they turned and headed across the beach to the forest. Hal and Thorn watched them go, waiting until they had disappeared into the shadows under the trees. Then they exchanged a quizzical look. It was a day of surprises, Hal thought.

"Let's go tell the others," Thorn said and they headed back to the stockade, where a crowd of curious faces now lined the fence.

• • • • •

"But I've got nothing to wear!" Lydia exclaimed when Hal told the crew they had been invited to a feast.

He cocked his head curiously. "You're kidding, aren't you?"

She allowed herself the ghost of a smile. "Of course I am. It's just I've heard that's the girly sort of thing young maids say when they're asked to a feast."

Hal raised his eyes to the heavens. "Loki save me from girly young maids then."

"No need to invoke the god," Stig put in. "From what I've seen, you're rarely bothered by girly young maids. Most of the ones I've seen are totally disinterested in you."

Which wasn't true, of course. As a matter of fact, Hal was quite in demand among the eligible girls in Hallasholm. He was, after all, a dashing and successful young skirl who had fought, and won, several battles. And he was the leader who had recovered the Andomal, the sacred belonging of the Skandians, from the pirate Zavac. That gave him a definite cachet among the young maids.

The fact that he was also the one who had allowed the pirate Zavac to steal the Andomal in the first place did nothing to reduce him in their eyes.

"Who's invited?" Edvin asked.

Hal and Thorn exchanged a quick glance. That hadn't been stipulated.

"I think all of us," Hal said and Thorn nodded agreement.

Stig frowned. "Shouldn't we leave someone here to guard the camp?"

Hal hesitated. He had been thinking over that question himself. "From whom?"

Stig shrugged. "How about these Ghostfizzers they mentioned?" he asked. "They sound unpleasant."

"It's Ghostfaces," Hal told him. "And I get the impression that they're not around all the time." He chewed on his lip thoughtfully. "I think we'll all go. It might be insulting to leave someone to guard the camp. After all, there's nobody to guard it against, other than our hosts."

"And if they want to rob us, they can simply kill us at the feast and take everything," Ulf said.

"What a ray of sunshine you are," Hal replied.

PART THREE

THE MAWAGANSETT

chapter twenty-two

The rest of the day passed slowly, the hours seeming to crawl by. The crew were excited about the prospect of meeting the local inhabitants and spent most of their time discussing what might happen, what the locals might be like and what sort of food they might be served.

"Goats' eyes," Jesper averred with the tone of one who knows. "They'll probably serve us goats' eyes. It's a great delicacy."

"I'm not eating anything that's looking back at me," Stefan said emphatically.

Ingvar, however, regarded Jesper with a small frown and shook his head in wonder at the other boy's stupidity.

"What makes you say that?" he asked. Jesper regarded him back, with the lofty expression of one who knows he is talking utter rubbish but refuses to admit to it.

"It's a well-known fact," he said. "Goats' eyes are highly prized among foreign people."

"What foreign people ever gave you goats' eyes?" Ingvar challenged and Jesper hesitated. He hadn't planned on having to defend his statement to this degree but he wasn't giving in now.

"The people of Arrida," he said. "Remember how they served us goats' eyes at the feast after we took the city of Tabork?"

"I recall that they served us minced goat meat and salad and flat bread," Stefan said slowly. "I didn't see any goats' eyes."

"Maybe not. But they saw you," Jesper told him.

Then Ingvar challenged his assertion again. "These people look nothing like the Arridi."

"They've got dark hair," Jesper said defiantly.

"Maybe so. But the Arridi are tall and slender people. These Mawagansett are quite stocky and muscular. At least the ones we've seen are."

"So who's to say the ones we haven't seen aren't tall and slender, like the Arridi?"

Ingvar shook his head in resignation. "Will you *ever* admit you're wrong?" he asked, but Jesper shook his head.

"I never am," he said.

Ingvar turned to where Hal and Thorn were discussing the invitation to the Mawagansett village. "Hal, would it be all right if I threw Jesper in the bay?" he asked.

Hal looked up, considered the request and nodded. "Any time you like, Ingvar," he said. "I trust your judgment."

Ingvar nodded in satisfaction and turned back to look at Jesper. The big boy had recovered his spectacles after the fight with the bear, but he wasn't wearing them now. He often didn't for close work or short-distance viewing, and his blue eyes seemed to bore into Jesper. As the former thief met his gaze, he could see a sense of resolve there and realized he was only seconds away from an undignified ducking.

"Well . . . ," he prevaricated, "maybe I was mistaken about the goats' eyes."

Ingvar nodded several times. "Maybe you were."

Stefan chuckled. But Jesper wasn't giving in so easily.

"It'll be something different, you wait and see. Like larks' tongues, maybe."

"Or ants in honey," Ulf put in.

Wulf looked at him. "Who ever heard of ants in honey?"

His brother smiled as he sprang the trap. "Ants are always getting into the honey at home."

"But you don't eat them there," Ulf protested.

"You could. You just need a more sophisticated palate than you possess," Wulf told him.

Sitting a few meters away, Thorn couldn't help smiling. "Nice to hear things are back to normal," he said.

Hal nodded. His crew had been a little subdued over the past week or so. Now that they were talking and teasing one another again, with Ulf and Wulf bickering good-naturedly and Jesper talking through his hat with a tone of total conviction, things felt more normal. It was probably the fact that they had made contact with other people, he thought. Up until Mohegas had arrived that morning, a sense of uncertainty had hung over all of them. Were they alone in this foreign land? Would the locals, if there were any, be hostile or friendly? Mohegas's visit had reassured them all and restored a welcome sense of normalcy to life.

"What's Edvin up to?" he asked. "He doesn't need to cook today."

After Mohegas and his two companions had left, Lydia had slipped away into the forest to hunt, returning with another of the large birds. Edvin had set to plucking and cleaning it and had Ulf and Wulf, who were on kitchen duty that day, dig him a large fire pit and set a fire to burn down to coals.

While he was waiting for this to happen, Edvin chopped some of the wild onions and herbs he had found growing in the forest and stuffed them into the plucked bird's cavity. Then he wrapped the large body in bark and proceeded to smear mud thickly over it, until it was completely covered. Hal and Thorn strolled over as he was raking the coals back in the fire pit to form a hole for the bird. He lowered it in and raked coals over the top of it again so that it was completely covered. He glanced up at Hal.

"I reckon maybe three hours and it'll be done," he said.

"But you don't need to cook. The locals have invited us to a feast," Hal told him.

Edvin shook his head. "You can't go to a feast empty-handed. Everyone knows that."

Hal looked at Thorn. "Did you know that?"

Thorn shook his head. "I didn't. But then, I am an ignorant man," he said.

"Maybe we could just take them some sweetmeats?" Hal suggested. "Taking an entire oggle bird seems a little extreme."

"What 'sweetmeats' would you suggest?" Edvin asked him. "Some of Wulf's ants in honey, perhaps?"

"Well, no . . . ," Hal admitted. "It just seems a little extreme to take a big bird like this."

"My mother does it when she's invited to a feast," Edvin said and Hal had to admit defeat. Mothers were, after all, the ultimate authorities on etiquette and proper behavior.

Eventually, the day was nearly over, and the shadows of the trees and cliffs behind the campsite stretched long and dark across the beach. As they reached the water's edge, Mohegas and his two companions emerged from the forest once more.

"Right, everyone," said Hal, "let's get moving."

The crew had spruced themselves up as much as they could. Even Thorn had consented to wash. Shirts were clean, leggings and jerkins had been brushed to remove any mud or dirt, and all of them wore their black knitted watch caps with the heron motif on the front. It was the nearest they came to a uniform and Hal did think it imparted a smart look to them.

Although they left their main weapons behind, they weren't completely unarmed, since they all wore their saxes in scabbards on their belts. That was normal behavior, Hal had decided. After all, Mohegas and his companions had worn knives when they visited earlier in the day.

Now, as the Mawagansett elder greeted them, raising his right-hand palm outward in a show of peace, they climbed over the two ladders and stood ready. At the last moment, there was a rattle and clatter of heavy paws on the ladder and Kloof scrambled over the palisade fence to join them.

Hal regarded her doubtfully. "Should we take her?"

Thorn shrugged. "Why not? She's one of the crew. And she fought the bear with us."

"Just so long as Mohegas doesn't have a walking staff that he treasures," Hal said. Kloof had been in trouble on more than one occasion in Hallasholm after chewing the Oberjarl's prized walking staff and his ax—a family heirloom that had been handed down from Erak's grandfather. Hal clicked his fingers, and Kloof, who had been watching him anxiously, as if guessing that she was being discussed, moved to sit obediently by his side.

"See?" said Thorn, grinning. "Butter wouldn't melt in her mouth."

"It's not butter in her mouth I'm worried about," Hal told him.

Mohegas studied Kloof with interest. "That is a big dog," he declared.

Hal shrugged. "She's very friendly," he said and Kloof, sensing that she was being discussed again, thumped her massive tail on the sand and lolled her tongue out the side of her mouth in what she took to be a disarming grin.

"She's a pussycat," Thorn added. It was an unfortunate choice of words. Kloof disliked cats and she growled at the word, a rumbling growl from deep in her chest.

"She doesn't bite," Hal continued, then added, "Unless you're a bear."

That reminded Mohegas of the fact that Kloof had taken part in the assault on the bear the previous day.

"She fought the bear with you," he said, and when Hal nodded assent, he continued. "Then she is welcome in our village as well."

Which seemed to suit Kloof just fine. She moved to stand by Mohegas, her tail sweeping back and forth. He stood his ground, although the sheer size of the dog, wagging tail or not, was a little unnerving. Kloof put her massive head under his right hand and jerked it up several times.

"She wants you to pat her," Hal said.

Tentatively, Mohegas stroked Kloof's head several times and she closed her eyes blissfully. When he stopped stroking, she pushed her head up into his hand once more. As he began to pat her again, she sat on his feet. He looked a little surprised.

"She does that too," Hal explained. "When you pat her, she doesn't want you to go away. So she sits on your feet to trap you."

"It's an effective tactic," Mohegas said gravely. Kloof's fifty-five-kilogram weight was settled firmly on his feet, making it difficult, if not impossible, for him to escape.

Hal clicked his fingers at the dog and gestured to the ground beside him. "Come here, girl."

Kloof reluctantly stood, releasing Mohegas, and moved to sit beside Hal. Mohegas looked relieved. He indicated his two companions.

"These are my nephews," he said. "Their names are Tamorat and Hokas."

As he spoke their names the two younger men inclined their heads. Hal nodded in reply. In Hallasholm, he would have stepped forward and offered to clasp forearms with the men. Here it seemed more fitting to simply raise his right hand, palm outward, as a greeting.

He then introduced the three Mawagansett to the rest of his crew. It seemed his instinct had been correct, as Mohegas greeted each of the Herons with the same palm-outward gesture that Hal had used. When the introductions were done, Mohegas gestured to the tree line, and the narrow path by which he and his companions had reached the beach.

"It is time to go," he said and began to turn away. But Edvin stopped him with a hasty cry.

"The bird!" he said. "We nearly forgot the bird."

Beckoning Ulf and Wulf to follow him, he hurriedly climbed back into the stockade and led them to the fire pit. While he raked away the coals that had covered the mud-plastered bird, Ulf and Wulf prepared a rectangle of canvas to carry it in. They laid it beside the fire pit on the sand and Edvin used a forked branch to roll the bird onto the center of the cloth. The mud was baked solid and almost white in color. It steamed with heat and he nodded, satisfied.

"Pick her up and let's go," he said, and the twins lifted it, then manhandled it over the stockade fence again to where the others were waiting for them. Mohegas, Tamorat and Hokas all looked at the twins' burden with interest. It looked like nothing more than a giant ball of baked mud.

"What is this?" Mohegas asked.

Edvin, a little breathless after the rush to retrieve the bird from the fire, made vague gestures in the air, intended to convey the shape of the bird's fanlike tail.

"It's an oggle bird," he said.

The tribal elder cocked his head uncertainly. "An oggle bird?" he repeated.

Edvin threw his head back and tried to imitate the call they had all heard. "You know—*oggle-oggle-oggle!*" he warbled.

Hokas recognized the sound and leaned forward to say something to Mohegas, whose puzzled expression cleared.

"Ah, yes. We call this a *comitarkinallita moricansett,*" he explained.

"*Comitarkin-a* what?" Edvin asked, frowning as he tried to get his tongue around the unfamiliar words.

"*Comitarkinallita moricansett,*" Mohegas repeated. "It means 'large bird with good meat.'"

Edvin frowned as he tried once more to repeat the words, and failed. "I think we'll stick with *oggle-oggle-oggle* bird," he said finally.

Mohegas smiled. "A wise choice," he said. "But why did you bring it? We have food in abundance."

Edvin assumed a stubborn look and Hal intervened hastily.

"His mother taught him this. She says you should never go to a feast empty-handed," he said.

Mohegas nodded slowly while he considered this statement. Then he smiled at Edvin.

"We must always obey our mothers," he said. "Bring your oggle bird with you by all means."

chapter twenty-three

The forest was dim and cool at this time of day. The Herons followed in single file behind Mohegas and his two companions as they led the way along a narrow game trail among the trees, meandering from side to side to avoid the larger trunks. After half a kilometer, the trail opened out into a wider track, where they could walk two or three abreast. Unlike the animal track, it led in a more or less straight direction to the northwest, and was obviously used frequently by the Mawagansett people.

With the extra room provided, the crew bunched up, walking now in small groups, looking around them and taking in these novel surroundings. Aside from Thorn and Lydia, few of them had ventured far into the forest to date and they were fascinated to see new and somewhat exotic varieties of trees and bushes, along with more familiar types, such as pine and spruce, that they would have found at home in Skandia.

There was little talking. An air of expectation hung over them, precluding any idle chatter. On one occasion, Lydia pointed to the left side of the track, where several deep grooves were evident in the bark of a tree.

"The bear," she said quietly, and they all looked as they passed the spot, noting the depth of the grooves and the height from the ground. It had been a very large bear, they all recalled. Jesper shuddered, remembering how, in the heat of the fight, he had charged unthinkingly at the huge predator, teasing it and challenging it, then turning to lead it down the beach. In hindsight, he realized how much at risk he had been when the bear finally had him backed up against the hull of the *Heron*. He recalled the slamming sound of the Mangler releasing, and the heavy thud as the bolt struck home, staggering the bear backward.

Just as well Hal's a good shot, he thought, although in the moment, with the adrenaline flowing in his veins, he hadn't considered what might have happened if Hal had missed. Now, as he did, his blood chilled. He looked at his skirl, who was striding purposefully behind Mohegas, and muttered a small word of thanks.

"What was that?" Stefan asked. He was walking beside Jesper and thought his shipmate was addressing him. Jesper shook his head, dismissing the morbid thoughts that had been bothering him.

"Nothing," he said. "I hope this feast is good."

"If it's not, we can always eat Edvin's oggle bird," Stefan said comfortably.

Near the head of the small procession, Lydia raised her nose and sniffed as a new and homey smell reached them through the forest.

"Wood smoke," she said. Thorn and Stig sniffed as well. She was right. They could smell the smoke of the fires in the Mawagansett village.

"We must be getting close," Stig said.

And then, rounding a sharp corner in the trail, they found themselves facing their hosts' settlement.

It was placed in a wide space of cleared land, fringed by the ever-present trees of the forest. There were fifteen to twenty sizeable huts, covered with animal hides or large sheets of bark. They were rectangular in layout, with pitched roofs thatched with pine branches and more hides. From the look of them, deer hide was the most common building material available to the locals.

Each hut was two meters high at the lower part of the pitched roof. The upper slides sloped up to a roofline that was three and a half meters from the ground, so there would be ample room for a tall man to stand erect inside them. They were obviously family dwellings, measuring eight meters long by five wide, and they seemed to be permanent structures. The Mawagansett were obviously not nomadic. Smoke rose from several of the huts, emerging from smoke holes at the rear, where the hide roof covering had been pulled aside to allow it to escape.

In front of the neat lines of huts was a cleared communal ground, the most prominent feature of which was a large circular fire pit, filled with smoking coals and meat roasting above the fire. Hal saw several haunches of venison, along with plump rabbits and ducks on spits. There were several large fish wrapped in damp bark and leaves, set in the coals to steam, while smaller fish—river trout, he thought—were spitted on green sticks and suspended over the glowing coals. In addition, there were vegetables steaming in clay pots—squash, beans and corn.

Between the fire pit and the huts were the Mawagansett people themselves.

They stood silently, watching the newcomers as they emerged from the trees. Hal estimated there were between eighty and a hundred people assembled in several rows, with men and women equally represented, and perhaps thirty being children of varying ages.

All were dressed in similar fashion to Mohegas, Tamorat and Hokas. Fringed deer-hide overshirts and leggings for the men, with skirts replacing the leggings in the case of the women. In some cases, individuals wore cloaks fashioned from animal fur—wolf skins and the pelts of smaller animals that had been tanned and sewn together. The cloaks looked soft and comfortable, Hal thought.

An expectant silence fell over the clearing. Then Mohegas called out a one-word command and the assembled people began to sing.

They sang in their own language, not the common tongue, so the words were indecipherable to the Herons. But the melody was unmistakably warm and welcoming, and the singers fell into a natural three-part harmony. Lydia repressed a smile as she watched some of the boys in the front rank of villagers trying to emulate the deep baritone sounds of the older men, tucking their chins down onto their chests and frowning with the effort of forcing their piping young voices into a lower register.

Mohegas turned to face the Herons. They had spread out in a single line to face the villagers as they sang.

"This is a song of welcome to you," he said. "It says, share our fire. Share our food. Share our love and thanks."

"That's quite beautiful," Thorn said softly.

Lydia turned to regard him with some curiosity. She didn't equate Thorn with the ability to appreciate poetry. Hal, on the other hand, knew that his old friend had a definite sentimental streak. He nodded agreement with Thorn's comment.

The song ended on a long drawn-out note that was beautiful to hear. The women, and some of the younger children, added a high fourth harmony to this note and the combined sound rang out around the clearing, infused with a natural vibrato and filling the evening air.

Finally, without anyone seeming to give a signal, it ceased, and the sound rang on in their memories. Spontaneously, the Herons broke into applause and Hal stepped toward them, his right hand raised in greeting.

"Thank you, Mawagansett people," he said in a clear, carrying voice. "Thank you for this beautiful welcome."

Smiles broke out among the ranks of the assembled villagers, and then two children, a boy and a girl, were ushered forward by their parents. Each carried a small posy of yellow and blue flowers. Uncertainly, nervously, they advanced on the line of strangers, seeking out one in particular.

Jesper, expecting the tributes to be handed to Hal or Thorn, raised his eyebrows when the children bypassed those two and stopped in front of him, proffering the flowers.

"For me?" he said, the surprise all too evident on his face.

The children piped up in unison. "For the first one to fight the bear. You have our thanks. You own our lives. You will be known to us as Hawasansat, the first to fight the bear."

Jesper realized that these must be the two children who had been cowering in the branches of the tree when he launched his attack on the bear. Truth be told, he didn't recognize them. Events the previous day had been a little hectic and he hadn't been taking too much notice of what the children looked like. Awkwardly, he accepted the two bunches of flowers.

"Well, thank you," he said uncertainly. Nothing in his life so far had prepared him to be honored in such a way and he was totally ignorant of local customs or etiquette.

He held the flowers to his breast and decided that it might be appropriate to bow. He bent at the waist and bowed deeply. It seemed he had picked the right response as a concerted cry of approval came from the assembled tribespeople.

It was a signal for the Mawagansett to break ranks and swarm forward to surround the newcomers, slapping them on their backs, smiling and, in the case of the women, hugging them.

One rather attractive matron singled out Thorn, and embraced him warmly, seeming unwilling to release him. The old sea wolf was beginning to enjoy himself. A little too much, Hal thought, as he saw his friend return the embrace with interest. He coughed sharply and Thorn looked up.

"Remember my mam," Hal said. Thorn looked sheepish, and disentangled himself from the woman's embrace.

"Ah . . . yes. Correct," he said. He smiled at the woman and patted her hand. "Very nice of you, my dear. Very nice. But I'm more or less spoken for, you know?"

Obviously, she didn't know. She reattached herself to him and he looked helplessly over her head at Hal, mouthing the words, *What do I do now?*

"Don't enjoy it so much," the skirl told him. Then he was almost swept off his feet as a tall and statuesque younger woman threw her arms around him, drawing him to her with a strength that forced most of the air from his lungs.

He tried to wriggle out of her embrace, but the more he squirmed, the tighter she held him, eventually stooping, as she was half a head taller than he, to plant a smacking kiss on his cheek.

"Thank you," he said breathlessly. The tight embrace was making it difficult to get a decent breath. Finally, Mohegas, failing to hide the smile on his lips, spoke gently to the woman and she released him suddenly, causing him to stagger back a few paces.

"This woman is the aunt of the children you saved," he told Hal, and the young skirl nodded to the woman.

"Well . . . thank you. It was a pleasure to help them. They seem like nice children," he mumbled. He watched her warily, as she seemed ready to renew her hugging and kissing onslaught at any moment. She beamed at him, then, realizing his comparative youth and understanding his embarrassment, she backed away, still grinning. She said something in her own tongue to a woman nearby and the two of them laughed heartily.

"What did she say?" Hal asked Mohegas. He could feel his cheeks aflame with embarrassment.

The Mawagansett elder shook his head, smiling. "Best if I don't tell you, I think," he said, and Hal had to be content to leave it at that.

All around him, the crew were being greeted and welcomed by other members of the tribe. The largest group was around Jesper, with everyone wanting to take his hand, pat his shoulder or slap him on the back. He was undoubtedly the hero of the hour. And Hal, thinking of how he had stood up to the bear, decided that Jesper deserved all the praise and adulation he was getting.

Then a loud voice cut through the hubbub that surrounded them. But the speaker didn't use the common tongue. He spoke in Skandian, with an accent that told them this was his first language.

"Thorn! One-handed Thorn! By the great Warbling Walrus of Skod! Is that really you?"

chapter twenty-four

The ranks of the Mawagansett parted to allow a figure to pass through them, his right hand held out in greeting.

With the exception of the young woman who had so enthusiastically welcomed Hal, the tribespeople tended to be short and stocky in build. This newcomer was at least a head taller than the majority of them. He was dressed in the hide overshirt and leggings that the men wore, and his hair was parted in the middle, to hang in two long braids on either side.

But, where the Mawagansetts' hair was black, his was gray-blond, and his face, while tanned and weathered by years of sun and wind, wasn't as dark as theirs.

His eyes were a startling blue and his mouth was curled in a smile of welcome and surprise as he reached Thorn. He went to grasp his right hand, realized there was only a wooden hook there and clumsily switched to his left hand, seizing Thorn's arm halfway up the forearm and pumping it exuberantly.

"Thorn One-Hand!" he repeated. "I never thought I'd see you here." He paused and considered, then added, "In fact, I never thought you'd still be alive! Last time I saw you, you seemed determined to drink yourself to death."

"Well, as you can see, I stopped," Thorn said, taking no offense. At one stage in his life, that had been his intention. He peered closely at the lined face in front of him, but try as he might, he couldn't place the owner. "You must be Orvik?" he said, remembering that Mohegas had told them the name of the Skandian who had come out of the sea some twelve years prior.

Orvik beamed. "Haven't been called that in too many years," he said. "But how did you get here? Did you sail from Skandia to find me? And who are all these boys?" he added, looking curiously at the youthful faces that surrounded them. The Herons had crowded around to see this mysterious Skandian.

Thorn held up his left hand to stem the tirade of questions.

"Just a moment!" he said. "You have the advantage of me. You seem to know me. But I can't recall you—although your face is a little familiar." He frowned, trying to imagine the face some twelve years younger, with fewer lines and a shock of blond hair instead of the dirty gray color that it was now.

"I was called Eelcatcher back then," the gray-haired man told him. "Orvik Eel—"

But Thorn, with a rush of memory, interrupted him and finished the statement. "—catcher! Orvik Eelcatcher!" he said, and the man's face broke into a beaming smile.

"That's right!" he said, delighted to be recognized—or at least, remembered.

"You were in Arnulf Sharkfighter's crew," Thorn said slowly, as more details emerged from his foggy memory.

Orvik nodded enthusiastically. "That's right. Third oar on the old *Wolf Foot*."

"*Wolf Foot*," Thorn said slowly, his brow furrowed as he recalled more facts from the past. "She went raiding one summer and never returned. Everyone assumed she'd been lost at sea." He looked around the faces that surrounded them, searching for more familiar features. "Did any of the others survive? Are they here?"

The beaming smile faded from Orvik's face and he shook his head sadly. "I'm the only one," he told them and Thorn regretted his impulsive question. Of course, Mohegas had made no reference to other Skandians living with the tribe.

"What happened?" Hal asked, seeing Thorn's momentary embarrassment.

Orvik looked at him curiously, noticing the young face and the clear, intelligent eyes. He glanced back to Thorn. "Who's this?" he asked.

Hal smiled to himself. Skandians weren't renowned for polite conversation. They tended to come straight to the point. Evidently, Orvik hadn't lost that tendency in his years with the Mawagansett.

Thorn, who had been asked this question many times before, placed a hand on Hal's shoulder in a sign of affection and respect.

"This is Hal Mikkelson," he said. "You remember Mikkel, don't you?"

"Indeed I do!" Orvik replied instantly. Mikkel had been one of

Skandia's foremost warriors until he was killed on the same raiding voyage during which Thorn had lost his hand. Orvik looked more closely at Hal. Mikkel had been a big man, whereas Hal was shorter and slimmer than the average Skandian. "He's not too big, is he?"

Hal shook his head. There was that renowned Skandian tact once more, he thought.

Thorn squared his shoulders aggressively. "He's just fine," he stated. "He's our skirl." There was a warning note in his voice, but Orvik missed it.

"He's barely out of short pants," Orvik said, frowning. Then he was somewhat startled as Stig pushed forward and faced him, standing just a little closer to him than politeness dictated. And while Orvik was tall, Stig was even taller and broader in the shoulder.

"I'm out of short pants," he said threateningly. "And I'm happy to obey Hal's orders as skirl. He's an expert navigator and helmsman. And a great ship designer. He built our ship, as a matter of fact."

Orvik realized belatedly that he might have overstepped the mark with his comments on Hal's youth. The young warrior facing him seemed to be no older than Hal. But he was bigger and broader and had an easy athletic grace about him that told the old Skandian that he would be a fighter to be reckoned with.

He also realized that the other members of the crew had stepped forward to join Stig, standing in a half circle just behind him. Their displeasure was all too evident.

"Take it easy, boys," Hal said quietly and the crew relaxed somewhat, all save Stig, who remained bristling and angry at the affront to his friend and skipper.

Orvik held up an apologetic hand. "No offense meant," he said. Then, seeking to change the subject, he added, "What happened to your ship?"

He addressed the question to Thorn, but the one-armed sea wolf deferred to Hal.

"Nothing happened to her," Hal replied. "She's hidden in an inlet at the southern end of the beach. We were caught in a huge storm as we were leaving Hibernia and driven thousands of kilometers to the west. We were almost out of water by the time we reached this shore. We landed in the bay back there"—he gestured over his shoulder in the direction of the bay—"and set up a camp. We hid the ship until we could make contact with the locals."

Orvik's eyes burned with a sudden light of hope. "So your ship's intact?" he asked. "You'll be heading home one day then?"

"One day. Yes," Hal told him. "As soon as this nonstop wind out of the northeast changes direction. It's dead foul for the course back to Skandia."

Orvik nodded several times. He was well aware of the prevailing wind, and his twelve years here had taught him about the weather conditions.

"It'll shift within the next five or six weeks," he told them. "Always does at this time of year. Then it'll be out of the southwest."

There was a murmur of interest from the assembled Herons.

"That'll be perfect for the trip home!" Stig said.

Hal nodded thoughtfully. A southwest wind would be ideal. He felt a vast sense of relief. They would be going home after all, he thought.

Thorn returned to Hal's original question. "What happened

to *Wolf Foot* and the rest of your crew?" he asked. Once more, a sad look overtook Orvik's lined features.

"We'd been raiding on the west coast of Hibernia," he said.

Thorn nodded. *Wolf Foot* had been lost before Erak had banned the practice of raiding, and the west Hibernian coast had been a favorite hunting ground for wolfships—despite the fact that the weather could prove unpredictable there, as the *Heron* had found to her cost.

"Problem was, we were doing too well. Plenty of booty and gold. The Hibernians didn't expect a raid that late in the season. And we overstayed our welcome. By the time we headed for home, the weather had shifted and we were hit by the mother of all storms from the northeast."

The Herons exchanged a quick look. It sounded like the conditions they had struck just a few weeks before.

"I've never seen such wind and waves," Orvik said. "The sail blew out in the first few minutes and we were riding under a bare mast, and still being driven south and west."

Thorn interrupted sympathetically. "We know how that feels," he said. "Sounds like the storm that hit us."

Orvik met his eyes and nodded. "Put out a sea anchor to try to slow down our drift, but the hawser snapped after an hour or two and we just kept sliding farther and farther out into the Endless Ocean. Some of the lads began to fear we'd be driven right off the edge of the world, onto the giant turtle's back. And that'd be the end of us."

He paused reflectively. His eyes had a faraway look as he remembered that terrible storm so many years before.

"Then we sighted the coast, a few kilometers north of here. At first, we thought we were safe, but then we realized there was nothing but rocks and shoals there and we were being blown down onto them. We tried to row, but the wind and waves and tide had us and we couldn't make any headway. We just swept down on that coast—and the rocks that were waiting for us there. Then we struck.

"Half the crew were lost in that first impact with the rocks at the foot of the cliffs. The undertow was terrible and they were sucked back into the ocean. The rest of us scrambled ashore somehow as the ship broke up.

"Sharkfighter led us along the base of the cliffs, just above the water's edge, until we found a narrow path leading to the top."

"That was lucky," Hal put in, and Orvik turned those blue eyes on him for several moments before he responded.

"You would think so. We certainly did. But when we scrambled up the path to the top, they were waiting for us." His voice was grim as he recalled the event.

Thorn asked the obvious question. "They? Who were 'they'?"

"The *Imsinnis skassak,*" he replied. "That's what they call themselves. It means 'Ghost Face.'"

The Herons exchanged a look. This was the second time they'd heard the name.

Orvik continued. "They're a tribe from north of here. Savage, warlike and ruthless. Anyone who's not one of them is an enemy and that's how they treated us. They kill without mercy. They were fully armed, with clubs and lances and bows. We had our saxes and nothing else. And they outnumbered us two to one.

"As Sharkfighter led the way onto the top of the cliffs, they charged out of the trees and started stabbing and hacking at the crew. We were all exhausted, of course, and could hardly put up a fight. I saw my shipmates going down before the attack and I turned and ran."

He stopped, lowering his eyes as he remembered the shame of the moment. "I left my shipmates to die," he said, his voice almost inaudible.

It was Stig who dropped a hand on his shoulder to comfort him. "No sense in sacrificing yourself," he said.

Orvik raised his gaze, seeing only compassion in the younger man's eyes. "That's what I've tried to tell myself ever since. Anyway, I ran, and one of them saw me. They came after me like the hounds of hell, yelling and screaming for blood. I went inland, running downhill as fast as I could go." He allowed a faint smile to touch his lips. "I was always a fast runner," he added.

"So you managed to outrun them?" Hal asked, but Orvik shook his head.

"They would have caught me. They were gaining on me when I reached a high bluff. There was a long drop before me, with a river at the bottom. And behind me were the Ghostfaces. I hesitated for a second or two, then I decided. I jumped off the bluff, hoping I'd get out far enough to reach the river below."

Again he paused, then continued. "Have you ever jumped into water from a great height?" he asked and the surrounding audience shook their heads. He nodded. "I thought I'd hit the water and it would break my fall. Instead, it nearly broke my legs. It was like jumping onto hard ground. I went way under, with the breath knocked out of me. It seemed to take forever to make it to the surface again and all the while, I was gulping and swallowing water. I came up, spluttering and gasping. The current had carried me ten meters farther downstream from where I'd hit the surface. I floundered there like an exhausted fish, flailing at the water. Above me, I could hear the Ghostfaces shouting and cursing after me. None of them were willing to risk that jump. Not that it mattered, of course. I could only swim a few strokes and I knew I'd drown. Then my hand touched something. It was a log, being carried by the current. I hauled myself onto it and collapsed. Some of the branches snagged in my jerkin and held me in place. Apparently, I drifted for several days, half unconscious, half drowned.

"When I came to, I had drifted downriver into the bay yonder." He indicated the direction of the large bay *Heron* had sailed into.

"I washed up on the beach where the Mawagansett found me, more dead than alive, and with my lungs and stomach full of seawater. They brought me back here, pumped me out and wrapped me in blankets and furs to get my blood flowing again. I was unconscious for three days. I'd come half awake every so often and they'd spoon-feed me with hot broth. And their healer would recite spells over me and burn eagle feathers and strange spices in the hut where they had me. Don't know how much good they did, but I eventually woke and began to regain my strength. They called me Polennis—it means—"

"Man Who Swims," Thorn put in.

Orvik nodded. "Of course, Mohegas told you. That's how they found me, washed up on the beach like a piece of worthless flotsam." He looked around the circle of brown-skinned faces. The

Mawagansett were patiently allowing the newcomers time to hear his story.

"They're good people," he said. "Kind and generous. I've been with them now for twelve sun cycles, sorry, years," he corrected himself and smiled. "And in all that time, there's been no prospect of my returning home. Not until now."

chapter twenty-five

At a signal from Mohegas, the group began to move toward the feast circle, set out around the fireplace in front of the village huts.

The children swarmed around the Herons, studying them with unabashed curiosity. Mohegas and several of the other adults admonished them, but not too severely. When this happened, the children would withdraw a few paces, but within a few seconds, they would gather around the strangers once more. Thorn's wooden hook aroused great interest. One of the more daring boys reached out to touch it and Thorn rounded on him with a ferocious expression, clacking the gripping hook open and shut like a deranged lobster. The boy recoiled, as did those around him. Then, when Thorn burst out laughing and held out the hook for further inspection, they warily crept back closer to him.

Ingvar was another subject of interest. Tall and massively built, he towered over the other members of the crew. Compared with the Mawagansett, who tended to be short and stocky, he appeared to be a giant. He was wearing his spectacles and the children found the black lenses fascinating. Even when he removed the spectacles, thinking the children might turn their attention from him, the sight of his piercing blue eyes roused further comment, as although most of the Skandians were blue-eyed, Ingvar's were a particularly brilliant color. But the children used their own language, not the common tongue, so Ingvar had no idea what they were chattering about.

Stefan, with his ability to mimic voices and other sounds, was an enormous favorite with them. At one stage, he stopped, threw his arms wide and intoned, in a perfect impression of Mohegas's serious tones:

"I am Mohegas, mighty king of the Mawagansett people!"

The group of children close to him took a step back, looking nervously to where Mohegas had turned at the sound of his own voice. When a wide smile cracked the elder's normally serious face, the children relaxed, taking it as permission to laugh themselves.

Before the laughter died down, Stefan followed up with a perfect imitation of the cry of the bird they now knew was called a tur-gay.

"*Oggle-oggle-oggle!*" he cried and the children laughed delightedly. It *did* sound exactly like the cry of the big bird, Hal thought.

Lydia seemed to agree. "Do that again and I'll put a dart through you," she said dryly.

At that, Stefan decided to move on to another impression. This time, he produced the shattering, snarling roar of an angry bear. With squeals of fright, the children scampered away from him, stopping some five meters away, studying him to make sure he hadn't suddenly turned into a bear. Then, as he grinned and made a whimpering, pleading sound, for all the world like a dog begging forgiveness, they began to giggle and gathered around him again, pleading for more impersonations.

But Stefan was a consummate showman and he knew the first rule of a successful entertainer is to leave the audience wanting more. Regretfully, he shook his head and patted his belly.

"I'm hungry," he said. "No more voices until I've eaten."

Now that Stefan had mentioned food, Hal realized how hungry he was, and how delicious the scents arising from the grilling food were. Mohegas and the other adults ushered their guests to their places round the feast fire, and Hal sat on a folded blanket to the right of Mohegas. Thorn was on the elder's other side, with Orvik sitting by him in case there was a need for translation—although so far this hadn't proved necessary. The other Herons sat on Hal's right, interspersed with members of the tribe. Presumably, judging by their age and the amount of gray in their hair, those closest were members of the elders' council, Hal thought.

As Ulf and Wulf took their seats, there was an expectant giggle from half a dozen children surrounding them.

Ulf cocked his head at the young ones. "What's so funny?" he asked.

"They've probably never seen twins before," Wulf remarked.

His brother nodded. "Yes. That'd be it. They probably think we're gods or something," he said loftily.

Wulf scowled. He wished he'd thought of claiming divine status. But he tried to resume the ascendancy by one of his unfounded statements of "fact."

"I imagine so. It's a well-known fact that twins are totally unknown among foreign people," he said, with that tone of certainty that only expert liars can produce.

He felt a tap on his shoulder and twisted round to see who was there. His jaw dropped as he beheld an incredibly pretty Mawagansett girl of around eighteen years, standing behind him, offering him a platter of assorted pieces of meat and roasted vegetables. Beside her, and offering another plate to Ulf, was an identical girl, with an identical platter.

"I am Millika," said the first girl, smiling warmly. "I have been assigned to serve you at the feast."

"And I am Pillika," her twin said. "I have been asked to serve your brother."

"How unusual," Ulf said to his brother. "Millika and Pillika. Their names are almost identical. You don't see that every day."

"What about Ulf and Wulf?" Lydia said, from her position three places away. The twins regarded her, frowning.

"What do you mean? Our names are totally different," said Ulf.

"That's right," Wulf joined in. "There's no *W* in his name." He jerked a thumb at Ulf as he said the words.

Lydia shook her head wearily. "The phrase 'dumb as a post' takes on a whole new meaning with you two around."

Ulf and Wulf shrugged, then turned back to Millika and Pillika, reaching for the plates they were offering. It was perhaps significant that they selected identical pieces of roast venison to begin their feast.

Each of the Herons was assigned a member of the tribe to serve them at the feast. In Ingvar's case, several of the older children squabbled to have the right. Mohegas finally intervened and assigned them to a rotating schedule.

Lydia was delighted to be attended by a strapping young man. Hal felt a strange twinge of jealousy as she greeted the young man with a dazzling smile. Then he shook himself mentally. Why am I jealous about Lydia? he asked himself. We're shipmates, friends, fellow warriors. Nothing more. Yet he couldn't shake off that feeling of irritation as he watched the unquestionably good-looking Mawagansett attending to her.

A platter of snacks was suddenly thrust in front of Hal and he turned, a little startled, to see the smiling face of the young woman who had greeted him so enthusiastically when they arrived. Instinctively, he edged a little away from her, fearing she might try to continue the rib-cracking hug she had subjected him to. He gingerly took a piece of roast bird from the platter.

"Um, thank you," he muttered.

She beamed. "I am Sagana," she said. "We thought you were Ghostfaces when we first saw you. I'm glad that you're not." She smiled at him and slipped away.

Hal frowned. This was the third or fourth time that someone had mentioned the mysterious Ghostfaces. He turned to Mohegas.

"The Ghostfaces. These are the people who killed Orvik's shipmates?" he said.

Mohegas hesitated, then deferred to Orvik with an inviting hand gesture. It was a complex matter and he feared his grasp of the common tongue might not be up to the explanation. Orvik considered his answer for a few seconds, then began. The Herons all leaned in to hear him. Some of the Mawagansett, Hal noted, looked away, casting nervous glances over their shoulders in case the Ghostfaces might suddenly materialize out of thin air. It was a touchy subject, he realized.

"As I told you, they live to the north of here," Orvik said slowly. "About ten days' travel by canoe. There are a lot more of them than the Mawagansett. They'd outnumber these people by at least three to one. A raiding party, or war party, is usually made up of more than a hundred warriors. They travel down the main river, which lies east of here, in fleets of canoes, raiding and killing as they go. There are four or five other tribes settled along the river north of here and they all suffer the same fate."

"Why not band together to fight them?" Thorn asked.

Orvik shook his head. "There's never time to organize it. They move quickly and silently and they travel by night. They've usually raided and burned two or three of the other villages before we even know they're here. Then it's our turn."

"What do you do?" Hal asked.

Orvik shrugged. "There's not much we can do. We can usually muster only twenty or so warriors with any skill in weapons. And we're facing four times that number. Best we can do is hide in the forest until they're done. If they catch us, they kill the men and take the women and children prisoner, to use them as slaves. If they can't find us, they strip the village of any food and vegetables. They destroy our crops and burn down the houses. Eventually, they get tired of the game and head back north."

"And then what?" Edvin asked.

"I've only seen one Ghostface raid," Orvik said. "That was . . ." He paused, thinking, then continued. "Eight years ago. Is that right?" he said in an aside to Mohegas, who nodded gravely. "Yes. Eight years. But I'm told it's always the same. After they've gone, the Mawagansett pick up the pieces, rebuild their homes and start over again. Usually it means a pretty hungry winter, as the food stocks have all been stolen."

Thorn shook his head angrily. As a former raider himself, back in the old days when wolfships marauded through the known world, he knew that a lack of resistance like this would only encourage the Ghostfaces to repeat the action anytime it suited them. But he said nothing.

It was Stefan who raised the question that they had all wondered about. "Why are they called Ghostfaces?" he asked, and there was a murmur of agreement from the other Herons.

This time, Mohegas supplied the answer. "They paint themselves to look like ghosts," he said. "They shave their heads completely, then paint their faces with white clay, putting black circles around their eyes so they resemble skulls." He gestured toward Ingvar's spectacles. "When we first saw the big one, the black circles he wears over his eyes made him look like a Ghostface—that and his pale skin. Then, as we watched Wooden Hand"—he gestured toward Thorn—"and She Who Throws a Spear"—this time the gesture was toward Lydia, who smiled at the description of herself—"we realized that you were not Ghostfaces, but more like Polennis here."

"Why didn't you make yourself known then?" asked Lydia.

Mohegas shrugged. "We still weren't sure. We didn't know

where you had come from. At that point, we had seen no sign of your ship, so we assumed that you had traveled overland from the south. You seemed to be well armed and well organized and we thought you might be the advance party for another raid. You all had the look of warriors about you—even you."

Lydia inclined her head, taking the comment as a compliment.

"So we decided it was best to stay out of sight and observe you—to see what your intentions might be. Then, of course, two naughty children brought things to a head, and we realized that you would be good people to have as friends." He paused and gestured around the feast circle. "And here we are," he concluded. "But enough talk of enemies and Ghostfaces. It has been eight years since we have seen them. By now, they have probably forgotten all about us."

There was a murmur of agreement. Thorn looked down, shaking his head. "Or they may be thinking it's time for another visit," he said. But he kept his voice low so that nobody would hear him.

"So let's eat in good fellowship!" Mohegas said. Several of the older women moved to the cook fire and began carving more slices of delicious, juicy-looking venison from the spitted deer haunches.

Stig, whose stomach was rumbling at the sight and smell of the food, felt a light hand on his shoulder. He looked around into the most beautiful pair of eyes he had ever seen.

Her dark eyes were set in an oval face. Her skin was light brown and unblemished, and her nose was straight with the mouth full lipped and perfectly formed. The beautiful face was framed by long, glossy black hair, parted in the middle and worn in braids.

The girl, who appeared to be in her late teens, was slim and long-legged and she moved with a supple, catlike grace as she lowered herself to kneel behind him.

"I am Tecumsa, your server," she said. "Can I fetch you some deer meat?"

Her voice was soft and warm, in keeping with the perfection of her face and figure.

"I am . . . Stig," Stig croaked, his voice catching in his throat.

She smiled at him. "Welcome, Stig."

And in that moment, for the first time in his life, Stig fell hopelessly, irrevocably in love.

chapter twenty-six

The rest of the evening was an unqualified success as the Mawags—as Hal discovered they were more familiarly known—and the Herons enjoyed one another's company. The food was excellent, and if the Skandians had any regret, it was that the locals had no knowledge of coffee. But they were offered an herbal tea that they found quite pleasant to the taste, and for those who wanted something different, there was pure cold water and pressed fruit juices.

Perhaps the highlight of the meal was the moment when Edvin revealed his mud-baked oggle bird. Ulf and Wulf had left it wrapped in the canvas sheet they had used to carry it, and it had retained most of its heat. As Edvin unwrapped the unprepossessing sphere of dried, whitened mud, the women of the tribe gathered round him curiously, while he explained the cooking technique.

"The mud seals the bird," he told them. "So all the juices and fragrances are kept inside, and the bird cooks in them, staying moist and juicy. I noticed these birds are low on fat content and can dry out when they're roasted."

Several of the older women nodded agreement. It was one of the disadvantages of the bird. The flesh was delicious, but incautious cooking could cause it to dry out. Edvin's technique was a fascinating approach to the subject and they crowded closer as he took his saxe and struck the hardened mud sharply with the hilt. The mud cracked in a long, uneven line around the bird. Edvin struck it again, opening another crack at right angles to the first. Then he used the tip of the blade to flick several large segments of mud away, revealing the bark wrapping underneath.

"The bark keeps the wet mud away from the flesh," he explained. "After all, you wouldn't want to eat a muddy bird, would you?"

Several heads shook in agreement. That had been one of the reservations they had felt about this method of cooking. As Edvin now used the saxe to open the bark and strip it away, a cloud of delicious-smelling steam rose from inside. Mouths watered all round the feast circle, and now the men of the tribe gathered round as well, some of them actually licking their lips at the delicious fragrance of the bird.

Edvin uncovered more of it, revealing the golden-brown skin, and a low chorus of appreciation went round the circle. Then he quickly jointed the bird, placing legs, thighs and wings on a large platter supplied by one of the women. Once that was done, he continued with the razor-sharp saxe, deftly carving thick, juicy slices of breast and thigh meat and placing them on the platter with the legs.

"Hop in," he said, gesturing with the knife, and the assembled Mawags and Herons needed no further invitation.

Hal moved quickly. "Better grab some or there'll be none left," he said.

Thorn eyed the flashing blade of Edvin's saxe as he continued to reduce the big bird to a large pile of delicious meat slices. "Hope he cleaned that knife after our last battle," he said. But the thought didn't deter him from seizing a wing and several slices of dark meat from the thigh.

There was just enough to give each of the adults a small sample of the roast bird. People drifted back to their seats, savoring the juice-laden, fragrant meat. The flavor of the onions and herbs that had been stuffed into the cavity and then trapped inside the mud shell had permeated the flesh, adding their own delicious highlights to the meat. Everyone agreed that it was an excellent method of cooking. Within a few minutes, the huge bird was reduced to a pile of stripped bones.

For the first time since they had arrived in this unknown land, the Herons found themselves really relaxing, reclining on their elbows around the fire and exchanging stories with the Mawags. Ulf and Wulf were fascinated by the ministrations of the Mawag twins, Millika and Pillika. The girls were extremely vivacious, laughing long and often at the feeble sallies of the two sail trimmers.

Ulf had gravitated to Millika. At least, he thought she was Millika. He whispered in an aside to his brother: "This one's mine. She's prettier than her sister by a long way."

"You must be blind as well as stupid," Wulf told him. "Anyone can see that Pillika is much prettier."

The two girls exchanged a secretive smile. So did several of the Mawags who were watching the little tableau with interested amusement. They had noticed, as Ulf and Wulf had failed to do, that some minutes earlier, the girls had switched places and partners. Millika, who had been wearing a red leather headband, had surreptitiously handed it to her sister, who quickly donned it.

The result was that Ulf, who had begun the feast with Millika, was now being served by Pillika. And Wulf, who assumed his partner was Pillika, was actually sitting beside Millika. It was a familiar sight for the Mawags. The girls had been playing this trick on boyfriends and dance partners since they were thirteen years old.

"What we should do," said Ulf, "is change places just for a laugh, so they don't know who's who."

He was somewhat surprised by the outburst of laughter that greeted his words. The Mawags, of course, had understood every word, even if the two girls pretended not to have heard.

Oblivious to this byplay, Stig sat cross-legged, facing the beautiful Tecumsa, totally absorbed by her loveliness and grace. For her part, she was equally fascinated by this tall, muscular young man from an unknown land across the sea. She could see that he was a warrior, and she guessed that he was an expert in the craft. She also noted how the rest of the crew deferred to him—with the exception of Hal, their leader, and the one-armed, shaggy-haired older man. Those two treated him as an equal and that indicated to her that he was one of the senior members of the Skandian hierarchy.

Not that he needed any such status to impress her. He was

handsome and blond and moved with the grace of a natural athlete. And he had a ready smile and a delightful sense of humor that had her constantly breaking into helpless laughter.

As the night wore on, the two had eyes only for each other. The other Skandians and most of the Mawags noticed and smiled indulgently.

Most, but not all. There was one Mawag who eyed the smiling couple with hot, angry eyes. Orvik, who was familiar with the social undercurrents in the Mawagansett tribe, noticed and wondered whether he should say something. Then he shrugged his shoulders. It wasn't his part to interfere, he thought. All the same, he wondered whether Stig's obvious attraction to Tecumsa, and her reciprocal interest in him, would eventually cause trouble.

Several days passed and the Herons and the Mawags were now bonded as friends. There was a good deal of to and fro passage between the village and the campsite by the beach. Edvin had been adopted by the women of the village, who were fascinated to see a man cooking—and cooking well. They gave him free run of the large vegetable garden they maintained behind the village, where they grew beans, squash, onions and the strange vegetable called corn they had eaten at the feast. It was cylindrical in shape, and covered in delicious small golden kernels. Its outer layers consisted of fine, silklike threads covered by thick green leaves. Roasted over the coals of a fire, it had a deliciously sweet flavor. The kernels could also be ground to make a fine flourlike substance, and Edvin began baking bread with it. The vegetables added a welcome new dimension to the Herons' basic meat diet.

Orvik arrived one morning with Mohegas and several of the other elder men to inspect the *Heron* itself, where it was concealed in the narrow inlet beyond the camp.

The Mawags, of course, had never seen *Wolf Foot,* the ship on which Orvik had sailed. It had been wrecked several miles farther north. And nobody had been present to witness the *Heron*'s arrival. Their concept of a ship was limited by their experience of the bark-covered canoes that they used to travel up and down the river and to fish in the bay. These were small, flimsy craft made from spruce frames, with birch bark glued and sewn in place over them. They were light and handy craft but they would be dwarfed by the graceful ship moored in the inlet. The men clambered aboard, wondering at the solid deck planking beneath their feet. In a canoe, one had to tread carefully to avoid putting a foot through the bark skin.

On this craft, one could step anywhere without fear of doing damage. They inspected the long oakwood oars, making a mental comparison with the light birchwood paddles they wielded in their canoes. All in all, they thought, the foreigners had a completely different take on the subject of water transport.

Orvik, however, was at first somewhat disappointed.

"She's not very big," he said. Then he realized that this might be taken as a criticism and hastily amended his statement. "I mean, compared with a wolfship. We were pulling fifteen oars a side on *Wolf Foot.* Here you've got only . . ." He hesitated, counting the rowing positions. "Four a side."

"Four on one side, three on the other," Hal corrected him. He wasn't offended by the older man's comments. He'd heard them all before when he first built *Heron*. "When Ingvar's rowing, he counts as two oarsmen."

Orvik looked doubtful. "Seven rowers. Eight if you count Ingvar as two. Is that enough to row upwind?"

Thorn smiled. "We don't row upwind. We sail."

Orvik regarded him with disbelief. "You can't sail upwind," he said.

Thorn inclined his head. "This ship can. She was designed by a genius."

"Oh, and who would that be?" Orvik wanted to know.

Thorn jerked a thumb at Hal. "That would be Hal. He came up with a sail plan that will run rings round a square-rigged wolfship." He could see the skepticism in Orvik's eyes and he gestured for Hal to explain the advantages of the *Heron*'s fore and aft sail rig.

They moved for'ard and Hal demonstrated how the twin yardarms could raise a triangular sail on either side and how, with their rigid leading edges, they could point into the wind.

"Of course," he said, "she won't sail dead upwind. But we can tack back and forth and zigzag our way."

Mohegas, listening keenly, didn't understand much that was said. But he could see Orvik's growing acceptance of what he was being told and realized that this ship, and its young designer, were something very special. He gestured to a large shape in the bow, covered in a canvas shroud.

"What is this?" he asked.

Hal smiled. He was enjoying showing off his successful inventions. He reflected ruefully that there had been more than one unsuccessful invention over the years, and he'd borne the brunt of ridicule when they'd failed to measure up to expectations. So when one worked, he felt he owed it to himself to boast a little.

"This is what we call the Mangler," he told the Mawag elder. He had repaired the thongs he had cut during the fight with the bear. He loosened them now and stripped the cover away, revealing the massive crossbow, which seemed to crouch malevolently on its mounting. He demonstrated the salient features of the weapon, showing how it traversed through an arc of forty-five degrees to either side of the bow, and how the massive arms were cocked.

"Ingvar takes care of that," he said, grinning. "He's the only one strong enough to haul the cord back."

Next, he opened the locker behind the weapon and showed them a selection of the heavy projectiles that the bow could shoot. Mohegas weighed one in his hand.

"This is what you used to kill the bear?" he said.

Hal nodded. "Exactly."

Orvik looked at the weapon with great interest. "I've never seen a ship carrying a weapon like this before," he said.

Thorn nodded, slapping his hand on the smooth wood of the Mangler.

"Hal designed this as well," he said. "We used it to defeat Zavac a couple of years ago."

Orvik shook his head, frowning. "Zavac? Who's he when he's at home?"

Thorn smiled, but without humor. "He's not at home anymore," he said. "He was a pirate and he raided Hallasholm and stole the Andomal."

Orvik's eyebrows shot up. The Andomal was the Skandian

nation's most precious artifact. Before he could ask the obvious question, Thorn continued.

"We chased him across half the world. Finally cornered him and fought him. His ship was the size of a wolfship," he explained. "But Hal outmaneuvered him and shot him and his crew to pieces with the Mangler here, and got it back."

As ever, when he boasted about Hal's achievements, Thorn didn't think it necessary to explain that his young friend had allowed the Andomal to be stolen in the first place. That was a minor detail, he thought.

Orvik regarded the young skirl with new respect.

Hal shrugged diffidently. He enjoyed showing off his inventions, but he was less eager to boast about his achievements.

"Let's get back to the camp," he said, and led the way to the boarding plank that connected the ship to the bank.

He glanced back as he reached the shore. Mohegas was still standing in the bow, regarding the massive crossbow with a thoughtful expression. Then, realizing he had been left behind, he hastily followed them to the bank.

chapter twenty-seven

As they emerged from the trees onto the beach once more, Hal became aware of an angry voice, coming from close by the campsite. A young Mawag warrior was standing by the access ladder, shouting in his own language and obviously demanding entrance. An imperturbable Ingvar stood at the fence, barring access with his voulge. The sun glinted on the razor-sharp steel head of the weapon, and the young Mawag viewed it warily.

Well he might, Hal thought. Ingvar and the long-handled, heavy weapon were not a combination to be taken lightly. The young skirl quickened his pace as the Mawag began shouting again.

Ingvar said nothing. His face was impassive. His eyes were concealed behind the dark circles of his spectacles. As the young tribesman took a pace toward the foot of the access ladder, Ingvar lowered the voulge so that it was pointing directly at the Mawag's chest. If the tribesman kept moving forward, he would impale himself on the point.

"We'd better get up there," Hal said.

Behind him, he heard Orvik say quietly, "It's young Simsinnet. I was afraid something like this might happen."

Hal glanced quickly back at him, an annoyed expression touching his face. If Orvik had foreseen there might be trouble, it would have been a good idea to have mentioned it, he thought.

As they came within speaking range, Mohegas called out in his own tongue and the young man looked around, a little shamefaced, and took a pace back from the ladder. Now that Hal had time to take stock of him, he could see he was around eighteen years old. He was stocky and muscular.

"What's going on here, Ingvar?" Hal demanded.

The big youth glanced at Hal, then indicated the Mawag with the point of his voulge. "This character turned up a few minutes ago and started yelling for Stig. I told him Stig wasn't in the camp but he didn't seem to believe me. He started yelling in Mawag and tried to climb the ladder. I wasn't having that, so I asked him to stop."

Hal couldn't repress a smile. "With your voulge?"

Ingvar hesitated, then nodded. "It seemed like the most compelling argument."

Hal turned to Mohegas. "What's the problem?" he asked. "Why is he so angry?"

The tribal elder made a dismissive gesture, glaring at the young man named Simsinnet. "Simsinnet is a fool. He is being discourteous. It is nothing. I will deal with him."

But Hal wasn't prepared to leave it at that. It obviously wasn't nothing, as Mohegas claimed. If he or one of his men had done something to offend the young Mawag, he wanted to know about it. Mohegas might be embarrassed by Simsinnet's behavior, but Hal wasn't going to let him brush it aside. He turned to the old Skandian castaway a few paces behind him.

"Orvik, you speak their language. What's this fellow so angry about?"

His tone conveyed his annoyance that Orvik might have seen trouble brewing and failed to alert him to it. The older Skandian hesitated, then reluctantly came clean.

"He's angry at Stig about the girl. He's been courting Tecumsa for the past six months—not that she's returned his interest. But he seems to think he has some kind of claim on her, and Stig has come along and got in the way."

"Does he? Does he have any claim on her?" Hal asked. It would be incredibly awkward if Stig had come between a betrothed couple.

Orvik shook his head. "No. As I said, she hasn't returned his interest. But he's understandably miffed that a stranger seems to have won her heart. You know how young men can be," he added.

Hal nodded, although in fact, he had no idea how young men could be, being a young man himself, and without any real experience in matters of the heart.

Mohegas began shouting at Simsinnet again, making angry, dismissive gestures and obviously telling him to go back to the Mawag village. Hal put a hand on his arm to stop him. It wouldn't do any good to simply send the young man away with his anger festering. This situation needed to be resolved, he thought. He looked at Ingvar.

"Where is Stig?" he asked. He felt a rush of anger at his first mate. Couldn't he simply have stayed away from the Mawag girl until it was time for them to head home? Why did he have to jeopardize their position by alienating this young Mawag? For although Mohegas was intent on stopping this affair, he had no doubt that Simsinnet would have friends among the younger Mawags who would take his side, and a tide of resentment could well rise up against the Skandians, driving a wedge between them and the Mawagansett tribe.

"He went for a walk down the beach a while back," Ingvar told him. Then added, "He was with the Mawag girl."

Simsinnet obviously understood him, but was more at home expressing his anger in his own language. He began shouting angrily again. Mohegas shouted back and the younger man eventually fell silent, although there was a dangerously sulky look to his face.

"This isn't good," Orvik said quietly.

Hal rounded on him. "Isn't it? I hadn't noticed," he said sarcastically. "And if you saw this coming, why didn't you give me a heads-up?"

Orvik opened his mouth to say something, couldn't think of a worthwhile reply and closed it again. Thorn saved him.

"Here they come now," he said and all eyes turned to follow the direction he was pointing with his hook. Stig and Tecumsa were strolling hand in hand at the water's edge, making their way back to the campsite. As the group watched, Stig said something and the girl laughed and touched his shoulder with an intimate gesture.

"Oh, Orlog's horns!" Hal muttered.

Thorn was grinning. He'd seen this sort of thing many times

before in his youth. Young men and young women, they couldn't help but stir things up, he thought.

"Does Orlog have horns?" he asked mildly. "I'd only ever heard of his teeth and claws."

Hal glared at him. It was all very well for Thorn to joke, he thought. "Orlog has horns if I want him to have horns," he said shortly. "And a big scaly backside as well, if I say."

Simsinnet had started to move toward the young couple approaching along the beach, but a sharp command from Mohegas stopped him.

Hal addressed Orvik again. "So what's likely to happen here?"

Orvik shrugged. "From what I know, he'll want to fight Stig for the right to court the girl," he replied. "But I could be wrong. Maybe he'll just give him an earful and forget it."

Hal studied the young Mawag. He was fit and hard muscled and he didn't look like the type who would be content to "just give Stig an earful," he thought.

"Fight?" he asked Orvik. "You mean Stig will have to kill him?" It never occurred to him that Stig would lose a fight. He had seen his friend in battle too many times to doubt his skill and ability. But if he was forced to kill Simsinnet, it could drive a serious wedge between the two groups—and the Herons were outnumbered about eight to one, he thought. But thankfully, he saw Orvik shaking his head.

"No. It won't be a fight to the death. No weapons. They'll fight hand to hand."

That was something to be thankful for, Hal thought.

By this time, Stig and Tecumsa had come within easy speaking distance. Stig looked amused and puzzled by the group of people around the access ladder to the compound. Tecumsa, Hal noticed, took one look at Simsinnet and looked a lot less than amused.

"What's the trouble?" Stig said good-naturedly. Then a storm of angry dissent broke over him. Simsinnet pointed an accusing finger at him and Tecumsa and started shouting. She shouted back, and Mohegas joined in as well, shouting louder than the two of them. They spoke in the Mawag tongue. Hal glanced angrily at Orvik, who attempted to translate.

"He's saying she's his girl. She says she's not and how dare he assume she is. Mohegas is telling them both to behave. Simsinnet says he and Tecumsa have had 'an understanding' for the past six months. She says he might have understood that but nobody told her—"

"All right. I get the general gist," Hal muttered. But now events took a turn for the worse as Simsinnet aimed a long, angry outburst at Tecumsa. He took a pace toward her and that was enough for Stig. He stepped between them, raising a hand to stop the angry warrior.

"That's enough of that!" he said warningly. "Just back off, feathertop!"

The last word was a reference to the two eagle feathers Simsinnet wore in a deer-hide headband. Simsinnet may have missed the meaning of the word, but the tone of derision was all too obvious. He stooped and grabbed a handful of beach sand.

"Oh no . . . ," Orvik began, and Mohegas shouted a warning.

Too late. Simsinnet hurled the sand in an arc at Stig, so that it sprayed across his chest. The young Skandian flushed with anger and took a pace forward, his fist raised. Hal, sensing from Orvik's and Mohegas's reactions that there was more to Simsinnet's gesture than simply throwing sand, shouted an order.

"Stig! Hold it right there!"

There was a time when Stig's notorious temper would have flared out of control and he would have launched himself in a fury at the Mawag. But since those days, Stig had learned discipline—and he'd learned that when Hal gave an order, he expected it to be obeyed. He stopped, looking angrily at his skirl.

"It's a challenge," Hal told him, guessing that that was what the gesture meant.

Orvik confirmed it for him. "It's a formal challenge to fight," he said. "If you accept, you have to throw a handful of sand back at him."

"Well, fine," Stig said, stooping, gathering a handful and throwing it at Simsinnet in one motion. "Let's get to it. I'll fetch my ax and shield."

Simsinnet smiled in satisfaction. "No weapons," he said, reverting for the first time to the common tongue. "We fight man to man. Bare hands."

"Suits me," Stig replied, realizing that this was to be a formal, organized contest, and not a simple brawl on the beach. "Name the time and place."

The time was an hour after noon and the place was the open ground in front of the village, between the huts and the fire circle. Stig sat on a low stool while Hal bound his hands with deer-hide strips to protect them, leaving the fingers free to grip but padding the knuckles. Orvik knelt beside them.

"Is there any way we can stop this?" Hal asked. "This can only cause bad blood between us and them."

But surprisingly, Orvik shook his head. "Not really. In fact, it might clear the air. Nobody will blame Stig for reacting to the challenge. They'll respect him for it. Simsinnet is regarded as a great fighter."

Hal sighed, shook his head and went back to fastening the bindings on Stig's fists.

"How will he fight?" Stig asked. "Is there anything I should look for?"

"He'll try to grapple you," Orvik told him. "He'll go for a choke hold or an arm or leg lock. Anything to disable you or force you to submit. He's a wrestler and he's good at it. He can throw you flat on your back in a second."

"That's not going to happen," Stig said. "Will he box? Will he throw punches?"

Orvik shook his head. "They don't know anything about boxing."

Stig looked at him for a few seconds. "They're about to learn," he said grimly.

A horn blast sounded from across the open space. Romanut, the Mawagansett battle leader, a man considerably younger than Mohegas, called for the combatants to take their places.

Stig rose and a chorus of encouragement came from the small group of Herons gathered around him. He stripped off his shirt and handed it to Hal. No sense in giving Simsinnet anything to grab hold of. Dressed in a knee-length pair of breeches and flanked by Orvik, Thorn and Hal, he made his way to the circle in the sand where the fight would take place. As they approached, Simsinnet emerged from one of the huts, accompanied by three retainers. The rest of the tribe gathered around the fighting ring. Some, but not all, cheered on their man. Hal noticed that Mohegas's lips were a tight, angry line. Tecumsa and several of the tribe's young women also stood silently, watching with keen interest.

Simsinnet was dressed only in a loincloth. His muscular body glistened with oil.

"Not very sporting of him," Stig muttered to Hal.

A hush fell as the two combatants faced each other, each standing at the edge of the circle.

Knowing that the rules, which were basic, had been explained to both youths, Romanut raised the horn to his lips again and sounded a long blast. When the horn ceased, it was the signal for the fight to begin.

The long, pealing note stopped abruptly. The sudden silence was almost shocking. Stig stepped forward a pace, left leg advanced slightly, fists raised in the classic boxer's pose. Simsinnet, who had never seen this before, hesitated a second, then, screaming a war cry, he leapt high in the air and charged across the sand, his arms curved into a wrestler's grappling pose.

Stig could see the fury on his face and, in a brief moment of recollection, he remembered how Thorn had taught him never to fight angry.

As the onrushing Simsinnet came close, Stig stepped toward him, inside the grappling arms, and shot out a straight right. It hit Simsinnet flush on the jaw, with all the force of Stig's upper body and shoulder behind it, augmented by Simsinnet's own hard-charging momentum. Simsinnet straightened up instantly, his eyes glazing, his arms suddenly dropping to hang slackly by his sides. Stig saw the light of awareness go out in his eyes, saw his knees begin to buckle under him. Quickly, the tall Skandian stepped forward, wrapping his arms around Simsinnet's upper body and lowering him to the sand, to forestall any further injury. Then he straightened and took a pace back, glancing around the suddenly silent onlookers.

"And I think we're done," he said quietly.

chapter twenty-eight

Remarkably, Orvik's prediction proved to be correct. Once the fight was over, the Mawagansett people regarded Stig with a mixture of awe and respect. The speed and power with which he'd finished the fight, which had lasted barely ten seconds, was discussed at length, and in admiring tones, around the cooking fires.

Simsinnet was a champion fighter and an expert warrior. Most of the tribe had expected him to win the fight, although not all had been happy about the prospect. The Skandians had won the friendship of the tribe. They were popular and good-natured.

And, of course, they had saved the two children from the bear and removed the bear itself as a threat to the community.

Simsinnet, on the other hand, although he was well liked, was seen as something of a hothead. And many of the tribe's women resented his high-handed assumption that Tecumsa was his property. Mawagansett women were independent and enjoyed equal status with their menfolk. And they made their own decisions about whom they might marry. As a result, many felt that Simsinnet had got no more than he had been asking for.

To his credit, Simsinnet seemed to learn by his experience. He still wasn't sure how Stig had defeated him. The whole thing had happened so quickly that he never clearly saw the straight right fist that Stig shot out. All he remembered was a devastating blow to the jaw, then blackness that lasted for several minutes. When he came to, he gazed around and found he was lying on a pallet in one of the huts. Mohegas and the tribe's healer were bending over him and there was a throbbing pain in his jaw.

"What happened?" he asked blearily.

"You lost," Mohegas told him. "The stranger Stig hit you with a massive blow. You're lucky your head didn't come off."

Simsinnet rubbed his jaw, moving it from side to side to ease the stiffness that was already setting in. "I'll fight him again . . . ," he began impulsively, although in truth he didn't want to go through this a second time. But as he tried to rise, Mohegas put a hand on his chest and pushed him back down on the pallet.

"You won't," he said firmly. "You challenged. You fought. He won. You know that is an end to this matter."

Simsinnet sank back glumly. Mohegas was right. Once a challenge had been taken up and the fight had been settled, that was it. There was no continuance of the bad blood that had existed between the two combatants; it was required of the loser that he make peace with his former opponent and set the feud aside. The Mawags were a small, tight-knit community and had no room for ongoing enmity.

"Once your head has cleared a little, you will seek him out and make peace with him," Mohegas ordered.

Simsinnet nodded. The instant pain in his jaw and head made him wish that he hadn't.

"He must be a mighty warrior," he said, feeling his jaw again. Hothead that he was, he had been involved in several fights before and he had never lost.

"He is," Mohegas told him. "It's no shame to be defeated by him."

"Did Tecumsa see me defeated?" Simsinnet asked plaintively.

Mohegas held his gaze for several seconds until the younger man looked away. "You offended her," he said gently. "Of course she saw the fight. But she was concerned that you might have been seriously hurt."

Simsinnet's face brightened at the news. "She was? She was worried about me?"

Mohegas shook his head slightly. "Don't get your hopes up. Of course she was concerned. She likes you. But I think she loves the stranger."

"Oh." Simsinnet turned his face away. He could feel tears threatening to force their way out and he wasn't having that. "I'll make my peace with him after I've rested for a while," he said, and closed his eyes before the tears could appear.

Mohegas patted his hand gently. "Don't leave it too long," he said.

• • • • •

The Mawags kept a dozen canoes drawn up on the bank of the stream that ran behind the village. Hal borrowed one and, accompanied by Orvik, paddled down the creek to the bay, then across to the northern headland. As they passed the middle head, Orvik pointed north to the wide river mouth they had sighted when they first entered the bay.

"That river runs inland and swings north. It's the Mawags' main thoroughfare if they want to trade with other tribes."

"Are there many other tribes on the river?" Hal asked. The recent mention of the Ghostfaces had him a little anxious about the prospect of meeting other tribes in this unfamiliar land. Orvik pursed his lips as he considered the question.

"Maybe five or six," he said. "They're small groups, like the Mawags. Probably all came from the same basic tribe in the beginning. Their languages are very similar and they can all make themselves understood."

"So they're friendly?" Hal asked.

Orvik grinned, guessing what he was getting at. "All except the Ghostfaces," he said. "They're from a lot farther north. When they've raided in the past, they've used the river to attack the other villages. They'll come down in a fleet of twenty or thirty canoes. They arrive by night and attack. We're at the end of the chain, so at least we get some warning that they're coming. In the past we've managed to take whatever we could and hide in the forest."

"But you say they haven't raided in, what, eight years?" Hal asked.

Orvik nodded. "They used to come every two or three years,

according to the Mawags. Maybe they've found other people to prey on," he added hopefully.

Hal pursed his lips thoughtfully. If the Ghostfaces hadn't been seen in eight years, there was little reason to suspect they might reappear now.

"That'd be all I need," he muttered to himself. Then, as they drew level with the inside of the northern headland, he steered the canoe into its lee and ran it up on a narrow strip of sand. Together, he and Orvik walked around the headland to the seaward side, where he studied the prevailing wind.

"Still out of the northeast," he said grimly. "The worst possible direction for us."

To head home, of course, they would have to sail northeast, straight into the teeth of the wind.

"I thought you said you could sail upwind," Orvik said.

Hal shrugged, tossing a small piece of dry seaweed into the air and watching it blow back behind him.

"Not dead into the eye of the wind," he explained. "We have to zigzag across it, and that takes a lot longer. With the distance we have to go to reach home, we'd run out of food and water before we were halfway."

Orvik shaded his eyes and peered directly into the wind, feeling the spray from the waves spattering against his face. The salt air and the spray evoked memories in him, of a life he had led years ago.

"Well, the elders say the wind is due to change soon," he said. "It always does around this time of year. It backs into the southwest."

"That'll be ideal for us," Hal said. "We can sail on a reach across it, and our leeway will take us to the north. If only they could tell us when it's going to change."

"Mohegas says at the time of the next new moon," Orvik told him. "And he's usually right about these things."

"Can't come too soon for me," Hal said. The new moon was two weeks away. "We'd better get back and see what new disasters have happened while I've been away."

He was pleasantly surprised to find that no trouble had occurred while he'd been on the headland. He had begun to feel as if every time he left the camp, something happened that required his urgent attention.

But things were absolutely normal when he returned. Mindful of Mohegas's prediction, he singled out Edvin and Lydia.

"We're going to have to start laying food aside for the return trip," he said. "That means I'll need you to bring in more meat, Lydia, and you can start smoking it or salting it, Edvin."

They both nodded. "I think smoking will be best," Edvin said. "We don't have enough salt to preserve a lot of meat—and we'll need a lot."

Hal gestured to the bay. "Couldn't we boil it out of seawater?" he asked.

Edvin looked doubtful. "It'd take a lot of seawater and a lot of boiling to get enough. I'll get the lads started building smoking racks." He looked at Lydia. "Deer meat will be best. And more of those big birds."

Lydia nodded. She glanced toward the tree line and slowly stood up. "Hullo. What's he want?"

Hal followed the line of her gaze and also stood, a sense of wariness flooding through him. At the entrance ladder, Simsinnet stood, talking to Ulf, who was on duty there. As he watched, he saw Stig emerge from the sleeping hut and begin to walk to the fence line. Hal hurriedly followed, arriving in time to hear Ulf's explanation.

"He says he wants to talk to you, Stig," the twin said. "He appears to be unarmed."

As he heard the last statement, Simsinnet held out his hands, palms outward. There were no weapons visible. Hal noticed that he wasn't even wearing a knife.

"We don't want trouble," he said to the Mawag. Ulf and Stig looked around at him as he spoke. Neither of them had heard his approach.

Simsinnet smiled and shook his head. "No trouble. I come as friend."

Stig glanced at his skirl. "Let him in, Hal. If he acts up, I can always knock his block off again."

Simsinnet's smile broadened. He seemed amused by the phrase. "Yes. Knock my block off," he repeated, touching his bruised jaw gingerly.

Hal gestured for Ulf to allow the Mawag to enter. Ulf, who had been blocking access to the ladder, stepped down and moved aside. Simsinnet climbed the outer ladder and descended the inner one. He stepped toward Stig, who took half a pace back. Simsinnet held out his right hand.

"You are a great warrior," he said. "You fought me and beat me. It was my honor to fight you. It will be my honor now to call you friend."

Stig hesitated. "I knock him out and he wants to be my friend?"

Hal shrugged. "Seems like a good enough reason to me," he said. "The way you whacked him, he'd be crazy to want to keep you as an enemy."

"I have no claim upon Tecumsa," Simsinnet continued. His sincerity was obvious. "I will stand aside for you. And I will be your friend, if you will have me."

Seeing Stig was still doubtful, Hal interrupted quietly. "Orvik said this is their way. Once a challenge has been issued and taken up, the two opponents either become friends, or the loser leaves the tribe and goes away."

Stig twisted his lips. Admittedly, this sort of thing wasn't unknown among the Skandians. He'd seen a lot of friendships forged after a fight—friendships that lasted for years.

"Shake his hand, Stig," Hal urged. He'd been thinking along similar lines.

Stig suddenly grinned and stepped forward, seizing Simsinnet's forearm in a spontaneous gesture. "Honored to have you as my friend, Simsinnet," he said.

The Mawag grinned. "Feathertop," he corrected, gesturing to the two feathers in his headband.

Stig held up his hands in agreement. "Feathertop," he repeated.

chapter twenty-nine

In addition to his daily cooking chores, Edvin was now kept busy preparing and preserving meat for the journey home. Stefan, Jesper and Ingvar had constructed a smoking chamber for him, consisting of a wood framework covered by dampened birch bark. At the base was a fire pit that he kept filled with charcoal. A water tray was placed above that and the upper three layers were wooden racks where he arranged the meat to smoke. The smell was delicious and he was hard put to stop his shipmates sampling the smoked meat as it came out of the chamber.

"If you keep 'sampling,' we'll have no food left for the journey," he told them angrily. They grinned unapologetically and tried to "sample" some more. Edvin had a long pair of wooden tongs and he found them amazingly useful for cracking knuckles. The sampling soon stopped.

Lydia, of course, spent most of her waking hours in the forest, tracking game and bringing it in to be smoked. As each day passed, and the birds and animals grew more wary of the silent figure slipping through the trees, she had to go farther afield. But the forest teemed with game and she continued to provide for their daily needs, as well as providing for the trip home.

Thorn, Hal and Stig went over the ship with a fine-toothed comb, looking for any sections of rigging that might have frayed or rotted, checking seams for leaks and, where they found them, re-caulking them.

The standing rigging—the heavy cables that supported the mast and yardarms—was in good condition. It had been well tarred before they left home and the thick black coating had protected it against rotting. The running rigging was a different matter. The halyards and sheets that controlled the twin sails were, by nature of their function, subjected to constant friction and strain as they were hauled in and out, running through wooden pulleys. The continual rubbing against pulleys and deadeyes chafed the rope, removing the protective tar coating and causing weak spots. These were scrupulously located and replaced.

As a final precaution, Hal had the ship towed round to the beach and ran her up onto the sand at the peak of high tide. As the water receded, *Heron* was left high and dry, canted over to one side on her keel. The crew scraped off the barnacles and weeds that had accumulated on the hull below the waterline, and caulked and sealed the seams of the planks to make them watertight.

Now that they had made contact with the local inhabitants and knew they had nothing to fear from them, Hal was content to beach the ship to carry out this work. Previously, the concept of having his precious *Heron* stranded and helpless on the beach when the forest might well conceal enemies had been an anathema to him.

In his spare time, Stig spent many hours in the company of Tecumsa. The two were often seen strolling hand in hand through the forest or along the beach. From time to time they took a canoe out onto the broad expanse of the bay. In addition, Stig often ate with her family, sitting round the cook fire outside their hut and laughing and joking with her parents. They had instantly accepted the tall blond stranger into their family circle, and treated him like an old friend. Tecumsa's younger brother, who was aged twelve, looked up to Stig both figuratively and literally. He hero-worshipped the muscular young man. For Stig, whose early life growing up in Hallasholm had been one of rejection and shame, this was a novel and thoroughly delightful experience. He warmed to the family atmosphere that surrounded and embraced him.

And of course, there was Tecumsa herself—beautiful, affectionate, independent and high spirited. She was the ideal companion and their relationship deepened rapidly.

"What's he going to do when it's time to leave?" Hal asked Thorn, as they watched the young couple sitting close together in the Herons' compound, laughing over something Tecumsa had said.

The grizzled old warrior said nothing. He studied the two happy young people and shook his head slowly.

Because now the concept of leaving, of going home, which had once seemed less than a remote possibility, was becoming more definite every day. As the stocks of provisions mounted and extra water jars were filled and stowed aboard ship, an air of expectation began to seize the Herons. Once the prevailing wind changed, it would be possible for them to set sail for their distant homeland. They had no doubt that they would reach it safely. Their faith in Hal's skill to find the way back across half the world was rock solid.

Orvik had sensed the expectation among his young countrymen. He had made himself useful as they prepared the ship, and taught Edvin the art of making pemmican—a mixture of dried meat, berries and fat that would keep for weeks and provide emergency rations if their smoked meat supplies were exhausted. As the Herons became more and more eager to be on their way, Orvik became increasingly silent, until one day he approached Hal.

"Would there be room for me on board?" he asked, nodding to the ship where it lay moored just off the beach. With no apparent threat in the vicinity, Hal had elected to move the ship permanently from concealment in the inlet. Having it close to hand made it easier to load food and water aboard.

"Well, of course!" Hal said immediately. "We'd be delighted to have you with us!"

Surprisingly, his statement seemed to cause the old Skandian further perplexity. He had grown used to his new home among the Mawags. He had made many friends among the tribe members, particularly Mohegas, and now the prospect of leaving them for good weighed down on him nearly as much as the prospect of being stranded among them permanently had done.

He wandered away from the beach, troubled in mind. When there had been no chance of returning to Skandia, he had longed for the familiar sights and sounds of his home country. But now he was loath to leave his friends among the Mawags. From his conversations with the crew of the *Heron,* he sensed that many things had changed back in Hallasholm. Wolfships no longer raided countries to the west and south. Instead, Erak had set up the Skandian fleet as a kind of international naval defense force, fighting pirates and escorting unarmed trading vessels from other countries through areas where they might be attacked by freebooters.

In addition, it seemed that many of the people he had known were gone—either dead or moved away. He had asked Thorn about several of his old acquaintances and the one-armed sea wolf had responded with a negative shake of the head. Of course, his closest friends, the members of his own brotherband, had all perished when *Wolf Foot* had gone down.

The more he thought about it, the more he began to think that perhaps his rightful place was here among the Mawagansett.

As the days passed, there was a good deal of visiting back and forth between the Mawagansett village and the camp on the beach. Sometimes the Herons were invited to the village as a group, sometimes as individual guests of Mawag families. Naturally, the Skandians reciprocated, inviting friends among the villagers to sample Edvin's excellent meals. Ulf and Wulf were constant visitors to the village, spending time with Millika and Pillika. The girls' friends and family were continually amused by the fact that the Skandian twins never realized how often the two girls switched identities on them. Strangely, the Mawagansett had no trouble telling Ulf and Wulf apart—something their shipmates had never managed to do.

• • • • •

One evening, Hal, Thorn and Lydia were sitting, waiting for Edvin to announce that the evening meal was ready to serve, when they were surprised by the appearance of Tecumsa in the camp. She was alone, which was remarkable in itself, as she was almost invariably accompanied by Stig. She noted Hal's inquiring look and smiled at him before he could ask the obvious question on his mind.

"Stig is eating with my family," she said. "I wanted a chance to talk to the three of you." She held up a covered tray she had been carrying. "I have brought food for us."

She glanced around and noted that the rest of the crew were watching. She nodded her head to a spot on the sand a few meters away. "Let us sit there," she said, "so we can talk in private."

Curious to know what she wanted to discuss, the three of them rose and moved down the beach a little, then sat expectantly by her. She set the tray on the ground between them and removed the cloth cover. Three covered clay bowls were revealed, along with four smaller wooden bowls and spoons. She lifted the lids on the clay bowls and they savored the delicious smells that wafted out. There was a savory rabbit stew, a bowl of mixed vegetables—corn, sweet potato and beans—and a thick soup of spiced fish and shellfish. She deftly apportioned the soup out among the platters and passed them around.

Hal took a spoonful, snatching in a breath to cool it. He smiled at her.

"Delicious," he said and she nodded in acknowledgment of his reaction.

"My mother made it," she said. Then she smiled. "She's a better cook than me."

"I can see why Stig spends so much time at your family's hut," Thorn said, rapidly spooning the soup into his mouth and spraying droplets around as he spoke.

Lydia regarded him with a raised eyebrow. "Try to get some of it down your throat," she said archly, and he grinned at her, totally unabashed, wiping his mouth with the back of his hand.

Hal set down his empty soup bowl and Tecumsa gestured for him to help himself to the other food. Seeing Lydia's bowl was empty as well, he reached across for it and spooned a mix of the rabbit stew and vegetables into it before handing it back and serving himself.

Tecumsa watched with interest. "Why do you do that?" she asked.

Hal shrugged. "My mam would wallop me if I didn't serve a lady before myself," he explained.

Tecumsa nodded, storing that information away. "In our tribe, all are equal," she said.

Thorn grinned at her. "We're all equal too," he said, reaching for the rabbit stew. "It's just that Lydia is more equal than the rest of us."

Lydia rolled her eyes and said nothing.

Hal tasted the rabbit, which was even better than the fish soup. Then he set the bowl down and regarded the beautiful young Mawagansett. "So, Tecumsa, what's this all about?"

She smiled at him innocently. "Don't you like my food?" she asked. There was a teasing note in her voice and he couldn't help smiling at it.

"The food is excellent. But I'm thinking you didn't come here simply to feed us."

He also couldn't help noticing, not for the first time, how very beautiful she was. Her skin was olive and faultless, and her eyes were the deepest brown, with a hint of mischief in them.

"You are Stig's friends. I want to get to know you better. I want you to be my friends as well."

Thorn burped cheerfully. "Keep bringing us meals like this and that won't be a problem," he said, reaching for the rabbit stew.

Tecumsa smiled at him, then became serious. "I want to know about this brotherband of yours," she said, addressing the question to Hal. "These are a lot of brothers." She gestured toward the rest of the crew, sitting round Edvin's cook fire.

"We're not real brothers," Hal said. "Although in a lot of ways we're closer than real brothers, I suppose. We joined together to train and sail and fight together. We trust one another. We depend on one another. And we know that no member of the brotherband would ever let the others down."

"Stig told me you formed this band," she said.

Hal nodded slowly, thinking back to the day that now seemed so long ago.

"Yes," he said. "We were all people who were rejected by the other brotherbands forming that day. Nobody else wanted us, so I guess we just decided we wanted one another. That's probably why our bond is so strong."

"And they went on to become the champion brotherband of that year," Thorn said, his pride in his young friend's achievements obvious. Hal made a dismissive gesture.

Tecumsa glanced at Lydia, who was watching Hal closely. "But you? You're hardly a brother?" she asked with a smile.

Lydia smiled in her turn. "I joined later," she said. "I guess I'm a sister to the brotherband—sort of an honorary member."

"There's nothing honorary about it," Hal retorted quickly. "You're as much a member as anyone else."

Lydia nodded her head, taking the comment as a compliment of the highest order. "Thank you," she said simply.

Tecumsa turned her attention now to Thorn. "You're not one of the brotherband, are you?"

Lydia laughed. "In a way, he's the biggest reject of them all," she said.

Thorn favored her with an amused look. Then he turned to Tecumsa.

"For once, Lydia is right," he said. "I had given up on myself and was lying out in the snow hoping to die when Hal's mother took pity on me and saved me."

Tecumsa tilted her head to one side, looking curiously at him. "How did she do that?"

He grinned widely. "She had Hal throw a bucket of water over me," he said.

Tecumsa made a small moue of surprise. "An unusual way to solve the problem," she said, obviously amused.

Thorn nodded agreement. "She's an unusual woman."

"When you say you had given up on yourself, what do you mean?" she asked.

Thorn considered his answer for a second or two, then spoke. "I felt sorry for myself. I felt the world had done me a great injustice."

"Because of your poor hand," she said simply, reaching out and gently resting her fingers on the wood of his hook.

Hal and Lydia froze, anxious to see how Thorn would respond. People usually didn't mention his missing hand. Somehow, they sensed it was not a subject for discussion. But there was no sense of idle curiosity in Tecumsa's words, only kindness and sympathy. And her dark eyes showed a level of compassion and awareness that precluded Thorn's taking offense. He glanced down at her slim fingers on the wooden hook, polished smooth but showing the scars of many months of use and hard wear.

To Hal's and Lydia's great relief, he smiled at the young woman. "Yes. Because of my hand."

"You must have been terribly saddened," she said. "Stig says you were a great warrior."

Before Thorn could reply, Hal answered. "He still is."

Tecumsa smiled at him. "Stig says that too." Then she turned back to Thorn. "So what is your role with this brotherband?"

"Oh, I train them. I discipline them. I kick their backsides when they're lazy and yell at them when they're stupid," he said, then added, "At times I do a lot of kicking and yelling, believe me."

She looked deep into his eyes. "And yet I think you're not as mean and bad tempered as you pretend to be," she said.

Thorn colored slightly and said nothing.

Lydia stepped into the silence. "Oh, he is, believe me. He's quite horrible at times."

Tecumsa's dark eyes switched to hold Lydia's gaze. "And I sense that you have a great affection for him, and he for you," she said.

Now it was Lydia's turn to redden as she realized that the

Mawag girl had seen through their constant bickering and teasing, and seen it for what it was—an expression of deep fondness.

"Well, maybe he's not all *that* bad," she said, looking away from those grave, steady eyes that were locked on to her own.

Hal laughed quietly. "I'm glad someone has finally seen through you two frauds," he said.

They continued talking in this way for another hour, answering Tecumsa's questions about the brotherband, how they worked together, the ship and how Hal could navigate with such accuracy from one point to another. Most of the latter was described by Thorn and it became apparent to the young woman that the old sea wolf held the boy in the deepest respect and admiration. They discussed Stig, and his amazing skill in battle, and how he and Hal had become friends. She was aware of the story of how Hal had saved Stig from drowning, but she wanted to hear him tell it, and was impressed by his self-deprecating manner. Many Mawagansett young men would have been boastful about such an achievement, she knew.

At length, the evening drew to an end, by which time they had all been captivated by Tecumsa's beauty, sensitivity and natural, unaffected warmth. If she had wanted them to become her friends as she had stated, she had succeeded beyond all reasonable expectation. They accompanied her back to the track through the trees that led to the Mawagansett village and made their farewells there.

"I'll walk you back to the village," Hal said impulsively, but she smiled and shook her head.

"I'll be quite safe. Stig is waiting at the bend in the track there."

And, looking up, they could see his tall form leaning against a tree. She hurried to him and they joined hands and disappeared into the darkness.

"What a remarkable girl," Thorn said softly. Then he smiled. "If I were a few years younger . . ."

"You'd still be old enough to be her father," Lydia finished the statement for him.

chapter thirty

It was some days after the meeting with Tecumsa when Hal broached the subject of returning home with Stig. It was early evening and the first mate had returned from a fishing trip with Simsinnet, laden with fish for Edvin's smoking chamber. As the Mawag warrior bade them a cheerful good night and headed for the trail through the forest, Hal watched his friend deftly cleaning the fish, then splitting them so they could be laid on the smoking racks.

"He seems to be a nice enough type," he said, gesturing toward the departing Mawag, who was bidding some of the other Herons good night.

Stig nodded. "Amazing how well you can get on with someone when you start out fighting them," he said. "We have a lot in common, as it turns out."

"I suppose when we go home, he'll start courting Tecumsa again," Hal said, trying to sound casual about it.

Stig looked up quickly, a frown creasing his forehead, and said nothing.

"I mean, it's not as if you're planning on marrying her or anything, is it?" Hal continued.

Once more, Stig didn't reply. For Hal, the silence was unbearable. It seemed to indicate that there was something important going on—something for which he was unprepared. When Stig finally spoke, it turned out he was right.

"I'm not sure I'll be going home with you," Stig said.

Hal recoiled in horror. Of all the replies he'd expected, this one had never occurred to him.

"Not coming with us?" he exclaimed. "But you have to! We're your brotherband—your family. You were the first one I picked! You're my best friend."

Stig refused to meet his eye, shaking his head stubbornly. "Well, things change, you know?"

Hal was almost hysterical in his reply. "No! I don't know! How do things change? You're one of us. You're a Heron. That doesn't change!"

"But I love Tecumsa," Stig said in a low voice. It was the first time he had admitted the fact, even to himself.

Hal made a desperate, helpless gesture. "Then bring her with us! She can come back to Hallasholm!"

But Stig was already shaking his head. "She wouldn't be happy there. Everything would be so strange for her."

"Everything here is so strange for you," Hal said, but Stig smiled sadly at him.

"Not really. I have friends here. There's Simsinnet and his circle, and Tecumsa's family has accepted me. I know I'll be happy here."

Hal felt tears stinging the back of his eyes at the thought of losing Stig—big, powerful, dependable Stig. He was the mainstay of the crew, Hal's strong right hand, always there when Hal needed support.

"But . . . ," he began. Then he couldn't think of anything further to say.

Stig reached across and gripped his shoulder, squeezing it firmly. "It'll be all right, Hal," he said. "It's not the end of the world. You'll find someone to take my place. Hallasholm is full of young men who'd jump at the chance to become a Heron."

"I don't want someone to take your place. I want you, Stig! Please say you'll reconsider." He was aghast at the thought of Stig's staying behind. It was as if the fabric of his world were being torn apart.

"Things change, Hal. People change. The situation changes. It's been a wonderful few years with you and the rest of the brotherband. But it's time for me to move on to the next phase of my life. And that's here with Tecumsa."

"What about your mam? She'll be devastated!" Hal said, desperate to change his mind.

Stig's face saddened. "Yes. I wish she could meet Tecumsa. But she'll understand." He smiled sadly. "You can explain it to her."

Then he rose and walked quietly away, leaving his friend devastated.

• • • • •

Hal slept badly that night, tossing and turning as he thought over what Stig had said. He remembered something his mother had said to him years before, when he had promised to always be beside her.

"You'll move on," she said. "Young men don't just marry their wives, they marry their families as well. It's the way of the world. Mothers know it and expect it."

He realized she was right. He resolved, however, to try to convince Stig to bring Tecumsa home with them. Lydia could help. She'd left her homeland and resettled in Skandia. She could tell Tecumsa what a good place it was to live.

But even as he had the thought, he was assailed by doubts. Lydia hadn't left any family behind in her hometown. And she had potentially blotted her copybook with the community leaders by liberating a batch of diamonds to pay the Herons for their services. She hadn't bothered to get permission for that and it could still be held against her. Tecumsa would be leaving her father, mother and brother behind—and an extended family of uncles, aunts and cousins. It wasn't the same at all.

"But we'd all help her fit in," he said. He wasn't aware that he had spoken the thought aloud until Stefan, on the other side of the tent, called softly to him.

"Are you all right, Hal?"

"Yes. Sorry, Stefan. Go to sleep."

He heard the other boy pull his blankets up and roll over. He tried to do the same but his mind kept churning. An hour before dawn, he finally dropped off, but he continued to mutter and toss fitfully in his sleep as he dreamed of sailing away from this foreign land, leaving Stig waving farewell on the beach.

Something woke him just after dawn. He sensed something new and he sat up, his head turned to one side to listen. Then he tossed the blankets back and rolled out of bed, slipping out of the sleeping tent and walking toward the palisade. Ulf was on sentry duty and he looked at his skirl curiously. Hal hadn't told the rest of the crew about Stig's shattering revelation, but most of them knew something was amiss with their leader.

"You all right, Hal?" he said, unconsciously repeating Stefan's earlier question.

Hal didn't answer. He sniffed the early morning air. "Did you hear something?" he asked.

Ulf shook his head, yawning. "No. But I'd like to hear Wulf coming to relieve me," he said. "Why do you ask?"

Hal walked a few paces away from Ulf, head raised, listening, sensing. Something was different, he thought. Then it came to him. Since they'd been here, the northeasterly wind had driven the waves through the narrow headland into the bay, sending them rolling onto the beach. The gentle rush of waves breaking had formed a constant background sound to their world. And the trees behind them had stirred and rustled with the wind, sounding like more waves breaking.

Now the waves were stilled and trees were silent.

The wind had shifted to the southwest.

chapter thirty-one

As the rest of the brotherband awoke, they all became aware of the changed conditions. Even Lydia, who was not as attuned to the variations in wind and weather as the rest of the crew, noticed something was different.

"The wind has backed," Ingvar told her. "We can go home."

There was a general air of elation in the camp as the Herons realized that the time was fast approaching when they could sail for Hallasholm. Only Stig appeared somewhat downcast, as the prospect of saying good-bye to his friends loomed ever closer. He walked off by himself, head down and shoulders hunched. Hal watched him go, his own heart heavy.

Thorn sensed there was something amiss between the two friends. He took Hal by the elbow and led him a little way down the beach, to a spot where they could speak privately.

"All right. Out with it. What's the trouble between you and Stig?" he asked. He expected to hear that they had quarreled over some minor matter but Hal's answer left him dumbfounded.

"He's planning to stay behind when we go," the skirl told him miserably.

"Stay behind? Where? Here? What are you talking about?"

"He says he's in love with Tecumsa," Hal told him.

Thorn stroked his beard thoughtfully at the words. He remembered a time when his friendship with Mikkel, Hal's father, had been disrupted by the advent of a beautiful young slave named Karina. The two friends had got through the disruption, but for a time it had been touch and go, and Thorn had thought their friendship might not survive.

"Oh . . . ," he said now, understanding the anguish on Hal's face and Stig's downcast appearance as he walked off down the beach. "That makes things difficult. Is he sure he wants to do this?"

Hal shrugged helplessly. "He seems to be. He's obviously thought it through. He says he has a place here with her and her family. Says he can be happy here."

"I'm sure he can. She's the sort of girl who would make any man happy," Thorn said.

"I wish she'd never been born!" Hal exclaimed viciously, but Thorn laid a restraining hand on his shoulder.

"I felt that way once," he said, and when Hal looked at him curiously, he added, "About your mother."

"My mam?" Hal said, surprised. "Why would you hate her?"

Thorn didn't answer immediately. Instead, he asked a question of his own. "For a start, you don't hate Tecumsa, do you? Not really?"

Hal hesitated, about to argue, then lowered his eyes. "No. She's a terrific girl. And I'm sure she'll make Stig very happy."

"That's what I realized about your mother when Mikkel wanted to marry her. I felt I was being cut out of his life."

"But you weren't, were you? They were still around and you could still see my father whenever you wanted to. This is different. Once we leave, I'll never see Stig again."

"You could always come back," Thorn suggested.

Hal shook his head. "No. I'm not keeping any sailing notes on how to get here." He saw Thorn's surprised look. It would have been standard practice for Hal to keep sailing records—courses, currents, wind conditions—on the way home so that the voyage could be retraced. Hal explained, "If we came back, others would follow—more and more of them. I don't think the Mawagansett want an influx of strangers from the other side of the world barging in on their lives, changing their customs, bringing new ways with them.

"It's been all right with just ten of us, but think how it would be if a hundred, or two hundred Skandians came here. The place would change, and not necessarily for the better. The Mawagansett have been good to us and it wouldn't be fair if their kindness ruined their world."

Thorn regarded him with admiration. "I've always said you're a thinker," he said. "That's a very wise attitude for someone of your age."

Hal essayed a sad smile. "Yeah, well, who knows? Maybe Stig will change his mind when the crunch comes."

"Maybe," Thorn agreed. But he didn't sound convinced. Tecumsa was not a girl you changed your mind about, he thought, and he sensed that Hal felt the same way.

They walked side by side back to the campsite, where Edvin was serving breakfast. They each took a slab of toasted corn-flour bread and a few slices of smoked river trout. They had finally run out of coffee, but the pot was filled with a rich herbal tea. It was a hot and comforting drink and they took a mug each and sat on the ground, their backs against a log, to eat.

Lydia joined them, looking around curiously. "Where's Stig?" she asked. Then, answering her own question, she said, "Probably off with Tecumsa." She liked the Mawagansett girl. She felt a proprietorial interest in both Stig and Hal. They were like brothers to her, and initially she had viewed Stig's growing attachment to Tecumsa with some reservations. But the more she saw of Tecumsa, the more she liked her, for her openness, her honesty and her cheerful attitude to life. She did wonder what would happen between the two of them now that the time had come for the *Heron* to leave. But it was only idle speculation. At heart, she assumed Stig would say farewell to the young woman. It would be sad, but it would be bearable. She shrugged away the thought. We'll cheer him up when the time comes, she thought. That's what friends do for each other.

Neither Hal nor Thorn replied to her, so she settled down to eat her breakfast.

Edvin, who had now served breakfast to all the crew who were gathered around the cook fire, filled a plate of his own and moved to join Hal, Thorn and Lydia by their log.

"When do you plan to get away?" he said to Hal.

The skirl looked up at the ridge behind them, where the tops of the trees were bending to the south wind.

"No rush," he said. "You've got plenty of time to get the ship fully provisioned."

Edvin considered the statement. "We're pretty well stocked," he said. "I'd like to get in a few more jars of water and some fresh vegetables, and then we'll be ready."

They had filled the water casks already—the leaking one had been repaired—and the Mawagansett had provided them with large clay jars to hold extra water. There was still room for a few more and Hal wanted to carry as much water as possible with them.

"We'll give it a few days," he told Edvin. "I want to be sure this change isn't temporary."

Edvin nodded agreement. That made sense, he thought. They wouldn't want to set sail and then find the wind back in the northeast, blowing them away from their destination.

They finished their meal without further discussion. Not for the first time, Hal reflected on how lucky they'd been to have Edvin in the crew. No matter where they were, or what supplies were available, he seemed capable of turning out appetizing, nourishing meals whenever asked.

"I suppose he'll tell me he wants to stay here and open a restaurant with the Mawag ladies," he said gloomily to himself. He placed his dirty plate and mug on a wooden rack to be washed. Stefan and Ingvar were detailed for kitchen duties. One of the perks of being skirl was that he didn't have to take his turn at menial camp chores. Of course, this was balanced by the fact that, in the event of an emergency, he could find himself at the tiller for eight to ten hours at a stretch.

He walked down to the palisade and studied the bay. The wind was holding steady from the south. The small rollers were no longer being pushed in between the headlands. Looking down the beach, he saw Stig slowly returning to the camp, walking in the firm wet sand by the water's edge, head down and shoulders hunched.

"I know how you feel," he said softly. Then a cheerful voice interrupted his gloomy thoughts.

"Good morning, Hal."

He looked up, a little startled. Simsinnet was standing just outside the palisade, by the entry ladder. These days, they didn't bother to raise the outer ladder at night, but Simsinnet still thought it would be a breach of protocol to enter the stockade uninvited.

"Good morning, Simsinnet," Hal said, and gestured for him to enter. "Come on in."

But the young Mawag shook his head. "Mohegas has asked if you will come to the village," he said. "You and Thorn and Stig."

Hal cocked his head curiously. It was unusual for the elder to request that all three of them come to the village. He reflected that it might have something to do with the change in wind direction.

"Is there some problem?" he asked.

Simsinnet shrugged. "He didn't say. But a messenger came in last night from the north. That might be what he wants to discuss."

Hal turned and caught Thorn's eye. The old sea wolf had noted Simsinnet's arrival and was watching with interest. Hal beckoned to him and pointed to the trail leading to the village. Thorn made a gesture of understanding and began to walk down the sand to join them. Hal mounted the inner ladder and stood poised at the top. Stig was still several hundred meters away. Hal put his fingers in his mouth and emitted a piercing whistle.

Simsinnet grinned. "I wish I could make that noise."

Stig, hearing the signal, looked up and Hal beckoned him urgently. The tall first mate increased his pace, jogging through the sand to the camp.

"What's going on?" Thorn asked.

"Mohegas wants a meeting," Hal said.

Thorn nodded. "Probably wants to ask when we'll be leaving."

Hal shrugged. "That's what I thought. But Simsinnet seems to think it's about a messenger who arrived last night."

They climbed the ladders and descended to the beach outside the palisade, waiting for Stig to join them. Simsinnet greeted him cheerfully and Stig nodded in reply. He met Hal's gaze with an inquiring look of his own.

"Mohegas wants to talk to us," Hal explained. Then Simsinnet led the three Skandians toward the path that wound through the forest to the Mawagansett village.

The sun hadn't risen high enough yet to penetrate far into the forest and they walked through the dark green shadows in silence. Small birds and animals scampered out of their way and the undergrowth around them was alive with the sound of panicked rustling.

At last, they emerged from the shadows into the clearing where the Mawagansett huts were arranged in neat rows. Those tribespeople who were up and about greeted them as they headed for

Mohegas's hut, but Hal sensed an air of tension about them. They seemed on edge and the usual smiles were absent.

"Something's wrong," he said quietly to his two friends.

Mohegas emerged from his hut as they approached, doubtless informed of their presence by one of his two guards. He stooped to pass under the low doorway and stood in the early morning sun waiting for them. As they reached the hut, he greeted them, then beckoned them inside.

It was warm and smoky in the hut. The fireplace at one end had a smoke hole in the roof above it, but not all the smoke managed to escape. They followed Mohegas to the circle by the fireplace and sat cross-legged, while his wife, Pacahan, served them with hot mugs of herbal tea.

Stig and Thorn deferred to Hal, waiting for him to open the conversation. The young Skandian came straight to the point.

"What's up, Mohegas?" he asked.

Mohegas took a deep breath, as if stating the problem were somehow going to make it more real.

"The Ghostfaces are raiding again," he said. "They're already in a village five days to the north of here, and they're on their way south."

PART FOUR

THE GHOSTFACES

chapter thirty-two

Both Hal and Stig reacted with surprise, the latter muttering a curse. Of course, thought Hal, his friend was committed to the Mawagansett people now and he felt the threat of the Ghost tribe's approach keenly.

Thorn remained unperturbed, as ever. He went straight to the practical question that the problem raised.

"What do you plan to do?" he asked.

While Mohegas shrugged, Stig answered impulsively.

"We'll fight!" he declared. His features were flushed with anger at the thought of these white-painted marauders threatening his adopted home.

Mohegas raised an eyebrow. "There are over a hundred of them," he said. "All warriors. We can raise barely forty. And our young men are trained more for hunting and fishing than warfare."

"You have fifty if you count us," Stig replied. "And we are trained to fight. Plus we have better weapons than the Ghosts'. That'd go a long way toward balancing the numbers."

The Mawagansett had spears and arrows and clubs. But they had no iron. Their spearheads and arrowheads were made from stone or flint. Their clubs were hardwood or stone. Presumably, the Ghosts' weapons were made from similar materials. The Herons' axes and swords would be far more effective in a fight. Plus, as Stig said, the crew were trained to fight, and to fight as a unit. That would do a lot to redress the inequality in numbers. The tribal elder looked inquiringly at Hal and Thorn, who remained expressionless. Stig was overlooking one vital fact, and, after a few seconds, Mohegas voiced it.

"The wind is from the south," he said. "You can leave anytime. This is not your fight."

Stig reacted angrily. "It's our fight all right! You've been kind to us. You've welcomed us into your country. We're not going to turn and run now that you're facing trouble!" He appealed to Hal. "We're not, are we? We're not going to desert these people. They're our friends!"

Hal shook his head. "No. We're not running. If the Mawags need help, we'll give it."

Stig subsided, relieved. He had simply assumed that because he was willing to stay and fight, his shipmates would support him. Mohegas's statement had suddenly made him realize that he might well be on his own.

"Will you fight?" Thorn said, addressing the gray-haired Mawag.

Mohegas hesitated, looking away from them, glancing round the neat, warm little hut. This was his home. He was happy here and the thought of leaving it for the Ghostfaces to burn and pillage left a sour taste in his mouth.

"In the past," he temporized, "we've always hidden in the forest when they came."

"And watched them destroy your homes," Thorn said evenly. "I can't believe you enjoy that."

Mohegas's brows came together in a dark line. "I hate it," he said. His voice was low, but the venom in it was all too obvious.

"Well, perhaps this might be the time to do something about it," Thorn said. "I've trained my boys to fight and they're good at it. I'd say that ten of us are a match for any thirty white-faced, bare-bummed tribesmen. Presumably they don't know we're here, so we'd have the advantage of surprise. And if we give them a good bloody nose this time, they might think twice about raiding here again."

Mohegas looked thoughtful. "Perhaps if we could borrow your special weapon," he said thoughtfully. "The one you call the Maggler?"

"Mangler," Hal corrected him. He considered the idea. "It would certainly give them a nasty shock. But whether it would be enough to turn the tide, I'm not sure. Maybe . . ." He hesitated. A thought was taking shape in his mind. It wasn't fully formed yet, just the beginning of an idea. Thorn and Stig both looked expectantly at him. They recognized the distracted, slightly distant expression on his face.

"What is it?" Thorn asked, but Hal waved the question aside.

He needed a few more moments to think. Thorn made a cautionary gesture to Mohegas, and the Mawag leader nodded. The three of them sat watching Hal for several minutes as he sat, head bowed, mind racing. Then he finally looked up. The question he asked took them all by surprise. As ever in such situations, his mind had raced off at a tangent.

"Your bows," he asked Mohegas. "What wood do you use for them?"

The Mawag's eyebrows shot up. He hadn't been expecting that question. "It's from a local tree, but I'm not sure what you would call it. It's tough and springy and we use hide to reinforce it."

Hal nodded thoughtfully. He'd seen the local bows. They were short and thick-limbed. The wood used was powerful and tough and the bows spat out arrows with surprising speed and power for their size.

"Could you make bigger ones?" he asked. "Perhaps ones that were this long?" He spread out his arms, indicating a length from fingertip to fingertip. "And a lot thicker? Maybe twice as thick as your normal bows?"

Mohegas considered. "I don't see why not," he said. "We'd simply have to use thicker branches. But nobody could draw a bow that size. The wood would be too stiff," he pointed out.

Hal waved the objection aside. "Never mind that," he said. "I can sort out a way to draw them." He turned to Thorn with a new question. "Thorn, is the village a reasonable defensive site?"

Thorn screwed up his lip thoughtfully. "Not as it is," he said. "But if we built a palisade like the one at our camp, we could make it a tough nut to crack. We could anchor each end at the stream that runs behind the village, and set stakes in the shallows to discourage attackers from going around the ends."

"Very well, here's the idea. We build a palisade round the village." Hal looked round and saw a large piece of bark in the pile of firewood and kindling. He took it and raked a piece of charcoal out of the edge of the fire, using it to sketch on the bark.

"We can use the materials from our camp to do it," he said. "I don't want the Ghosts to know we've been here when they arrive." He looked at Mohegas. "While that's happening, we get your men to make maybe ten big crossbows, like the Mangler. I'll give them a plan. They only need to be basic. We don't need the training and elevating gears and we can set them on simple wooden tripods. Can your men do that?"

He sketched a rough diagram of a simplified Mangler set on a wooden stand.

Mohegas studied it for a few seconds. "I don't see why not."

Then Hal marked two lines on the bark, one to either side of the defensive half circle he had drawn, and facing in toward the palisade.

"We place them in the forest, out of sight, and off to either side, so they can provide a cross barrage on the Ghosts when they attack the palisade."

Stig whistled in admiration. "That *would* give them a nasty surprise," he said. "Ten big crossbows hitting them from either side, and from behind. We could cut them to pieces."

"Shaping ten big bows in a few days might be difficult," Mohegas warned. "The wood is tough to work and we have only flint knives."

Again, Hal waved the objection aside. "I've got iron tools," he said. "Adzes and drills and saws and planes and shaping knives. That'll speed things up."

"You'll need to design a new trigger mechanism," Thorn pointed out. "We don't have time to build one like you have on the Mangler."

The Mangler's trigger was an arrangement of carefully shaped circular cogs made from thin wood and set in a hollowed-out part of the crossbow's body. It required a degree of fine detail work and adjustment that would be nigh impossible on ten bows in the time they had left.

Hal nodded. "I've got an idea there too," he said. Already, his fertile mind could see a simplified trigger mechanism to hold the bowstring in place, then release it. "Once the first bow is completed, select ten or twelve shooters and have them practice with it."

Mohegas nodded gravely. He eyed the young foreigner with new respect. He had been surprised that one so young could be in command of his crew, particularly the older, bearded man with one hand. Now that he saw how quickly Hal's mind worked, and how he could prioritize actions, he realized that he was a remarkable young man indeed.

"I'll have Ulf and Wulf help your men with the bow building," Hal continued. "They're both handy with tools and they've each got a good natural eye for line and form."

"Wouldn't it be better for you to help out?" Stig asked. "You're the best craftsman we have, after all."

Hal nodded. "That's true. But I'm going to be otherwise engaged," he said. Before Thorn could ask the obvious question that sprang to his mind, Hal turned back to Mohegas.

"Now, see if I've got this right. When these Ghosts have attacked in the past, they've come downriver in canoes?"

Mohegas nodded confirmation and Hal continued. "They come out into the bay and cross to land at the beach—pretty much where we have our camp—then strike inland?"

Again, Mohegas indicated that this was correct.

Hal tapped his front teeth with the piece of charcoal, thoughtlessly smearing his lips and teeth with black. Thorn smiled. Sooner or later, he'd notice, he thought, and then wonder how it had happened.

"Here's what I'm thinking," Hal said. "We'll moor the *Heron* out of sight just inside the northern headland. When the Ghosts' canoes are out on the bay, I'll take Ulf, Wulf and Edvin with me and create a little havoc among them. The ones that escape will land and head for the village, where you, Thorn, and you, Stig, will be waiting for them with the rest of our lads. And Lydia, of course."

"You're not taking Ingvar? How will you load the Mangler?" Thorn asked.

Hal shrugged. "I won't need it. I'll ram the canoes and run them down, so long as I have a little wind to play with."

"You'll be in trouble if any of the Ghosts get aboard while you're doing this," Stig pointed out.

Hal smiled. "That's why I'm also taking Kloof," he said. That seemed to answer Stig's query.

"Coming back to my previous point," Thorn said, "why won't you be able to help the Mawags build the extra crossbows?"

"I thought the three of us—Stig, you and I—might take a canoe upriver to get a look at these Ghostfaces," Hal said. "And maybe slow them down a little."

A wolfish smile came over Thorn's face at the thought of taking the fight to the enemy. He always preferred to do that, instead of fighting a purely defensive battle. He idly stroked the wooden hook on his right arm, imagining the extra weight of the huge club that he wore there when he attacked an enemy force.

"That sounds just perfect," he said.

chapter thirty-three

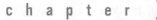

Simsinnet came with them as a guide. They took one of the canoes from the row drawn up on the sand behind the village and paddled down the stream to the bay. The canoe was light and responsive and, with four of them paddling, it fairly flew across the bay to the mouth of the river that led north, into the interior.

Hal had left the twins with a quickly drawn plan for the proposed crossbows and told them to use any of his tools they needed. He knew they would take care of them. Work on the bows was well under way when the four departed. The designs were simple and the bows would be finished quickly. Only the trigger mechanisms required anything resembling fine work. He indicated that the body of each bow should have two holes drilled through it, at the point where the bowstring would be held. A block of hardwood, with two wooden pins protruding from it, would fit against the underside of the bow, with the pins projecting up through the two holes. These pins would restrain the bowstring once it was drawn.

The block would be held in place by a piece of pliable hide, and a flattened piece of wood would be inserted between it and the bow to act as a lever. This was placed over a wooden piece that would form a fulcrum. When the longer end of the lever was depressed, the shorter end would pull the block down, so that the pins released the bowstring on the top of the bow. The pliable leather strap would then retract, pulling the block and the two pins back up to the loading position again. It was a simple but efficient design, and once more, Mohegas regarded the young Skandian with admiration.

Thorn had seen the look and grinned at the older Mawag. "It's what he does," he said.

Mohegas shook his head. "Remarkable."

Hal had picked the time when the tide began to flood to make their departure. The river was tidal for the first five kilometers, with the incoming tide creating a bore, or small wave, which ran upriver, riding over the top of the prevailing downstream current. They rode the flooding tide, flying past the land on either side, until the bore died away. Then they bent their backs to the paddles and drove the canoe deeper inland, against the natural flow.

The messenger who had brought word of the Ghostfaces' approach had said they were five days away. But in the intervening time, they had probably moved closer.

"How many villages are there between the Ghostfaces and the bay?" Thorn asked Simsinnet.

"They were a day away from the Pallikan village when the messenger left. After that, there is only the village of the Limigina people. That's another day or so closer to us."

Thorn chewed reflectively on his mustache as he wielded his paddle. Simsinnet admired the man's dexterity, holding one end of the paddle in his wooden hook and driving the blade through the water with his uninjured left hand and arm.

"Mind you," the young Mawag added, "we're probably traveling a lot faster than they are."

That made sense. Their canoe was lightly laden, with all four of them paddling. The Ghostfaces would have heavier-laden canoes, filled with supplies and weapons and booty. And it would take longer to muster a group of over a hundred men each day and get them moving downriver. There'd be delays—whether it was equipment lost or left behind, or the inevitable sluggards among the group who were never ready on time. Moving a large body of men was a ponderous business.

Another thought struck Simsinnet. "On top of that, they often stay in a village for several days to feast and celebrate their victory."

"Some victory," Stig grunted. "A hundred men against twenty or so." The other villages on the river were smaller than the Mawag encampment, mustering only fifty or so inhabitants at the most.

Thorn nodded. "We'll need to move faster than them when we start back downstream," he said.

Hal turned to look at his friend. Thorn was in the rearmost seat of the canoe.

"What do you have in mind when we do see them?" he asked.

The old sea wolf shrugged. "Dunno yet. I'll wait to see the situation. But we need to find a way to slow them down. That'll give the Mawags a chance to get the new bows made, and the palisade in place."

They paddled until long after dark, then pulled quietly into the bank to camp for the night.

"Maybe we should keep moving?" Stig said. "I can keep paddling for hours yet." But Thorn quashed the idea.

"We don't know what we're getting into," he said. "We could find ourselves in a fight when we run into the Ghosts and we don't want to be exhausted from paddling if we do. Besides, if we rest for a few hours, we'll move all the faster tomorrow."

They had a quick meal of smoked venison and cold river water, then rolled into their blankets. Thorn set a watch. It would be foolish not to with an enemy somewhere nearby.

"Since you're still fresh as a daisy," he told Stig, "you can keep the first watch. Give me a shake when the moon is overhead."

The moon was a quarter way through its traverse across the heavens, sending a pale, cold light down onto the surface of the river. Stig glanced up to the overhead point Thorn had indicated and nodded. That would give the one-armed warrior three hours' sleep. He wrapped his blanket round his shoulders. It was chilly without the exertion of paddling to keep the blood flowing. He found a convenient flat rock to sit on, resisting the urge to lean his back against one of the many fallen trees that lined the riverbank. If he got too comfortable, he might well fall asleep—in spite of his assertion that he could keep paddling through the night. As his companions' breathing became deep and regular, he marveled at

Thorn's instinctive ability to match his breathing to the existing conditions. In their campsite, or on board ship, when there was no risk of impending danger, Thorn would snore like a bull walrus with a broken nose. But here, with the possibility that enemies might be nearby, he regulated his breathing to an almost-inaudible sigh.

Gradually, the natural noises of the forest, which had stilled when the four men had pulled the canoe ashore, began to reassert themselves. He heard small animals rustling the branches and leaves of the undergrowth and once, he heard a sudden commotion at the base of a tree five meters away. His hair stood on end and his hand tightened around the haft of the ax cradled across his knees. Then he heard the self-satisfied murmur of a hunting owl and, a few minutes later, its triumphant hoot.

There'd been no sound of its swift passage through the air as it swooped on its prey. The owl's wing feathers were soft and pliable and created almost no noise in passing. The only sound had been the rustling in the undergrowth as its powerful talons had settled on the mouse, or vole or squirrel, that was now being borne away to feed the raptor's young. Stig smiled. He liked owls. They were efficient hunters and killers.

I'll wager Lydia admires them, he thought to himself, and smiled once more at the comparison between the girl hunter and an owl.

He glanced up and saw, to his surprise, that the moon had almost reached the position Thorn had indicated. The light was overhead now, and unimpeded by the trees. It flooded the river and the cleared space on the riverbank with silver luminescence. The shadows under the trees seemed all the more impenetrable as a result.

He took one last look around to make sure it was all clear. He had been scanning the surrounding terrain constantly, without even thinking about it, throughout the passing hours. He rose to his feet, pulling the blanket tighter around himself, and walked softly to where Thorn lay, kneeling beside him to wake him.

"Stig?" the sea wolf said, and Stig shook his head in admiration. Thorn had a sixth sense, even when he was sleeping, that told him when someone approached.

"Your watch," Stig told him and the shaggy-haired warrior tossed his blanket aside, instantly awake and ready.

"Get some sleep, Stig," he said, and rose to his feet.

As Stig rolled into his blanket and lay down, he was aware of Thorn moving silently around the clearing where they were camped, checking the perimeter for any sign of danger. How does he move so silently? Stig thought. Thorn was big and bulky and well muscled. Yet he moved as light-footed as a haymaking festival dancer. He was still wondering about it when he fell asleep.

Simsinnet had the last watch and he woke them at first light. They had a quick breakfast—smoked meat and cold water once more.

"Coffee would be nice," Stig said.

"No fire," Thorn said.

Stig gave him a wan smile. "No coffee either," he said, then added, "That'll be one thing I'll miss."

"And not my smiling face in the morning?" Thorn inquired.

Stig allowed his smile to widen. "Definitely not that."

They were soon back on the river, paddling smoothly northward. They moved a little more slowly on the second day, without the impetus of the tidal bore behind them. But the banks still glided past them with impressive speed.

Simsinnet kept them close to the eastern bank now. There was a twofold reason for this. Close to the bank, they were out of the main river current that would slow their upriver progress. And if danger suddenly threatened, they could slip quickly into the concealment of the reeds that lined the riverbank, or the overhanging trees.

But once again they saw nothing of the raiding Ghostface tribe. The forest on either side of the river was still and peaceful, the silence broken only by the call of birds or the occasional splash of a leaping fish. The river gurgled against the thin bark sides of their canoe, and they could well have been the only people alive on the earth.

The sun slowly rose and dispelled the chill of the night from their hands and shoulders. The constant thrust of their paddles through the water set the blood flowing as well, and before they had been on the river for an hour, they were all thoroughly warmed up.

When the sun was high overhead, Simsinnet guided the canoe under the overhanging branches of a willow and held it in place against the current.

"Eat now," he said, and they opened their supplies of dried meat.

"I could get used to this," Hal said, struggling to bite off a piece of the tough meat. He noticed that Simsinnet held the meat in his teeth and cut it off close to his mouth with his flint dagger. Must try that next time, he thought.

Stig looked at him, considering his statement. He found the dried meat quite unpalatable, although he knew it was nourishing. "Really?" he asked.

Hal smiled. "Yeah. In about twenty years or so."

They both laughed and Thorn frowned at them.

"Keep your voices down," he ordered and they both nodded sheepishly. They were, after all, in enemy territory.

"Sorry, Thorn," Hal whispered.

Thorn grunted. Jokes and banter were all very well for morale, he thought. But they did tend to distract one from the situation at hand. And this was a situation where he definitely did not want distraction.

Simsinnet gave a signal. Hal swallowed the last tough chunk of dried meat, took a final swig from his water skin and stowed it away. Simsinnet heaved on the branch he was holding, sending the canoe sliding out onto the river again. Before it lost momentum, they all dug their paddles into the surface of the water. The slender craft gathered speed, the gentle *bok-bok-bok* of ripples against its bark skin beginning once more.

It was late afternoon when Hal uttered a low warning and stopped paddling. The others all looked at him and allowed the canoe to drift off its headway. It gently began to turn broadside on to the current as the skirl sat on his thwart, his head tilted back and nose raised, sniffing the air.

"Smoke," he said and they all sniffed in turn. Thorn was the next to sense it.

"You're right," he said. "Wood smoke."

Then Simsinnet and Stig could smell it as well. The canoe, without any motive power, had drifted out toward the center of the river. A quick gesture from Simsinnet had them paddling once more, until they were back in the shelter of a grove of willows.

"How far to the Limigina village?" Stig asked Simsinnet.

The Mawag youth hesitated, studying the land around them, looking up to the sky, then frowning. "Not far," he said eventually. "Maybe two hours' paddling. Maybe less."

"Well, it looks like the Ghostfaces are there before us," Thorn said. "Let's keep the chatter down from now on."

Which was a little unfair. His companions, since his warning earlier in the day, had been silent, with only an occasional soft grunt of exertion.

Thorn dipped his paddle into the water and the others followed suit. Once more, the canoe curved out from its place of concealment and continued upriver, hugging the eastern bank. The smell of smoke became stronger. Then, as the sun fell, they became aware of a glow in the sky ahead of them, reflecting off the base of several low-lying clouds.

"Eyes peeled, everyone," Thorn whispered. "Looks like we're nearly there."

chapter thirty-four

They continued paddling for another hour. The sun had dropped behind the tall trees flanking the river and the shadows embraced the water. But the loom of light over the treetops became stronger as the daylight faded and they began to hear the faint murmur of voices as well—voices that were raised in song—and the throbbing of drums.

"Sounds like a party," Stig murmured.

Simsinnet turned toward him. "Not one that you'd want to be invited to," he said grimly. "It's the Ghostfaces celebrating their victory."

The sounds grew louder as they continued upriver, and eventually, they could see the flicker of flames and firelight through the trees.

"Time we went ashore," Thorn said quietly.

They steered their canoe under the shelter of a large clump of willows. The singing and drumming continued as they tied the canoe firmly to one of the overhanging branches and slipped over the side into waist-deep water. Silently, they heaved themselves up onto the bank and stood waiting while the water dripped from them. Simsinnet watched, fascinated, as Thorn replaced his wooden hook with the massive war club Hal had fashioned for him. The Mawag was armed with a stone-headed ax and a flint dagger. Stig had his ax and Hal his sword. Both the younger men had shields as well.

"How far to the village?" Thorn asked quietly, although there was little chance they'd be heard over the sound of chanting and drumming. Simsinnet hesitated, getting his bearings, then pointed into the trees.

"Maybe fifty meters farther upriver," he said. "And another thirty inland. There's a sand strip where the Ghostfaces will have beached their canoes," he added.

Thorn nodded and gestured upriver. "We'll go along the bank until we're level with the village," he said. He gestured to Stig's ax. "When we get there, I want you to put holes in their canoes. That should hold them up for a day or two while they repair them. I'm going to head for the village itself. I'd like to get a look at these bald-headed bogeymen. Hal, you stay and watch Stig's back while he's wrecking the canoes. Simsinnet, you come with me."

His three companions nodded and he gestured for the young Mawag to lead the way along the bank. They fell into single file behind him as they moved. With each few meters, the firelight grew more vivid and the sound of the celebrating Ghostfaces increased.

After thirty meters, they could see the flames through the trees, leaping some twenty meters into the air.

"That's some bonfire," Stig muttered.

"Shut up," Thorn ordered. There was no chance he could be heard in the village, of course, but the Ghosts might have set a guard over the canoes. Finally, they emerged from the trees into a cleared space on the riverbank. As Simsinnet had predicted, there was a narrow sandy beach where a row of canoes was drawn up out of the water.

Hal counted them quickly. "Eighteen," he said. He noted that the Ghostface canoes were bigger than the one they were traveling in. Each would hold five or six men and their baggage.

Thorn nodded. He stepped closer to Stig so he could speak quietly, but still be heard above the pounding drums and the strident chanting voices from inland.

"Put a decent hole in each," he said, "below the waterline."

Stig nodded and Hal added to Thorn's instructions. "Break the frames as well. That'll take longer to repair than a simple patch over the hole."

Stig glanced at him, his eyes reflecting the leaping firelight from the village, and nodded his understanding once more.

"Right. Get to it. I'm taking a look at the village. Come on, Simsinnet," Thorn said, and he turned away, moving silently into the leaping shadows cast by the flames of the giant fire. Simsinnet followed behind him. As they disappeared into the shadows, Hal gestured to the far end of the line of drawn-up canoes.

"Start up there and work back toward where we are," he said. That would make their getaway, if they needed to make one in a hurry, quicker and easier. They began to move quickly along the line of canoes, half crouching, scanning the flickering shadows around them for some sign of a guard. It seemed unlikely to Hal that the Ghostfaces would leave their canoes untended. But then, he thought, maybe they felt they had nothing to fear. According to Mohegas, none of the local tribes had ever shown signs of resistance. And presumably, the Limigina had either been captured, killed or driven off. They would see no point in damaging their enemies' canoes.

They reached the end of the line and Stig went to work, bringing his ax down in a series of efficient, destructive strokes. The birch bark covering of the canoes provided negligible resistance to his razor-sharp ax head, the light framework only a little more.

It took him only a few seconds to disable each canoe and he made his way along the line quickly, leaving a gaping hole in the bottom of each of the small craft.

Hal faced inland, in the direction from which any danger was likely to come. He had slipped his shield over his left arm. His sword was drawn, the blade glittering red in the light of the massive fire.

The attack, when it came, was from an unexpected direction. Four Ghost warriors burst out of the trees by the riverbank, from the same direction the small Skandian raiding party had come. One of them shouted a challenge, infuriated by the sight of strangers disabling their canoes.

Had they been thinking clearly, one or more of them might have headed for the village to bring help. But the Ghostfaces were so accustomed to quick, easy victories that they misjudged their opposition. There were four of them and only two interlopers. Shouting their war cries, they charged.

They were certainly a fearsome sight, Hal thought. Their shaved heads were completely covered in white paint, highlighted by black paint around their eyes and in the hollows of their cheeks. The overall effect was startlingly like a skull. In the uncertain light, Hal could see how an opponent might be unnerved by their terrifying appearance. All of them were naked to the waist, with deer-hide leggings and the soft shoes the Mawags called moccasins.

Their leader was a few paces ahead of his companions. He was a huge warrior, and the whites of his eyes gleamed madly in the black paint surrounding them. He drew back a massive war club and swung it overhand at Hal.

The village was like a scene out of a nightmare. Lit by the leaping flames of the massive bonfire, augmented by several fires burning among the villagers' huts, the Ghostface warriors formed a huge dancing circle, leaping and gyrating to the rhythm of the pounding drums. A large cauldron stood in the middle of their dancing circle, just clear of the fire. From time to time, a dancer would stagger to it, dip a drinking gourd into it, throw back his head and pour the contents down his throat.

"They brew a strong drink from fermented corn," Simsinnet whispered in Thorn's ear. In truth, there was no need for whispering, as the drums and the chanting were near deafening.

Thorn peered off to one side of the dancing circle. In the shadows, well out of the glare of the firelight, a dozen men knelt on the ground, heads bowed, eyes down. Their hands were tied behind their back and a rawhide thong was looped around each man's throat. Several meters away, a larger group of women and children were restrained in the same way. A Ghost warrior strode among them, armed with a wooden club, a knife in his belt. From time to time, he would lean down, thrusting his grotesque features close to one of the men's faces, and shout insults and abuse. His victims endured his taunts stoically.

"What's happening there?" Thorn asked, although he thought he knew.

Simsinnet indicated the women and children. "They'll be taken away as slaves."

"And the men?"

"When the Ghosts have finished their dance, they'll be executed," Simsinnet told him, his mouth a grim line. Thorn said nothing for several seconds, but his expression grew harder.

"Oh, will they indeed?" he said. "Keep an eye on those dancers for me." And he glided away, moving silently through the group of captive men, staying in a half crouch as he approached the Ghostface sentry from behind.

"Good evening," he said as he reached the sentry, and stood upright.

Thinking that one of the prisoners had loosened his bonds and moved behind him, the Ghostface swung round in a fury, drawing back his club to strike. Thorn took half a second to study the deathly white features and glittering eyes sunk in their black circles.

"You *are* ugly, aren't you?" he said conversationally.

The sentry was momentarily nonplussed at the sight of a completely foreign figure. This was no member of the Limiginas, or of any other local tribe. He was tall and broad-shouldered. His hair was gray and wild and untrimmed. He was bearded and his skin was white. The Ghostface turned his head toward the circle of dancers, twenty meters away, and drew breath for a warning shout.

He never uttered it. Thorn's club-hand, a heavy ball of hardwood, shot forward in a jab and smashed into his solar plexus. The breath was driven out of him in a massive, explosive *whoof!* and he doubled over, letting his war club fall from his hands. Thorn thrust his own war club out to the side and rapped it smartly against the sentry's temple—not hard enough to break the bone and kill him, but enough to knock him unconscious. The man sagged at the knees and collapsed sideways onto the dirt.

Quickly, Thorn dropped to a crouch beside the nearest prisoner and, drawing his saxe with his left hand, sliced through the rawhide thongs that restrained him. The man said something to him but Thorn shook his head, not understanding. As he freed a second captive with two quick slashes of his saxe, he glanced around and jerked his head toward Simsinnet, summoning him closer. The young Mawag hurried to join him, and Thorn spoke quickly.

"Tell them we're setting them free," he said, and Simsinnet hastily passed on the message in the local tongue. Thorn saw the captives' eyes shine with new hope. Simsinnet went to work with his own knife, cutting the cords that held the prisoners captive.

Thorn glanced at the fallen sentry and saw a knife in his belt. He reached down and ripped it free. The blade was flint, roughly shaped, but surprisingly keen. He handed it to the first prisoner freed and indicated for the man to cut more of his companions loose.

"Tell them to cut the women and children free and be ready to move. When the Ghostfaces head for the river, they're to run into the forest and escape. The Ghosts will follow us, so they'll have a good head start."

Hastily, Simsinnet relayed his instructions. A torrent of questions escaped the prisoners, but he waved them down. Gradually, the captives fell silent and sat still, aside from one, who crept among the women and children, cutting them free and cautioning them not to make noise.

One of the Limiginas asked a question and Simsinnet relayed it to Thorn, jerking his thumb at the fallen sentry. "What do we do with this one?" he asked.

Thorn reached down and rolled back the man's eyelid with his thumb. He was out cold. "I'd rather he remained alive, so he knows it wasn't these people who set him free," he said. "It'll do them good to wonder who the long-haired, white-skinned strangers are. But if he makes a move or tries to raise the alarm, tell them to kill him."

Simsinnet repeated the instructions. The former captive looked at his erstwhile guard and touched the point of the flint knife to his thumb. Obviously, he was hoping the man would regain consciousness.

"Tie him up," Thorn ordered and Simsinnet repeated the instruction. Reluctantly, the Limigina took one of the discarded lengths of rawhide and lashed the man's hands and feet tightly together.

Thorn took one last look around. Already, most of the men and half the women and children had been freed.

"Tell them to wait for the signal, then run like blazes and scatter into the forest," he said.

Simsinnet frowned. "How will they know the signal?"

Thorn grinned at him. "Oh, they'll know it. Now let's get back to the riverbank."

chapter thirty-five

The huge warrior brought his war club arcing down, and Hal raised his shield to deflect it. There was a ringing shriek as the club slid across the steel face of the shield, and the Ghostface, his features contorted in a snarl, stumbled, off balance, as his wild swing met with no real resistance.

As he did, Hal lunged quickly with his sword, the blade darting out like a striking snake and taking the man in his midsection. The sword went home, and Hal saw the contorted face suddenly relax into a surprised look. He withdrew the sword and the warrior fell to his knees, hands clutching his abdomen.

The second Ghostface was already on him, swinging a stone-headed ax through a horizontal arc. This time Hal reversed his movements, using his sword to flick the ax high over his head, then bringing his shield up horizontally and driving it forward, so the steel and timber edge slammed into the Ghost's jaw. The man stumbled. His eyes rolled up in his head and he crashed over, falling across the body of his companion.

Hal sensed that Stig had moved up from the line of canoes to stand beside him. The third Ghostface lunged forward with a long lance. Stig caught it neatly in the gap between the ax head and its shaft and twisted violently, tearing the weapon from his attacker's grasp. The Ghostface reached for the knife in his belt and stepped toward Stig. As he did, Hal pivoted beside him and hit him above the ear with the hilt of his sword. A third body was added to the growing pile before them.

The fourth Ghostface hesitated, his eyes and mouth wide-open in sudden fear as he realized he was seriously outmatched. Three of his companions had been dispatched in as many seconds by this strange pair of warriors, and now he was facing odds of two to one. He turned to run and found his way blocked by another white-skinned stranger. Before he could react, the newcomer slammed forward with a wooden club, hitting him full in the face and hurling him backward to join his companions.

Simsinnet stood, eyes wide with shock at the speed and power the three Skandians had just demonstrated. Four of the Ghostfaces lay sprawled in a heap on the sand—one dead and the others incapacitated. And it had all happened so quickly that Simsinnet had barely had time to half draw his knife from its sheath. Sheepishly, he pushed it back home now, shaking his head. The Skandians seemed to have taken the whole matter in their stride, he thought, and he began to realize that, with ten such warriors helping them, the Mawagansett might have a good chance of handing the hated Ghostfaces a serious defeat.

Thorn interrupted his thoughts, jerking a thumb at the canoes. "Finished?" he asked Stig.

The tall young man shook his head. "Five to go. We were a little . . . distracted," he said, grinning.

Thorn made an impatient gesture. "Well, there's nothing to distract you now. Get on with it."

Stig grinned. If he was waiting for any words of praise from Thorn, he was waiting in vain. As far as the old sea wolf was concerned, Hal and Stig had done no more than he expected of them. Thorn had been taking on odds of two to one all his fighting life.

Stig stepped back to the nearest undamaged canoe and brought his ax down in a crunching blow, smashing a frame and punching a large slit in the bark. He struck twice more, enlarging the slit into a large triangular hole. Then he moved on to the fourth-last canoe in line to repeat the process. Thorn pointed to the far end of the line, where they had begun their destruction.

"Pile some brushwood up there so you can light a fire," he said to Hal. Obediently, the skirl jogged back along the line of damaged canoes and began to gather dry brushwood, piling it up between the first and second canoe in line. Thorn watched for a few seconds, then dropped to one knee beside the inert forms piled on top of one another.

The first Ghostface, who had been the leader of the attack, was already dead. Hal's sword stroke had been fatal. The second was mumbling incoherently, his eyes unfocused. The third, whom Hal had knocked unconscious with his sword hilt, showed signs of recovery. Thorn pulled him upright, shoving one of his companions clear of the man's body, and slapped him lightly on the cheeks.

"You! Wake up! Come on! Get over it. You're all right," he said.

The man groaned and his eyes flickered open, startlingly white against the black paint surrounding them. He saw the bearded, grizzled face of a devil only a few centimeters from his own and uttered a shrill cry of fear.

"Tell him to shut up," Thorn snarled to Simsinnet, and the Mawag repeated the instruction. The Ghostface's eyes flickered toward him and the moment of panic subsided. At least this was a living human being, he thought. He nodded rapidly and the cries of fear died away to a mere whimper.

"Tell him I'm going to let him go," Thorn said, and as Simsinnet repeated the message, a ray of hope dawned in the stricken warrior's eyes. Thorn snorted in contempt.

"Amazing, isn't it?" he said. "Here he is, all painted up like a scary skull head yet he's frightened out of his wits by me."

"I don't blame him," Simsinnet muttered.

Thorn grinned at him. "Oh, I'm not that bad when you get to know me." He raised himself and looked down the line of canoes to where Hal was piling brushwood for a fire.

Stig finished work on the last of the canoes, leaving a thirty-centimeter-square hole in the bark bottom of the little craft. He replaced his ax in its belt loop and walked up the beach to join Thorn and Simsinnet. The Ghostface, seeing another white-skinned demon figure approaching, cowered back.

Stig contrived to look insulted. "What's his problem?" he asked Thorn.

"Obviously, he thinks you don't need a bald head and white paint to look scary," Thorn told him.

The Ghostface stammered a question and Thorn looked at Simsinnet. "What did he say?" he asked.

The Mawag replied with a grin. He was enjoying seeing the raider getting some of his own medicine. "He asked if you're going to eat his heart," he said.

Thorn appeared to consider the idea, but then shook his head.

"I doubt it," he said. "After all, I said I was going to set him free."

"He thinks you're tricking him. That when he tries to leave, you'll kill him and eat his heart."

Thorn scratched his head. "Why is he so obsessed with having someone eat his heart?"

Simsinnet shrugged. "That's what demons do," he replied.

Thorn shook his head angrily. It did nothing to allay the Ghostface's fear. "I'm not a demon. I'm just me."

"You're a big old pussycat," Stig put in, grinning.

Thorn turned a baleful eye on him. "Just be very careful, my friend," he said warningly.

Stig's grin widened.

Thorn turned back to Simsinnet and said very carefully, "Tell him I'm not going to eat his heart."

Simsinnet hesitated. "Should I say you're not a demon?"

Thorn considered the question for a few seconds, then shook his head. "No. It might be good to keep him thinking that. But tell him I'm not a full demon."

"Tell him Thorn's a semi-demi-demon," Stig said cheerfully.

Thorn ignored him. "Tell him I won't eat his heart. But I might nibble on his fingers and toes if he doesn't get moving when I tell him."

"Why do you want to set him free anyway?" Stig asked.

Thorn gestured toward the line of wrecked canoes. "I want them to know that this wasn't done by any of the Limiginas who got away when they first arrived. If they think it was done by mysterious strangers—"

"Semi-demi-demons?" Stig put in.

Thorn paused before replying, giving the young man a withering look. "If you must. If they think that, they won't take reprisals against any Limigina they recapture."

Stig thought about that and nodded thoughtfully. "That's quite a good idea," he said. "But won't it warn them that we're working with the Mawags?"

Thorn shrugged. "I don't see why it should. The Mawagansett village is thirty kilometers away from here. Why should they connect us with them?"

"I suppose not. Maybe you could have Simsinnet tell this rooster"—Stig gestured to the quaking Ghostface, who was watching them nervously, totally unaware of what they were saying—"that we came down from the sky to eat their hearts."

"Not a bad idea." Thorn glanced at Simsinnet. "Tell him something along those lines, Simsinnet. It might convince them to get out of here as soon as they can."

The Mawagansett warrior nodded. He addressed a few words to the Ghostface, who cringed a little away from Stig and Thorn. Stig bared his teeth at the man and he cringed further.

"Now tell him that we're going to burn their canoes, and if they don't put the fire out, they'll be trapped here where we can get them," Thorn added. Simsinnet translated and the Ghostface nodded his understanding. Thorn stood and dragged the white-faced raider upright by the arm. He waved to Hal to set the fire and saw a flash of flint on steel from down the beach. Then, a few seconds later, a tongue of flame leapt up from the first of the canoes. Thorn waited till the fire took hold, then shoved the Ghostface in the direction of the village.

"Run!" he shouted. The man hesitated, and Thorn made a threatening gesture with his club. That did the trick. The Ghostface turned away and made off at a shambling run toward the village.

Thorn looked up and saw Hal pounding back along the line of canoes to join them. He gestured to the trail that led along the bank to their own canoe.

"Right. Let's get going!" he said.

They slipped into the shadows between the trees, running back to where they had left their canoe. If they got away before the Ghostfaces saw them, Hal thought, the enemy would have no idea where they had gone.

As they reached the moored canoe, the drums and chanting stopped, dying away quickly. They could hear one voice shouting hysterically—probably the man Thorn had let escape. Then a roar of outrage sounded and they could hear the sound of many bodies shoving and crashing through the undergrowth to the beach.

The four of them slipped into the water again. Simsinnet held the canoe level while his companions climbed aboard, then leapt lightly into his seat and released the rope that held them to the willow branch.

They shot out onto the river, and an angry shout behind them told them they had been seen.

"Dig those paddles in!" Thorn ordered, hurriedly replacing his club-hand with his wooden gripping hook. Hal glanced over his shoulder. On the strip of beach farther up the river, he could see three or four of the canoes being launched into the shallows. Their crews scrambled aboard as soon as they were afloat, then cries of surprise and rage carried to them as their weight caused the canoes to sink into the river, water pouring through the holes Stig had cut in them.

"That should hold them up for a day or two," Hal said.

"Save your breath for paddling," Thorn told him.

They dug their paddles deep into the water and the canoe sped downriver, its speed boosted by the current. They rounded a bend and soon they could only see the glow of the Ghostfaces' fire against the sky.

"They seem to have stopped singing," Stig remarked.

chapter thirty-six

This time, the current was with them and they sent the canoe flying downriver, the banks flashing past them with amazing speed as the light strengthened and a new day dawned.

Around mid-morning, Thorn came to a decision. "Simsinnet and Hal, you two rest for a while. Stig and I will keep paddling. Then you can relieve us."

Gratefully, Hal brought his paddle inboard and stowed it. His shoulders and upper arms were burning with the effort of driving the canoe through the swift-running water. He was fit and young, but the action of paddling was an unfamiliar one, calling for a different set of muscles from rowing—which he was more accustomed to. There was no room to stretch out in the little craft, but he slumped forward on his seat, letting his head and arms hang loose and his body relax. Simsinnet, he noticed, was doing the same thing.

"Let me know when you want us to take over again," he said.

Thorn gave a short bark of laughter. "Oh, don't worry. I will."

Their speed was reduced with only two of them paddling, but they still managed to move downriver at a respectable rate. They continued in that fashion for the next six hours, with two resting and two paddling. As dusk closed in on them, Thorn ordered a halt while they ate a quick meal of dried meat, washed down with cold river water from their canteens. But even then, they didn't pull in to the bank, letting the swift river current sweep them farther along toward the ocean. Simsinnet kept his paddle across his knees as he ate and drank, occasionally using it to keep the canoe heading straight downriver and out in the middle of the current.

"Right, let's get paddling again," Thorn ordered as they finished their hasty meal. "We'll give it another three hours, then we'll stop for a few hours' proper rest."

"You think we're far enough ahead of them?" Stig asked.

Thorn inadvertently glanced back over his shoulder at the dark, smooth water behind them. "I think they're probably still back on the beach," he said. "It'll take hours for them to repair their canoes. They'll have to repair the frames you smashed, then cut patches of new bark to cover the holes and stitch them in place. Then they'll have to seal the stitches somehow. What'll they use for that, Simsinnet?" Had they been in Skandia, they would have used molten pitch for the task. Here, he wasn't so sure.

"Wax," Simsinnet replied. "They'll melt wax and smear it over the join to make it completely waterproof."

Thorn grunted. "And then they'll have to wait for that to harden," he said. "It'll all take time. But in the meantime, let's put a few more leagues between us and them."

He paused, paddle raised, and waited for Simsinnet to call the stroke. The four paddle blades dipped into the water. The canoe seemed to hesitate for a second as its prow turned back on course, then it shot away at speed, the ripples beating a rapid tattoo on the hull.

They continued that way as the sun set and darkness settled over the river. The tree-lined banks were dark and featureless. Only the smooth, black water stretching out in front of them was discernible in the dim light of the stars. But the river was free of snags and shallows—at least any section shallow enough to impede the canoe, with its minimal draught. Simsinnet kept them out in the center, where the current was strongest and visibility was clearest, and they kept paddling, the silence broken only by the light splash of their paddles, the burble of water along their hull and the rhythmic grunting of the four paddlers as they set their blades into the water in an unvarying pattern.

When the three-quarter moon rose over the tall trees flanking the river, it came as something of a shock, with the abrupt flood of light striking them with an almost physical impact. Suddenly the river was bathed in its cold, pale light and the water changed from black to silver. Close to the horizon as it was, the moon appeared to be huge. Hal gave an involuntary grunt of surprise at the sight of a massive, white orb hanging just over the treetops. Simsinnet turned from his position in the bow as he heard the skirl's exclamation.

"The moon is a goddess to us," he said quietly.

Hal nodded in appreciation. "I can see why. It's beautiful. It seems to be alive."

"Save the poetry for later," Thorn called crisply. "We'll keep paddling until the goddess has gone past her zenith."

The bright light of the moon threw the shaded banks into a starkly contrasting darkness. It was almost impossible to make out any features. The moon soared high above them, gradually diminishing in size as it moved farther and farther away from the horizon. Eventually, Thorn called a halt.

"Take us into the shore, Simsinnet," he ordered, and the Mawag warrior swung the canoe toward the bank, where he could just make out the white line of a small sandy beach. The prow grated ashore and they stepped out into the shallow water.

"Get some rest," Thorn ordered gruffly. "I'll take the first watch."

But Hal demurred. "I'll do it. You need sleep as much as any of us."

Thorn looked at him for a moment without speaking, then nodded. "You're right," he said. "I do and I will." He spotted a fallen log at the edge of the tree line and stretched himself out beside it, using it as a pillow. He pulled his shabby old sheepskin vest a little tighter around himself and sighed contentedly as his eyes closed.

"Don't fall asleep," he warned Hal, and promptly did so himself.

Simsinnet had taken the final watch and he roused them. Stig stretched his stiff muscles as he rose, raking his fingers through his unruly hair and swigging from his canteen. He eyed the water skin distastefully.

"What I could really use," he said, "is a strong mug of coffee."

"We've been out of coffee for weeks," Hal pointed out.

His friend scowled at him. "Well then, even a mug of that wishy-washy tea the Mawags make," he said.

Simsinnet grinned at the remark. "Better not let Tecumsa hear you say that," he said. "She prides herself on her tea making."

Stig grunted. "I'm going to have to find something we can roast to make a drink that's vaguely like coffee," he said. "Maybe I can use corn kernels."

"Good luck with that," Thorn told him, and jerked a thumb at the canoe. "Let's get back on the river."

They quickly repacked their bedrolls, stowing them in the canoe. The night had been cold and Hal found himself wishing he had carried an extra blanket. He was stiff and chilled, and his arm and shoulder muscles ached. But he shrugged the discomfort aside.

"I've been through worse," he muttered, remembering the terrifying days and nights when the *Heron* had been smashed and battered and driven by the massive storm. It had seemed then that he would never be warm and dry again. With an occasional groan from the two younger Skandians, the four of them resumed their places in the canoe and shoved off. They continued downriver in the cold of predawn.

"Now my feet are wet," Stig grumbled.

Thorn made a sympathetic clucking sound with his tongue.

"Poor baby," he said. "When we get home, Uncle Thorn will tuck you up with a hot rock in your blankets."

In spite of himself, Stig found himself grinning at the shaggy old warrior's cooing tones. "Would you really do that, Thorn?"

Thorn eyed him with a fierce smile. "Right after I bash you over the head with it," he said.

They fell into the rhythm of paddling once more, and soon their muscles loosened and their bodies warmed with the constant exercise. The sky in the east began to lighten and pale ribbons of pink light stretched across it. Then the sun rose. Like the moon the night before, it soared into sight above the tall treetops lining the eastern bank and its instant warmth penetrated their bones.

"Not far to go now," Simsinnet said, surprising them. Hal had assumed they would have hours more paddling to do, but he'd neglected to take account of the following current that was aiding their passage.

As if triggered by the Mawag's words, the river began to widen, and as they rounded one last bend, they could see the broad waters of the bay ahead of them. Involuntarily, they stopped paddling and sat back on the narrow wooden seats of the canoe.

It's good to be home, Hal thought. Then he smiled wryly at the idea that he could have come to think of this bay, so far from Skandia, as home. A voice hailed them from the riverbank and interrupted his musing. A canoe, a little smaller than their own and manned by three paddlers, was shooting out from the bank toward them. Without thinking, he dropped his hand to the hilt of his sword, where it rested against his seat—it was too long to wear in the close confines of the canoe.

"They're friends," Simsinnet said quickly, sensing his movement.

As the canoe drew closer, Hal could make out the now-familiar garments of the Mawagansett tribe. The three occupants were all armed, each one carrying one of the short bows over one shoulder, and a quiver of flint-headed arrows over the other.

Quickly, they drew alongside and smiled their greetings.

"Welcome back, Simsinnet," the warrior seated in the stern called out as the two craft drew together. "Did you find the Ghostfaces?"

"Found them. Fought them. Our friends here"—he indicated the three Skandians—"wrecked their canoes and disabled half a dozen of the Ghostfaces."

The paddlers looked at Stig, Thorn and Hal with new respect.

"So they're not coming?" the youngest of the three asked. "They've turned back?"

But Thorn quickly stifled his hopeful suggestion. "Oh, they're still coming," he said. "They'll be along in a few days. What are you three doing here?" he continued, although he thought he knew the answer.

"Mohegas posted us here to watch for your return. Or the Ghostfaces," the first speaker said, adding the second comment after a short pause.

"Just in case we didn't make it?" Thorn asked.

The warrior grinned a little sheepishly. "Yes," he admitted.

"Well, keep an eye out for them," Thorn replied.

They watched as the sentries turned back toward their

concealed observation post on the bank. Then they took up their paddles once more and sent the canoe surging out onto the broad waters of the bay.

Hal felt his heart surge as he saw the neat little ship moored on the opposite shore.

That's home, he thought, no matter where in the world I find myself.

chapter thirty-seven

Now that they had reached their destination, they eased the pace and sent the canoe gliding across the bay toward the *Heron*. They beached the little craft close to the ship and hauled it up onto the sand. Hal glanced around.

"The lads have been busy," he said. The palisade was gone, and the sleeping hut, as well as Lydia's separate accommodation, had been dismantled and removed. Walking up the beach, the only sign he could see that the area had been occupied was the blackened rocks where Edvin had sited his cook fire. Even they had been scattered, so that there would be no clue to warn the Ghostfaces that people had been camping here.

Thorn glanced around the empty former camp and nodded approvingly. "They've done well," he said. "I assume the palisade has been moved to the village and reassembled there." He indicated the narrow opening in the trees that marked the path leading to the Mawag settlement. "Let's go see."

They had been rowing for hours, day and night, and they made their way wearily through the shadows under the trees. They reached the Mawag village to find a scene of bustling activity.

Jesper, Stefan and Ingvar were working with a group of Mawag young men, putting the finishing touches to the palisade, which stretched in a wide semicircle to enclose the village. One of the new crossbows was assembled on the meeting ground in front of the village, and Lydia was instructing another group in the art of aiming and shooting—and the equally critical art of reloading. Like the Mangler, Hal had designed the new bows with extended cocking levers to give the loader as much mechanical advantage as possible in drawing the thick bowstring back to settle it over the trigger mechanism. One of the Mawags was bent over the bow, with Lydia beside him, coaching him as he lined it up on its target—a tightly bound bundle of branches standing fifty meters away. As they watched, they heard the wooden slam of the trigger releasing and the bow's arms springing forward. A bolt flashed away from the bow, streaking across the intervening space to smash into the bundle of branches, hurling it backward for several meters. Lydia slapped the shooter on the back in congratulation. The young Mawag grinned and stepped reluctantly away from the bow.

"Next shooter," Lydia said crisply, and another warrior stepped up eagerly, reaching for the cocking handles. "Help him," Lydia ordered and a third Mawag took one of the levers.

The two tribesmen heaved on the levers and drew the cord back, the arms of the bow and the cord itself creaking under the strain. Then they settled it snugly over the retaining pegs protruding above the body of the bow.

"Bolt," Lydia ordered, and the second man reached down to a small pile of heavy hardwood projectiles, placing one in the shallow trough cut along the top of the bow, and engaging the notch at the back with the cord. Hal stepped forward curiously. There was something unusual about the bolt. It had no fletching, he saw.

Lydia glanced up and saw him approaching. Her face lit up in a smile—welcome tinged with relief. "You're back," she said.

Hal grinned, looking down at himself, as if to make sure he was really there. "Apparently, we are," he said. He indicated the bolt loaded into the crossbow. "No fletching?"

Lydia shook her head. "I decided to speed things up," she said, unclipping the bolt from the crossbow's cord and handing it to Hal for him to study. Instead of the three vanes that he placed on the back end of his bolts, there was a large feather attached by a short piece of cord. Lydia took it and held it out behind the bolt.

"The feather streams behind the bolt as it's released and keeps it flying true, without toppling," she said. "It's not as efficient as fletching, but it does the job. We'll be shooting at pretty close range and we don't need pinpoint accuracy."

Hal nodded reflectively. "That's true," he said. "Good thinking."

Lydia continued. "The bows have been relatively easy to construct. Ulf and Wulf have done a good job and the Mawags are good carpenters. But the bolts were holding us up. Setting the vanes in place is a fiddly job and we need as many bolts as we can manage."

Hal handed back the projectile. "Let's see," he said, gesturing toward the bow. Lydia placed the bolt in the groove once more and signaled for the shooter to take his place. The bow sat on a framework of four legs and was mounted so that it had only a small amount of traverse and elevation travel. But that would be sufficient for the job they had to do. The shooter crouched behind it, nestling the butt of the bow into his shoulder and peering at the target.

"I put a simple V backsight and blade foresight on it to help them aim," Lydia explained. "There's no adjustment but they're getting used to allowing for drop over the distance."

Hal nodded and glanced at Stig, who had joined them and was watching with interest.

"Looks like you're not the only inventor anymore," Stig said, and Hal nodded.

"When you're ready, Harowatta," Lydia said. The Mawag's hand tightened around the trigger lever. The two pins slipped down into the body of the bow, releasing the cord, and the tensioned arms slammed forward.

The bolt shot away and Hal saw that Lydia was right. The big feather streamed out behind the heavy wooden bolt, keeping it flying true. Like its predecessor, the bolt slammed into the bundle of branches being used as a target. There was a splintering sound as it drove through the thin branches, smashing some and pushing some aside. This shot was dead center and the target skidded back on the hard-packed ground for a meter or so.

"Nice work," Hal said to the shooter, who grinned appreciatively. Then, turning back to Lydia, he asked, "How many bows are ready?"

"Six," she replied. "With another two that should be finished today. We've been training all the shooters on this bow. It was the first completed. By now, they're getting pretty accurate."

"So I saw," Hal said. He waved a greeting to Jesper and Stefan, who had just noticed their arrival. Stefan turned and said something to Ingvar, who was lugging a bundle of long, sharpened stakes that would be set facing out from the palisade. The big lad looked up, saw Hal and waved, a huge grin spreading over his face. Hal waved in reply, then turned back as Lydia spoke.

"Did you see the Ghostfaces?" she asked.

Hal nodded. "I figure they'll be along in about three days."

But Simsinnet wasn't prepared to let it go at that. "Did we see them?" he asked. "We didn't just see them! Hal, Stig and Thorn took on six of them and just"—he hesitated, holding his hands out uncertainly as he sought the correct word—"*demolished* them!" he concluded.

Lydia grinned. "Yes. They're good at that," she said, glancing affectionately at Stig. "Particularly Mr. Muscles here and the dreaded Hookyhand." She used a term that Thorn had applied to himself several years previously, when introduced to the king of Araluen.

Simsinnet was a little taken aback at her casual acceptance of her shipmates' prowess. "Hal too!" he insisted excitedly. "He killed one and knocked another cold, in a matter of seconds. I've never seen anything like the three of them!"

Hal and Stig shrugged diffidently as Lydia turned to them. "Wait till he sees Ingvar in action," she said and they both nodded. Then she turned back to the waiting group of shooters clustered around the crossbow. "Well, I'd better get back to it if the Ghostfaces are on their way," she said.

Hal nodded agreement. "And we'd better report in to Mohegas, and make sure everything will be ready for our guests."

They crossed the gathering ground, heading for Mohegas's hut. The older Mawagansett had been informed of their return and met them halfway, reaching out to clasp the arms of each of them in greeting.

"It's good to see you safe!" he said, smiling. "Did you find the Ghostfaces?"

Hal reported on the location of the enemy and the actions they'd taken to slow them down. Again, Simsinnet enthused over the fighting skills his three companions had demonstrated.

"So perhaps this won't be a one-sided battle this time?" Mohegas said. Hal, Thorn and Stig all shrugged, but Simsinnet agreed heartily with the tribal elder.

"Believe me, Uncle," he said—*Uncle* was a term of respect among the tribespeople—"this time, the Ghostfaces are going to get the shock of their lives."

Mohegas studied the three Skandians for a few seconds. They weren't boastful or arrogant, but he could see a calm confidence about them. They knew their own capabilities and they trusted their skill in fighting. Simsinnet could be right, he thought. These were trained warriors and ten of them would make a big difference in the coming flight. Ten of them, he thought, and eight of the massive crossbows that he'd seen constructed. As he had the thought, they heard the *SLAM!* of another shot and a ragged cheer from the warriors practicing their skills. Obviously, that one had gone home as well and done more damage to the target.

"I'm glad you're with us," he said simply.

Thorn replied with a wolfish grin. "Let's make sure the Ghost-faces aren't," he said.

Satisfied that preparations were proceeding satisfactorily, the four travelers rested for the remainder of the day, catching up on the sleep they had lost during their arduous journey downriver. Hal awoke refreshed the following morning, but his arms were still stiff and his shoulder muscles were aching. Stig was in the same condition. Thorn seemed immune. His powerful muscles seemed to be able to take any exertion in their stride.

"It's the result of clean living," he said, in a superior tone.

Hal raised an eyebrow in his direction. "It may be the result of many things," he said. "I doubt clean living is one of them in your case."

Tecumsa produced a powerful-smelling salve that she rubbed into Stig's and Hal's arms and shoulders. The liniment had a burning effect, but it soon eased the cramps and pains that assailed them. Thorn sniffed the air close to the two friends, a pained expression on his face.

"Maybe you two should try clean living in the future. You smell like a stable full of donkeys."

Many years before, on a raid in Iberion, Thorn had seen and, more importantly, smelled donkeys. The memory lived on. Stig and

Hal, however, stared at him, uncomprehending. Donkeys were an unknown quantity in Hallasholm.

"What do donkeys smell like?" Stig asked.

Thorn shook his head, trying to dispel the powerful aroma that wafted from his two young friends. "Like you two—but not as pungent."

It was a little disconcerting to have Thorn, who was not the most fragrant of people, commenting on their personal freshness. But Tecumsa's salve had a wonderful healing effect on their stiff muscles, so Hal decided it was worth the insults.

"Let's take a look at where the boys have placed the crossbows," he said.

Lydia, Ingvar, Stefan and Edvin took them on a tour of the site. They had set the eight crossbows up in two batteries, one on either side of the village, inside the tree line facing the palisade, with each set at a forty-five-degree angle to it. From those positions, they would be able to enfilade the attacking Ghosts as they tried to storm the palisade, raking them with bolts from two angles.

Each crossbow had a respectable pile of heavy bolts set next to it. Hal picked one up and examined it. The shaft was hardwood and there was a sharp flint warhead bound to the tip. As he had seen previously, the other end was equipped with a large feather to stabilize the bolt in flight. Each crossbow had a dozen bolts lying beside it, ready to shoot.

"That's nearly a hundred shots we can take at them," Hal mused. "And chances are, each bolt will account for more than one of them."

"Chances are, once we start shooting, they'll turn back and attack us," Thorn pointed out.

Hal nodded. "We'd better build some defenses here as well," he said. "A hedge of sharpened stakes pointing outward should do the trick." He glanced at Stefan. "Can you organize that?"

Stefan nodded. "I'll get some of the Mawags onto it immediately."

Hal turned to Lydia. "You can take command of things here. Thorn, you take the other battery." He gestured to where the other four crossbows had been set up in the trees. Lydia and Thorn both nodded assent.

Stig tilted his head curiously. "Where do you want me?"

"You take command at the main palisade. And have a force of half a dozen Mawag warriors ready as an emergency squad, in case the Ghostfaces break through at any point along the defenses."

"Where will you be?" Lydia asked.

Hal gestured in the direction of the beach. "I'll take Ulf, Wulf and Edvin with me. We'll hide the ship inside the north headland and get among the Ghostfaces' canoes once they're committed. We'll ram and sink as many as we can." He chewed his lip thoughtfully. "I'll have to wait until all the canoes are out of the river and in the bay. Then I'll attack them from behind," he said. "That means you'll have to cope with probably half the attacking force—the ones who make it to the beach before we can attack them."

"That shouldn't be a problem," Thorn said, and the others murmured agreement.

Hal glanced at Thorn. "Have I forgotten anything?" he asked.

The grizzled old sea wolf shook his head. "I think that covers everything. Of course, once the fight starts, a whole lot of things will happen that we haven't foreseen. It always happens that way."

The others all regarded him solemnly. Past experience told

them that what he said was only too true. Then Stig broke the silence.

"Well, even if we get it half right, we'll make sure they won't be coming back," he said.

"And if we get it all right," Hal replied, "we'll make sure they won't be going home."

chapter thirty-eight

They're coming!" Ulf shouted, his voice cracking with excitement or anxiety—or both.

It was the third day after Hal and the others had returned from their expedition upriver. Mohegas had dispatched a series of two-man teams to watch for the enemy's approach, spacing them up the river, about two or three kilometers apart. Upon seeing the fleet of canoes coming downriver, each pair of observers was to light a signal fire, then flee—either inland if they felt the Ghostfaces were too close, or downriver by canoe if they felt it was safe to do so.

The Ghosts, having paddled over a long distance, would move more slowly than a single light canoe with two paddlers and only a short distance to cover.

Now Hal saw a thin spiral of smoke rising from what was the

sixth and final observation post, on the bank of the river as it widened into the bay. He knew the river before that point stretched in a straight line for two kilometers, which meant the Ghostface fleet was now less than two kilometers away. As he had the thought, he saw the small two-man canoe streak away from the bank and head for the far beach as fast as its crew could paddle.

He, Edvin and the twins were aboard the *Heron*, moored just inside the northern headland. Each day, they had crossed the bay by canoe, bringing Kloof with them, and waited aboard the ship for the first sign of the approaching enemy. The ship itself was festooned with creepers and leafy branches to break up its outline and make it more difficult to spot. The yardarms were lowered, but ready to hoist once the Ghostface fleet of canoes had emerged from the river and were on the broad surface of the bay, where they would be vulnerable to attack from the *Heron*.

Shading his eyes against the mid-morning glare, he peered across the bay to the beach, where he saw an answering thread of smoke rising from close to the beginning of the tree line—confirmation that the signal had been received. The sentry on duty there could just be seen, running into the shadows under the trees and heading for the village to spread the warning.

"Let's get ready," he said, and his three companions all checked their weapons. There was a sudden air of tension on board the little ship that Kloof seemed to sense. Her hackles rose around her neck and she emitted a low, whining growl.

"Steady, girl," Hal told her, stroking the top of her head to calm her. He didn't want her barking and possibly warning the approaching enemy of their position.

"Shall we get rid of the covering, Hal?" Wulf asked, moving toward the intertwined creepers and branches that covered the ship.

Hal shook his head. "Leave it for the moment. I want all the Ghosts' canoes out on the bay before we reveal ourselves. If they sight us too soon, some of them might head back up the river and escape."

The fast, handy canoes would make better time upriver than the *Heron*. The banks were close together, restricting the wind and making it impossible for the ship to follow a straight course. Out on the open water of the bay, it would be a different matter. Her sails would give her a considerable speed advantage over the canoes. She could swoop down on them, ramming them and smashing their fragile hulls at will.

His stomach tightened into a knot as he awaited the first sign of the enemy. It's always the way, he thought. You get the first warning and everyone's on edge immediately. Then nothing happens. He shaded his eyes again, straining to see the mouth of the river and some sign of movement there. But still, there was nothing.

When the sentry had run into the village, breathlessly spreading the word of the Ghostfaces' approach, there had been an immediate bustle of activity. Thorn smiled grimly as he watched the villagers rushing here and there. There was no real need for the rush. Everyone was ready for the attack—and had been for several days now. The eight crossbows were deployed in the trees to either side of the village. Each was placed so that it had a clear sight line through the trees. There had been some debate as to whether the trees should be cut down to provide a wider angle of shot for the bows but

Thorn had vetoed the idea. The bows would be easier to spot if the trees were cut back. As it was, the first shattering impact of the bolts would seem to come from nowhere, and everywhere. And in the event that the Ghostfaces turned to attack the batteries, the close-set trees would prevent their attacking in a concerted line.

Now he watched as parents hurriedly chivvied their children into huts in the center of the village, where the young women and older tribespeople would care for them during the battle.

"No need to rush," he murmured. "They won't be here for at least an hour."

Lydia, at the other crossbow site, echoed his thoughts. This was always the hardest part, she mused, waiting for the attack. And, like Thorn, she knew that there was still plenty of time to wait. She watched as the Mawagansett warriors began to take their places at the barricade of intertwined branches and sharpened stakes that ringed the village. She could make out Tecumsa as the young woman gathered a group of small children and led them to the relative safety of the central huts. The day prior, Tecumsa and a group of half a dozen other young women had approached Lydia.

"Will you fight the Ghostfaces?" they asked.

When she nodded confirmation, Tecumsa stepped forward. "Teach us to fight too," she said, and the others chorused agreement.

Their faces fell as Lydia shook her head. "I can't teach you in such a short time," she said. "And if you try to take a place at the barricade, you might well distract your warriors. They'd be concerned for you, and it might cost them their lives."

She saw them realizing the truth of what she'd said. But they were disappointed, she could tell.

"This much I can teach you," she said, and their eyes lit up with interest. "Arm yourselves with weapons you can handle easily. Spears would be best. They're lighter than clubs or axes, and if an enemy warrior does break through and attack you, they'll keep him at a distance."

The girls nodded, eyes intent on her, taking note of every word she said.

"Attack in pairs if you can. Jab at them. Stab them. Use the point of the spear. Aim for their legs and thighs. It's harder to counter a stroke there. If you wound them, you'll put them out of the fight just as surely as if you kill them."

She paused. She could see her words had sunk in. The girls' eyes were still intent on her.

"One more thing," she said, "and this is the most important part, and the hardest. *Do not give ground.* No matter how frightened you are—and you will be frightened—no matter how fierce they appear with their skull faces and black eyes—do *not* retreat. Attack them. Go forward all the time. Scream at them. Hate them. But most of all, *attack* them. They won't be expecting it. They'll expect you to scream in fear and run away. Don't do it. Go forward. Always forward."

She saw Tecumsa mouthing the word with her, saw the girl's jaw set and the resolve in her eyes. She's not going to run from the Ghostfaces, Lydia thought.

Now she looked at the warriors grouped around the four crossbows.

"Everyone ready?" she asked, and they chorused an affirmative. She could see they were tense and nervous and she smiled encouragement at them. "They won't be here for at least an hour," she said. "Just relax and take it easy. There'll be plenty to do when they arrive."

Several of the young men nodded nervously back at her and it occurred to her for the first time that she had probably been in more battles than any of them.

"We'll be fine," she said, still smiling. "I can't wait to see those pasty-faced bogeymen when we start shooting them down." Like Thorn, she realized the value of denigrating the enemy, of making light of their terrifying makeup. Some of the men smiled uncertainly back at her.

Stefan and Jesper, who had been assigned to accompany Lydia, nodded to her, understanding what she was doing. Stefan yawned and rested against one of the crossbows, idly twirling his ax. The massive weapon spun and caught the rays of the sun that filtered through the trees. It seemed as light as a feather in his hands. The casual demeanor of the two Skandians communicated itself to the Mawags. They had heard from Simsinnet of the skill these foreigners showed in fighting. Following their example, the tribesmen relaxed a little.

Stig paced calmly behind the palisade, looking for weak points in the wooden wall where the Ghosts might penetrate. His shield was still slung over his back. From time to time he made an encouraging comment to the warriors as they stood ready, flint-headed spears and wooden clubs in their hands. Most of the men had shields of deer hide stretched tightly across a wooden frame. Approximately one in three was armed with one of the Mawags' short, powerful bows and a quiver bristling with arrows slung over the shoulder.

"Don't waste arrows," he said. "Wait till they're close and then shoot. And remember, when you hear the horn signal, get down."

They nodded in reply. He saw several moistening their lips. Dry mouth, he thought. A common problem before a fight.

The horn signal he'd mentioned was an important idea Hal had added to the defense. When the crossbow batteries were about to shoot, Lydia or Thorn would sound a blast on a horn. When they heard it, the defenders were to crouch below the palisade. That way, any bolts that missed the enemy wouldn't strike down the defenders instead.

He felt a light touch on his arm and turned to see Tecumsa behind him. He smiled at her and nodded his head toward the huts.

"You should be back looking after the children," he said gently. She smiled back. He could see she was nervous, but trying hard not to show it.

"I wanted to wish you good luck," she said. "Stay safe, my love."

She stood on tiptoes and kissed him lightly on the lips. Some of the nearby warriors chuckled aloud and whistled at the show of affection. It was unusual among the Mawagansett, he knew. Her lips were soft and their touch was fleeting. But even after she had stepped back from him, he could feel their touch on his own.

"I'll be fine," he said. "You take care of yourself."

She smiled again, then turned and ran back into the village, threading her way through the lines of huts until she came to one of the largest, where the children and young women were gathered. She paused at the doorway and waved a hand to him. He raised his own right hand in salute, then she slipped inside the hut and was lost to his sight.

"I'll see you when this is over," Stig promised quietly.

The time passed with agonizing slowness. Hal paced the deck of the little ship, looking constantly toward the mouth of the river. But there was still no sign of the Ghostfaces. The smoke alarm signal was already dwindling. It was now nothing more than a thin gray ribbon rising into the sky. Soon, it would be gone as the fire died down.

He looked across the bay toward the south to check on the wind for the tenth time since the Ghostfaces had been sighted. The wind was from the southwest, of course, as it had been for some time now. The first hundred meters or so of the southern part of the bay were smooth and undisturbed, sheltered by the high headlands that enclosed the bay. He could see the treetops on the bluffs swaying in the wind, however. Then, beyond that hundred-meter point, the wind eddied down and ruffled the surface of the water into a series of wavelets. He'd have plenty of wind to maneuver, he thought.

"There they are," said Edvin, drawing Hal's attention back to the river. He felt a jolt of adrenaline as he saw the first canoes making their way onto the waters of the bay. He shook his head in disappointment as he saw that the Ghostface fleet was traveling in line astern, one canoe at a time. He'd hoped they might bunch up and clear the river sooner. This way, the leading canoes would be almost to the far beach before the last of them emerged from the river.

"Well," he said quietly, "Thorn and Stig will just have to take care of the first wave."

He had no doubt that his friends could handle the Ghostfaces' attack. Even without the demoralizing effect of the eight giant crossbows on the enemy, the Skandians would provide a stiffening to the Mawags' defense. They were highly trained and skilled, and their iron weapons were superior to the flint- and stone-edged weapons of the tribespeople. All the same, it would have been a neater solution if the Ghosts had bunched up, and he could have attacked the entire fleet of canoes before any of them reached the beach.

Would have been, could have been, he mused. That was always the way when it came to a battle. Things never worked out quite the way you hoped.

He saw a movement out of the corner of his eye. Ulf had moved to the main rope holding the concealing screen of creepers and branches in place.

"Not yet," Hal said. "Let them get fully committed first."

chapter thirty-nine

The first of the canoes had grounded on the beach, their crews spilling eagerly out of them. The expedition leader, a warrior known in the Ghostfaces' tongue as Holds a Black Lance, waited impatiently. When the first six canoes had grounded on the beach, he hastily mustered his men, thirty-two of them in all, and led them at a trot to the path through the forest. The six canoes had carried the pick of his men—the best warriors and the fastest paddlers. The first of the following canoes was still only halfway across the bay, with others straggling behind it.

"They can follow when they get here," he told his second in command, a short but massively built warrior known as Crusher of Heads, by virtue of the heavy stone ax he wielded.

The man smiled cruelly. "All the more booty for us," he said.

Neither of them expected any resistance. If things went as they usually did, the local villagers would have fled, leaving their homes and possessions for the invaders.

Black Lance was familiar with the terrain. He had been on a previous raid against the Mawagansett village and he led his men through the dim shadows beneath the trees, their feet pounding the soft, leaf-matted ground as they jogged in two files, chanting a cadence as they went.

They emerged into the bright sunlight at the cleared gathering ground in front of the village and stopped in surprise.

They had expected a deserted, defenseless village, filled with plunder ready for the taking. Instead, they found themselves facing a defensive stockade, a chest-high tangle of brushwood and branches that surrounded the neat lines of huts, terminating at either end at the stream behind the village. The newly sharpened ends of stakes protruded like a porcupine's quills, threatening any incautious attacker. Black Lance could see more stakes placed in the shallow water of the stream behind the village, preventing access in that direction.

His face flushed with rage as he saw the heads and shoulders of the Mawagansett tribesmen above the palisade—and saw the weapons they brandished in defiance. He gestured for his men to form in a long line facing the barricade. A frontal assault was the Ghostfaces' usual method of attack, relying on their ferocity and bloodthirsty reputation to chill the hearts of any enemies. His men readied themselves. The palisade was a mere twenty meters away and they poised, ready to begin a concerted rush. Black Lance decided to give the Mawagansett one last chance to surrender peaceably—and be hacked down as a result.

"Mawagansett people!" he shouted in his own tongue, knowing they would understand him. "Surrender to us now. This is your last chance! Surrender and we will spare your women and children!"

There was no answer, only a muted growl of defiance from the barricade. He tried one more time.

"Surrender now!" he demanded. "Otherwise we will kill you all! And you will all die slowly, in great pain!"

Silence from the village. Then a voice rang out in an unfamiliar tongue.

"You'll have to take us first, Baldy!"

He didn't understand the words, but his rage grew as he heard the chorus of laughter from behind the barricade. Then a strange figure rose above the top of the palisade—a pale-skinned, pale-haired figure, wielding an ax with a strange, silver-glinting head and bearing a huge round shield on his left arm.

Black Lance hesitated, feeling a chill of fear down his spine. This sounded like one of the strange demons who had attacked his camp several days ago. One of his men had survived the attack and described them to him. At the time, he had thought the man was lying to cover his own cowardice and had him put to death. Now here was exactly the sort of figure he had described—a warrior the like of which Black Lance had never seen. For a second, he considered retreating to the beach. Then he gathered his courage. To do that would be an invitation to his own men to depose and kill him. Demon or no demon, he had to go on with the attack. He heard his own men stirring nervously at the sight of the strange warrior and he screamed at them in rage.

"Ghostfaces! Attack now! Kill the Mawagansett! Kill the Pale Hair!"

He raised his lance and charged ahead. It had been many years since the Ghostfaces had tasted defeat in battle. His men charged with him in an extended line, yelling vile insults and threats at the enemy and uttering the chilling, high-pitched, ululating scream that was the Ghostface war cry.

As he came closer to the barricade, Black Lance surreptitiously veered to his right, taking his line of approach away from the strange warrior. Let someone else take care of him, he thought. He saw the Mawagansett warriors inside the barricade readying themselves to repel the assault. He centered his aim on one young Mawag, and drew back his lance, ready to thrust.

Then he stopped, his heart rising into his throat with fear as another Pale Hair, this one with large black circles around his eyes, rose up from behind the barricade, directly in front of him. He was even larger than the first Pale Hair, and he held a strange type of spear ready—a spear with a head fashioned from that same glittering silver metal. The warrior smiled at him and rage filled Black Lance once more, overcoming his fear. He leapt forward.

"He's coming your way, Ingvar!" Stig warned.

"Let him come," Ingvar answered, holding the voulge diagonally across his chest in the ready position Thorn had taught him so many months ago.

The Ghostface was carrying a long, black lance, fitted with a razor-sharp flint warhead. He darted it at Ingvar now, but the big youth casually parried it with the voulge, flicking it aside. Then, with a speed that was remarkable in such a bulky frame, Ingvar lunged forward himself. But Black Lance was expecting the counterstroke and swayed to one side, so that the gleaming spear point slid past him, over his shoulder.

Then he realized his mistake, as Ingvar rapidly jerked the voulge back, snagging the Ghostface leader's bare flesh with the wicked hook on the back of the voulge's head. The razor-sharp iron bit deep into the muscles of Black Lance's upper back and dragged him forward, screaming in sudden agony. The lance fell from his hands as he threw his hands up, trying to quell the sudden pain in his back and shoulder.

Long hours of practice under Thorn's tutelage had made Ingvar a master of his unusual weapon, and taught him how to exploit its triple warhead to best advantage. The voulge was equipped with a spear point, a hook and an ax blade and now Ingvar jerked the hook free and raised the ax blade, chopping down in a short, controlled action at the off-balance attacker. He didn't need to take a long, extended swing. Had he done so, the ax blade would have removed Black Lance's head from his body. But Ingvar's powerful muscles put plenty of force behind the ax blade, even with a shortened swing.

Black Lance felt another jarring, agonizing impact, this time on his neck, just above his shoulder. He felt his knees weaken and he began to fall. His vision dimmed and he realized that he had just lost a combat for the first, and last, time. The last thing he saw was the pale-skinned demon above him, staring down at him with those black circles that seemed to contain no eyes. Then his own vision faded.

His men were shocked by the brief, brutal combat. They had never seen Black Lance bested in battle. Now he lay sprawled and lifeless across one of the sharpened stakes projecting out from the barricade. Involuntarily, the leading attackers took a pace back from the timber barricade.

In the trees, pacing behind the row of giant crossbows, Thorn watched the brief fight, nodding his approval at Ingvar's skill and power. His men were nervous, wanting to shoot immediately, and he spoke to calm them. The first volley was their best chance to do maximum damage. He wanted all the bows to shoot simultaneously, and all of them to be aimed carefully. After that, he knew, the shooting would become more ragged.

"Not yet," he cautioned his men. "Wait till they're bunched up in front of the barricade, and then make sure of your aim." Several of the Mawags adjusted the alignment of their giant weapons, seeking out individual targets among the Ghostfaces. Thorn glanced at the warrior with the signal horn, saw he was nervously moistening his lips.

"Ready . . . ," he said, raising his arm.

Crusher of Heads, in command now that Black Lance had fallen, stepped forward, half turning to face his own men, and raising his massive ax.

"Ghostfaces!" he screamed. "Avenge our leader! Attack! Kill the Pale Hairs! We have them outnumbered!" The Ghostfaces stirred, their failing courage bolstered by his words. Then a strange thing happened.

A horn rang out from behind him to the left, and the faces of the defenders promptly disappeared below the barrier.

Crusher of Heads had no idea what was happening or why it had happened, but he saw his opportunity.

"Now!" he screamed, and surged, hauling himself up onto the tangle of branches and saplings, ax drawn back to smash the skull of any who dared to oppose him.

While Crusher of Heads and Black Lance led the attack at the center of the barricade, a small group of Ghostface warriors ran to the eastern end, crouching to keep out of the defenders' sight. As all attention focused on the main attack, three of them leaped, screaming abuse and war cries, onto the palisade, striking out at the startled defenders. In a matter of seconds, two Mawags fell back, one dead, the other seriously injured.

Inside the palisade, Orvik ran to the wounded man and half dragged, half carried him back from the fence. The old Skandian had been assigned the task of rescuing the wounded and getting them to safety. He had volunteered to fight alongside his adopted tribesmen, but both Mohegas and Thorn had shaken their heads. In his time, Orvik had been a valuable man in a battle, but the years had taken their toll. His movements were slow and his strength wasn't what it had once been. On top of that, the passage of years had seen his right knee stiffen so that it ached in cold weather, and the resilience of his muscles wither.

"You'll do better tending the wounded," Thorn had told him, and Orvik had reluctantly accepted the inevitable. Better to serve a useful purpose than to become a victory marker on a Ghostface lance, he thought.

He settled the wounded Mawag on a litter, arranging his arms and legs so the man was comfortable, and turned to call for one of the healers who were standing by to treat the wounded.

He never got the chance. One of the Ghostfaces, seeing the gray-haired old man tending to a fallen Mawag, screamed in fury and launched himself from the top of the barricade, over the heads of the defenders, and dashed toward him.

Orvik heard the scream and turned to face the charging Ghost, quickly drawing his saxe—the only possession he had come ashore with all those years ago. The brass and leather hilt felt solid and familiar in his hand. It was an old friend that had seen him through many battles, and he waited confidently for his attacker.

The Ghostface lunged underhand with his lance. But Orvik was an experienced fighter, with a score of successful combats behind him. He sensed the blow coming even before it was on its way and sprang lightly to one side, so that the lance would pass harmlessly by him.

At least, that was what his mind planned, but his body let him down. The unreliable right knee folded as he tried to leap aside, turning the intended graceful movement into an awkward stumble. He lurched forward, and felt a hot stab of pain in his stomach as the lance took him. He gasped in agony. Then, oddly, the area went numb and he felt no pain. He could sense the lance head tearing at his body as the enemy warrior tried to withdraw it. He locked gazes with the white-faced Ghost and allowed himself a grim smile. Then he slashed the saxe, kept razor-sharp over the years by dint of constant honing on a smooth rock, across the man's exposed throat in a killing stroke.

The Ghostface emitted a gurgling scream and fell facedown on the hard-packed dirt. A moment later, Orvik fell across him. In his last moment, he realized that his right knee no longer troubled him.

Crusher of Heads heaved himself up onto the suddenly unprotected barricade. He felt a moment of triumph. The defenders' nerve must have broken, causing them to fall back in panic and disarray.

Then it seemed that a massive fist smashed through their tightly packed ranks. A heavy projectile took Crusher of Heads in the left upper arm, spinning him round and throwing him to the ground. Beside him, he saw another Ghostface transfixed by a bolt. Three others screamed and fell, wounded or killed as two more bolts tumbled through their ranks. Before he could make out what had happened, another horn blast sounded, this time from the forest to his right.

Once more, a barrage of projectiles smashed into the tightly packed attackers. This time, two Ghostfaces went down, but Crusher of Heads saw the violent impact of two bolts on the palisade itself, as they shattered the branches and timbers, sending splinters flying.

He turned to peer into the forest to his right, trying to see the source of the shooting. Before he could see more than a flicker of movement among the trees, another four missiles slammed into his men, once more from the left.

"They're in the trees!" someone shouted, pointing into the forest to their right rear. Crusher of Heads realized they would have to neutralize this unexpected attack or they would all be wiped out. He staggered upright, his left arm hanging uselessly, blood streaming down, and pointed his ax to the trees on their right, where he had seen movement.

"Follow me!" he screamed, and set off at a shambling run. He heard the footsteps of his men running behind him. A new sense of purpose filled him and he increased his pace, ignoring the agony in his arm. This was an enemy they could destroy. These were no pale-skinned demons. These, he could now see, were Mawagansett, huddled round four massive contraptions among the trees. And Crusher of Heads and his men had been defeating and killing Mawagansett since time began.

He blundered into a tree trunk, then staggered back toward the enemy line, having to thread his way through the trees and feeling the concerted attack of his men being scattered and dissipated. To his surprise, he saw that one of the people standing by the giant crossbows was a girl—slim, young and vulnerable. He screamed his hatred and lunged toward her.

He saw her right arm go back, then flick forward. He felt a jolting impact in his chest and staggered, slamming into a tree trunk and losing his balance. He slid down the trunk until he was sitting on the ground beneath the tree. A huge dart seemed to be protruding from his chest. He wondered where that had come from.

Cautiously, Stig raised his head above the palisade, ready to duck back instantly. There had been no double blast of the horns—the prearranged signal for the defenders to take their posts once more—but the barrage of bolts seemed to have stopped. Grimly, he realized that if he was wrong, he would be too late to take cover again. To his left, he saw a group of about ten Ghostfaces plunging into the trees toward the spot where Lydia's battery was sited. He heard the clash of weapons and the cries of the wounded. Then he glanced to the right and his heart froze.

Another small party of Ghostfaces, about half a dozen in all, had taken advantage of the fact that the defenders had dropped below the palisade while the crossbows were shooting. They were swarming over the western end of the barrier, hacking and thrusting at the Mawags who crouched behind it, taking them by surprise and scattering them in confusion. One of the attackers fell back as a Mawag thrust with a lance at him, but the other five cleared the barrier and struck out around them, felling the surprised defenders and scattering them as they retreated from the sheer savagery of the attack.

Stig saw Mohegas ten meters away, gesturing wildly to him, and pointing to the village. He couldn't hear what the elder was saying, but, as he turned farther to the right, his heart leapt in horror.

Three of the Ghostfaces had survived the brief fight at the palisade. And now they were dashing in among the neat rows of huts, shoving doors open, checking inside, then continuing on their way when they found the huts unoccupied.

But there was one they were heading for that wouldn't be empty, Stig knew. That was the large hut in the center of the village.

The hut where the children and women were assembled.

The hut where Tecumsa was helping to guard the children.

With a hoarse cry, Stig set his shield more firmly on his left arm and, with his ax in his right hand, began to run toward the rows of huts. But, even as he did, he realized that the Ghostfaces had too big a lead over him.

This was a race he couldn't win.

chapter forty

Hal watched as the last of the canoes emerged from the river into the bay. Including the six that had already landed on the far beach, he counted seventeen canoes. There had been eighteen drawn up on the beach by the Limigina village and he waited several seconds to see if a final canoe would emerge.

But there was no sign of another craft and he reasoned that Stig must have smashed one beyond repair. Either that or the fire he had set had caught one of them and destroyed it before the Ghosts could save it from the flames. Whatever the case, there were now eleven canoes strung out in a ragged line, heading for the beach. It was time for them to move.

"Get rid of this mess!" he ordered, hacking at the tangle of creepers and branches that had served to conceal the *Heron* from view. The other three set to with a will, and the mass of foliage was sent flying over the side into the water.

"Cast off, Edvin," he ordered.

There was no need to give orders to Ulf and Wulf. They were already hauling the starboard yardarm and sail aloft, the slender yard rising in a series of rapid jerks. As the wind caught the unrestrained sail, it flapped and billowed wildly. Then, as Edvin darted ashore and released the two mooring lines, the twins heaved in on the sheets; the sail filled, then hardened. They were close to the rocks and the starboard side of the ship grated unpleasantly against them as the wind forced it toward the shore. Then Hal heaved on the tiller and the taut sail powered them out and away from the headland, gathering speed as they went. They were on a reach, their best point of sailing, with the wind from abeam on their port side. The bow rose and fell on the small swell within the bay, dashing spray up to either side as the ship cut into the water on the downward thrust.

The last canoe in line was only twenty meters away. There were five warriors on board, Hal could see, all of them armed with clubs and axes. He stooped to peer under the sail as they bore down on the unsuspecting craft, angling the *Heron* so she'd come in behind them and slightly to their left.

At the last moment, something warned the rear paddler and he turned, a look of horror forming on his face as he saw the seemingly huge craft behind them, its sharp prow slicing through the waves, throwing spray high in the air to either side.

He yelled a warning to his companions, but the warning came too late. *Heron* rose on a small wave, then her forefoot came plunging down, slamming into the frail timbers of the canoe and smashing them, opening a gaping hole close to the stern, then riding over the canoe and driving it under, spilling its crew out into the bay.

There were cries of alarm and fear as the *Heron* rode up and over the canoe, rolling it over and leaving it upside down in her wake, surrounded by the bobbing heads of her surviving crew members. Hal counted three survivors in the water. The others must have gone under when *Heron* smashed the canoe.

"No need for the Mangler," he said to Edvin with a savage grin, then he heaved on the tiller to set course after the next canoe in line.

This crew, alerted by the shouts of fear, had seen what had just happened to their comrades and tried to avoid the onrushing ship. Hal brought the bow around to follow their course, once again aiming for a strike on the canoe's stern quarter. At the last minute, the paddlers heaved their craft to one side, avoiding the axlike bow that bore down on them by a matter of a few meters, and sliding down the starboard side. Cursing, Hal put all his weight on the tiller and dragged the *Heron*'s bow violently to port, causing the stern to slew wildly to starboard as a result. The hull caught the canoe side on, slamming into it, collapsing it and capsizing it. Again, he heard cries of defiance and screams of terror. He glanced quickly astern and could see only two heads bobbing in the water beside the swamped canoe. Obviously, there were many among the Ghostfaces who couldn't swim.

He looked for the remaining nine canoes and saw that they were still heading for the beach—and now they were more than halfway there. Stern attacks were too difficult, he thought. They gave the canoes too much opportunity to twist away from the *Heron* in the last few meters. He'd have to get ahead of the other canoes, then begin a series of broadside attacks, leaving them less chance to evade him.

"Sheet home!" he yelled to the twins, and headed the ship to the southwest, on a slightly divergent course to the remaining canoes, which were heading west. *Heron,* with her sail sheeted home tightly, fairly flew across the surface of the bay, sending spray fanning high to either side as she cut through the waves. She rapidly overhauled the desperately paddling canoes, the crews of which were now all too aware of her presence. Hal, eyes narrowed in concentration, judged distances and angles as the little ship overtook the canoes. Then, when he judged the moment to be right, he swung her about to go downwind, calling to Ulf and Wulf to let the sail out to starboard as far as it would go.

Driven by a stern wind, *Heron* swooped down on the leading three canoes, which were in a staggered line-abreast formation.

"Couldn't be better," Hal muttered grimly. With any luck, he'd be able to smash his ship into all three on the one pass. He saw that the nearest canoe, which was slightly in the lead of the others, was gaining on him, moving right to left across his bow. He waited, letting the crew think they had escaped, then brought the *Heron* to port, angling his course in front of the fleeing canoe.

He judged it perfectly. The canoe, initially to starboard, continued to move from right to left, placing itself directly under the *Heron*'s bow. There was a splintering crash as the ship slammed into the canoe's hull at right angles. More screams of fear and anger, and he felt the ship shudder slightly as it drove the canoe under the surface.

They swept past the wrecked craft and he aimed for the next in line. They tried to evade him, but he was too close and moving too quickly. With another splintering crash, *Heron* sliced off the forward section of the canoe, from a point about a meter short of her bow. Water rushed in and the canoe sank immediately. The canoes were fast and maneuverable, he thought, but their light frames and birch-bark cladding gave them little chance against the solid oak of the *Heron*'s bow.

He looked for the third canoe in that leading bunch and muttered a curse. He'd hoped to take all three in one pass, but that had been wishful thinking. The crew of the third canoe, seeing their two companions smashed and driven under, had swung away to the east, back toward the river mouth. If he went after them now, he'd be leaving the way open for the rest of the fleet. His best course now was to swing left in a wide arc, staying ahead of the canoes, and repeat the attack he had just carried out.

He swung to the east, then, yelling orders to Ulf and Wulf, brought the *Heron* round, tacking upwind as close as she would lie. Knowing that he would need all the speed he could muster for his next maneuver, he let the bow fall off a little, and sensed the ship accelerating. He held that course for a few minutes, glancing back over his shoulder to keep track of the Ghostface canoes, then heaved the tiller over to swing to port.

"Let fly!" he shouted at the same moment, and Ulf and Wulf released the sail, spilling the wind out of it and presenting no resistance to the headwind as the bow of the ship swung to port.

With only a limited crew, he didn't have time for fancy sail handling. Normally, as the ship came across the wind, he would have lowered the starboard sail and raised the port one. But he didn't have enough men and all he could do was hope that his speed and momentum would carry the ship through a 180-degree turn, allowing the starboard sail—now unrestrained and flapping and whip cracking in protest—to fill so that he could run down on the canoes once again.

The bow was swinging. It moved quickly at first, but it was beginning to slow as it crossed the wind's eye and began to fall off downwind. Now it was barely moving at all, and he thought, for one horrible moment, that the momentum hadn't been enough to carry her through the complete turn. If that was the case, they would be caught, heading into the wind with the sail flapping uselessly and with no way for it to power them back downwind.

Then the bow came all the way around and the sail began to fill as the wind came from behind it.

"Sheet home!" he yelled, although there was no need. Ulf and Wulf knew their job by now and they gradually hauled the sail in, trapping the wind and harnessing its power. As they did, *Heron* began to surge, her bow rising and falling once more.

And ahead of them were four more canoes, paddling desperately to reach the shore before this terrible nemesis swept down on them.

Heron smashed into the nearest, with the now-familiar pandemonium of shouts and screams and rending wood. Hal felt the impact through the soles of his feet, transmitted through the planks of the ship. The second canoe had accelerated and was now to port. He adjusted the tiller and drove the bow into it from dead abeam. The canoe actually split in two, with the two halves rising out of the water momentarily, to be visible on either side of the bow. He searched the bay for another target, then heard a cry of warning from Wulf.

He looked for'ard. Two Ghostface warriors were clambering over the bow, dropping onto the deck as he watched. They must have leapt for the bow at the last moment, he realized. They hesitated, getting their bearings in these unfamiliar surroundings, then their eyes settled on the twins tending the sail amidships. The Ghostfaces had lost their principal weapons in the crash, but they both had long flint knives in their belts and they drew them now, moving purposefully toward the sail handlers.

Wulf was caught up with the mainsheet, trying to keep the *Heron* powering through the waves. Ulf stood and drew his saxe as the two Ghosts approached. His ax was too far away to reach in time. They saw the gleam of metal in his hand and hesitated. Then they separated to take him from two angles.

"Take the helm!" Hal yelled at Edvin. He let the tiller go and dashed forward, drawing his sword.

As he released the tiller, the ship yawed wildly, trying to fly head to wind. It was as well it did. The unintentional action caused the deck to lurch violently, and one of the Ghostfaces stumbled, falling into the rowing benches on the opposite side of the ship to where Ulf was waiting.

The other Ghostface struck underhand at Ulf with his knife. Ulf parried with his saxe, and a startling shower of sparks flew from the contact as steel and flint blades met. The Ghostface warrior had never seen that happen before and he flinched, dropping his eyes from Ulf to his blade.

It was a mistake. As the Ghostface lost focus, Ulf's saxe slipped forward and took him in the side. The man grunted in surprise and pain, then looked down at the blood welling from the long slash in his side and fell to the deck.

But now his comrade had regained his feet and dashed under the sail to attack Ulf. Hal was still several meters away and he yelled a warning to his shipmate. Ulf turned, caught his foot on a trailing length of rope and stumbled backward. The Ghostface's eyes gleamed with triumph and he stepped toward him.

To be met by a hurtling mass of black, brown and white fur as Kloof launched herself at him. Fifty-five kilograms of snarling, ravening dog slammed into the Ghostface and drove him back, sending him crashing to the deck planking. His knife flew from his hand and was lost somewhere below the rowing benches. Desperate with fear, he scrambled backward, away from the huge dog. Kloof crouched, ready to attack again. Her massive jaws opened, revealing huge, lethal teeth.

With a cry of utter terror, the warrior rolled to his feet and hurled himself over the railing, into the bay.

Hal put a hand down and helped Ulf to his feet. He re-sheathed his sword and smiled at the twins.

"That was exciting, wasn't it?" he said. Kloof padded over to him, rumbling and growling contentedly. She liked nothing more than scaring the daylights out of an enemy, he thought. But she would have liked to get a bite or two in before the man fled.

Ulf reached down to her and fondled her head, ruffling the fur about her ears.

"Good dog, Kloof," he said. "He certainly wasn't expecting that."

Wulf glanced up at them from where he was still tending the mainsheet that controlled the sail.

"If you're through playing with the dog, would you mind giving me a hand with the sail?" he said sarcastically.

Ulf grinned at Hal. "I'd better give him a hand. He's something of a weakling and the wind might blow him away."

Wulf opened his mouth to reply. But he was forestalled by a shout from Edvin, at the steering platform.

While the tiller had been momentarily untended, the ship had weathervaned into the wind and lost way. As she lay, rolling with the swell, two more canoes had pulled alongside, and now their crews were clambering over the bulwarks and onto the *Heron*'s stern.

chapter forty-one

Thorn paused to take stock of the situation. The village had been attacked by just over thirty men. Of those, eight had been killed or wounded by the barrage of bolts from the two crossbow batteries.

Another ten had turned to attack the crossbows Lydia was commanding, and he could see flashes of movement from the trees to his right as Lydia, Stefan and Jesper led the eight Mawags assigned to the crossbows in a spirited defense.

A further small group had breached the perimeter to the left, and he had seen Stig start off after them.

That left a small group of eight to ten Ghostface warriors in an uncertain group in front of the barricade. For once, he realized, the Mawags had their long-time enemy outnumbered. But that situation might not last for long. If Hal didn't succeed in stopping the rest of the canoes, reinforcements could arrive anytime. In every battle, he knew, a time came when one side or the other could make a decisive move. That time was now.

"Ingvar!" Thorn bellowed, and Ingvar's huge form rose above the barricade. His voulge blade was stained an ominous red, Thorn noticed. He'd seen how the big lad had dealt with the Ghostface leader, dispatching him with almost contemptuous ease.

"Yes, Thorn?" Ingvar was peering uncertainly at the tree line.

Thorn moved forward so he could be seen more clearly. He pointed at the huddled group of Ghostfaces between them.

"We've got them outnumbered. Attack now! We'll take them from the rear!"

Ingvar didn't reply. Instead, he raised the voulge over his head and turned to the men around him inside the barricade.

"Come on!" he yelled, and leapt onto the top of the palisade, scrambling down the far side and heading for the remaining Ghostfaces. Simsinnet was close behind him and the rest of the Mawags followed on his heels, rattling and clattering down the palisade with its close-knit screen of branches and saplings. Then Ingvar was charging into the small group of Ghostfaces, who turned, panic-stricken at the sight of him, to run.

And saw Thorn's men emerging from the trees behind them. Cornered, confused, they turned back to face the first attack. Ingvar was upon them almost immediately. This time, he used the voulge in full, arcing sweeps, smashing through the flimsy shields the Ghostfaces carried, batting their stone and wooden weapons aside, then withdrawing the weapon and lunging at them with the spear point.

The momentum of his charge carried him through the small group, scattering them and leaving three mortally wounded. The Mawags behind him, led by Simsinnet wielding a long-handled wooden club, followed up on his attack. They put years of humiliation and frustration behind every stroke of ax or club, smashing into the enemy group, battering them and hacking at them with flint knives.

Thorn turned to the right, heading for the trees where Lydia's men were fighting off the Ghosts' attack.

Lydia brought down another of the attackers with a dart. Then she stepped aside as Jesper and Stefan charged into the attackers, followed by the eight Mawags who had been manning the crossbows.

Stefan smashed his ax into the enemy on either side of him, scattering them in panic. Jesper darted his sword in and out with lightning speed, proving the truth of Thorn's oft-spoken dictum, *Three centimeters of point is as good as thirty of edge any day.* Their big round shields effectively protected them from the Ghostfaces' attempted ripostes, and their razor-sharp steel weapons sliced and hewed through the light hide shields their enemies carried. Together, they carved a path through the attackers, with Lydia a few meters behind them, poised on a fallen tree trunk and ready to send a dart flying at any attacker who might look likely to break through their defenses.

In truth, their attack was so effective that there was little for their Mawag comrades to do. They followed the two Skandians as they rampaged their way through the Ghostfaces, their weapons at the ready but so far unused.

The critical moment came when Thorn and his men appeared behind the retreating Ghosts, with Ingvar and another group of Mawags close behind them. Stefan and Jesper let out a yell of recognition as the shaggy-haired old warrior hit the rear of the enemy's ragged line with the force of a battering ram. Caught between two irresistible forces, the surviving Ghostfaces did the only sensible thing.

They ran, skirting off to one side through the trees, heading for the beach where their canoes were drawn up, hoping to escape.

A hope that was dashed when they heard the implacable pounding of feet behind them as the four terrible foreigners pursued them, accompanied by a large group of Mawags.

Exhausted and terrified, the small party of Ghostfaces emerged into the sunlight that flooded the beach. Their canoes were still drawn up above the high-water mark. And now, they saw with relief, an additional three craft were pulling into the shallows, their crews spilling out into the ankle-deep water and turning to drag their canoes ashore.

Farther out in the bay, a strange craft could be seen. It was the length of four canoes and sat much higher out of the water. Two canoes were tied to the stern of the vessel, and they could hear faint sounds of combat carrying across the bay.

The new arrivals from the canoes looked at their panicked comrades in surprise as the latter dashed down the beach to greet them.

"Back in the canoes!" one of them shouted, his voice high-pitched with terror. "The enemy are right behind us!"

Fist of Stone, the lead paddler on the first canoe to land,

laughed scornfully. The only enemy here were the Mawagansett, and they had never shown any effective resistance to the Ghostfaces in the past.

Of course, the appearance of the strange ship cruising the bay was a matter of some concern. But the three canoes had effectively escaped its attack. The Mawags would be easy meat.

"You're women!" he sneered. "Women who run in fright from a few Mawagansett! Step behind us, little women. We'll protect you. After all—"

His voice died away as a group of warriors burst out of the trees and stopped, surveying the beach. Fist of Stone had fourteen men with him, not counting the terrified group who had just joined them. He estimated that there were approximately twenty warriors facing him. They were mostly Mawagansett, but four of them were pale haired and pale skinned. Not four, but five, he realized as he caught sight of a slim figure behind them. Then his surprise mounted as he realized the fifth stranger was a girl.

"Form a battle line!" he ordered his men, gesturing with his wooden club to indicate where the line should stand. As they hurried into position, he raised the club defiantly. He felt a vague twinge of unease at the sight of the men facing him. Ghostfaces were used to fighting with overwhelming numerical superiority. If anything, they were slightly outnumbered here. Still, the majority of their enemies were Mawagansett, whom he dismissed as frightened rabbits, useless in a battle. He turned to voice the thought to his men.

"Kill them!" he ordered. "They're only Mawagan—"

He got no farther as he felt a tremendous blow in his side, just above his hip. He looked down in surprise to see a meter-long dart had hit him there, and blood was coursing down his left side.

Lydia had an uncanny knack for spotting an enemy commander, and as her target sank to the sand, there was an uneasy murmur of fear from his men. Thorn turned to Jesper, Ingvar and Stefan.

"Arrowhead," he said quietly, and they formed up behind him, Ingvar on one side, Jesper and Stefan on the other, so that they created a V formation, with Thorn at its head. Thorn's face set in an almost blissful smile as he uttered his favorite command.

"Let's get 'em."

The four paced out down the beach, followed by the ragged formation of Mawagansett warriors. They didn't run. They advanced steadily at walking pace, and that was all the more terrifying for the Ghostfaces who awaited them. The sand squeaked under their boots, and bright sunlight glinted off their weapons.

As they came closer, the Ghostfaces began to shrink back, instinctively gathering closer together—a movement that merely restricted their own ability to use their weapons. The Skandians were a terrifying sight and some of the Ghostfaces recalled the story they had heard of demons. A low wail of fear rose from the tightly packed Ghostfaces, and Thorn recognized that this was the moment to strike.

"Now!" he roared, bounding over the last few meters and bringing his mighty club-hand smashing down on one of the warriors in the front rank. The man's knees buckled and he went down. Beside him, Thorn saw Jesper slashing at another enemy, sending him staggering backward in a desperate attempt to avoid the sword as it sliced through his lightweight shield.

"Use the point!" Thorn growled, slamming his club into another warrior's ribs and hurling him to the side. At the same time, Stefan crashed his ax down through a Ghostface's utterly inadequate defenses and into the warrior himself, then jerked it free as the man screamed in pain and fear and sank to the ground. Jesper, suitably chastened, lunged and took his man in the midsection.

Ingvar needed no direction from Thorn. His voulge darted in and out, alternately stabbing, hooking and chopping at the enemy.

In a matter of seconds, four of the Ghosts' best warriors were dead or disabled. Coupled with the startling loss of their leader, it was all too much for the remaining invaders. A cry of terror swept through them and they turned and ran. Thorn stood back, gesturing after them to Simsinnet and the other Mawagansett, eager for revenge on their hated enemies.

"Go get 'em," he said.

The Mawagansett force surged forward, clubs, lances and axes raised, and hurled themselves upon the retreating Ghostfaces.

Thorn turned and smiled at his companions.

"I think our work here is done," he said. Then he glanced out to the bay. "Wonder how Hal is doing?"

Hal, Edvin, Ulf and Wulf stood shoulder to shoulder across the raised center deck of the *Heron* as the Ghostfaces scrambled aboard. There were nine men in the two canoes and they bunched up in the narrow space where the stern of the ship tapered down to a point.

"Don't give them room to move," Hal ordered. "Keep them cramped in the stern." Then he gave the order he'd always wanted to issue.

"Let's get 'em, boys!"

He and his three companions surged forward, pinning the boarders back into the confined space of the stern, smashing into them with their shields, then swinging freely with axes and swords as the Ghostfaces desperately tried to get out of one another's way and find room to wield their weapons.

Within a few seconds, the numbers were more or less even as each of the Herons dispatched one of the enemy, leaving four Skandians facing five Ghostfaces. Now the fighting became more difficult as the Ghostfaces had room to swing their clubs and axes. But still, the superiority of the Skandians' weapons gave them an advantage. They battered, stabbed and hacked at the enemy, forcing them farther back into the cramped triangular space at the stern. One of the Ghostface warriors slipped past them, hurling himself in a forward somersault that carried him under their weapons. He rose to his feet behind them, a massive war club ready, his eyes alight with triumph as he measured the distance to Ulf's unprotected back.

Then he screamed as Kloof leapt, hitting him in the chest with her forepaws, her teeth and jaws slashing and snapping at him.

He rolled across the deck, desperate to escape her. He came up on one knee, and as Kloof gathered her hindquarters under her for another leap, he chose the path that so many attackers had chosen before him.

With a desperate leap, he sprang to the bulwark and vaulted over it, landing in the sea overside with an enormous splash. Kloof, barking furiously, stood on her hind legs, her forepaws on the bulwark, snarling after him as he splashed awkwardly away from the ship, sheer terror lending him the ability to swim.

Two more of his comrades sank to the deck, wounded. The remaining pair hesitated, then dropped their weapons and scrambled back over the side, dropping into one of the canoes tethered there, setting it rocking wildly. Water poured over the low bulwarks before they managed to right it and shove themselves clear of *Heron*'s side. Their floundering companion, the warrior who had only just evaded Kloof's jaws, called to them for help. But they ignored him, seizing paddles and dragging the half-swamped craft sluggishly back toward the river mouth. Gradually, his cries died away, ending with a bubbling groan as he sank beneath the waves.

"Let 'em go," Hal said. Then he saw with a start of alarm how close to the rocks *Heron* had drifted during the brief but desperate fight. He leapt toward the tiller, signaling for Ulf and Wulf to take the sail under control once more. Edvin, unbidden, seized one of the long oars from its rack and hurried forward, in case he needed to fend the ship off the rocks.

As it turned out, they brought her under control seconds before this was necessary—although it was a matter of only a few meters. Hal, heaving a huge sigh of relief, swung the *Heron*'s bow toward the beach, where he could make out the distinctive figures of Thorn, Lydia and Ingvar. Jesper and Stefan had stayed with the Mawagansett to hunt down the retreating Ghostfaces. He could see a struggling group farther along the beach where the Ghosts were making a last, desperate stand. As he ran the bow up onto the sand, the struggle ended. Three of the Ghosts were left alive to surrender.

Hal leapt down from the bow of the ship onto the sand and embraced his friends. Thorn gestured to the bay, where the wrecked hulls of several canoes were slowly drifting out to sea with the falling tide.

"That seemed to go well," he said.

Hal nodded. "A few got past us," he admitted. Then he looked around, seeing Stefan and Jesper trudging wearily up the beach to rejoin them. Stefan had a slight wound in one leg and had his arm around the smaller youth's shoulders for support. A cold hand seized Hal's heart as he realized someone was missing.

"Where's Stig?" he asked.

chapter forty-two

Stig sped through the village, running light-footed and barely noticing the weight of his ax and the heavy shield on his left arm. He took a direct route, hurdling over the fireplaces and stools that stood in front of the huts and turning down the central lane that led to the hut where he knew Tecumsa and several other women had taken refuge with some of the children.

His heart skipped a beat as he saw the hut—and the three Ghostface warriors outside, hammering at a makeshift barricade of branches, bed frames and stools that had been erected in the doorway by those inside. As he watched, the central Ghostface, a stocky, heavily set warrior with a huge barrel chest and thick muscular arms, tore the last of the impediments aside, opening the way into the hut.

"You!" Stig challenged. "Stop right there!"

The three white-faced warriors turned in surprise. They hadn't expected to see anyone following them. They thought they had made their way into the village unnoticed by the main body of defenders.

Now they found themselves confronted by one of the strange, pale-haired warriors they had seen assisting the Mawagansett. And they all knew by now how well these strangers could fight. The heavy-set Ghostface said something to his two companions, then plunged through the door into the hut, tossing the last of the improvised barricade aside.

Stig heard a terrified wailing as the children inside screamed at the sight of the intruder. He redoubled his pace, charging at the two Ghostfaces who remained outside to block his path.

Running full pace, he slammed his shield into one and sent him flying backward. The other lunged at him with a long lance and Stig parried it with his ax, beating the point down and to the side.

Barely pausing, he swept the ax up and over into a vertical strike, a movement that required enormous strength and muscle coordination. But the Ghostface leapt backward just in time, and the ax blade missed him by centimeters. He withdrew his lance and was preparing for another lunge when Stig, recovering first, smashed the ax down onto the hardwood shaft, neatly severing it into two pieces. The Ghostface looked at his weapon in surprise. It was heavy hardwood and he had never seen an ax that could cut through it so easily.

While he was still wondering, Stig swept the ax through a

horizontal arc, slamming the side of the heavy head into the Ghostface's jaw. There was an ugly crunch and the man dropped, unconscious, to the sand, where he remained unmoving.

Stig turned to the hut. He could hear the screaming intensifying inside. Then he heard another voice. It was Tecumsa, shouting defiance at the warrior who had gone through the door. The sound of her voice galvanized Stig, and he started for the doorway.

But some sixth sense warned him and he half turned, bringing his shield up to block the long flint knife that the first Ghostface, now recovered and back on his feet, lunged at him. The knife scraped on the wood, gouging a huge rent in the cowhide covering. Then Stig spun and delivered a killing blow with the edge of the ax, taking the man in the ribs and dropping him to the sand as well.

He leapt through the door, clearing the tangle of stools and cook pots that had been used to block the entry. His eyes were unaccustomed to the dim light inside for a few seconds, and he hesitated just inside the door, peering owlishly around.

Then his eyes adjusted and he gasped at the scene that greeted him. Eight or nine children and three older women were cowering back against the far wall of the hut. One of the women, he could see, was working with a knife to cut a rent in the tough deer hide of the wall so they could escape.

Between them and the menacing figure of the Ghostface leader, Tecumsa crouched, a long, flint-headed lance in her hands, held parallel to the ground and darting out at the warrior's legs, groin and then face, in a series of lightning jabs. As she jabbed the lance at him, she shuffled forward in small steps, constantly advancing and giving him no chance to reply. He parried her thrusts desperately, watching through slitted eyes for the moment when she would make a mistake and leave herself vulnerable.

Stig's heart lurched with fear. Tecumsa had the advantage for the moment, he could see. But he knew she was facing an experienced warrior and that advantage would be short-lived. His only chance was to distract the Ghostface, to turn the man away from Tecumsa to face him.

"You!" he shouted. "Fight me, you coward!"

But his attempt to distract the Ghostface had tragic results. Tecumsa, until now intent on the enemy warrior, heard the voice of her beloved Stig and looked toward the figure silhouetted in the doorway.

"Stig!" she cried, the relief all too evident in her voice. And, momentarily, she stopped the constant jabbing and lunging with the lance.

The Ghostface reacted instantly, seizing the opportunity she offered. He swung his stone-headed ax at her, sweeping down to crush her skull.

But Tecumsa was agile and young and she leapt to one side as the deadly weapon whipped down, so that it merely grazed the side of her head. Instantly, blood sprang from the wound, but Stig could see it was only a glancing blow, and not the death stroke the Ghostface had intended. Tecumsa gave a cry of pain and fright and staggered back. Before the fearsome white-painted warrior could follow up, Stig was upon him.

The Ghostface parried desperately as Stig rained blow after blow down on him. The ax was a glittering wheel of light, one stroke blending into another as the Skandian used all his strength and skill to overwhelm the Ghostface. The skull-faced warrior barely had time to strike back. The few blows he managed to land were treated with contempt, deflected by the big round shield on Stig's left arm, or blocked by the heavy ax, which seemed to have a life of its own, moving at blinding speed.

Tecumsa watched fearfully, one hand to the side of her head, trying to stem the flow of blood. Like all scalp wounds, it bled prodigiously. But she knew it wasn't a major injury. One of the other women advanced and handed her a soft piece of cloth. She held it to her head, stopping the flow. Her vision was a little unfocused, but she knew that was merely a side effect of the head wound.

The Ghostface was breathing heavily now, his breath coming in giant gasps that set his shoulders heaving and his chest rising and falling. But it was less the result of exertion and more of fear. He was facing an opponent more skilled than he, armed with superior weapons. There could only be one result to this fight.

And it came as he swung a clumsy blow with his ax and missed completely, staggering and spinning halfway round with the momentum of the awkward stroke. His small shield had been smashed to tatters in the first moments of this engagement and he was unprotected.

Although he was still young, Stig had fought many battles in his life. In the heat of a massed conflict, it would be a matter of striking out at those who faced him, beating down their defenses and dispatching them as quickly and as efficiently as possible.

But in single combats, he had often chosen to spare an enemy when he found him open and at his mercy, using the flat of his ax head to stun his opponent. This time, with the memory of that savage blow aimed at Tecumsa fresh in his mind, he felt no such compunction.

He swung the ax in a fierce, controlled strike that caught the Ghostface between his right shoulder and his neck, biting deep into his upper body. The stone ax fell from lifeless hands and the Ghostface, his eyes already glazing, toppled to one side like a rag doll.

An involuntary sigh of "Aaaaaaah!" came from the assembled children and women who were watching. Tecumsa, still interposing her body between the huddled children and their would-be attacker, smiled at him and mouthed his name.

He felt his heart swell with love for her, and relief that she was still standing. He dropped his weapons and moved to her, sweeping her into his arms and kissing her repeatedly. She sank into his embrace, and the children and the other women came to gather around the two of them, throwing their arms around them and speaking their names in joy and relief.

Gently, Stig touched the side of Tecumsa's head, where the shallow graze was still bleeding, although nowhere near as freely as it had initially.

"I'm all right," she assured him, smiling up into his eyes, seeing the concern and love there. "He only grazed me. I barely felt it."

"You're sure?" he said, his voice catching in his throat. The thought of anything happening to her was unbearable. But she smiled again and nodded.

"I'm sure."

With a sigh of relief, he released her and stepped back, gently disengaging several of the children who had their arms around his waist and were seeking his attention.

"Did you see her, Stig?" one of the older boys asked excitedly. "She kept going forward and shouting at the Ghostface, just the way Lydia told her."

"Yes. I saw her." He smiled.

"She's very brave. Are you proud of her?"

"More proud than you could know," he told the boy and he looked up, still smiling, to catch Tecumsa's eye. The smile froze on his lips as he saw her shaking her head uncertainly, the back of her hand to her forehead. She took a step, staggered and looked at him.

"Stig?" she said, her voice full of sudden fear, and he was instantly by her side, his arms around her to steady her. Gently, he laid her down on a pile of blankets and knelt by her side, holding her hand and stroking her beautiful face. She was very pale, he realized, and her eyes didn't seem to be focusing properly.

"Stig . . . ," she repeated. "I love you, Stig."

"I love you too, Tecumsa," he said, his voice breaking. He looked up to one of the older women. "Fetch someone!" he shouted. "She needs help."

The woman nodded and darted out of the hut, followed by several of the children. He could hear her yelling for help as she ran up the laneway between the huts to the palisade. The village healers were there, he knew, ready to tend to any of the warriors who might be wounded in the battle.

He squeezed Tecumsa's hand reassuringly. "Help is coming," he said.

She smiled vaguely. "That's nice," she said.

Then her eyes slowly closed and she simply stopped breathing.

chapter forty-three

Alerted by the children, Hal found his friend some minutes later.

Stig was cradling Tecumsa's lifeless body in his arms. He sat on the floor of the hut, bending over her, tears running in torrents down his face. Hal, glancing through the door and taking in the tragic scene, motioned for the others to remain outside while he entered.

He went down on his knees beside his weeping friend. His heart was torn in two for Stig. He knew how much his first mate had loved the beautiful Mawagansett maid, knew how he saw her as the beginning of a new chapter in his life, free of the shame that he perceived followed him in Hallasholm because of the treachery of his father. Here, in the foreign western land, he was well regarded and loved without any taint of family history to affect him.

"Stig," he said softly, "I'm sorry. So sorry."

But Stig didn't seem to hear him. He continued to rock slowly back and forth above Tecumsa's still body, little whimpers of grief escaping him. Hal touched him gently on the shoulder.

"Stig," he said, and finally his friend looked up at him, a depth of sorrow in his eyes such as Hal had never seen.

"I loved her, Hal," he said, the words seeming to be wrenched from him. "I loved her so much and I couldn't save her."

In the back of Stig's mind was the hideous thought that he might have actually been responsible for her death. He had shouted at the Ghostface to distract him but had succeeded only in diverting Tecumsa's attention from her desperate attack on the invader. If he hadn't called out, an insidious worm of guilt whispered, she would still be alive. But that thought was so dreadful, he couldn't begin to admit to it, couldn't voice it to his friend.

Hal, wisely, said nothing. There were no words for a moment like this. All he could offer was his friendship, his support and, most of all, his presence beside his oldest and best friend.

They sat thus for some minutes, then a shadow blocked the sunlight coming through the doorway and Thorn entered, his movements surprisingly quiet for someone so bulky. He knelt on the other side of the stricken first mate and put his left arm around the young man's shoulders. Finally, he spoke, his usually rough and raucous voice surprisingly gentle.

"Come on, lad, it's time to take her to her family."

Stig looked up at him and, like Hal, Thorn was stricken by the devastating sadness in those eyes.

"He barely touched her, Thorn. He just grazed her, that's all. He nearly missed completely." He looked down at the pale face of the young woman. "But she's dead."

Thorn gripped Stig's shoulder with his left hand. "Sometimes that's the way of it, lad. I've seen men suffer shocking wounds and survive with no ill effects. With others, a mere scratch can kill them. There's no understanding it. Don't try."

"He barely touched her," Stig repeated.

Thorn reached down and gently disentangled Stig's hands from Tecumsa's still form. "Aye. It's a terrible thing. But it's time to let her go. Her family needs her now."

Reluctantly, Stig allowed Thorn to release Tecumsa from his embrace. Then the bulky old sea wolf came to his knees, slipped his arms around Tecumsa and rose to his feet, cradling her to him. Slowly, Stig rose, his eyes riveted on the beautiful face. Hal stood as well. There was a huge lump in his throat, and he felt tears stinging the backs of his eyelids. He blinked them away, then stopped. Let them fall, he thought. Tecumsa deserved them. Stig deserved them.

Slowly, the three friends made their way out into the uncaring, bright sunshine. Stig blinked and looked around himself. How could the sun shine so brightly, so cheerfully, on such a dreadful day?

"Come on, Stig," Thorn said. "Let's take her to her mother."

Walking three abreast, with Thorn in the middle carrying Tecumsa, they made their way down the lane between the huts, heading for the hut where Tecumsa's parents, shattered by the news of their daughter's death, waited for them.

The rest of the Heron brotherband followed them in a silent, somber procession, heads bowed in sorrow for their shipmate.

Four days later, Tecumsa's body, wrapped in clean scented robes, was laid to rest in accordance with the Mawagansetts' customs.

Inside her parents' hut, the tribe's senior holy man prayed over her, wafting the smoke from a burning eagle's feather and a smoldering pot of herbs over the funeral bier. The immediate family, accompanied by Stig, stood and witnessed the brief ceremony. Then, at a signal from the priest, four of the tribe's young men, led by a weeping Simsinnet, entered the hut and raised the bier on which she lay to shoulder height and carried her out of the hut, where the tribe, and the Herons, were standing in several lines, forming a guard of honor.

They processed past the other Mawagansett, and the Skandians, who bowed their heads in respect as the bier passed. Tecumsa's people, Hal noticed, held their heads erect, watching the young woman as she began her final journey.

When everyone had witnessed her passing, the burial party, consisting of the priest and his assistants, the four bearers, Tecumsa's family and Stig, set out for a secluded grove in the forest where the tribe had their cemetery. Normally, an outsider and a nonbeliever such as Stig would not have accompanied them. But Tecumsa had loved Stig, and so did her family, so he was included.

In a quiet grove in the forest, a small hut had been constructed from a timber frame covered with bark. It was just big enough to accommodate the bier on which Tecumsa lay and it stood among a score of similar structures, in varying stages of repair. Half a dozen were obviously brand-new, and they held the remains of the warriors who had been killed in the Ghostfaces' attack. Some were crumbling and on the verge of collapse. They had clearly been there for years.

The priest explained the tradition to Stig as he saw him looking at the derelict huts. "Soon we will collect the bones from those huts and they will be buried in the communal resting place with those of the rest of the tribe. Eventually, the same will be done for Bird of the Forest."

This was now the name by which Tecumsa was known. The Mawagansett believed that if a deceased person's name was spoken, the spirit might be called back, to wander, lost and alone, between this world and the next.

Stig nodded, looking round the peaceful grove. In the surrounding trees, birds flitted and sang. It was a beautiful spot, he thought. She would have loved it. He felt a gentle touch on his shoulder and looked down into Simsinnet's compassionate eyes.

"I loved her too, brother Stig," said the Mawagansett. "Thank you for trying to save her."

Stig nodded, a huge lump in his throat preventing him from speaking. His heart was leaden. He bowed his head before the hut where Tecumsa's body had been laid to rest and said his own private farewell. He had loved her so much, he thought. He wondered whether he would ever love anyone again.

Then, as the priest and the family began to intone their final salute and farewell to Bird of the Forest, he turned on his heel and strode back through the trees toward the village. Suddenly, all he wanted was to be with his own people.

Mohegas and Hal stood together on the beach as Edvin supervised the final stages of *Heron*'s provisioning, which had been interrupted by the arrival of the Ghostfaces. A dozen Ghostface prisoners formed a line, supervised by the Herons, carrying the final fresh food and water supplies on board. They were the few who had surrendered on the beach, accompanied by survivors from the canoes who had been picked up from various spots around the bay.

Hal nodded in their direction. "What do you plan to do with them?" he asked. If the tables had been turned, he knew, the Ghostfaces would have killed their captives. But Mohegas had other ideas.

"We'll keep them as prisoners and take them upriver to rebuild the villages they destroyed," he said.

"That's a wise decision," Hal told him.

Mohegas nodded gravely. After a few seconds, he said, "You're leaving today?"

"I think Stig would prefer that," Hal replied. "The tide's due to turn soon. We'll go out with it."

"And will you ever return?" Mohegas asked.

Hal smiled at him. "Would we be welcome?"

The Mawag elder hesitated, not wanting to cause offense. He chose his words carefully. "You, yes. But others might follow you who would be less so. After all, your people are warriors and your steel weapons are far more effective than our stone ones. I'm not sure we would welcome such visitors."

"I thought not," Hal said. "That's why I will keep no records for this voyage. Nobody will know how we came here, or how we returned."

Mohegas nodded approval. "I think that would be best."

chapter forty-four

Hal realized that Ulf, Wulf and Stefan had approached and were standing, seeking to catch his attention. He glanced from them to the two canoes drawn up on the beach behind them and raised his eyebrows in a question.

"Everything's ready, Hal," Stefan said.

Hal nodded to Mohegas and moved to join his shipmates.

In one of the canoes, Orvik's body was laid out, his arms crossed over his chest and his old, worn saxe clasped in his right fist, its bare blade still stained with the dried blood of the Ghostface Orvik had killed. He was wearing a fine shirt of deer hide, leggings of the same material and knee-high moccasins. The small boat was piled high with firewood, soaked in oil. Several jars of oil were placed at key points along the hull. Thorn stood by the canoe, making a few final adjustments to the combustibles in it. Hal and his companions joined him and together they began to shove the laden canoe down to the water. Thorn and Hal stepped aboard as the canoe floated free. They took up their paddles while Ulf, Wulf and Stefan boarded the second canoe to accompany them. They paddled swiftly across the bay, toward the open sea.

They stopped just before the mouth of the bay and pulled the two canoes alongside each other. Thorn and Hal stepped across into the second canoe while Ulf held the funeral craft alongside. They bobbed up and down on the small waves for a few moments, then Hal took his flint and steel and struck sparks into a handful of tinder that Thorn held. The old sea wolf blew on it until it flared into flame, then leaned over the gunwale and tossed the burning mass into the bottom of Orvik's canoe. For a second, nothing happened. Then flames shot up and began licking at the oil-soaked wood. At a nod from Hal, Ulf shoved the funeral craft clear and they watched as the ebbing tide began to draw it out to sea. Wulf and Stefan kept their canoe steady with their paddles.

The flames licked higher and a banner of black smoke rose above the canoe. Then Hal made a signal and they all took up their paddles and headed back to the beach.

Mohegas was waiting for them, his face impassive. He stared across the bay to where the black pall marked the path of Orvik's last voyage.

"This was a good farewell," he said.

Hal nodded agreement. "It's our way."

Thorn shaded his eyes with his hand and peered across the bay. The canoe was still afloat, but before long it would burn to the waterline and disappear.

"You know," he said, "I don't think Orvik would have been happy back in Hallasholm. Too many things have changed, and most of the people he knew are gone now."

"He was happy here," Hal said, and smiled at Mohegas. "He told me so," he added.

Mohegas didn't reply directly, but gestured back toward the trees.

"Here is another who would have been happy here," he said. "It's sad that fate chose otherwise."

Stig was striding down the beach toward them, his face set in a grim expression. His shield was slung over his back, and a satchel containing his personal effects was over one shoulder. His bedroll had already been taken aboard by the others.

He stopped as he reached them and bowed slightly to the Mawag elder.

"Mohegas," he said, "thank you for your friendship."

Mohegas returned the salute. "Thank you for helping us defeat the enemy," he said, gesturing toward the downcast Ghostface prisoners. The face paint had been roughly wiped clear by their captors and they made a sorry-looking bunch, with streaks of black and white smearing their faces.

Stig turned to Hal. "When can we leave?"

Hal glanced across the bay, studying the pattern of wind ruffling the surface. "Tide's just turned," he observed. "We can get going right away. Get on board."

Word had spread that the foreigners were leaving, and the Mawagansett began to gather on the beach. Millika and Pillika, faces wreathed in smiles, embraced Ulf and Wulf with considerable warmth. The four had spent a lot of time together over the past weeks. Ulf felt he had to own up to the subterfuge he and his brother had carried out.

"I have to confess," he told Millika, or perhaps it was Pillika, "we often switched places on you girls."

Millika's smile widened. "We know," she said. "So whenever you did, we switched places back. And sometimes we did it when you didn't."

The two Skandians looked suitably confused. The girls solved the problem by embracing both of them again—twice—and giggling.

Hal smiled. "I've never seen those two taken aback quite so much," he said.

Ingvar, standing close by, replied gruffly. "It'll do them good."

Apart from that moment of laughter, it was a subdued farewell, overshadowed by the sadness of the two funerals, so different in nature. More and more of the villagers streamed out onto the beach as the Herons went aboard. Jesper retrieved the beach anchor, leaving the ship attached to the shore by just a meter or so of keel grounded in the sand. Without consultation, Thorn took Stig's normal place at the stroke oar and called a command to the other rowers. Stig took up a spot in the stern of the vessel, close by Hal on the steering platform.

"Oars!"

There was the usual rattle and clatter of wood on wood as the oars were taken from their storage racks and raised vertically.

"Ready!" Thorn called and the oars were lowered to the horizontal as one and set in their oarlocks. Mohegas, watching, was put in mind of an eagle preparing its wings for flight.

"Back water!"

The rowers strained, heaving their oars in a reverse stroke that dragged the bow free of the sand with a slight sucking sound. Released, the little ship glided back for several meters until Thorn judged they had enough room to turn.

"Back starboard. Forward port. Stroke!" Thorn ordered and the *Heron* turned in her own length under the opposing forces of the two banks of oars. Onshore, the Mawagansett people moved forward involuntarily until they were standing right at the water's edge. Softly, they began to sing, a song of farewell to their friends.

The plaintive, beautiful notes carried across the water to the Heron brotherband, contrasting with the practical sounds of the peremptory commands from Thorn and Hal, the clatter of oars being unshipped and stowed and the squeal of halyards through the blocks as the sail was raised and clunked into place.

Hal judged the angle to the gap between the headlands, and the leeway that the ship was making as the port sail took effect. He adjusted the tiller so that they'd go out through the bay entrance on one tack. *Heron* settled on the course he'd selected and began to move faster and faster.

Stig stood, a little apart, one hand resting on the sternpost, staring back at the group of people on the beach as the singing began to fade, obscured by the background sounds of the ship in motion—the creak of the rigging, the swish and thump of the waves.

He remained there as they passed through the gap between the headlands and felt the southwest wind strengthen. The first real rollers passed under their keel as they left the sheltered bay.

Instinctively, he swayed with the motion of the ship, still staring back at the beach. They passed a small patch of blackened, burnt timber floating on the surface, marking the spot where Orvik's canoe had finally settled beneath the waves. Then the land was a long green line low on the horizon as they moved farther offshore.

Finally, when the land sank below the horizon, Hal called to him gently.

"I could use a spell on the tiller here," he said.

Stig nodded, moving to take control of the ship, glancing up at the sail and the wind telltale on top of the mast, getting the feel of the wind strength and direction. He twitched the tiller slightly and made a small adjustment to their course. Hal smiled. A new helmsman almost invariably did that. He dropped a hand on his friend's muscular shoulder.

"Take us home, Stig."

Epilogue

This time when they arrived home, there would be no celebrations, no raucous saga to be sung describing the crew's exploits while they had been away. Hal timed their approach to Hallasholm so that they slipped through the harbor entrance close to midnight.

Their arrival was noted only by half a dozen sleepy harbor guards. One of them ran down the stone-flagged wall to greet them as they moored the *Heron* in her usual spot.

"We thought you were dead!" he said.

Hal gave him a tired smile. "So did we, at times."

"Well," said the guard, "there'll be a big celebration to mark your return. People will go wild!"

Hal's smile faded. "I don't think so. We'll just go quietly to our homes. Keep an eye on the ship, will you? We'll come back and stow things properly in the morning."

And so, singly and in pairs, the crew slipped ashore and made their way through the darkened streets to their homes. Around the town, lights could be seen going on in their houses and cries of joy and surprise, and tears of relief, could be heard. Hal, Thorn and Stig were the last to leave the ship.

"Tell Mam I'll be along directly," Hal said quietly to Thorn. "I'll walk home with Stig."

He was deeply concerned for his friend. Stig had barely spoken to any of his shipmates on the journey home, beyond those remarks necessary for the running of the ship. He was obviously still mourning the loss of Tecumsa, but seemed unable to speak about it.

They set off together for the small cottage Stig shared with his mother. When they reached it, there was a light shining inside. Stig's mother was a light sleeper and usually retired late. Hal told Stig to wait, then knocked and went in. Briefly, he described the events of the past few months to Stig's mother, telling her of her son's love for the Mawagansett girl and her death. That way, he spared Stig the pain of going over the details himself.

Stig's mother came out to where her son was waiting. She folded her arms around him and led him inside.

"I'll be going," Hal said.

She touched his arm in a gesture of gratitude. "Thank you, Hal."

He shrugged and turned away.

The woman regarded her son with sorrow in her eyes. So young, she thought, and yet he'd seen so much tragedy and pain in his life: Her husband had been disgraced, leaving Stig to grow up bitter and fatherless. Now this girl had been killed before his eyes, breaking his heart. How could someone so young bear such sadness, she wondered. Then she looked toward the shadowy figure of Hal, walking head down back to the village.

Because he has friends like that, she told herself. That's how he bears it.

The following morning, on his regular early morning walk, Oberjarl Erak and his friend Svengal were amazed and delighted to see the salt-stained, weary little ship moored alongside the mole. On board, they could see Hal, Ingvar and Edvin setting the ship to rights, furling and stowing the sails, taking any remaining supplies out of the hull to go ashore.

"You're back!" Erak bellowed from fifty meters away. "Welcome home!"

Hal rose from the task of furling the port sail around the yardarm and waved a greeting as the Oberjarl thundered along the mole toward them. He retrieved a package of papers, wrapped in oilskin, from the ship's strong box and stepped ashore to greet the huge Oberjarl, who instantly enveloped him in a bear hug. He staggered a few paces as Erak released him, then was engulfed by Svengal, whose face was lit by an enormous smile.

"We thought you were dead," Erak said, and he dashed the back of his hand across his eyes, unashamed by the tears that had formed there.

"Four wolfships were lost in that storm," Svengal put in. "How did you survive?"

Hal shrugged. "We ran before it," he said. "Out into the Endless Ocean."

"And where have you been all this time?" Erak wanted to know.

Hal went to answer, then realized that half a dozen bystanders were listening and recalled his pledge to Mohegas.

"I'll tell you later," he temporized, and handed Erak the oilskin packet by way of changing the subject. "Here are the contracts from Hibernia, all signed and sealed. And Sean of Clonmel has agreed to hire three ships for a two-year period to keep their coast free of slavers and Sonderland raiders."

Erak weighed the packet in his hand. He couldn't stop a grin bursting out over his face. He had been devastated when the *Heron* hadn't returned. The Herons were his favorite crew, and Hal was his best-loved skirl. He sensed that Hal had more to tell him, but not in such a public place.

"Come up to the Great Hall when you're ready," he said. "You can give me your report then."

Hal nodded. "I've a few things to attend to first."

Erak made a magnanimous gesture. "Whenever you're ready."

Later that morning, toward midday, Hal was surprised when Stig entered the cozy little eating house his mother kept. He rose hurriedly from the table where he was writing his report for the Oberjarl.

"Stig! Come on in! What can I do for you?"

The muscular first mate hesitated. He'd removed his Heron watch cap as he entered the eating house anteroom. Now he turned it nervously in his hands.

"Actually, I wanted to speak to your mam," he said.

Karina, who had been in the adjoining kitchen and heard voices, entered, catching the last comment.

"I'm here, Stig," she said gently. She and Stig were close. They had enjoyed a special relationship since he and Hal had become friends. She gestured for him to accompany her back to the kitchen and take a seat by the big, scrubbed pine table. Curious, Hal followed them, standing just inside the doorway, leaning against the frame.

"What is it, Stig?" Karina asked. Hal, of course, had told her about Tecumsa and she sensed that was why he was here. He started to speak, stopped, started again, then finally managed to say:

"You lost your husband."

She nodded, thinking she'd been right in her supposition. "I did," she said calmly. Stig looked down at the scarred surface of the work table, running his forefinger along a groove cut by a cleaver years before. He seemed unable to proceed, so she encouraged him gently.

"And you lost Tecumsa," she said.

He looked up at her then, anguish filling his eyes. "How do you get over something like that?" The words seemed to erupt from him. "It's been over a month! And I can't forget her!"

Karina reached out and placed one of her hands over his.

"Do you want to forget her, Stig?" she asked, and he shook his head, his eyes lowered now. Karina continued gently. "When we lose someone we love, it leaves a giant hole in our lives. It's like a wound, an open wound in our soul. If you try to forget the person, that wound festers. You can't push the memories aside as if they'd never existed."

"Then what do you do?" he said miserably.

"You remember her. You remember her for the wonderful

times you had together. You cherish those memories as you cherished the person herself. And you learn to cope with the loss. You don't ever forget, but each day, it becomes a little easier to bear the loss." She paused. "Ask yourself this: Do you wish you'd never met her?"

He shook his head without hesitation. "No," he said.

She smiled kindly at him. "Then you will gradually accept that the joy of knowing her, of spending time with her, is more than worth the pain of having lost her."

He nodded slowly. Her words made sense, he thought, and the logic eased the pain in his heart a little. Perhaps not completely, but a little.

"Karina," he said, "how did you become so wise?"

Her smile widened. "I'm a mother. It's my job."

She took his hand now and raised him from his seat, leading him toward the kitchen window.

"Another thing, Stig," she said. "Lean on your friends to help you through this. Talk about her with them. Remember her with them. Or just let them be with you and lend you their silent support and companionship. You'll find that it helps."

She drew back the curtain and Stig was surprised to see a small group of people seated on the grass slope outside the kitchen.

Ingvar, Stefan, Jesper, Edvin, Ulf, Wulf and Lydia were all sitting there. His brotherband. His friends. Hal straightened up from where he leaned against the door frame and joined Stig by the window. He looked at his mother, puzzled.

"How did you know they were there?" he asked.

She inclined her head in a mysterious gesture. "I told you. I'm a mother." Then she patted Stig's shoulder and pointed to the silent, waiting group. "Go and join them. They're here to support you."

The crew looked up as Stig and Hal emerged from the kitchen and came down the steps to join them on the grass. Some of them muttered a greeting. Others simply nodded as Stig sat on the soft grass, then they all moved a little closer, forming a tight circle around him. Including him. Drawing him in. Giving him their strength. As the day wore on, they continued to sit in that small, intimate circle around Stig. Little was said among them. Lydia sat beside him, holding his hand in both of hers. Hal sat on his other side, one arm across his shoulders. The others simply sat, ready to lend him their support if he needed it. Ready to talk if he wanted to. To listen if necessary. Or simply to sit in companionable silence, letting him know they loved him.

And he drew strength from their silent company. Strength to cope with the terrible loss he had experienced. Strength to pick up the pieces and go on. Strength to remember Tecumsa and think about her with joy in the remembering, mixed with the sadness of his loss.

The sun passed over the mountain behind the town and the shadows grew longer. He looked at the faces around him. They were his friends. But they were more than that. They were his brotherband, he thought, tied together by an unbreakable, if invisible, bond that would last for the rest of their lives. He smiled. It was a sad, wan little smile. But it was a smile, nevertheless, and that was something they hadn't seen from him in weeks.

"I'm lucky to have you all," he said.

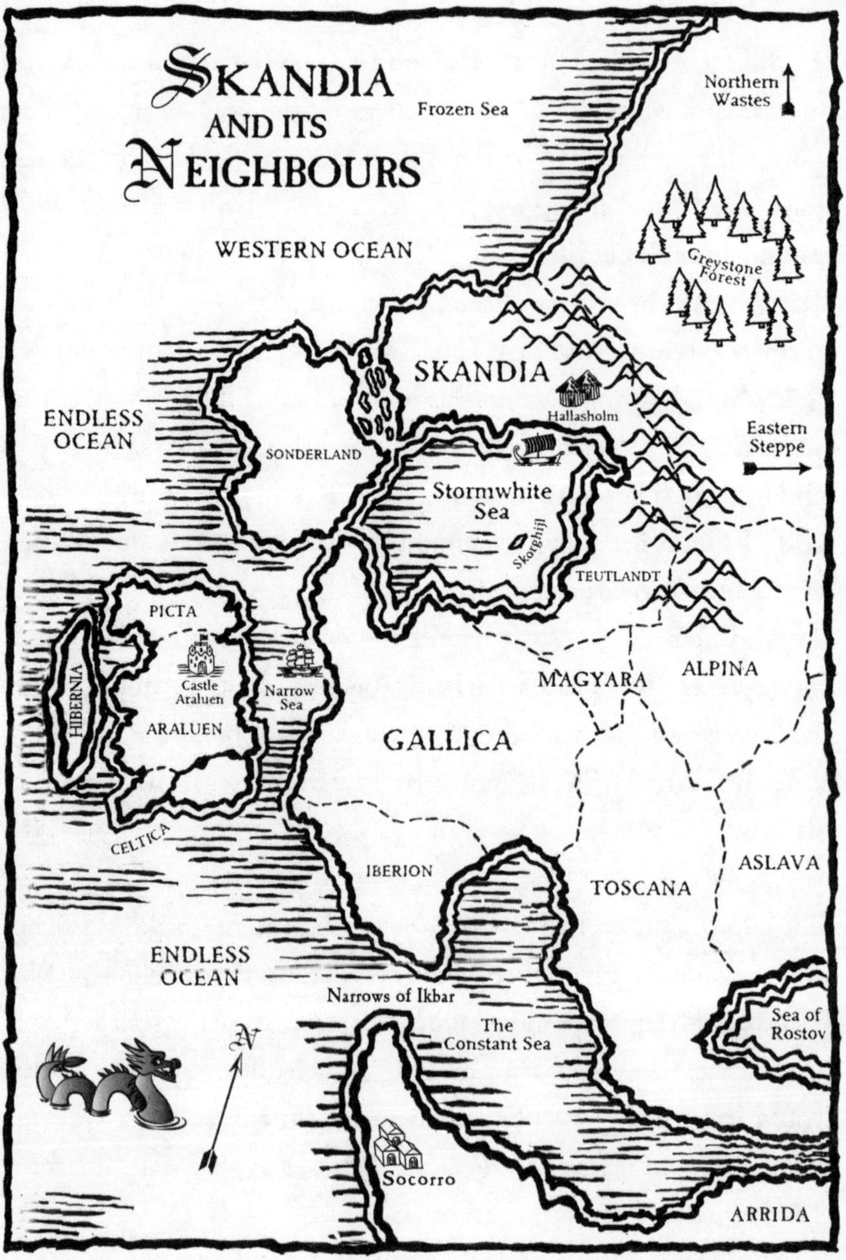
Skandia and its Neighbours
Frozen Sea
Northern Wastes
Western Ocean
Greystone Forest
Skandia
Hallasholm
Endless Ocean
Sonderland
Eastern Steppe
Stormwhite Sea
Skorghijl
Teutlandt
Picta
Hibernia
Castle Araluen
Narrow Sea
Araluen
Magyara
Alpina
Gallica
Celtica
Iberion
Toscana
Aslava
Endless Ocean
Narrows of Ikbar
The Constant Sea
Sea of Rostov
N
Socorro
Arrida

Author's Note

I would ask readers to bear in mind that the world of Brotherband, and Ranger's Apprentice, is not the real world. It's a fantasy world, although it's similar in many ways to our own.

This is particularly relevant when it comes to indigenous people referred to in the book. Astute readers will quickly identify the real-life groups who have inspired the fictional ones. But please remember, they're not intended to be identical. For this reason, I haven't used any identifiable language to create the words and descriptive phrases used by my indigenous people. They are all fabricated.

I have tried to avoid any stereotypes or potentially offensive words and phrases, be they about appearance or behavior. If any references or phrasing cause offense, please understand that this is totally unintentional, and forgive me for my ignorance.

John Flanagan

About the Author

JOHN FLANAGAN grew up in Sydney, Australia, hoping to be a writer, and after a successful career in advertising and television, he began writing a series of short stories for his son, Michael, in order to encourage him to read. Those stories would eventually become *The Ruins of Gorlan,* Book I of the Ranger's Apprentice epic. Now with his companion series, Brotherband, the novels of John Flanagan have sold millions of copies and made readers of kids the world over.

Mr. Flanagan lives in the suburb of Manly, Australia, with his wife. In addition to their son, they have two grown daughters and four grandsons.

You can visit John Flanagan at
www.WorldofJohnFlanagan.com